Praise for
The Beginning of Everything

"Journalist Josh Green sees what others can't. After years of suppressing the visions he doesn't trust or understand, he agrees to help an old friend find his missing daughter. In *The Beginning of Everything*, Charles Salzberg has crafted a tight thriller with a supernatural edge that explores the ultimate mysteries of the forces that shape us, and how the things we want most expose us to the biggest risks."

—Dennis Tafoya, author of *Dope Thief*
(made into an Apple TV series)

Praise for
Canary in the Coal Mine

"*Canary in the Coal Mine* is a terrific old-school crime novel with a machine gun pace. It delivers style and satisfaction on every page."

—Peter Blauner *New York Times* bestselling
author of *Slow Motion Riot*

"*Canary in the Coal Mine* is terrific. Salzberg has hit it out of the park. Love the writing style, and the story really draws you in. Pete Fortunato is a formidable character, strong enough to open a new series. Flawed, lovable, ballsy, smart. As with Salzberg's prior works, he has a knack for making his heroes real, which makes their jeopardy real, too. So, say hello to Pete Fortunato, a modern PI who thinks on his feet and has moves like classic noir that reads like the noir version of *Midnight Run*."

—Tom Straw, author of the Richard Castle series (from the ABC show), and *Buzz Killer*

Praise for *Swann Dives In*

"I always love it when I come across a new private detective to admire and worship, someone who is brave where I'm weak, someone who gets his hands dirty while I keep mine clean. Henry Swann is such a detective and he tells a great story. For fans of hard-boiled mysteries or just plain old good fiction, I'm sure you'll love *Swann Dives In*."

—Jonathan Ames, author of *Wake Up, Sir!* and the creator of *Bored to Death*

Praise for *Swann's Down*

"Psychics, double-crosses, missing persons—Charles Salzberg's latest Henry Swann book has it all. *Swann's Down* is a gritty, no-frills PI novel that brings to mind greats like Reed Farrel Coleman's Moe Prager and Michael Harvey's Michael Kelly. Whether this is your first Swann adventure or the latest, you won't want to miss the brass-knuckle punch that is *Swann's Down*. Trust me."

—Alex Segura, author of *Blackout* and *Dangerous Ends*

Praise for
Man on the Run

"Salzberg's bad boy, Francis Hoyt, is a character right out of a Michael Mann movie—professional, manipulative, accomplished. Love him or hate him or both, he's a character for the ages as is the novel. The stakes couldn't be higher as the cat and mouse game moves to the Left Coast in Salzberg's compelling *Man on the Run*. A superb mix of action, suspense, psychopathology. One part heist movie, one part psychological thriller, three parts great character and blend. Salzberg's superb *Man on the Run* will keep your head spinning from the first page to the last."

—Reed Farrel Coleman

"*Man on the Run* grips you from the opening page and doesn't let go. The plot will leave you breathless with anticipation as a master burglar and a crime podcaster try to outwit and outmaneuver each other before an outrageous heist. There's nothing better than smart characters, with smart dialogue, going head to head. You won't want to miss a twist or turn."

—Michael Wiley, Shamus Award-winning writer of the Sam Kelson mysteries

"Francis Hoyt, Charles Salzberg's brilliant burglar anti-hero from *Second Story Man* is back on the prowl in *Man on the Run*. Old-school crime meets the podcast age as Hoyt tangles with a true-crime reporter as well as fellow felons and the law. LIke his hero, Salzberg is a total pro who always brings it home."

—Wallace Stroby, author of *Heaven's a Lie*

"It's a battle of wits and nerves as a cop, a robber, and a journalist dance around each other weaving a tapestry of deceit and suspense. Salzberg's dialogue flows like water until it finds truth in this most entertaining read."

—Matt Goldman, *New York Times* bestselling author

"Smart, sly and compelling, with a fascinating main character—the very definition of intelligent suspense."

—Lee Child

Praise for
Swann's Lake of Despair

"Smart, satisfying, even profound, this is exactly what every mystery reader is looking for: A terrific story, full of wit and originality, and a master class in voice. Charles Salberg is a true talent, and his Henry Swann is a classic—complex, hilarious, and completely charming."

—Hank Phillippi Ryan, Mary Higgins Clark Award winner for *The Other Woman*, and Agatha Award winner for *The Wrong Girl*

Also by Charles Salzberg

Henry Swann Mystery Series

Swann's Last Song
Swann Dives In
Swann's Lake of Despair
Swann's Down
Swann's Way Out

Stand-Alone Novels

Man on the Run
Canary in the Coal Mine
Second Story Man
Devil in the Hole

Novella

Triple Shot (Twist of Fate)
Three Strikes (The Maybrick Affair)
Third Degree (The Fifth Column)

Nonfiction

On a Clear Day They Could See Seventh Place: Baseball's Worst Teams
From Set Shot to Slam Dunk: The Glory Days of Basketball in the Words of Those Who Played It

THE BEGINNING OF EVERYTHING

CHARLES SALZBERG

A REGALO PRESS BOOK
ISBN: 979-8-89565-659-4
ISBN (eBook): 979-8-89565-660-0

Cover Design by Jim Villaflores

Publishing Team:
Founder and Publisher – Gretchen Young
Managing Editor – Caitlin Burdette
Production Manager – Kate Harris
Production Editor – Rachel Paul

As part of the mission of Regalo Press, a donation is being made to National Pain Advocacy Center, as chosen by the author. Find out more about this organization at https://nationalpain.org/.

This book, as well as any other Regalo Press publications, may be purchased in bulk quantities at a special discounted rate. Contact orders@regalopress.com for more information.

Regalo Press
New York • Nashville
regalopress.com

Published in the United States of America
1 2 3 4 5 6 7 8 9 10

"In the child, consciousness rises out of the depths of unconscious psychic life, at first like separate islands, which gradually unite to form a 'continent,' a continuous landmass of consciousness. Progressive mental development means, in effect, extension of consciousness."

—*Carl Jung*

Daniel

"Ain't she a little young for you, Danny-boy?"

"She's my kid, asshole."

She's standing a couple feet behind me, to my right, her arms folded across her chest. He leers at her like she's an underage girl dressed in one of those Catholic-school uniforms, not well-worn faded blue jeans and a Yale T-shirt.

"If you say so."

"I say so."

"So, what's she doing here? This here's between you and me, Danny-boy. I don't like an audience."

"Live with it."

He stares me down. Or tries to. I've been around too long, seen too much to be intimidated by this two-bit punk. The company I keep is definitely the downside of doing what I do. Under other circumstances, I might play along. But this is my kid, not some cutie-pie along for the ride. For a split second, I wonder if maybe I'm making a mistake bringing her along. But that's the point, isn't it? To give her an honest look at the kind of life I lead and why she should run, not walk, back to her Ivy League life.

Finally, when he sees he's getting nowhere, he gives it up.

"Okay, okay. Let's talk turkey."

"That's what I'm here for," I say.

"You don't mind talking about this shit in front of…" He jerks his thumb in her general direction. "…the kid."

I look back at her. Her arms are folded across her chest. I can't tell if she's in shock or enjoying herself.

"Nope."

"Okay. Your funeral, if something goes wrong." He looks over my shoulder. "What's that they say? Little pinchers have big ears."

"Talk to me, not her."

"Okay, man. Relax. But if something goes wrong, it's gonna be because you screwed up, not me. When do we get started?"

"Soon." I rub the thumb of my right hand against my index finger. At that moment, it occurs to me that maybe I ought to check to see if he's wired. I doubt it. But better safe than sorry. In this world I live in, you trust nobody. Even if he's not wired now, he might be in the future. This'll put him on notice as to how thorough I am. In the end, I'm doing him a favor.

"Mind if I pat you down?" I say.

"What's a matter, you don't trust me?"

"It's not you, Teddy. I don't trust anyone. Two things can happen if I do, and neither one of them is good."

Josh

Those Damn Chickens Always Seem to Find Their Way Home

The call comes just before 1 a.m., only minutes after I've shut down for the night. Not a problem. It's not like I have to be somewhere in the morning. Or afternoon. That's the way it is when you're out of work. Of course, if you ask, the answer you'd get would be that I'm not out of work. I'm a freelancer between jobs.

Don't believe a word of that story. I don't. Why should you?

"Sorry to call so late, man, but I need your help."

It's my best friend, Tony, and I don't have to be a mind reader to know it's something serious. His voice sags under the weight of desperation. Besides, no call that comes after midnight is a good one. My father would have made that 9 p.m. Anyone calling after that would have heard, "Too late," and then the phone would be slammed down. Got to where if I was expecting a call, I'd hover by the phone and catch it just as it began to ring.

I'm not sure why, but this thought runs through my mind.

He's going to ask me to do something only he knows I can do. Something I don't want to do…

I've been dreading this day ever since my secret slipped out early in our friendship. And if, in a moment of weakness (or maybe it was strength?), I let slip my deepest, darkest secret, whose fault is that? To paraphrase Chaucer, my chickens have come home to roost. It was only a matter of time.

To his credit, in the over fifteen years we've been friends, Tony's never once asked me about it. Not how it works. Not what it's like to have it. Not why I have it. As far as he's concerned, it's just another piece of who I am. Like someone with a deathly fear of heights. Someone who avoids stepping on sidewalk cracks to save his mother from breaking her back. Someone who never sleeps on his left side lest he put too much pressure on his heart.

Nevertheless, I cling to them. These are the building blocks that make me who I am. Besides, what's the harm? Why should I, of all people, tempt fate?

"What's up?" I ask as I reach over and turn on the lamp on my night table. Like most everything else in my life lately, it doesn't cooperate. I twist the little knob three, four times, but nothing happens. So, I give up and remain in darkness. Just another something that doesn't work the way it's supposed to.

"Can you meet me for breakfast in the morning?"

"Just tell me what it is now," I say, as I slide my butt back so I'm sitting upright, leaning against the headboard, staring at the huge, dark outline of the humongous flat-screen TV pinned to the wall opposite my bed. "I'm up and wide awake."

"It's not something I want to talk about on the phone," he says, his voice lowering to a whisper.

I can't say no to Tony. And I can't make up some lame excuse, because he knows me well enough to know I'm a terrible liar. Believe me, I've tried. I just don't seem to have the essential lying gene.

"Okay. Sure."

"I'll come down to you. How's eight o'clock at Friedman's?"

I make a quick calculation. Even if I can fall asleep immediately after I hang up, I'll get, at best, four or so hours sleep. No problem. I'll just pencil in a late-afternoon nap.

"You got it."

I hang up. I slide my butt forward until I'm back in a supine position. I close my eyes in an attempt to return to where I was before Tony's call. But it's impossible to sleep.

Elvis remains in the building.

Josh
Cat Busts Out of Bag

My secret leaked early in our budding friendship. Unplanned. Unexpected. The way secrets often reveal themselves. You only have to let your guard down for a moment. Secrets are like that. They have an energy and power all their own. And they seek air, like a forest fire, which is essential in keeping them alive. If no one knows you have a secret, do you have one?

We were having an after-work drink, something we did occasionally when we bumped into each other while reporting the same story. At the time, we worked for rival small-market local Connecticut newspapers. He was telling me about this missing kid case in Stamford he was working. Horrible tale. A parent's worst nightmare. Six years old. In a playground. One minute he's there. Next minute he's not. Faster than the speed of sound. Now you see him, now you don't. Weeks into the disappearance, the cops have no leads, so they finally accede to the pleas of the frantic parents to call in a local psychic. Just to prove they're doing everything they can and get the parents off their backs.

Tony shook his head, then emptied what was left of his beer. "I can't believe the cops said yes. What a fucking waste of time."

I said nothing, my mind racing toward another subject to hide behind, which I immediately realized is the tip-off I might be hiding something. Never try to hide something from a trained investigative reporter. Everyone has a tell. Whether it be a slight movement of the eyes, a tiny hesitation, a hand to the face. Fuck! I should've simply smiled and said, "That's fucking crazy, man." But I didn't. And so that's the very moment I knew my goose was cooked.

Tony's face lit up. Nothing gets by him. He knew he'd struck a nerve. Better yet, a possible story. "Can you believe that shit?" he said, which was an obvious invitation to keep the subject alive. To keep me wiggling on the hook.

I hoped he'd move on. But I knew better. What made Tony a good reporter—an excellent reporter—also makes for a difficult friend. He knows everyone has a secret. Sometimes more than one. He's made a living out of stripping those secrets bare. It's like talking to a shrink. They're always searching for the subtext, the truth behind the lies we tell ourselves. With guys, it's a plus not knowing what your friend is really thinking. Unlike women, we don't bond by sharing secrets; we bond by keeping them.

Unfortunately, at the moment, none of this was uppermost on my mind.

"You don't believe in this phony psychic crap, do you, Josh?" he asked, nailing me with his laser-like deep brown eyes, which seemed like they might penetrate the deepest, darkest recesses of my mind. Looking back, I know I had no defense to keep him out.

What I should have said was, *No way, man.* I should have been listening to that annoying little voice in my head that kept repeating, *Shut the fuck up, Josh. Just shut the fuck up!*

But that voice was overruled by another annoying voice that screamed, *Tell him! Tell him! You've kept this secret long enough. You need to share it with someone or you'll fucking explode.*

"Do you?" he pressed.

"I guess I do," I mumbled.

He stared at me. An old tried-and-true trick. Using silence as a tool to make me talk. I knew what he was doing but by this point, like it or not (and I didn't), I was a willing coconspirator. The conveyor belt was moving forward too swiftly, no way I could jump off. I thought about the classic *I Love Lucy* scene at the chocolate factory. Except this wasn't funny. This was as serious as it gets.

"Well, to be honest, I've kinda had a few weird episodes over the years."

"Episodes? What kind of episodes?"

Is it too late to stop?

"I'd rather not talk about it."

The look on his face was, *Is this guy for real?*

"Don't want to talk about it, huh?"

I shook my head, no. Now, only when it was too late, did I vow to keep my mouth shut.

I didn't expect him to drop it, but I underestimated him. The conveyor belt stopped. I didn't have to jump off. Later, much later, I realized he knew that to pursue the subject would ruin our budding friendship, a friendship he'd obviously began to value. Shared secrets do not cement friendships between people. It demolishes them. And so, he chose friendship over curiosity. By honoring my silence, we would become good friends. Best friends. The kind of friend who allows the other friend to keep and protect a shared secret.

In the end, the toothpaste was out of the tube. It could never find its way back in. And I swear I knew it at the time: There was a very good chance that eventually it would come back and bite me in the ass. Turns out, I was right.

Over the years, I've told myself it would have happened eventually. If not Tony, then someone else. I was married for a short time, but since communication, or lack of it, ruined the relationship, I was able to hide it from her. But it's almost impossible to keep a secret like that to yourself. After a while, it's not a secret anymore. It's a curse. An almost unbearable burden, and only by sharing it can the curse be lifted. Not the burden. No, the burden remains. Forever. And so, as counterintuitive as it might sound, in order for it to remain a secret, someone besides me had to be in on it. Tony was in the right (or wrong) place at the right (or wrong) time, so he became my coconspirator. Silence bonds us together. Like superglue. I hope.

To be honest, after all those years keeping it to myself, it's a relief. For too long have I been Clark Kent, and I can't spend the rest of my life looking for off-the-beaten-path telephone booths to change in. For the record, there are no phone booths left in Manhattan. The phone company hauled away the last couple from the Times Square area in late spring of 2022.

And so, Tony doesn't ask annoying questions, probing for what it is and how it works. After a while, as a result of our shared silence, I'm able to convince myself that our exchange never happened, which would explain why he's never brought it up. But more likely, it's because bringing it up would make it as real for him as it is for me. It would drive a wedge between us and eventually become the stake in the heart that tears it apart. It's only much later that I realize by sharing my secret I'm making Tony not only my coconspirator but also an unwilling accomplice. It's now his burden to keep my secret as much as it is mine. But for some reason this feels okay. Who would have known that a secret shared makes it bearable?

Over the years, it's remained *our* unspoken secret. Nevertheless, every so often, in the middle of a conversation, I'll glance over to find Tony staring at me, probably recognizing what he interprets as a faraway, spaced-out look in my eyes. When he sees I've caught him red-handed, he'll smile and whisper, "Are we entering the *Twilight Zone,* Josh?"

I suppose it can look that way. Here but *not* here. And every so often, he's right. I am in the *Twilight Zone*. But on those rare occasions, I do not own up to it for one very simple reason. A discussion of said zone will lead nowhere good. Instead of bonding me with people, it sets me apart. I don't want to be apart. I've spent most of my life trying desperately to connect with people rather than having them back away slowly, as if I've got some deadly, highly communicable disease. That's why I keep this *thing of mine* on the down-low. I don't want to become defined by it. Even though, let's face it, I am, even if only by me.

At the time of the call, Tony had left the world of print journalism and was now executive producer for a local TV news show. I'm in the midst of a self-imposed exile from the writing business. I'd like to say it's by choice, but that would be stretching the truth. The magazine where I was a contributing editor shuttered six months ago, part of a growing trend. Being a magazine journalist is like being a coal miner, but without the black lung. There's still work out there, somewhere, but it gets scarcer and scarcer, harder and harder to find. And so, I decided to take the opportunity to start a new life. The problem is, I'm not sure what life that will be. I don't really have any real marketable skills, and when I take pen to pad and try to list my dream professions, I don't get much past general manager of a baseball team, which ain't gonna happen. Fortunately, I've managed to save a little dough and that, plus my weekly (temporary) unemployment check and a cheap rent-stabilized apartment, keeps me afloat. But the clock is ticking. I hear it, and it's getting louder and louder.

And so, to keep up my spirits and have something to tell people who ask, I'm starting to write a novel. It's not going particularly well. At the time I get the call from Tony, I've been working on it a couple months. I've managed to write a first chapter and a bunch of random scenes, but since I don't outline (how can you outline if you don't know where you're going?), I'm not sure how they fit in the big picture.

And so, I spend much of my day treading water: reading, binging streaming services, listening to podcasts, and wandering the city. The only thing that keeps me tethered to reality is my weekly lunches with Tony.

But who knows how long those'll last?

Josh
Sticking My Nose Where It Doesn't Belong

When I arrive at Friedman's, the Upper West Side's version of an upscale diner, a few minutes before eight, Tony's already sitting in the front booth. For a weekend brunch there are packs of hungry diners lined up outside waiting for a table. But for a weekday breakfast, the place is virtually empty, offering us plenty of privacy, as well as an open invitation to sit there as long as we like.

Tony is huddled over a cup of coffee, staring out into space. He doesn't bother looking up from his trance as I slide in across from him. Only when I'm comfortably in place does he acknowledge my presence.

"Thanks for coming, man," he says in a slightly hoarse, whispery voice that reminds me of Kiefer Sutherland in *24*.

Tony lives in Westchester with his wife, Rachel, and their two kids. When I was married, Morgan and I—she's been out of the picture almost six years now—would occasionally take Metro-North up to spend time with Tony and Rachel. Eventually, when it was apparent my wife didn't particularly like either of them or

Westchester, the trips became painful, and eventually they ended. Only later, after our divorce, did I learn from Tony the feeling was mutual.

To the outside world, we look like two average forty-somethings touching base before heading off to work. But in truth, neither of us is anywhere near average.

If you look up the word "restless" in Webster's, there's a good chance you'll find a photo of Tony. His life reminds me of that Sinatra song, "That's Life." Over time, Tony's added a few more professions, and I'm pretty sure he's not finished yet.

Back in the '80s, he was a moderately successful child actor. When his voice began to change and he found hair growing in places it had never grown before, his career—which included a stint as one of the Lost Boys in a *Peter Pan* revival on Broadway, a small part in a Tom Cruise flick, and a meatier role in *Once Upon a Time in America*—was supposed to launch. But when he took his agent's (bad) advice and turned down a role in a TV movie because his name wouldn't be above the title, his star began to fall. The film helped launch the career of the two young stars, while Tony's acting career pretty much came to an abrupt end. Turns out it was no tragedy, since any career Tony chooses comes with an expiration date.

In college, Tony studied journalism, then scored a gig as a reporter on a financial magazine. That lasted two years. Next, it was a small, suburban Connecticut newspaper, which is how we met. It was my first job, and I looked up to Tony, who, only a few years older than me, was pretty much yin to my yang. He was outgoing and ambitious. I was shy and barely motivated. And yet, we bonded and he became an unofficial mentor, a valuable source of journalistic knowledge. I relied on him, since I had no formal training for the job, having fallen into the profession only because it seemed to be one of the few things I could do with a liberal arts education. After a couple years, he tired of journalism. Without any discernable reason (unless you count an obsession with *Perry Mason* reruns or the "order" part of *Law and Order*), he burned to be a lawyer, which didn't surprise me. It fit perfectly with his narcissistic streak. He dreamed of being a prosecutor, ridding the world of evil while bringing justice to the downtrodden. I didn't believe it for a second. Not that he was lying, but more because it came off as simply playing a heroic figure on a high-stakes stage to perform on. Years later, when he was telling me about this part of his life, I said, "You should have used Shakespeare's advice from *Henry VI, Part 2*: 'The first thing we do, let's kill all the lawyers.'"

He enrolled at Duke Law School. After graduating in the top 10 percent of his class, he snagged a job in the prosecutor's office in Durham. That's where he met Rachel, a Connecticut transplant who was on the mayor's staff. She likes to say it was disinterest at first sight. He claims she's lying. I'm guessing the truth lies somewhere in between.

Restless as ever, the law only held his attention for a few years. "I couldn't see myself prosecuting penny-ante crooks, pederasts, rapists, and thieves for the rest of my life," he explained. "It was getting fucking depressing." Could be true. But if you ask me, it was because his dreams of holding a jury in his thrall died when he realized most of his time was spent pleading out cases for the lottery of life losers.

And so, the curtain came down on the law.

The next act came when he decided his real future was in radio, and after a short job search—his background as an actor certainly helped—he found work at the North Carolina public radio station as a field reporter, occasionally substituting as host of a local talk show offered by the affiliate. The audience loved him at the very time he was having a tough time loving himself.

Two years later the music began to play again, signaling it was time to find a new chair. So, after marrying Rachel, they moved back up north to Connecticut where he got that job on a local newspaper and then, after he became bored with journalism, he took a job as a producer for a TV news show. By this time, I'd left the paper, moved back to the city, and was picking up work as a freelance magazine writer and occasional ghostwriter. Now that we were back in the same geographical area, we began our weekly lunch tradition. I didn't mind taking Metro-North up to his neck of the woods, but Tony preferred traveling south, to the city where he was born. He claimed it gave him a few hours to pretend he was single again, with all sorts of possibilities in his future. Turns out, Tony's pretty good at pretending.

Usually, he's the life of the party that is our weekly lunch, but this morning he is expressionless and unusually contemplative. I don't need a crystal ball to know something is seriously wrong. The thing is, with Tony, a bit of a hypochondriac and equal opportunity malcontent, there's always a long laundry list of things that could be bugging him.

My first guess is that something's wrong between him and Rachel. On the surface, they seem to be the perfect couple. All the more reason to think something's amiss. But if it is that, I certainly don't want to find myself in the middle. And as for giving advice? Well, my track record speaks for itself.

"What's up, my friend?" I ask, girding myself for what could be a self-pitying litany of dreams and ambitions quickly disappearing, as well as various physical and emotional ailments that are betraying him, or at least slowing him down.

He stares at me for what seems like an eternity. I squirm in my seat, wishing I'd thought of some excuse to have turned him down. Frankly, I'm an expert at that. As a kid, I held the unofficial record for sick days in elementary school. I'd catch my parents while they were still sleeping, complain of a sore throat, and if they insisted on taking my temperature before agreeing to let me stay home, no problem. For some mysterious reason I consistently show ninety-nine to one hundred degrees, barely above normal, good enough to skip school that day.

Finally, he breaks the silence. "You're not doing that thing you can do, are you?"

I know exactly what he means.

"I have enough trouble knowing my own mind, much less reading someone else's." He smiles but says nothing, so I quickly add, "Besides, that's not something I can do. Read people's minds, I mean. You know that, right?"

The waitress—young, pretty, wearing a blue tank top, faded jeans, and rocking a two-tone green and red spikey hairdo—suddenly appears holding one of those glass coffee pitchers.

"Coffee?" she asks.

"Sure," I say. I need a pick-me-up since being out of work has resulted in erratic sleep patterns. I'm staying up too late and, without somewhere specific to be, sleeping much too late into the day.

"You boys up for some breakfast?" she asks in a tone too cheery for this early in the morning. Maybe even for any hour of the day.

I look over at Tony, who's now somewhere else. He looks awful. Unshaven. Hair disheveled. Like he hasn't slept or showered in days.

"I think we're good for now," I say.

"No problem, gents. I'll be back with your coffee in a jiff. Maybe by then you'll have worked up an appetite."

I don't know whether to prod Tony or let him go at his own pace. I'm treading unknown territory here. Never do I have to coax a complaint out of my friend. Normally, they tumble from his mouth like a torrential midsummer rainstorm. But as loquacious as Tony is, he's not one to share his inner life. I can't be sure he even has one. I'm going to have to let him go at his own pace. Except that even though I don't have anything particular planned for the day, I don't want to spend too much of it face-to-face with him in a diner. Sometimes, being with Tony can suck the life out of you. I'm hoping this is not one of those times.

"What's the problem, man?"

His face tightens. He closes his eyes. When he finally opens them, he says, "It's Allie."

Tony's got two kids. A boy, Jason, ten, and Allie, who's nineteen. Allie is Rachel's daughter from her first marriage. Rachel's husband died in some kind of tragic automobile accident a couple months before Allie was born. Two years later, Tony met Rachel. They fell in love, married, and a year later he formally adopted Allie, making him the only father Allie's ever known. I didn't know Rachel or Allie back then, but after she married Tony and became pregnant with Jason, she named me the godfather. I should have been flattered, but I was afraid it came with certain responsibilities I wasn't anxious to take on. Fortunately, I was assured it was mostly an honorary title. "Look," explained Tony, "you only have to worry if Rachel and I both go at the same time. It's more like a ceremonial type thing." I'm not sure I believed that, but I couldn't refuse them.

Allie's a brilliant kid, but she can be trouble with a capital T. She got herself suspended from two high schools. Typical rebellious kid stuff. Smoking in the girl's bathroom. Tacking up *The Communist Manifesto* on a hall bulletin board. Cutting classes. Wearing inappropriate attire, whatever that is. I chalk it up to her being particularly high-spirited, bored with suburban life. I see it as a good thing, this reluctance to conform. But then I don't have to clean up her messes.

"What's that school she's at?"

This is a running joke between us, and it usually elicits a giggle, a grin, a smirk. Not this time. Silence. That's because Tony's not all there. He's sitting across from me, but actually he's a million miles away. In an effort to engage and get this thing moving, I answer my own question.

"Oh, yeah. Yale. That's one of those hoity-toity Ivy League schools, right? How much was it you guys had to donate to get her in? Less than the couple million Jared's dad kicked in, I hope."

No reaction. If I were to wave my hand in front of his eyes, I doubt he'd flinch. As much as I want to stay out of Tony's business, out of everyone's business—including my own—I'm a friend and I want to help. Presumably that's why I'm here. So, I wish he'd get to the point.

"She's not in trouble again, is she?"

He looks up, and the pupils of his eyes are little black pellets. Scary. Very scary.

"Maybe."

"Oh, God, she hasn't been suspended, has she?"

He shakes his head no.

"Flunking out?"

No again.

"So, what's the problem?"

He hesitates, as if he isn't quite sure he wants to talk about it. I don't have to be the Amazing Kreskin to know that in his own time he will. People rarely bring up something important then drop it. Which is a sure sign that whatever this is, it's pretty serious.

"Well," he starts, drawing out every word as if each has a life of its own, "she's…" He clears his throat. "Kind of disappeared."

Before I can respond, Little Miss Perky arrives with my coffee. She sets it down in front of me. "Well, you gents worked up that appetite yet?"

Too guilt-ridden to sit there with only coffee in front of us, I pipe up, "How about two orders of scrambled eggs and wheat toast?"

"Sounds good." She turns to Tony.

He waves her away. "Yeah, yeah. Sure. That's fine."

She smiles. We've made her day. As soon as she paddles off, I pick up the thread of our conversation.

"How do you 'kind of' disappear?"

"We can't get in touch with her. We don't know where she is."

The muscles in his face tighten. It's ridiculous, but I'm afraid he's going to cry.

"That's nothing new, right?" I say, making a feeble attempt to defuse the ticking bomb in his head. "I mean, she's on her own now. She's an adult. And she's always marched to the beat of her own drum. Besides, it's not like you guys need to know where she is and what she's doing every minute, right?"

"Tell that to Rachel. Besides, this is different. That's typical teenage shit. Calls unanswered. Texts ignored. Damn cell phones. They're on them all the time, so you'd think they'd answer the fucking thing when they get a call. But when she sees it's us, she ignores it. Maybe just to piss us off. Because she knows it does."

"I guess we were lucky we didn't grow up with cell phones. When we were out of the house it was pretty much out of sight, out of mind." I stop, suddenly realizing this might be one of the reasons our generation is so fucked up.

"It's been nearly a week and we haven't heard a word from her. That's unusual. Before she left for college, Rachel and Allie were constantly at each other's throats. That changed pretty quick once she was out of sight and on her own. I guess it was that absence growing fonder thing. Now, they're practically joined at the hip. They speak four, five times a week. Allie calls for advice. She calls for a sympathetic ear. She calls before she makes any decision, big or small. Between you and me, I think it borders on being a little...weird. I mean, suddenly, they're best buddies. But Rachel loves it. It's the relationship with her daughter she always wanted. That's why this is so disturbing for her. Every day that passes without hearing from her makes it worse. After two, three days, Rachel was frantic. She wanted to go up there and look for her. She called a bunch of Allie's friends, but no one's seen her or heard from her since last Friday. Rachel found out she hasn't been in her classes since last Thursday. That's never happened before."

"You think maybe Rachel's overreacting?"

He circles his index finger around the rim of his water glass, first clockwise, then counter-clockwise.

"I did at first. Now, I'm not so sure."

"You think something's seriously wrong?"

"Probably not. But..." He picks up his half-empty water glass, examines it, holds it up to the light as if he is checking for fingerprints, then puts it back down. "You never know. This fucked-up world today..." His voice trails off.

I think I know what's coming next. He's going to ask me to watch their son, Jason, take out the dog, and water the plants while they head up to New Haven to look for Allie. He needs a baby/dog sitter. I can do that. I don't want to. But I can.

"Have you called the cops?"

"You know the cops won't touch a case like this as early as it is. *College Girl Doesn't Phone Home.* Stop the fucking presses." He pauses a moment before adding, "That's what Rachel wanted to do right away, but I talked her out of it. Thankfully, there are no signs of foul play." He frowns. "Where does that come from anyway? I mean, what the hell is foul play?"

"I believe Shakespeare coined the phrase. Evil doing."

"Figures. Dude had his fingers in every fucking pie. Anyway, according to her roommate, she packed a bag and took off. Not exactly a sign of the crime of the century. Besides…" His voice trails off.

"Besides what?"

"Well, it's not the first time."

"First time for what?"

"It's nothing, Josh. Really."

"What kind of nothing are we talking about?"

"When she was a kid, junior high, high school, she hit the bricks a couple times."

"What does that mean?"

"You know. Ran away. All kids do it. It was never anything serious. It was usually the result of words between Rachel and her. The usual stuff, ridiculous when you look back on it. The first time, we called the cops. Second time, we didn't even bother. Since you've never been a teenage girl and don't live under the same roof with one, you wouldn't know that teenage girls love drama."

"So, she's on record as a runaway."

"That's what we think. So, you can see why it's not exactly a good idea to get the cops involved. At least not till we have some kind of proof she didn't go on her own accord."

"How can I help?"

I'm hoping the kind of help he wants from me is nothing more than a sympathetic shoulder to cry on. Reassurance that everything's gonna be fine. That they're overreacting. Wishful thinking, on my part, because that's not what he has in mind, at all.

He cradles his head in his hands and sighs.

Without lifting his head, he says, "If I'd let her, Rachel would be up there already. That would be absolutely no help. She's an emotional wreck. I convinced her she should let me go up while she stays home with Jason. In part, I have to admit, it's so I can get the hell out of the house. Me being there only makes things worse."

"Worse how?"

"She thinks I don't care enough, because Allie isn't blood to me. That I can't possibly understand what she's going through. That I'm not upset enough. That I'm not proactive enough. Shit like that."

"Is she right?"

He gives me a look. He's angry.

"Of course not. I love the kid. Always have. And she knows it. Whenever she accuses me of that kind of thing, she always apologizes for, her word not mine, 'overreacting.'"

"Sounds like a good idea, you going up there alone," I say.

He drains his water glass. He puts it back on the table but doesn't let go of it, as if waiting for it to be magically refilled. I can see the frustration and worry all over his face. Finally, he looks up, nailing me in place with his eyes, as he delivers the very words I do not expect to hear. "Not alone. I'm kinda hoping I can convince you to go up there with me."

This, I did not see this coming.

"Just out of curiosity, how were you going to convince me?"

He smiles. He knows he's already won the battle without a shot being fired. "By asking?"

"Why me?"

I know why, but I'm hoping I'm wrong.

"You know why," he says.

"Oh. That."

"Yeah. *That.* I've never asked you before, Josh…"

I don't let him finish.

"I hate to disappoint you, Tony."

"Disappoint me how?"

"Well, about this thing of mine."

"You won't disappoint me because I'm not sure I even believe in it. But maybe—who knows—maybe you can help. What about it?"

I don't hesitate.

"Hey, I've always wanted to go to Yale, and since it wasn't my grades that were going to get me there, here's my chance."

"I really appreciate it, J. What's your day rate?"

"Day rate?"

"Yeah. I'm paying you for this."

"You've gotta be kidding. I'm not taking money from you."

"Sure, you are. Because, if you don't, deal's off."

"You're my best friend, Tony. No way I'm letting you pay."

"No pay, no play. This isn't about you or our friendship, and I appreciate your position. But this is the way it's gonna be."

"So, you want me to be your employee?"

"I guess. Sure. But you'll find me a very easy boss. I stay in my lane and I'm excellent at delegating."

It makes me super uncomfortable, but I guess I kinda understand his position.

"A hundred a day."

He smiles. "I know that's a fucking lie. Even you, the worst negotiator in the history of negotiation, make more than that. But okay, one hundred dollars a day it is."

Various charities where I might donate it flash through my mind. But then again, charity does begin at home, and right now, I've got no work on the horizon.

The waitress arrives with two plates of eggs and toast. Before she's able to set them down, Tony pulls out his wallet, extracts a credit card, and drops it on the table.

Apparently, we are done.

Josh
It Is What It Is and That's All That It Is

Tony picks me up at the White Plains train station early Tuesday morning. I offer to take Amtrak up to New Haven to save him the time and trouble of picking me up. But he insists we drive up together.

Turns out, he wants the company. Scratch that. He *needs* the company.

I settle into the passenger's seat, strap on my seatbelt, and glance over at Tony. I can see he's on edge simply by how tightly he grips the steering wheel. His back is so straight I worry that if we hit a bump his head will go through the roof. I offer to drive, but he shoots that down, and not in a particularly kind way.

"No thanks, Josh. I've seen you at the wheel, and it ain't pretty."

A dagger thrust through my heart. Never, ever question a man's driving ability. That's worse than challenging his penis size. Or pointing out he's losing his hair. Truth is, he's right. I might not be the world's worst driver, but I'm close. I understand the mechanics. And the theory. Turn key. Check both mirrors. Acknowledge objects are closer in said mirrors than they appear. Or is it further?

(See what I mean?) Shift into drive. Hit the accelerator. Use the brakes if necessary. This is not the problem. Problem is, I have trouble concentrating on what's in front of me, much less what's behind and creeping up on me. My mind wanders. I can't quite master the art of looking forward and back at the same time. Ironic, isn't it, given my ability to see things well outside my own experience. Once I'm behind the wheel I have trouble distinguishing right from left. Trust me, it's a mess. You are safer in a car driven by Stevie Wonder than you are with me.

So, I don't argue the point. But I do remind him I have a license and can, in a pinch, take over if necessary.

"I can't imagine the circumstance that would make that necessary, Josh, but I appreciate the offer," he says as he peels away from the curb, heading for the highway.

He's stressed. His teeth are clenched and a vein pops out on his forehead. I'm not surprised. His daughter's missing and his wife is frantic. If it were happening to me, I'd probably scrunch up in a fetal position and try to make myself disappear. My first inclination when trouble arises is to look the other way, hoping it will somehow resolve itself. It never does. But that doesn't stop me from trying. Tony's first instinct is to charge into any and all burning buildings, in an attempt to save lives of people he doesn't even know.

It's my job to keep Tony's mind from going where it wants to go but shouldn't. I have so many questions about our upcoming adventure, questions I will hold off asking.

Soon, we're tooling up the Major Deegan, toward New Haven, at a speed that seems excessive. A glance at the speedometer confirms it: We're moving eighty-plus miles an hour. Speed doesn't bother me. Being stopped by the cops or being in the middle of a five-car pileup does. But I don't say anything. Tony has a lot on his mind, and I'm sure getting a speeding ticket is at the bottom of the list.

As much as I might want to, I can't keep my mouth shut forever. "So," I begin, by playing the empathy/sympathy card, "how's Rachel holding up?"

Tony, eyes still glued to the road ahead, slowly shakes his head back and forth. "Not so good. She's thinking the worst, of course. That she's hooked on all those true crime shows like *Dateline* and *48 Hours* doesn't help."

"Start worrying when she binges on *Women Who Kill Their Husbands.*"

I expect a laugh. I get nothing. I want to engage Tony so he'll stop living in his runaway imagination. But I'm in a losing battle. Tony keeps things bottled up inside. Me, not so much. My mother used to say, "Josh, you know what your problem is?" (Note: I did not ask, but that never stopped my mother from offering.) "What's on your lung is on your tongue." She didn't mean it as a compliment. We've had conversations, Tony and me, that touch on the issue, but like most men we change direction when the conversation comes too close to the bone.

I persist. Maybe if I keep him talking, it'll take his mind off his missing daughter.

Tony sighs.

"I don't know what the hell to do. Between you and me, J…" I hate it when he shortens my name to one letter, because I think it somehow diminishes me. My problem, not his. I've told him before—leaving out the part about being diminished—but this isn't the time to remind him. "I jumped at the opportunity to get the hell out of the house. I was going batshit, cooped up like that, not able to do anything about it. I'm as worried as Rachel is, so I'm grateful to be able to do something instead of sitting home, waiting by the phone."

"Yeah, that'd be tough," I say. But I'm not sure he hears me, because he keeps talking. A torrent of words tumbling from his mouth.

"We have to maintain some semblance of normality because of Jason. Don't want to get him upset. When they were living under the same roof, they fought all the time. But now that she's gone, they've suddenly bonded. He misses her. A lot. He asks about her all the time. I guess it's that whole absence making the heart grow fonder thing."

"Does he know what's going on? That Allie's missing?"

"Kid's smart as a whip. And super sensitive. I'm sure he knows something's wrong, but he doesn't know what it is. It won't be long before he figures it out. Rachel would protect those kids from any and every possible danger, realistic or not. And unlike me she isn't very good at hiding her feelings."

"You've had years of practice," I say. "Where does he think you're going?"

"We told him I'm on a shoot for a couple days. That's not unusual, so he's not asking questions. So, we're okay for now."

"So, other than my being such good company…"

He finishes for me. "Why are you here?"

"A question I ask myself every day," I say, lamely risking a joke I know isn't particularly funny. Jokes about folks like Descartes and Socrates rarely elicit laughs.

"In all the years I've known you, J, I've never once asked you about it, have I? Not once. Know why?" He doesn't wait for my response. "Because you're a friend, my best friend, and you asked me not to. And it's not that over the years it hasn't crossed my mind, J. But I respect your privacy. I figure if you ever want to talk about it, or want me to know more about it, you'd be the one to bring it up."

"I appreciate that, Tony. I don't mind talking about it with you."

I'm lying, of course. I don't want to talk about it with him or anyone. Even myself. Especially myself. The more I talk about it, the more real it gets. The more real it gets, the scarier it is for me. All my life I wanted to be different. To stand out. Just not this way.

I lean forward and I stage-whisper, "Okay, what is it you want to know?"

"I'm not sure where to start."

"Ask whatever you like, and if I don't want to answer, I'll plead the Fifth."

He taps the wheel several times, as if it's a keyboard and he's carefully composing his question. "Well, maybe we should start by explaining what it is you can do."

"You don't waste time, do you?"

"Buckle up, my friend. This is only the beginning. We've got at least an hour left on the road and unless you want to spend the time listening to me singing along with pop music…"

I throw up my arms in a gesture of surrender.

"Okay. Okay. Anything but that." I take a deep breath. "Let's start with this disclaimer. Even though I've lived with this thing since I was a kid, I still don't fully understand it. Part of the reason is, I don't want to. I'm afraid if I look too deeply into it, I'll fall into a black hole that'll suck me in and I'll never get out. I think it's best to tell you what I've experienced, what I think I might be able to do, and what I know I can't do."

I see his lips slowly form a Mona Lisa smile. The pressure builds. So much so that I can actually feel my blood pressure rising. I can't help but wonder what will happen to our friendship if I fail. More important, how will I feel if I fail?

"Don't leave out anything, okay?" he says.

Even though I've never needed a detailed explanation of what I can and can't do, it doesn't mean I don't have one. Not so much for other people, but for myself. Years ago, while in my late teens, I jotted down everything I knew about this *thing,* as well as everything I didn't know. Over the years, I occasionally take out the list, read it over, add to or subtract from it, then type it all over again into a document on my computer. When I upgrade my computer, I upgrade the list. I haven't done so in a few years, but I know it's ever-changing and incomplete. This thing of mine is organic. It seems to be in a constant state of growth. But maybe that means it can also shrink. Or even disappear. If that happens, I haven't quite decided whether that'd be a good or a bad thing.

I take a deep breath and begin with a disclaimer.

"First off, it's not magic, and I'm not infallible. I'm no quack nor am I scamming anyone."

"I don't think either of those things."

"I know. But it needs to be said."

"Of course."

"I honestly don't know how helpful I'll be, Tony. First off, I don't think of it as a power. It's an ability. Like a sixth sense. I think we all have it to some extent. First off, I can't see into the future and I can't read minds. What I can do is get a picture in my mind of things that have happened or are happening. Over the years, every so often, I've tried to understand it, to wrap my mind around what I can do and why I can do it, but I can't. The closest I can come is calling it a form of fact-based intuition. I'm not always accurate, but I think if I put my mind to it, I can get pretty close."

And so, for the next fifteen, twenty minutes, as we settle into a comfortable cruising speed heading toward New Haven, I lay it all out for him, trying to answer any questions he might have. And he has plenty.

I tell him that asking me when I first realized I have "the power" is like asking someone when was the first time they realized they could see. Or hear. Or smell. I'm uncomfortable talking about it, much less thinking about it, so I leave out specific facts, avoid nuances that'll just spawn more questions, and fudge the truth when it suits me.

"I don't remember how old I was, but I started having these very strange dreams. They were so vivid that when I woke up, I couldn't tell the difference between dream and reality. I remembered them in detail, and the details didn't fade like most dreams. At first, I thought everyone had them, that I wasn't a freak. After a while, I realized that wasn't the case. One day, I was watching the news, and they reported on a recent murder. As the commentator described it, it seemed very familiar. Like I already knew what was being described. When they showed the scene, it was surprisingly familiar. Finally, I realized the reason it seemed so familiar was that I'd dreamed something very similar the night before."

"Did you tell your parents?"

"You're the only one who knows, Tony. Including my ex-wife. To be honest, I'm a little embarrassed, even frightened by *it.* I mean, what if I introduce you to someone saying, 'I'd like you to meet So-and-So. He's a little different from you and me. He gets visions of past events that have nothing to do with his life and he speaks to dead people. What would you think?'"

"You talk to dead people?"

"Absolutely not. See, there's the problem: other people's expectations. I do *not* speak to dead people. I do not have a spirit guide. And I most certainly do *not* see them. In fact, I'm not so crazy about seeing and speaking to most of the live people I know, much less interact with dead ones. And I cannot foretell the future, so if you want to know who's gonna win the sixth race at Belmont, you'd do better picking winners by choosing the horse's name you like best."

"Too bad," he says.

"And it's not a superpower. I cannot leap tall buildings in a single bound, bend steel bars, stop speeding bullets. And I can't use my nonexistent x-ray vision to fulfill a preteen boy's fantasy of seeing women naked. What I have is no more a power than being able to crack your knuckles at will, cross your eyes on command, or wrap your legs around your neck is a power. It's more like a quirky trait. A trait I try to ignore whenever possible. I don't use it in my life, nor do I use it for other people. My life is complicated enough without getting mixed up in other people's. Besides, it's a little scary. It's a burden, and it comes with responsibility."

"Seems like a nice thing to have."

"It's not. And it doesn't make me feel special. It makes me feel *different.*"

"What's wrong with that?"

"The last thing I want is a constant reminder that I'm different from everyone else. I don't want people looking at me like I'm some kind of freak or, even worse, a conman. By the way, for the record, I'm neither of those."

From the expression on his face, I can see he doesn't totally get it. Why should he? I'm not sure myself.

What Tony really wants is ground rules: a handy list of the cans and cannots. So, as we cruise toward New Haven, this is what I try to give him.

I cannot touch or smell or be in the general vicinity of the garment or any possession of a missing person and then, like a reliable cadaver dog, lead folks to where the body is buried.

I do not fall into a deep trance, my eyes rolling back into my head, as I travel into some kind of mysterious room where I make contact with my spirit guide. In fact, I have no idea what a spirit guide is or does.

I do not speak in unfamiliar foreign tongues or gibberish that might pass for some exotic language I have no business knowing. Frankly, after a couple drinks I have trouble handling the tongue I've grown up speaking.

On the rare occasion when I do allow my mind to go where I do not want it to go, meaning thinking about this thing I have, I'm not always 100 percent right. Sometimes I'm in the ballpark. Sometimes I get it half right. And sometimes, I'm so far off you might as well consult one of those toy eight-ball fortune-telling globes. But most of the time, I don't even bother thinking about it.

I cannot turn this *thing*, this gift, this quirky trait, this curse, on and off at will. I can try, but more often than not, I will fail. Miserably. I cannot call it up at will, at least I don't think I can. So far, it comes to me randomly and unexpectedly.

I can, however, if I concentrate really hard and if the wind is blowing in the right direction (just kidding about the wind), I can try to cultivate a "scene" and tease it into existence. If, that is,

I'm of a mind to. But I don't and have never experimented much, exploring the ins and outs of what I can do. Practice might make perfect, but I don't practice, in part because I don't want to get it "perfect." I'm not sure why I haven't nurtured it. Maybe it's because I'm frightened by what I'm capable of doing. It's like I'm at the edge of a precipice and there's the almost overwhelming temptation to get closer and closer to the edge to see exactly what's down there. But what if I get so close I tumble in? What then? Will I get seriously psychically injured? Will I fall so deep I won't be able to get back up? Sure, I'm curious. But not curious enough to get any closer to the edge than I have to. And when Tony asks for help, the first thing that runs through my mind is: *How far will I have to go? How far can I go?* And if I try and fail, what will be the effects? This last bit is something I do not tell Tony. At this point, he needs to believe in me a lot more than I need to believe in myself.

I do not want to be defined by this thing. I do not want people to look at me and identify me as *the dude who's a psychic...*

Finally, the lightning round.

I do not say things like, *I see danger ahead...* or *I wouldn't take that flight if I were you.*

I do not perform cheesy parlor tricks, so don't ask me to regale you with Kreskin or Penn & Teller–like stunts. The fact is, you're more likely to guess the number between one and ten that someone's thinking of than I am.

I do not see things that aren't there.

I do not see things that are there but shouldn't be.

I do not see into the future.

I do not and cannot communicate with your late Uncle Joe, nor do I have a Native American spirit guide named Running Bear. Or Leaky Faucet.

So, what can I do?

I can somehow put myself into a scene that already exists somewhere in time and space. Not a scene that *will* exist. But one that *has* already existed or is in the process of existing.

By the time I finish, there's a look of bewilderment on Tony's face. Am I just making this even less comprehensible than it is?

"I'm not totally sure what you mean," says Tony who's obviously struggling to make sense of what I'm telling him. "How about an example?"

"Okay. Let's say we're sitting around, chatting about this and that, and you tell me about a walk in the park you took the other day. If I'm in the right mood, or rather the right mode, a picture might begin to develop in my mind. You are in that picture, and so am I. Only I'm not really there, I'm kind of hovering above it. I see things you see. I hear things you hear. I feel things you feel. In other words, for that moment, we are indistinguishable. I am you, and yet I'm still me. In that moment, I am that proverbial fly on the wall. While floating above you, I see everything, as if I'm a camera recording the moment. If I turn around, I can see three hundred and sixty degrees. Think of me as a drone following you and only you. But I have the ability to see things you don't see, because either you weren't looking or you weren't paying attention, or it's something that's taking place outside your line of sight. At that moment I can sense your pain, your delight, your confusion, your happiness, your sadness. But I cannot read what's going on in your mind. And, at least as yet, I can't hear what's taking place. Does this make any sense?"

"To be honest," he says, "none of it makes sense." He shakes his head. "But for some reason, that's reassuring. Maybe, like you, the less I know about the ins and outs, and the less I understand, the better. Maybe it's just a matter of being a believer."

"This may seem like a gift, Tony, but it's not. Think about it. How would you feel if you thought the person next to you could hop in and out of your life? I'll answer that for you: pretty shitty and totally creeped out."

"That it?" he asks, his fingers nervously tapping the wheel.

"There are probably more rules, caveats, and warnings, but because I've spent my life running in the opposite direction, I don't know what they are. Whenever *it* kicks in and I decide to go with the flow, I become more aware of what I can and can't do. It's like you know you can throw a baseball, but you aren't sure how far you can throw it and how accurately until you give it a try."

"You make it sound like a fucking burden."

I hesitate a moment before answering. I know the answer—it *is* a burden—but do I really want to turn myself into a victim?

"Since I don't talk about it, I can't say I'm burdened by it."

"So, when do you start using it? I mean, have you already started tuning in?"

Talking about this makes me anxious. But I know Tony's desperate, and if talking about it helps him calm down, I'll muddle through.

"It's more like it uses me. Sometimes I get images flashing through my mind, but unless I concentrate on them, they fade away. It's kind of like you're thinking about something and then, suddenly, your mind goes somewhere else and you have to stop yourself and get back to what you were originally thinking about. There came a time when I realized if I concentrate on an image, I can keep it with me for a while, and then I found I could actually enter the picture I was seeing. Kind of like being an astral visitor. I can enter that picture, look around, see everything from the point of view of the person whose reality it is as well as the overall scene. It's like I'm watching and participating at the same time. Does this make any sense?"

"Not sure."

"Let's face it. Bottom line, what you really want to know is how I can help find Allie."

"Right."

"I'm not sure. I can only promise I'll do my best. Have you told Rachel that's why you asked me to come with you?"

"She'd think I was out of my mind."

I laugh, because that seems like the appropriate response. Tony keeping my secret makes me feel closer to him. It also puts a lot of pressure on me.

"What did you tell her?"

"I lied. I told her you're one of the smartest people I know and that if you were with me, you'd pick up on things I wouldn't." He takes one hand off the wheel and passes his palm swiftly over his head. He smiles. "I think she bought it." Beat. "Because we both know that ain't true."

"Best case scenario, what do *you* hope to get out of me?"

"You make it sound so…transactional."

"It is. And that's fine. If I were in your position, I'd do the same thing. I'd throw everything against the wall and hope something, anything stuck. I can't imagine what it's like to have someone you love disappear into thin air."

I think I've fucked up. My talking about this is forcing him to face up to the possible consequences: that I can't help him find his daughter and that something is seriously wrong. Suddenly, he gets all quiet. This silence is broken only by the occasional thumping sound his thumbs make as he taps nervously on the wheel.

Finally, he gets to what's on his mind. "Okay. I was thinking that maybe with this psychic ability of yours, you might be able to get some sign of where she is. Or maybe you can help me figure out who's lying and who's telling the truth."

"You think people will be lying to you?"

He shrugs. "I think there's a good chance of it. If she is missing of her own accord, she probably confided in one of her friends, or her roommate, and I'm guessing she swore them to secrecy. And if something bad has happened to her, God forbid, it's not like anyone's gonna come right out and admit guilt. I need someone more objective than me."

"I'm not a human lie detector, Tony."

"I know that," he says, obviously annoyed at what he probably perceives at worst as hostility, at best negativity.

"At what point were you thinking about getting the cops involved?"

"Trying to avoid that as long as possible. I mean, what if it's something really simple? What if she actually told Rachel she was going away for the weekend but Rachel forgot? We don't want to jump the gun and look like a couple idiots."

"What if we find out it's something serious?"

"I guess that's when we call the cops. She's an adult. She can disappear if she wants to. There's no crime here…yet. But…" His sentence trails off.

"Wanna finish that thought?"

"Look, she does have that history of running away. Kid stuff, though. You know, when they pack a bag, take off, and don't get any further away than a few blocks. But that's a question the cops will ask, and the answer gives them an excuse for not following up immediately."

If that's the case now, and she comes back soon, I'm pretty much off the hook. This might simply be the rebellious Allie simply taking off with a new boyfriend or traveling down to the southern border to help immigrants sneak into the country.

Lesson over, we ride in silence. Tony in his world. Me in mine.

After a while, the silence, which is forcing me into my own head, is making me nervous. It doesn't help that I'm already starting to feel the pressure. And so, mostly to get out of my own head, I decide to fill the void with questions.

"Have you guys checked her social media? There's no such thing as privacy anymore. Everything is aired over places like Facebook, Instagram, and TikTok."

"First thing Rachel did was check her social media. Some funky dance routine's not gonna tell us where she is."

"And?"

"Try dialing into a teenager's head thinking you'll learn something about them and you'll see what I mean. It's all about convincing other people, and yourself, that you're living the good life, that you've got it better than your friends. Much better, your enemies."

"She's got enemies?"

He laughs. "Only kidding. She's probably too young to have real enemies. Not like us old timers. It makes me damn glad we grew up a generation before social media."

"So, you didn't find anything helpful?"

"Not a clue as to where she is, if that's what you're asking."

"When did she last post?" I ask.

"A couple days before she went off the grid."

So, there it is. As far as Tony is concerned, she's not missing, she's merely chosen to "go off the grid." Like it's her choice, and that conjures up the notion of a whole different ball game. No longer a victim of foul play, she's simply decided to go off and do her own thing. I have no idea where this is coming from until, after giving it some thought, I realize this is a lot more palatable concept than contemplating foul play.

"It's the first thing we thought of. I mean, these kids don't do anything without announcing it to the whole fucking world."

"What about direct messages? Maybe there's someone she confided in?"

"We'd have to know her passwords to get to those."

"Right," I say, as we fall back into our shared silence. A moment passes. "Maybe Rachel knows them?"

"I'll ask."

The thought, more like a wish, crosses my mind that when we arrive at Allie's dorm, she'll be there to greet us and we can all have a good laugh and go back to our lives.

Fat chance, right?

Josh
The Sound a Whiffenpoof Makes

I'm all talked out, and Tony, eyes still firmly fixed on the road ahead, is lost in his own thoughts.

For the past fifteen, twenty minutes there's been an awkward, uncharacteristic silence. Tony's worried about his wife and daughter. I get that. The stakes are high. If we're not able to find her, he doesn't know how he's going to face Rachel. And, after my rambling, possibly confusing, and probably ineffective attempt at explaining myself, he might be wondering why the hell he brought me into this in the first place.

The silence becomes too unnerving, so I find an NPR station. The spoken word now fills the empty spaces in the car, but none of the words are ours. Tony pretends to listen, while I stare out the window, preparing myself for failure. I start to wonder how long will it take me to find another best friend.

To make matters worse, I can't get comfortable. I'm restless. I'm jumpy. Something's not quite right, but I can't figure out what it is. A shrink once claimed I suffer from "free-floating anxiety."

"If that means I worry about everything all the time, then you're right," I said. And then, since I don't need to pay someone $150 an hour to tell me what I already know, I found a new shrink.

With way too much time to think, my mind drifts off to where it shouldn't go. I feel like a specimen under a microscope. I begin to wonder if Tony is testing me, looking for telltale signs of my *special gift*, which I consider a curse. Of course, I don't tell him that. But a simple question like, "Do you think we should look for a parking spot or put it in a garage?" feels like a challenge. Like if I don't give the right answer, I'll be voted off the island. *Get over yourself*, I tell myself as I fiddle with the seat position.

I don't know exactly what Tony's expectations are, but I doubt I can live up to them. I should have said no when he asked me to come along with him. But what kind of friend would I be if I didn't at least go through the motions of trying to help him?

We exit off 95 and pull onto the sprawling Yale campus. It's my first time, but Tony's been here at least twice before—once to take Allison to check out the campus, the second time to move her in—so he seems to know where he's going. Tony's legendary "parking karma" kicks in (he swears he's never had to spend more than five minutes looking for a parking spot) and sure enough we find a spot in front of The Whale Tea, a takeout/delivery joint across from Helen Hadley Hall, Allie's dorm.

"Should I stay here?" I ask.

I'm suddenly hit by a wave of fatigue. I can hardly keep my eyes open. My arms and legs are lead weights. *Am I having a stroke? A heart attack? A runaway blood clot?* You hear about this kind of stuff all the time. Healthy, middle-aged man suddenly passes away from an undiagnosed illness. *Am I going to die? Here, in a car parked across from a college dorm? Will this be my final resting place?*

I don't want to get out of the car. All I want to do is tilt my head back, close my eyes, and fall asleep. And, hours from now, wake up in my own bed.

"Come with me. Worst-case scenario, you get to stretch your legs and make believe you're back in college."

"That's a nightmare," I mumble as I unstrap myself and get out of the car. I'm standing on the sidewalk on the passenger's side. Tony's standing opposite me, in the street. He has a faraway look on his face. He's jingling the car keys in his right hand while his left hand rests atop of the half-open door. He's looking in my direction, but he's got this odd expression on his face. I'm not even sure he sees me. He reminds me of one of those frighteningly realistic commuter statues, carrying a folded-up newspaper under one arm, the other arm stretched outward, as if hailing a cab.

I walk around the front of the car and put my arm around his shoulders.

"You okay, man?"

He startles, then snaps to attention. "Yeah. I'm fine."

"For a moment there, I thought I'd lost you." Lost both of us, actually.

"So, you do care."

"Not really. Just figure it's the right thing to say." My arm's still around his shoulder, as I gently guide him in the direction of the sidewalk.

"For the record, J, you're like a brother to me," he says solemnly.

Where is this coming from? Am I supposed to say something back? I'm not sure how to react, so I do what I often do when I'm uncomfortable: make a joke out of it.

"I appreciate that, Tony. But I already have a brother and I haven't spoken to him in over five years. So, the last thing I need is another one not talking to me."

He smiles and pats me twice on the cheek. This, I hope, is as close as we're going to get to a Hallmark moment.

"Let's go," he says. Suddenly energized, he turns and heads toward the dorm. I follow a step behind. Just as we're about to enter the building, I tug on Tony's arm.

"What's up, man?" he says.

"Before we go in, I think we ought to get something straight."

"Like what?"

"I need to know what your expectations are."

"Expectations?"

"What's our strategy? What role you want me to take. And I'm warning you, Tony, if you expect miracles..."

He looks at me like I'm speaking a foreign language.

"Who said anything about miracles? Just...just chill. You do what you do, I'll do what I do. Capisce?"

"Yeah. That's fine. But I need to know exactly how you want me to act."

"We'll make it up as we go along. Jump in whenever you think you can help. Like maybe when you get a vision of where she is and what's happened to her." He hesitates a moment. "If anything."

I see fear in his face.

"You're expecting the worst, aren't you?"

"The worst?"

"About Allie."

"Aren't you?"

"Doesn't matter what I think."

"Right," he says, though I can't swear he's actually hearing what I say because despite the fact he's standing still, it appears as if he's in constant motion, his body charged with energy but without direction.

"One more thing, Tony. I need you to understand I'm not a circus freak who can turn it on and off at will. And remember, I can't read minds and I can't see into the future."

"Just do your best, okay?" He pats me on the top of my head, like I'm a kid, then turns and charges ahead into the building.

By the time I catch up to him, he's already explaining to the security guard at the front desk who he is and why he's here.

"I need to get into her room," says Tony.

The security guard, who looks like every male bank teller you've seen in every bank you've ever been to, shakes his head. "Sorry. I can't let you guys up there."

"I'm her father."

"That doesn't…"

Tony whips out his wallet and flashes his driver's license. "Here. Look. See. Same last name."

The security guy shakes his head. "Sorry, sir. I can't let you up without permission. Call your daughter and have her come down and she can either escort you up to the room or you guys can visit in the lounge. Better yet, take her out for a good meal."

Tony's ready to blow. Fearing he'll get us thrown off campus, maybe even out of the city of New Haven, I jump in, hoping to calm the waters.

"As a parent," says the guard, "aren't you glad we have rules about letting strangers up without permission? It's all about security, sir."

Tony doesn't react, but I do.

I lean into the guard, so I'm only inches from his face and in a conspiratorial fake whisper, and say, "Look, the reason we're here is my friend's daughter isn't responding to phone calls or texts. So, there's no point in calling or texting. But she's got a roommate, right?" I look at Tony and he nods yes. "So, maybe call the roommate and ask her to either come down to talk to us, or let us come up."

The guard looks dubious, but I'm chipping away at his resolve. "You got a number for the roommate?" he asks.

I look over to Tony, who's zoned out again. I put my hand on his shoulder and he snaps to attention.

"The roommate's number? Got it?" I say.

"Yeah." He takes out his phone, scrolls through until he finds the number, then dials it. "Straight to voicemail," he says, as he faces the phone toward the guard, so he can hear.

I turn to Tony and say, "Try texting."

"Right." His fingers fly across the tiny keyboard. Seconds later there's a ping.

"Wants to meet us in the backyard patio."

Tony shows the security guard the text and he points us in the right direction.

It's been more than twenty years since I've been on a college campus. The closest I've ever gotten to one of the elite schools was growing up on the Upper West Side in Manhattan, about a mile south of Columbia. For a time, as a teenager, I was heavy into the Beats, Kerouac, Ginsberg, Caleb Carr. So, I visited the West End Bar hoping I'd somehow be able to communicate with the ghosts of my heroes, hoping some of their talent might rub off. It didn't.

We find a small, round table with a couple wire chairs on the patio, shaded by a large tree just beginning to bloom. We sit.

"Name's Kevin."

"Who?"

"Allie's roommate."

"He's a guy?"

"He was when we moved Allie in. But with all this gender-bending, nonspecific shit today, you can never be sure. He. She. Her. Him. It. They. Them. Did you know there are seventy-eight gender pronouns?"

"I did not. How's this something you know?

"Get with the program, man. Get woke."

"I thought I was, but I guess not. This has something to do with gender fluidity, right?"

He nods.

"Aren't you impressed I know even that much?"

"You never cease to amaze me, J. Every time I think I've got you pegged as a no-nothing yahoo, you surprise the hell out of me. It's a nonbinary gender thing. Or genderqueer. You have a 'woke' teenage daughter, you damn well better be up on all the jargon. Fortunately, she's decided to stick with being female. At least for now. Unfortunately, we had to sit through a thirty-minute oral dissertation from Allie when she was a sophomore in high school about how clueless we were. Probably still are, if you ask her."

"Were you guys worried about Allie rooming with a guy?"

"We had the talk when she was fourteen when she had her first boyfriend. Besides, she's got a very specific type, and this guy's not even close."

I feel my face flushing. Listening to Tony talk about his daughter's sex life is weird. And it is at that very moment I am, once again, glad I don't have kids. The idea of explaining the birds and the bees to an adolescent, male, female, it, them, or whatever, scares the heck out of me. I'd be overwhelmed with embarrassment. My parents solved the problem by tossing a book at me. I had absolutely no interest, so I don't think I cracked it open for maybe a year. As it turned out, what I learned from my peers on the street turned out to be pretty accurate.

Kevin is not what I picture a Yale Kevin to be. He's tall. Over six feet. And he's wide, with the beginnings of what will be a beer belly if he doesn't watch what he eats...and drinks. I'm no fat shamer, but I can't help but project what he'll look like twenty years from now. Go to any city where people don't walk, and you'll get the picture. He's got a full head of curly reddish-brown hair and a thick, red beard. He's dressed like a lumberjack. Faded blue jeans, plaid flannel with the tail out. When I was in college, this outfit was a dead giveaway that you were a forestry student. At Yale, though, he could be studying anything.

Before Tony can introduce us, the kid, who's carrying a book, says, "Sorry, Mr. A, but I'm kinda pressed for time. Gotta get this book back to the library and then I'm supposed to meet with one of my profs. According to her, I'm having a little trouble understanding the difference between a metaphor and a simile. Like I give a shit. Like it's ever gonna come up at a job interview."

"We'll be quick, Kevin. This is my friend, Josh. He's helping out. I know you've already spoken to my wife, so you know the deal. Any idea where Allie is?"

He shakes his head. "Like I told Mrs. A, not a clue."

"When was the last time you saw her?"

"What's today?"

I'm hanging back, letting Tony take the lead. But there's something about this kid that doesn't seem right. For one thing, he doesn't appear to be very concerned about Allie. He seems disconnected. When I get a closer look into his eyes, I see his pupils are dilated.

"Tuesday," says Tony.

"Right," says the kid.

His head drops. He runs his hand through his thick, unruly hair. "I guess, maybe it was Friday?"

"You're asking me, Kevin? Was it Friday, or wasn't it?"

"Yeah. Yeah. Friday. Three, four o'clock."

"Did you talk to her?"

"You mean like did we have a conversation?"

This is beginning to resemble an Abbott and Costello routine.

"Mind my asking what you're on, Kevin?" I say.

"What's that supposed to mean?" Kevin replies.

Tony looks aghast, as if I'm going to blow the whole interview by alienating the kid. But I've already taken the leap, and once taken, there's no return. I'm wondering if what's going on with Allie has something to do with drugs.

"Your eyes are practically popping out of your head, Kevin. What's going on?"

"I got a prescription."

"For what?"

"What's it your business?"

"Easy," says Tony, putting his hand on both the kid's and my shoulders, as if completing a circuit connection. "Look Kevin, my daughter's missing. I don't have the luxury of continuing this meaningless back and forth shit. Maybe we should just call the cops. Would you like being questioned by the cops, Kevin?"

"Come on, man," he whines.

"I'm sure you can understand why Tony's so upset, Kevin.... Just answer a few questions and we'll get out of your hair."

"Ritalin."

"Excuse me?" I say.

"That's what I'm taking. Ritalin. I have ADHD. It helps me concentrate."

Yet another alphabet salad drug taken in an attempt to make sense out of the world. Maybe I should try it.

"Obviously, it's not working very well," Tony mutters under his breath.

I shoot Tony a look meant to signal that he should dial down the hostility.

"Listen, kid, this is serious," I say.

"What say we stop fucking around," says Tony, who cannot contain his anger any longer. "All we want is to find my daughter. Or at least make sure she's okay. I don't give a fuck about you, what you're on or off. I just wanna know if there's anything you can remember that might help us."

Kevin casts his eyes to the ground. "Sorry, man. Look, Allie and I aren't close. That's why we're the perfect roommates. She does her thing, I do mine. Neither of us gets up in the other's business. I'm sorry. I really am. But I don't know how I can help you guys."

"Tell us about the last time you saw her Friday," I say softly, trying to lower the temperature. I don't want him to fear us. I want him to want to help us.

"When I got back from class Friday afternoon, she was there. To tell you the truth, I was kinda surprised..."

"Why?" says Tony.

"Because we hardly ever see each other. She's either in class, at the library studying, or hanging with her crew."

"Her crew?"

"You know, like her friends."

"Like?" Tony says.

He shrugs. "Wish I could help you, man, but they're like *her* friends. I might know one or two of them by sight, but I don't know their names or how to find them."

"What was she doing?" I ask.

"Doing?"

"When you got back to the room. What was she doing?"

"Packing."

"Where was she going?" asks Tony.

He shrugs. "None of my business. I figured she was going away for the weekend. Home maybe?" His gaze moves from Tony to me and then back to Tony. "Obviously not."

"Did you ask where?"

"I think maybe I asked if she was going home."

"And she said?" says Tony.

He closes his eyes and tilts his head back. "She said no."

"What then?"

"I dropped it. First off, I couldn't care less. Second of all, I could see she was kinda in a hurry to get out of there and all's I wanted to do was crash. I hadn't slept in like a day or two. Besides, we don't have that kind of relationship. You know, like keeping track of each other.... Like I said. She does her thing, I do mine."

"Can you just put yourself back there for a minute, Kevin," I say. "Is there anything she said that might give a clue where she was going?"

He shakes his head. "Nope."

"What state was she in?" I ask.

"State?"

"Was she anxious? Angry? Happy? Sad?"

"Don't know, didn't care."

"And you have no clue where she was headed?"

"Like I already told you, no idea." He shifts his book from one hand to the other. I can see we're starting to lose him.

"Think, Kevin. It's really important," I say.

"I wish I could help you guys. I really do. Allie's cool, but like I said, she and me aren't that close. I don't mind her business and she don't mind mine. She's got this best friend. I think her name's Lisa something. Ask her. She might know something."

"How do we find her?" asks Tony.

Kevin shakes his head. "No clue. Look, like I said, I'm kinda in a hurry. How about I bring you guys up to the room and you can look around? Maybe you'll find something there. Like Lisa's last name?"

"I don't have a key," says Tony.

"Don't need one. Door's unlocked. Stay as long as you want. Just shut it when you leave."

I'm about to say something about how stupid it is to leave your door unlocked, but Tony is already on the move.

"Time to get this show on the road," says Tony.

Kevin takes off and we go back inside. Waiting for the elevator, I can see Tony is a bundle of exposed nerves.

"Does Allie have a boyfriend?" I ask.

Either Tony doesn't hear me or he doesn't want to answer the question. Instead, he channels his anxiety by punching the UP button a few more times with his closed fist.

"So, does she?"

"Does she what?"

"Have a boyfriend."

"You'll have to ask Rachel. That's not the kind of thing she talks to me about."

The elevator door opens, and two young women deep in conversation get off.

As soon as we step onto the elevator, I get an odd, unsettling feeling. I'm not sure what's going on. I take a step back, so I'm behind him. I'm not even sure he notices.

A picture begins to form in my mind. It comes unexpectedly, and it's disturbing. In the past, I'd simply force myself to think of something else, but today I'm on the job, so I go with the flow. I shut my eyes, hoping the image becomes clear enough so I can understand what it's about.

It begins as a blurry image, like one of those cheesy movie dreams. Slowly, it comes into focus. I'm floating up near the ceiling in what appears to be a dorm room. I watch as Allie silently shuffles back and forth from her closet to a chest of drawers to a blue canvas duffle bag open on her bed. I look to see what's behind Allie, and there's Kevin standing in the doorway. They're speaking to each other—I can see their lips move—but the scene comes minus sound.

It's like I'm wearing a pair of virtual reality goggles, putting me smack in the middle of the scene. It's freaky and mind-boggling the way I can maneuver my body simply by leaning one way or the other. Hovering in midair, I'm able to spin 360 degrees around the room. Suddenly, the ding of the elevator reaching our floor and the scene disappears.

Tony twists open the doorknob and we're in. The dorm room, which looks eerily familiar, is split in two, a common wall separating them. To the left is Allie's area, to the right Kevin's. Tony's been here before, so he heads straight into Allie's room while I stand in the small foyer. I glance into Kevin's room. Clothes are strewn over the bed and on the floor. There's an open laptop computer on a desk smothered in books and papers. The bed is unmade and it looks like it's been that way for days, maybe longer. And there's this musty, stomach-churning guy smell.

Allie's room, on the other hand, is in stark contrast to Kevin's. It's surprisingly neat, everything in its place.

"Something's definitely wrong here," says Tony, shaking his head.

"Wrong how?"

"It's way too neat. Allie's room at home always looked like a twister just hit followed by a cyclone. So, unless she has a housekeeper who comes in every day, this is plain wrong."

Either Allie's uncharacteristically tidied up before leaving for an unknown destination, or someone else did. But if so, who?

Tony takes a seat in front of Allie's desk and begins opening the drawers while I slowly circle the room, looking for something, anything that might provide a hint as to where Allie is.

With my eyes, I browse through the few dozen books lined up perfectly on a five-foot-high wooden bookshelf opposite her desk. They're mostly the same books I had to read in freshman English: Hemingway, Fitzgerald. Alongside them were authors like Margaret Atwood, Toni Morrison, Zadie Smith, Junot Diaz, Sherman Alexie, James Baldwin, and Ralph Ellison. Checking out these titles makes it feel like I'm drowning in a wave of nostalgia, sending me back in time twenty-five years.

"Find anything interesting?" I ask, peering over Tony's shoulder.

He shakes his head no. "Her laptop would help, but it isn't here."

"That's a good sign, don't you think?"

"How's that?"

"If she was snatched, the laptop would still be here. The fact that it's not means either it's been stolen or she took it with her. And if she's taken it with her, it means she expected to be gone for at least a few days."

"Maybe," says Tony, though I can tell by the tone of his voice that he's not totally convinced.

"I think wherever she is, she's there of her own volition. Remember what Kevin told us. No one packs for a kidnapping."

"Makes sense, I guess." He gives me a look I haven't seen before. It worries me.

"I know I'm here to use whatever it is you think I have to help find Allie, and that's fine. You know I'll do anything for you to help. But it makes me very uncomfortable the way you're looking at me."

"How'm looking at you?"

"Like you're judging me. And you know what, I can't deal with the expectations you're piling on me. The way you're looking at me creeps me out. The message I'm getting is that anything less than finding her makes me a loser."

"I'm sorry if you think that's what I'm thinking, J. I appreciate what you're doing. Even if it doesn't lead to finding Allie, it means a lot that I've got a friend who's going out on a limb to help. I don't know if I can control this judgmental look, but I need you to know that no matter what happens, I know you're doing your best."

"Okay.... I'm glad I said something," I say, patting Tony on the shoulder. "And I promise I won't keep anything from you concerning Allie."

I'm lying, of course. Because I know at some point I will hold back, not only to protect him and Rachel, but to protect myself.

"That's a promise, right?"

"Got a Bible handy?"

"That won't be necessary," he says as he turns his attention back to riffling through Allie's desk drawers.

"Any idea what we're looking for?" I ask.

He stops and swivels to face me.

"No fucking idea."

I plop down on the edge of Allie's bed.

"Too bad about the laptop," I say. "There might be some kind of schedule on it. Or a clue to what's going on. Ditto her phone. Back in the day, we had Rolodexes, date books, even journals. Today, everything's electronic." I pull my smartphone out of my pocket. "Our entire lives are dependent on this thing. Kinda scary, right?"

He slams the bottom drawer closed. He cradles his head in his hands. "What the hell am I going to tell Rachel? I can't go home without something," he says.

I don't need any superpower to feel his pain. Or his frustration. It's not my kid who's missing, but the responsibility he's put on me is almost unbearable. I desperately want to return to the days when no one knew my secret. I wish I'd never come clean about it with Tony, all those years ago. I may be able to see the past, but I can't change it. What I'm doing for Tony is forcing me to confront and embrace what I've always thought of as a curse. And as I sit here watching my best friend slowly dissolve into a pool of frustration and anxiety, I realize I have another role in this family drama: keeping Tony's spirits high, so he doesn't sink into total despair.

The stakes are almost as high for me, as they are for Tony and Rachel. I don't want to lie or shine him on, but for his sake, I do what I have to.

"Don't worry, Tony. We'll find something that'll help us find her. Let's talk to her friends and see what they have to say. Someone must know something."

Tony takes a deep breath. He wipes his eyes with the sleeve of his jacket. Has he been crying?

"Okay. But we're not leaving here before checking out everything."

He gets up and heads to Allie's closet.

"He's telling the truth," I say.

He stops and turns to face me.

"Who's telling the truth?"

"Kevin. She was packing a bag when he saw her."

"How do you know?"

I hesitate. Maybe I've said too much. Should I be straight with him? I know Tony well enough to know that feeding him lies will only make it worse. What he needs now is a sign from me that I might be able to help.

"Because I *saw* it."

I have crossed the Rubicon, and there's no turning back

"Saw it? What do you mean, *saw it*?"

I give him a look meant to say, *Isn't that obvious?*

"You mean that thing you do?"

I nod.

"You saw both of them in the room here? Together?"

I nod.

"And Allie was packing."

"Yes. Into a blue backpack."

"What was she putting in it?"

"Regular stuff. Clothing. Books. Like that."

"You can see those details?"

"Yes."

"What about her laptop?" he says, unable to hide his excitement.

"Didn't see it. But maybe she'd already packed it. I could only see what was going on when she and Kevin were in the room.... It's not like I can dial it back and forward."

"So, it's like you were actually in the room with them?"

"Yes. But I'm only an observer, Tony. I can't make people do what they haven't done. I can't get into their minds. I can't read their thoughts. I can't interact with them, at all.... I cannot change events that have already happened. And I don't hear sounds or conversations. At least not yet."

It's difficult to explain. And when I try it makes me feel like I'm some kind of two-bit fortune teller.

Tony falls silent. I don't have to be a mind reader to know he's trying to figure out how he can best use me and, most important, whether he can trust what I'm seeing.

We sit in silence until, after a minute or two, he turns his attention back to the closet and renews his search. I'm pretty sure this won't lead to answers. But doing something, anything probably makes him feel better.

So, I keep my mouth shut and do not interfere.

Josh
BFFs

It's midafternoon and spring has sprung early in New England. It's uncharacteristically warm, the temperature pushing seventy-five. Chalk it up to global warming.

Things are heating up for me too. Let's face it. I have a real problem when it comes to people's expectations. It's probably why I've had so many problems making relationships work. Truth is, I do much better on my own, probably because the expectations I place on myself are so low. But now Tony's forced me into a position where others are counting on me and, to be honest, that's an uncomfortable place for me to be.

And so, it's up to me to "man" up. To rise to the occasion. This might be what's called adult behavior, which I've struggled with most of my adult life. When the late, great Satchel Paige was once asked how old he was, he replied, "How old would you be if you didn't know how old you was?" My answer would be twelve.

Now, thanks to Tony, I can no longer hide from this *thing* I have. Not only do I have to face it head on, but I also have to make peace with it so I can use it to help find Allie.

Like the boxer Joe Louis once said about his upcoming opponent, Billy Conn, "He can run, but he can't hide," which is something I've done most of my life.

"Listen, Tony, why don't you call Rachel and ask her for a list of all Allie's friends, both here and back home. We'll need email addresses and phone numbers. Tell her we need it as soon as possible."

"She's gonna ask how we're doing. What am I supposed to tell her?"

"Tell her we're making progress and all indications are that Allie's okay. Strike that. Tell her we're sure Allie's okay. Don't tell her anything that'll make her panic. That's not gonna help anyone."

"Easy for you to say. She's like Torquemada. Once she gets me on the phone, she'll have me spilling every bean in the bag."

"Don't call. Email or text. That way, you can avoid getting into a conversation."

"Ha! You think that's gonna stop her?" he says as he leans up against the hood of the car, whips out his phone, and begins composing a text. "I guarantee within seconds after she gets this"—he waves his phone in the air—"my phone's gonna ring, and guess who it'll be."

"While you're at it, see if she has passwords for Allie's social media. Facebook, Twitter, TikTok, Instagram…"

"I doubt Allie shares any of that with Rachel. Even though their relationship has improved, they still have their good times and bad times. It's a mother-daughter thing. But who knows, maybe I'll be pleasantly surprised."

He sends the text, and sure enough, within seconds his phone begins to sing what sounds like a familiar tune.

"Who's that? Taylor Swift?"

He shrugs. "Blame Allie. She's the one who set up my phone. It only rings that way when I get a call from Rachel or Allie. Everyone close has their own song. Truth is, I don't need a song to know it's my wife calling. Hey, maybe I've got a little of that ESP thing too."

Before answering, he walks around to the driver's side. He gets in, then gestures for me to do the same. That's when it hits me. For the first time I begin to wonder if Tony has shared my secret with Rachel. She is, after all, his wife. I didn't share all my secrets with my ex-wife—maybe that's why she's my ex—but Tony has a different relationship. I want to ask, but think better of it. It's not the time to question his ability to keep a secret and his loyalty as a friend.

"Keep it short and sweet," I warn. He holds the phone far enough away from his ear that I can hear Rachel's end of the conversation.

"What's going on?" she says in a high-pitched voice that bleeds panic.

"We just spoke to Kevin."

"Does he know anything?"

"He saw her Friday. She was packing."

"Packing for what?"

"He doesn't know. But this is good news, Rachel. It means she left of her own accord."

"But it doesn't tell us where she is, why she left without telling me, or if she's okay," says Rachel.

"Honey, you've got to take it down a notch. We're all over this. All I need is that list so we can move ahead. You've got to stop thinking the worst…"

"We haven't heard from her in almost a week, Tony. I think that's pretty close to the worst, don't you?" Her tone has turned harsh. I feel for my friend. And even more for Rachel. Until we find Allie, this will only get worse, and Tony is an easy, available target.

Tony begins to tear up. I feel his pain. He loves and misses Allie, at least as much as if he were her biological father, and he's frustrated he can't do more to find her. No one wants to fail. Especially not in front of people we love. I've been thinking about bailing as soon as I can, but now I know there's no way I will abandon my friend. No matter what happens, I'm all in till the bitter end.

I can't listen to them anymore. It's way too private. I feel like I'm in the middle of a disintegrating marriage. I went through it once myself, no way I want to go through it again. I get out of the car and lean up against a nearby tree, waiting for Tony to finish. When he does, he leans forward and rests his head on the steering wheel.

I get back in the car.

"Let's get something to eat and then, as soon as Rachel sends the list, we'll get started."

He looks up. "You're a good friend, Josh. You know that, don't you?"

"I do my best," I say, even though I know it's not the truth. But I promise myself it will be. Over the years, I've failed myself way too many times. No way I'm going to fail my best friend.

We find a coffee shop not far from the dorm. Tony says very little and I welcome the silence. He hardly touches what's supposed to be a turkey and avocado sandwich. When the waitress comes to clear our table, I ask her to wrap it up for him. He puts his hand up and shakes his head no.

I hear *ping* coming from Tony's cell phone. It's Rachel, texting us the list. Now, finally, we can get back on the trail.

Josh
Pulling Teeth

Her name is Lisa Milano. Like the cookie. She's at the top of the list of half dozen names Rachel texts us. Ever organized, a remnant from her producer days, Rachel includes emails, phone numbers, and their relationship to Allie. The only exception is for someone named "Alex," for whom there's no contact information. Nor is there an indication of whether Alex is a he, she, they or them. The note next to his or her name simply indicates *new friend?* I make a note to have Tony reach out to Rachel for more information. There's no rush. We've plenty to work with for now.

What I thought or rather hoped would amount to maybe a day now looks like it's more likely two or three days we need to be in New Haven. Rather than commute back and forth, I suggest we find an inexpensive motel for the night. At first, Tony is resistant. He doesn't want to be away from Rachel and his son that long. He's afraid that left alone her imagination will run wild. Eventually, he gives in to the reality that there's no way we're going to find Allie in the next few hours.

"Okay if we share a room? I'm paying, of course," he says, as we approach the front desk of a Super 8 by Wyndham, about a mile and a half from the campus. At sixty-four bucks a night, it's quite the bargain. "It's not that I'm cheap or anything," he adds. "I just think it's a good idea so we can bounce shit off each other. But if you'd rather…"

People rarely say what they really mean, and Tony is no exception. Whether he'll admit it or not, I know he wants to keep me close in case I get a psychic newsflash. Or, perhaps, he doesn't want to be alone. Even though I prefer my own room and I'm more than willing to pay for it, I don't put up a fight.

"It'll be fun. Like a sleepover."

After we check in, we visit a CVS to pick up essentials like toothpaste, toothbrushes, and disposable razors. We have a good laugh about living in the same clothing for a few days, something we both own up to doing more than once back in the day.

Though I'm beat—it's already been a tortuously long day—Tony is anxious to keep going. He can't seem to unwind. He's like one giant tic. A bundle of energy. Every part of his body is in constant motion. I picture him as one of those off-shore wind turbines. While I check my email for messages, Tony is practically bouncing off the walls. He paces the room like a caged animal.

His unrest is contagious. While my body craves rest, my mind is active, jumping from one thing to another. I have to come up with something to keep him busy, so we can both calm down. Besides, we both need to find something, anything, that gives us even the illusion of making progress.

"How about we give this kid Lisa a call and see if we can meet up with her."

"Great idea," says Tony.

While he contacts Lisa Milano, I take the opportunity to visit the bathroom, where I splash water on my face. When I look into the mirror, I don't recognize the face staring back at me. It's the face of a man ten, twenty years older than me. Could I possibly have more wrinkles today than I did yesterday?

When I come back into the room, Tony is putting on his jacket.

"We're all set. She'll meet us at a coffee shop not far from here. Let's roll."

Twenty minutes later, we're seated at a table in the back of a Starbucks halfway between our motel and the campus. Tony, nervously thrumming his fingers on the table, keeps checking his cell phone.

"What time you say she'll get here?" I ask.

"Five."

"It's only five-ten, Tony. You know these kids have no sense of time. Just like my ex-wife."

"I gave her my cell number. She said she'd let me know if she was running late."

His eyes are glued to the entrance. Suddenly, he jumps up from the table, almost knocking his chair to the floor. "That's her!" he says as he heads toward the entrance. I wonder how he knows what she looks like, but quickly realize he's probably seen her picture on Facebook or Instagram.

She's a young, very pretty Asian woman with jet-black, shoulder-length hair. She's wearing skintight, faded jeans, a dark blue bulky knit sweater with a jean jacket over it, and calf-high black boots. She's got a small silver ring through her nose that matches her silver hoop earrings.

Tony escorts her back to our table but neglects to introduce me. I rise and offer my hand. "My name's Josh, and I'm this guy's keeper."

"Oh, yeah, this is Josh," Tony says dismissively, offering absolutely no explanation of who I am or why I'm here. "What'll you have, Lisa? Anything you want. My treat."

She smiles and mumbles some exotic coffee concoction I've never heard of.

"Josh, would you mind?" he says, jerking his head toward the counter. I sit there a moment thinking, *Is this what it's come to? Am I nothing more than an overage go-fer?* And then I realize it's because he doesn't want to take his eyes off Lisa, lest she take off. At that moment, all hope is invested in this young woman barely out of her teens.

I ask if she'd like something to eat.

"Like, here?" she says.

"Well, since that's where we are, then yes, like, here."

"Have you ever taken a good look at what they serve here? First off, it's, like, petrified, from like the Dark Ages. It might look like food, but it's like all chemicals. Check out the labels. You'll see what I mean. There's no actual food in it. And it's like been sitting under those lights in the counter for like a week."

I can't help but smile. This generation, so concerned about what they put into their bodies, while at the same time taking part in all kinds of dangerous, risky behavior.

As I turn to leave, Tony says, "Don't worry, J. We won't discuss anything important till you get back."

I know he's not saying this out of consideration for me. He's saying it because he doesn't want me to miss a single word, a thought, a gesture, in case there's something, anything, that sets off some kind of magical, mystical image tour in my mind. And there's something else. It suddenly occurs to me that Tony might also be using me as a kind of truth serum. He probably thinks I'll automatically know if someone's lying or holding back important information.

When I return with the kid's coffee, I find them staring across at each other in stony silence. Like they've been frozen in time, just waiting for me to return. I place the coffee in front of Lisa, then slip back into a seat between them.

"Let's get started," says Tony.

He's always been a topflight journalist, and now, for the first time, I'm seeing him work face-to-face. He knows what questions to ask and how to ask them. He has a goal and, like a heat-seeking missile, he stays on target no matter how many obstacles are thrown in his path. Good traits for a journalist, but maybe not so good when you're interviewing someone who wants to be anywhere but here.

"You know why we're here, Lisa. I'm looking for my daughter, Allison. Do you know where she is?"

"Who's he?" she asks, nodding in my direction, as if I'm not there. "You're not a cop, are you?"

I smile. "Only in my wildest imagination."

"He's an old family friend."

"So, why's he here? Where's Mrs. A?"

"Home with our son. Worried sick, by the way."

I know Tony well enough to see he's pissed. His teeth are clenched and the muscles in his jaw are flexing like a metronome. To his credit, he's holding it together. But how long will that last?

"Do you know where Allie is?"

"Nope," she says, flicking her long, black hair back. She grabs a couple packs of Sweet'n Low, tears them open, and dumps them both at the same time into her drink. Ironic that this introduction of chemicals into her body doesn't seem to bother her. She takes a sip and makes a sour face.

"Yuch. This sucks. Tastes burnt." She pushes the cup away.

"Live with it," Tony says, tossing her another packet of Sweet'n Low.

"When was the last time you saw her?" I ask, picking up the loose ball in an attempt to get us back in the game.

"Let me think," she says, nervously tapping her fingers on the table. Each fingernail is painted a different color, and when she thrusts her hand forward, I can make out a small tattoo of a Chinese symbol on her inside right wrist.

"She's been missing since Friday, Lisa, if that helps," I say. I can see she's nervous. Who wouldn't be with two men she doesn't know, asking questions, intimating by their presence that something bad might have happened to her friend. I need to slow things down and let her know she's in a safe place.

Tony removes a small notebook from his jacket pocket, one of the items he purchased at CVS a few hours ago. "This is embarrassing, but do either of you have a pen?" he asks.

"I do," says Lisa. She dips her hand in her large purse, rummages around, finds a pen, and hands it to Tony.

"So, what do you think, Lisa?" Tony asks as he opens his new notebook and folds back the cover. "Anything you can tell us. Even the smallest detail. Please don't leave anything out."

"I saw her last Thursday night. We met for a drink," she says in a monotone that does nothing to hide her boredom.

"Did she say anything about taking a trip?" Tony, pen poised in the air, asks.

"What kind of trip?" she says.

"That's what we need to know, Lisa," I say, learning forward slightly so she can't help but look into my eyes. I learned long ago that one of the rules of journalism is to always make eye contact. It creates a bond of sort, making it harder to lie.

"I don't know. She didn't say."

"What was her state of mind?" I ask.

I can see Tony's back on the edge. This isn't moving quick enough for him. But as a pro, he knows if he pushes too hard he risks losing her and any important information she might have. Now that we've fallen into some kind of bizarre tag-team wrestling event, it feels like my turn to take over.

"What do you mean?" she asks, her eyebrows lifting.

"Did she seem agitated? Happy? Worried? Sad? Angry? You're her best friend, Lisa." (Flattery.) "I'm sure you picked up on something she might have said."

"I don't think we're as close as you think we are."

"She talks to her mom about you all the time, Lisa," says Tony.

"Really?"

"Really. So, what was her state of mind?"

"Well, she seemed…I don't know. Excited, maybe? But at the same time, she was kind of subdued. At least for her. You know, like when you want something to happen but you're afraid if you talk about it too much, it won't happen. That you'll jinx it. That kind of thing."

"Women talk to each other, Lisa. Especially best friends. I'm sure she confided in you."

She hesitates. I think she's holding back, but I'm not sure. And if she is, I'm at a loss as to how to get her to open up. I glance over at Tony and see he's getting even antsier. I'm afraid he'll reach across the table, grab the poor girl by the scruff of her neck, and shake her till she coughs up everything she knows.

If she knows anything. And that's a big if.

"I'm sure you can understand how worried her parents are," I say. "All they want to know is that she's safe and sound."

The look of concentration on Tony's face is so disturbing I have to look away. I don't know who he's more frustrated with, me or Lisa. It feels like he's trying to break into my head and turn on my "power." Oh, man, what have I let myself get talked into? It's one thing looking for a missing person. It's another looking deep into yourself. It reminds me of a quote from Francois de La Rochefoucauld: "*Le soleil ni la mort ne se peuvent regarder fixement.*" Or, in English, "Neither the sun nor death can be looked at steadily."

I'm beginning to know exactly what that means and how it feels.

I turn back to Lisa. She runs her hand through her thick, black hair. She looks up, toward the ceiling, hoping, perhaps, to find the answer up there?

Finally, she breaks the silence. "You don't have to worry. I think she's fine."

"How do you know?" asks Tony.

She rolls her eyes.

"It's the kind of thing you know about a best friend. I don't feel any, you know, like, danger vibes. To be honest, I think you guys are making a pretty big deal over nothing. She's an adult, right? I mean, she doesn't have to check in every minute, does she?"

I can see Tony's seething, but before he can say something counterproductive, I jump in again to save the day, like my childhood hero Mighty Mouse. "Have you heard from her lately?"

"Not since that night."

"Then how can you be so sure she's fine?" says Tony, no longer able to contain himself.

"I just do, that's all."

"Lisa, please, tell us everything you know. Even if it seems unimportant," I say. "The longer it takes for us to find her, the more serious it becomes."

"Like, serious how?"

I don't want to say the words and I know Tony can't. So, we remain silent.

Finally, maybe out of pity, she throws us a bone. "I know you guys are worried. I get that. But I trust Allie. She's a big girl. You parents, you all treat us like we're still seven years old. We're not, you know."

Since I'm not a parent, I let Tony field this one.

"We know. We also know she's your best friend, and I'm sure you want to keep Allison's confidence. We get that. But under certain circumstances, when it's in the best interest of the person whose confidence you're keeping, it's okay to break your word."

"You make it sound like she's in serious trouble," she says. "Like serial-killer trouble."

"That's the point, Lisa," I say, realizing the playing field is not equal, what with Tony and me tag-teaming her. "We just don't know. All we want is to be able to contact her to make sure she's okay. The only way we can do that is with your help."

I've used all the words I have to convince her. I look over to Tony and he's writing furiously on his pad. He tears out a page and pushes it across the table to me.

Are you getting anything?

Just what I'm afraid of. He's more focused on me than he is on Lisa. I shake my head, take the paper, fold it in half, and stuff it in my pocket. This is exactly what I don't want. It's natural Tony should look to me for answers. That's what I'm here for. But I also know it's pointless for him to pressure me. It's at that moment I realize if I'm going to help find Allie, it's going to have to be on my own. I can't have Tony or anyone else breathing down my neck. Not only is it annoying, but when I don't have answers, it only makes me feel like a failure, like I'm letting my best friend down. Which, so far, is exactly what's happening. My mind is made up. I just have to figure out how I can separate from Tony, either continuing on my own or throwing in the towel altogether. That would leave taking it to the cops as his only alternative, which is something I think Tony wants to avoid, and I can't say I blame him. Once they've got it, it's public and it's official: Allie's in some kind of trouble. But the truth is, and Tony knows this as well as I do, there's no crime to report. Right now, she's just a college kid who took an unexplained trip, with absolutely no sign of foul play.

"Okay. I'll tell you everything I know. But, like, you'll see it's not much."

"That's all we ask, Lisa," I say, reaching out to pat her hand. But just short of her hand I stop, realizing the last thing I want to have happen is me being accused of condescension or, even worse, flirting with a woman less than half my age.

Lisa proceeds to tell us about a conversation she had with Allie a couple days before she left. As she's talking, I close my eyes as I try to put myself in the scene she's describing. But it's just not coming. I know the more I force it the less likely I am to get where I want to go.

"We were on our way to our fave bar to hang out with friends, but I could tell something was, like, bothering her."

"What?" asks Tony, leaning forward, trying hard not to miss a single word. A single nuance.

"I don't know. She just wasn't herself. She was kinda, like, preoccupied. Usually, we'd wind up talking about all kinds of shit. Guys we know, classes we take, professors we have, a concert we're looking forward to. Stuff like that. But like she just wasn't into it."

"Did you call her on it?" I ask.

She looks at me quizzically. "What do you mean, 'call her' on it?"

"You know, dig a little deeper."

"Oh. Yeah. I said, 'Hey, Allie, what's up? Where the hell are you?' She apologized. Said she'd heard from somebody about something that was a little confusing."

"Confusing how?"

"You know. Like, disturbing."

"Did she say what it was?"

"I tried to get it out of her, but she wouldn't go there. All she'd say is that it was a family matter."

"What kind of family matter?"

"She didn't say."

"And you didn't ask?"

"Why would I ask? It's like I'd be prying into her life. Unless she brings it up, that's just not cool."

"Was she upset about anything in particular?" I ask. "You know, grades?"

"Allie? Are you kidding? She's a friggin' genius. If I sat next to her in class and copied her notes, I'd be, like, the fucking valedictorian."

"Something her mother or father did? Or didn't do?"

She shakes her head no.

"What about guys?" asks Tony.

"She never had any trouble with guys. But she wasn't into anyone seriously. She was really into her classes. She used to say there's plenty of time later for guys. Right now, she said, they'd just slow her down."

"Sounds like her," says Tony.

"Any idea what she might have been referring to?" I ask.

Lisa shakes her head no. "Sorry.... Coulda been anything or anyone."

"Don't you girls talk about every little thing?" I ask.

"We girls?"

Oh, shit. I've struck a nerve. I only hope it doesn't fuck everything up. This weighing-every-single-word-you-say-lest-you-offend-someone is exhausting.

"Sorry. My bad. Women."

She glares at me, but chooses not to come after me. Seems like we've dodged a bullet.

"Has she been seeing anyone new lately?" asks Tony.

"Like a new guy?"

"Yes."

She smiles.

"You know, it's kinda weird talking about this kind of stuff with her dad."

"Stepdad," says Tony, as if this makes it less weird.

"Well, she's not a nun, if that's what you're asking. All I know is she's not in a place in her life where she's looking for anything serious."

Tony mumbles under his breath, "Thank God."

Lisa continues, "Allie never has trouble meeting guys. But she's not really interested in any of the guys around here. She says they're all babies. All they care about is drinking, getting laid, and finding the easiest schedule. Allie's all about getting the hell out as soon as she can, so she can start her life." She looks at Tony. "She's planning on summer school, so she can graduate early."

"Why so anxious to get out of here?" I ask. The next words out of my mouth are, I'm embarrassed to admit, "These are the best years of your life."

"Hope not," says Lisa, and I swear she's now looking at me like I'm some kind of alien space visitor.

"No offence," she says, "but you guys went to college, right?"

"In fact, I did," I say. "And I actually graduated in four years, though at times it was a little iffy."

"So, if you can remember that far back…"

"Ouch!"

"How did you feel about graduation?"

What the heck's going on? I'm being skewered by a college freshman. At this point, I can't help but play along. "Couldn't come quick enough. Didn't even make graduation ceremonies."

She flashes a huge grin. "Any more questions about why Allie wants out of here early?"

I check out Tony. He's shaking his head slowly back and forth. "So, we're paying close to a hundred grand a year and she can't wait to get the hell out of here?" he mumbles.

"Think of all the money you'll save, if she leaves," says Lisa. This isn't supposed to be funny, but damned if it isn't starting to be. I'm close to forgetting why we're here and why we're subjecting ourselves to the rapier wit of a teenager.

"See, Tony, I tell you that all the time. You gotta walk on the sunny side, man, always on the sunny side."

"Fuck you," he says. But he's smiling. Is he loosening up a little? Is talking with this young woman actually calming his nerves?

"Are you worried about her, Lisa?" I ask.

She hesitates a moment. "Not really. Well, maybe a little, but only because you guys are making such a big fucking deal out of it."

"You don't think it's a big deal?" says Tony. "Her missing and all?"

"What makes you think she's missing?"

"Because we can't get in touch with her."

"Oh. My. God. Maybe you guys should put that three-sixty app on her phone, or put one of those GPS chips in her like they do with dogs and cats. That way you'd know exactly where she is every minute of the day."

I can see Tony's this close to losing it. The kid's not on trial, and bullying her is not only counterproductive—it's just plain unfair.

"I wasn't worried before, but honestly, you guys are starting to worry me. Why couldn't it just be something simple, something ordinary. You know, like she's visiting a friend for the weekend."

"It could," I say, jumping in so Tony doesn't have a chance to give the more serious, expected parental response. "In fact, I'm guessing it is no big deal. But still, we have to make sure. You understand that, right? We're adults. Overreacting is part of the job description."

She rolls her eyes. "I guess," she says. I don't have to be a mind reader to know she doesn't really get it at all. Why should she? She's pushing twenty and thinks she knows it all. Adults are so easily spooked. At her age, you think you own the world and have a far better understanding about how it works than anyone with even a hint of grey in their hair. But while I've got her cooperating—sort of—I push it further.

"Is there anything else you can think of, Lisa, anything that might give us a lead as to where Allie went and why? To be honest, I don't completely buy that you didn't talk about what's going on."

She goes quiet. And then, "What if it's something she asked me not to talk about?"

"Under most circumstances you absolutely should keep the confidence of a friend. But this isn't a normal circumstance, Lisa. She's disappeared, without a word to her parents. All they want," I nod toward Tony, "is to make sure she's okay. In the end, it's not so much about breaking a confidence as it's making sure her parents aren't crazy worried."

She drops her head, and then, as if she's had some earth-shattering epiphany, she looks up. "Okay. But honestly, there really isn't much to tell. All she said is that someone gave her some information, and if it's true it would mean her whole life was a lie."

Sounds like typical teenage dramatics, but before I can follow up, Tony breaks in. "Told her what? What are you talking about?"

"I don't know."

"Come on…" he prods, as I reach across and put my hand on Tony's wrist, then squeeze, hoping to shut him down before we lose the kid altogether.

"What kind of information, Lisa?" I ask gently.

"Like I said, I don't know."

These answers are making Tony crazy, and crazy is not a good look when you're trying to get information. "What do you mean, you don't know?" says Tony, with no attempt to control his mounting anger and frustration. "There's no way she didn't tell you what it is."

"Well, she didn't," she says defiantly.

"Who was it who gave her this information, Lisa?" I ask as Tony slips into sulking mode.

She shrugs her shoulders.

"How about an educated guess?"

She shrugs. "I don't know. Could be anyone. She didn't go into detail. She was, like, too…" Lisa hesitates, obviously searching for the right word. "Too, you know, like, hyper. I didn't want to upset her, so I didn't make a big deal out of it."

I feel myself buckling under the growing weight of Tony's expectations. I want to bail, but I can't.

"Is there someone new in her life? You know, like a recent new friend or acquaintance? Like a new boyfriend, maybe?" I ask.

"Well, there's someone named Alex she met recently."

"Man or woman?" says Tony.

"Not sure."

"Tell us what you know about him or her," says Tony. "Please."

I look at Lisa and I see tears forming in the corners of her eyes. Tony's intensity is frightening her. She feels threatened and I can't blame her. Here she sits with two strange men pressing her for answers she obviously doesn't have. I want to reach over, put my arm around her, and try to comfort her. But in this "Me Too" climate, I'm not about to do anything that might be misconstrued.

"I honestly don't know anything about him or her. Maybe he or she's someone Allie bumped into at the bookstore, or the library. She was kinda friendly that way. Everybody liked Allie. Everyone wanted to be her friend."

"Anyone else in Allie's group of friends who might know who this Alex person is? Someone who might even have met him. Someone who can tell us who he or she is and describe him or her to us?"

"You don't get it, do you?" she says.

"Get what?" Tony says.

"That I'm telling you everything I know. I think you're making like way too much of a deal about this. I really wish I could help you…but honestly…" Her voice trails off.

"Do you think this Alex person has something to do with Allie's disappearance?" I ask.

"She hasn't disappeared," Lisa says sternly. "She's just, like, gone. I mean, she's not like some lost puppy. She's a grown woman, and she doesn't have to check in and out with her parents when she does something. Me either. Besides, what makes you so sure something bad's happened to her? Why do you people always jump to the worst possible conclusion?"

"Because we're parents," Tony says, lumping me into a class I'm not in or chances are will ever be in. "It's part of the job description. If you're ever unlucky enough to be one, you'll know exactly what I mean."

Lisa's hearing what Tony is saying, but she's not buying it. As far as she's concerned, we're the enemy, and if she does know more than she's saying, it's because she's not about to betray her friend.

We've hit a brick wall.

Josh
Back to Where You Once Belonged

We grab a quick dinner in a nondescript greasy spoon near the motel, then head back to our room. We're both beat, emotionally and physically, and our hastily devised plan is to get a good night's rest, then continue the hunt in the morning. The exact details of what form that hunt will take are to be determined.

For the past fifteen, twenty minutes, there's been only dead silence between us. I guess we're pretty much all talked out. At least I am. But there's one more thing to discuss, and I don't relish the conversation. I've got to word it just right so as not to offend Tony, while at the same time convince him of the wisdom of what I'm suggesting. I'm ready for some serious pushback, but I plan to hold my ground to the point where I'll threaten to go home if he doesn't agree. Best friend or not, I have every intention of carrying through on this threat.

While Tony's on the phone with Rachel, I'm in the shower. Instead of showing off my shower voice by crooning my favorite Dylan or Beatles songs—thanks to bathroom tiles, I can hold my own—I rehearse what I'm going to say to him. When I emerge from the bathroom, wrapped in a towel that smells of laundry powder, Tony is on the bed, leaning back against the headboard. His shoes are off, but otherwise he's fully clothed and staring intently at his iPad propped up on his lap.

I pull on my T-shirt and, my lower half still wrapped in the towel, I sit down on the edge of my bed. Although I know he's aware of my presence—how could he not be in a room barely large enough to hold two queen-sized beds, a desk, and a couple chairs—Tony doesn't bother looking up.

"Whatcha doin?" I ask.

"Checking Allie's Facebook and Instagram pages," he says, eyes still glued to the screen.

"You have her passwords?"

"Rachel gave them to me."

"I'm surprised Allie shared them with her."

He looks up, flashes an evil grin. "My wife can be very sneaky when she has to. Good thing I've never cheated on her, because if I did, she'd know it in a New York minute."

"Isn't this kind of an intrusion on Allie's privacy?"

The minute the words escape from my mouth I realize how ridiculous they are. Me talking about civil and personal rights while he's searching for his daughter.

"When you've got a teenager in your house, there is no such thing as privacy. Do you have any idea how many crazy people there are out there? How many bad things a kid can get into?"

"More than a dozen but less than a billion?" I joke. "Does Allie know Rachel has her passwords?"

"Don't know. But Allie's smart enough to be careful about anything she posts. She learned that the hard way."

I'm curious as to what the "hard way" was, but I realize that's a topic for another day.

"How do you know she doesn't have another page. Maybe under another name?"

"I'm sure she does. She's smart and devious, a lethal combination. That's how teenagers roll. It's like that old joke they used to tell about Lyndon B. Johnson. How do you know when he's lying? When he touches his forehead, he's telling the truth. When he runs his hand through his hair, he's telling the truth. When he smiles, he's telling the truth. But when he opens his mouth, he's lying."

"Thinking back to my own lying, tumultuous teens, I'd say that's pretty much spot-on. Find anything interesting?"

He shakes his head. "Not yet. What was that kid Lisa's last name?"

He wants it so he can scour her social media, searching for clues. I can try to talk him out of it, tell him how wrong it is, that it's a gross invasion of privacy, and that it could easily be counterproductive, especially if Allie figures out what he's doing. Or I can just play along.

"Milano. Like the cookie."

"Oh, yeah." His index finger flies across the keyboard.

I reach out across the gap between our queen-sized beds and grab the iPad from his hands.

"Hey, man…what the fuck?"

"We need to talk."

"We're not breaking up, are we? Dammit, I knew this day would come."

"Don't think I haven't considered it. But not yet."

"Then what?"

I sit back down on my bed, cradling the still warm iPad in my lap.

"We've been buddies a long time, Tony, so I'm not going to insult you or our friendship by lying. This," I say, extending the palms of both hands, "is not working."

"What's *this*?"

"Look at us. Two middle-aged men who don't know what the fuck they're doing, sitting in a cheap, shitty motel room…"

"It's not that bad, considering. Believe me, I've stayed in worse."

"You know what I mean. You're using me as a tool to find your daughter. I don't blame you, and I want to help as much as I can. But this just isn't working for me."

"You're bailing?"

"Depends."

"On what?"

"The pressure you're putting on me is shutting me down when I should be opening up," I say, trying to make myself heard over the high-pitched voice in my head screaming over and over again, *Get rid of him! Get rid of him!*

"Pressure? What pressure?" And from the look on his face, I suddenly realize he truly doesn't have a clue. Tony's always been a bit of a narcissist, which is probably one of the reasons he's such good company. But it also limits his vision to within three or four feet surrounding him. I must choose my words carefully, making sure not to offend him, while making myself perfectly clear.

"Whenever we're with someone you look at me like I'm a human lie detector. It doesn't work that way, Tony. I can't perform at will, like a trained seal."

"Are you saying you can't do what I thought you could? That it's all one big, fat fucking joke?"

"You think I made this all up? That I'm a fake? Why? To entertain people? To take something from them? Trust me, this is no picnic, my friend. No one in his fucking right mind, unless they're gonna use it to prey on people, would want this thing, once they see how it can fucking ruin your life. It's not a gift, it's a curse. But if I'm ever gonna be okay using whatever this is, now's the time. If I can help find Allie, I don't care if everyone knows about it. So, I'll do what I can, my friend. All I ask is that you be patient with me and not expect miracles."

His body, which lately seems to be in constant motion, suddenly calms. Like his battery is slowly losing juice.

"Any suggestions?" he says.

"As a matter of fact, I do. First thing tomorrow morning, you're going home."

"You gotta be kidding…"

"Let me finish. You go home, and I stay here and continue the search. In the meantime, you and Rachel do what you have to do, which means anything and everything you can think of to find her. I suggest you try getting the cops involved. Even if they won't do anything, I think it's important to make sure there's an official record and that Allie's on their radar. Meanwhile, I'll be way more productive if I do my thing without you. Think of it as a two-pronged attack."

Tony can be a closed book. Most times I have no idea what he's thinking. But this is one of the rare times I do: He's pissed.

"I guess I interfere with this secret power you've got?" He begins to imitate the *Twilight Zone* music, even though he knows I hate when he does that. Or maybe he does it *because* he knows I hate it. I don't mind that his anger has turned into sarcasm and scorn. Actually, it's to my advantage if he thinks what I can do is a big fat lie. Still, I can't help feeling attacked and marginalized.

"I'm not quite sure why you're belittling me, Tony, while at the same time you want my help."

I strike a nerve. He leans his head back against the headboard with a thump. Immediately, I regret my harsh, insensitive words. I remind myself to cut him some slack. His daughter's missing, and he probably feels like I'm abandoning him.

"Am I doing that?" he asks. His tone softens. He turns into a contrite little boy who's messed up and is called on it.

He drops his head, so it appears as if he's praying.

Finally, he takes a deep breath and slowly exhales. "If that's the way it comes off, I apologize. It's the tension, man. I guess it's starting to get to me. But do me a favor, Josh. Don't hold back. If I'm doing something that pisses you off, don't be afraid to call me on it."

"You don't have to apologize. I get it. I can't imagine the pressure you and Rachel are under. Your most treasured possession, your kid, is missing. I get that. But I honestly believe if we continue the way we've been going that by the end of the week we'll kill each other. Then everyone loses. I think I can be more efficient without you. But I promise to stay in constant touch."

He gets up from the bed, goes over to the window, and pulls back the draperies. He stares out into the darkness. We overlook a five-story parking structure, so there's not much to see. Especially in the dark.

He turns around to face me.

"Do you have a plan or are you just gonna wing it?"

"I've got the beginnings of a plan," I lie.

"Wanna share it with me?"

"Nope."

"I think I have a right to know your strategy, Josh. She's my kid, remember?"

I don't have a strategy or a plan, but that doesn't stop me from coming up with one on the fly, just to satisfy him. "I'll talk to as many of her friends as I can find, create a timeline, then try to trace her footsteps. For what it's worth, Tony, I don't think she's trying to disappear. Maybe she's doing something she knows you guys wouldn't approve of. Once I figure out why she's disappeared, we'll have a better chance of figuring out where she is."

"Unless there's someone else involved in her disappearance." He stops, then drops the ticking bomb. "You think she's alive?"

He wants me to reassure him that Allie is fine. It would be easy to say yes, but that would cross a line and create a troubling precedent.

"Well?" he presses.

I make a decision that's against my better judgment. If that exists.

"I do."

It's not a lie if I believe it, right?

"Why? Why do you think that?"

I must be careful what I say. The longer Allie remains missing, the more serious it is. I know this. Tony knows this. Rachel knows this. Still, it falls on me to keep these nasty thoughts out of theirs heads as long as I can.

I sit down next to him on his bed and throw my arm around his shoulder. I have to convince myself before I can convince him. I reason, if she is dead, wouldn't I have had a vision of it?

"I believe she's fine, Tony. I really do."

"Does this mean you've *seen* her? In your head, I mean."

"Right now, it's just a good old-fashioned gut feeling. We'll find her. You'll see…"

I only wish I could be persuasive enough to convince myself.

Josh
Me and My Shadow

As soon as Tony drives off into the sunset (it's actually early morning and there's a thick, grey cloud cover), I become aware of a lump in the pit of my stomach. For someone with abandonment issues—that would be me—it's never easy watching people leave. Of course, I know he's not abandoning me—for one thing, it's my idea he go home—but I can't help feeling I'm being abandoned.

With Tony gone, I'm having a bad case of buyer's remorse. Why did I agree to help? I know he's my best friend, but I also know I'm totally unqualified for this job. Sure, I'm a journalist, which means I have skills akin to tools wielded by professional detectives: experienced researcher who can follow leads. But that's not why Tony's asked for my help. His request is based solely on an ability I don't quite understand, not to mention know how to use effectively, if at all.

Why didn't I go back with him? Why didn't I say, "Sorry, my friend, but I don't know what the hell I'm doing. I'll probably just get in the way. You need professional help." What if I fail? How will he feel? How will I feel? How will it affect our friendship? And who will save Allison, if she even needs saving?

Self-doubt plagues me. It always has. I can't remember the last time I felt adequate to a task thrust upon me. I am the poster boy for imposter syndrome. But the stakes were never this high.

All these doubts bouncing off each other in my head are trumped by one thing: Tony is my best friend, and even if I fail I owe it to him and our friendship to at least try.

As I stand there, frozen in place from a lethal combination of anxiety and doubt, my thoughts wander back to Tony. Heading south, in the direction of New York City, Tony will exit the highway at one of those toney, largely interchangeable Westchester towns that serve as bedroom communities for commuters. He'll arrive home to Rachel and their son, and a world turned upside down and inside out. Until they get the cops involved, everything falls on me. Not because of what I've done in the past, but because of what Tony believes I can do in the future. This despite the fact that I've offered absolutely no proof of what I can do, nor could I if asked. And if there's anyone more uncertain about the possibility of my success in tracking her down, it's me.

The irony does not elude me: Now it's me who feels like running away and getting lost.

I need a plan. Not only a plan on how to proceed, but also a plan on how I'm going to gracefully extricate myself from this mess.

Writing things down, making a list, has always served me well. First on the list is to find a quiet place where I can get my thoughts in order. That turns out to be a tiny hole-in-the-wall coffee shop not far from the motel, where I grab a cup of bad, lukewarm coffee and a half-stale croissant, probably left over from yesterday.

It's the midmorning lull, and the joint is nearly empty. Only a few people drinking coffee, sitting at small tables reading, or staring blankly at their laptops. I find a table up front, near the window. I pull out my notebook, grab the pen I've appropriated from the motel, and begin by scribbling "1" at the top of a blank page. It's the way, as a journalist, I've always worked. Gather my research, then put it in the order I'm going to use it.

Writing the number one has always filled me with joy. It's a sign of hope. A sign of forward movement. A sign of promised progress (if you have a one, it stands to reason there'll be a number two, and so on). It's like turning the key and hearing the engine engage. To celebrate, I take a bite of my croissant and wash it down with a slug of so-so coffee that set me back five bucks.

Now the hard work begins.

Forty-five minutes and two refills later (what can I say? My body craves caffeine, and it doesn't care how it gets it), I've only managed to jot down half a dozen things, a very sketchy blueprint for how I'll proceed.

1. Back to A's room, see if I've missed anything.
2. Contact people on A's list of friends.
3. Create as much of a timeline of the 24 to 48 hours before A disappears.

I'm not sure why, but something is drawing me back to Allie's room. Gnawing at me is the feeling we missed something. As I walk in the direction of Allie's dorm, an image of Allie's bookshelf begins to form. I stop and close my eyes. The image slowly focuses until it becomes fixed, and suddenly, I'm back in Allie's room, no more than six inches away from the bookshelf. I scan the titles, but I keep coming back to a copy of *The Great Gatsby*, F. Scott Fitzgerald. There's something about that book. But what?

After a few moments, the image fades, leaving me apprehensive. Anxious. Lightheaded, I grab onto a lamppost for balance and support.

After several moments, I continue in the direction of her dorm.

I'm in luck. The security guard at the front desk is the guy from yesterday, and he recognizes me. "Find her yet?" he asks.

"Not yet. But it would really help if I could get back into her room. Can you call up and see if her roommate's there."

"Don't have to. Saw him leave 'bout an hour ago."

"Gee, that's too bad. I left something really important up there and I'm headed back to the city..."

"Well...seeing as I kinda know you, and seeing as you were here with her daddy the other day, I'm gonna break protocol and let you up. But I don't know how you're gonna get in. Less'n you got a key."

I'm hoping I don't need one, because chances are Kevin's left the door unlocked. But I don't want to say that. So, I lie.

"Know what, her father did leave me with a spare room key." I pull my own set of keys from my pocket and wave them in front of him. "So, if it's all right with you, my friend, I'll just head up..."

When I reach Allie's room, I say a little prayer and twist the knob. The door swings open and I'm in.

I sit on the edge of Allie's bed and close my eyes, in an attempt to clear my mind. Usually, these visions come without warning. I've never tried to summon them before, and it makes me feel like I'm in some cheesy horror flick where a bunch of kids sit around a Ouija board trying to connect with the spirit world.

It's only a matter of seconds before a picture begins to come into focus. It's the image of *The Great Gatsby* sitting on the shelf, between a copy of *The Sun Also Rises* and *As I Lay Dying*. I open my eyes and take a deep breath. I know what I have to do next, but I hesitate. My first real test. Is the book there?

I stand up and approach Allie's bookshelf. My eyes drift across the titles and, sure enough, there it is, tucked between Hemingway and Faulkner, a paperback copy of *The Great Gatsby*. A chill that starts at the small of my back quickly moves up toward my neck. *Relax, Josh,* I tell myself. *This still might mean absolutely nothing. You probably saw the book yesterday and it stuck in your mind. Besides, who knows if it has any significance?*

I pull the book from the shelf. It seems slightly warm. Like it's giving off some kind of weird energy. Or am I imagining it? It seems so tacky, such a cliché. Way too woo-woo. I tell myself, *Get a grip...*

I begin to flip through the pages, several of them with handwritten notes in the margins, and buried about halfway through, there's something acting as a bookmark. It's a letter, folded neatly in thirds. It's the first page from one of those genealogy DNA services. It's addressed to Allie. It begins with one of those corny greetings, thanking Allie for signing up. At the bottom of the page it announces that results can be found on the following pages. But there are no other pages.

This feels significant, though I'm not sure why.

I sit back down on the edge of Allie's bed and stare blankly into space. This shit is becoming real. There's something going on, something well past my comprehension. I'm drawn to this book for a reason, and the reason probably has to do with the letter I'm holding in my hands.

Should I call Tony? Or, should I wait till I find something more concrete, something that can actually help find Allie?

I realize I can't keep this to myself. I have to share it with someone, and Tony's the obvious choice.

Tony picks up almost immediately, like he's anticipated my call.

"What you got, Josh?" he asks in a surprisingly lively voice.

"Do you know anything about Allie contacting one of those DNA ancestry websites?"

"No. Why?"

"Ask Rachel."

"She's here. I'll put you on speaker." I hear him shouting, "Rachel, it's Tony. He wants to know if Allie's ever said anything to you about contacting one of those DNA ancestry sites?"

Her voice comes through loud and clear.

"No. Why? Does this have anything to do with where Allie is?"

I don't want to lie, but I can't say anything about what I've "seen," because she'd have no idea what I'm talking about. And yet I feel Rachel needs some kind of good news and this might be it.

"I think it might, Rachel. Do you know anything about this DNA thing?"

"No," she says, but there's a slight hesitation in her voice.

"Please, Josh, please tell us everything you know," she quickly adds, her trembly voice reflecting her concern.

I've said enough. Maybe too much. I know she's desperate to engage, to grasp at any straw of hope, but I don't want to get into a prolonged discussion. "I'm sorry, Rachel. Right now, there's nothing else. Tony, can you take us off speaker?"

"Okay," he says, and immediately that hollow, echoing sound is gone.

"Listen, I know it's tough, but you really can't say anything at all to Rachel, or anyone else, about this, this thing of mine. I'll just be some crazy dude who thinks he has this ridiculous superpower..."

"Of course. But be honest with me, Josh. Do you think this is important? That it might have something to do with Allie's disappearance?"

"Honestly, I don't know, but it could."

"So, we're making progress?"

I'm not sure what to answer. I don't want to give false hope, and yet I sense they need some hint that all is not lost. And so, I lie. "Yes."

"That's great, man. Really..."

"Have you contacted the cops, Tony?"

"We have. But you know the drill: 'It's too soon to get involved...' blah, blah, blah. She's still a kid to us, but she's an adult to the rest of the world. And they say there's no reason to believe there's anything criminal going on. They want us to wait another forty-eight hours and then if there's a reason for them to get involved, they will. But I'm not giving up. I've got some contacts in the FBI. I'm gonna to reach out to them."

"Good idea. You certainly don't want to put all your eggs in my basket."

"What's next?"

"I'll stick around here another day or so. Speak to anyone I can find who might know something."

"Josh, I can't tell you how much we appreciate what you're doing. If you need anything, and I mean anything, please let me know."

And it's there that our conversation ends.

Josh
If There's a Haystack There Must Be a Needle

I find one of those sticky note pads on Allie's desk and scrawl, *Kevin, it's Josh from yesterday. I'm in Allie's room.*

I stick the note on the front door to alert Mr. Mountain Man. In case he gets back while I'm still here, I don't want to startle him.

I whip out my trusty notebook and prepare to create another list. I tear out the old list, crumple it up, and shoot it, like a basketball, into the trash can by Allie's desk. Being only three, four feet away it shouldn't be difficult but instead of an easy score, the surrogate basketball hits the rim of the trash can, seems to balance precariously on the edge for a moment, then tumbles to the floor.

Practically a slam dunk and I still can't manage it. Is this the paranormal's way of preparing me for failure?

I pick up the crumpled paper, drop it in the trash, then return to my spot on the edge of Allie's bed. I stare at the blank page, like I'm hoping words will mysteriously appear. No dice. I shut my eyes and try to clear my mind, hoping if I do an image will appear with a huge finger pointing me in the right direction. Good plan. Only it's not happening either.

I can't simply will myself into a state where I can summon images on command. At least not yet. Perhaps, with practice, I might be able to exercise more control. But since I've spent most of my life pretending this thing of mine doesn't exist, I know very little if anything of how it works and how to work it.

Finally, I give up.

I check my watch. It's almost 12:30. I've still got most of the day.

I pull out Rachel's list. At the top is the name Kent, with a note that he's Allie's ex-boyfriend. I call the number Rachel provided. He picks up on the fourth ring.

"Yeah?"

"This Kent?"

"Who's this?"

"Josh Green. I'm a friend of Allie's parents."

"So?"

"Are you aware Allie's missing?"

"What do you mean missing?"

"She's disappeared, without leaving a word, and no one seems to know where she is."

"We're not together anymore, so how would I know anything about that?" His tone is combative. I wonder if this is a sign that he either knows where Allie is or has something to do with her disappearance. The spurned boyfriend and all.

"You sound like you don't give a shit, Kent," I say.

"It wasn't a pretty ending."

"Sorry about that," I say, flashing back to all the non-pretty endings I've had since the day I was old enough to ask girls out. That kind of hurt never goes away. "I'd still like to talk to you, Kent. I'm here, in New Haven. Any chance we could meet up?"

"I'm kinda busy."

Kid's acting like a dick. But I need his cooperation, so I play nice.

"It would be great if you could carve out a little time for me today, Kent. Ten, fifteen minutes, tops. I can come to wherever you are. We just want to make sure Allie is safe."

"I should just fucking hang up on you."

"Don't do that, Kent." I want to add, *because I'll hunt you down, and when I find you it won't be pretty.* Instead, I try to appeal to his better angels, hoping he has at least one. "Allie's parents are worried sick. It's not about you and Allie. It's about her safety and the peace of mind of her family."

"You're practically accusing me of having something to do with you not being able to find Allie?"

"I'm sorry you feel that way, because it's not true."

"Yeah, well, I haven't seen her in weeks, so I don't know how I can help. And why can't we just do this on the phone?"

Because I want to look you straight in your eye, you little fucker. I want to see your body language. I want to look into your eyes. Into your soul. That's why.

"Ten minutes, Kent. That's all I'm asking."

The line goes silent. I think maybe he's hung up on me, but when I check my phone, I see he's still on the line.

"I got a class at one. We can meet around twelve-thirty. In front of Bass. It's underground, so I'll be at the arch, near the bicycle rack. Know where it is?"

"I'll figure it out."

Despite getting lost twice, I manage to arrive with a couple minutes to spare. Kent is already there, leaning against the wall behind the bike rack, his eyes glued to his phone.

He's small, maybe five-five, five-six in the morning, before we shrink a little from the stress of the day. He's dressed like most every college kid. Blue jeans, blue sweatshirt with YALE emblazoned in large, gold letters, and black high-top Chucks. He's got a beaten-up red knapsack strapped to his back. Accuse any kid of wearing a uniform and they'll ream you a new asshole. But don't kid yourself; it appears as if they've all received the same dress code memo.

"Kent, I presume."

He looks up.

"I don't have long. Got a class at one."

"I'll make it quick. Like I said on the phone, Allie's missing."

He shrugs. "Why should I care?"

"Listen, kid..."

"Kid?"

He's got this obnoxious, arrogant thing that makes me want to punch him in the face. Instead, I take the high road.

"Sorry. Poor choice of word. How about young man?"

Now, I feel like punching myself in the face.

"Funny," he says. But he's not laughing.

"Listen, Kent, take it from me, you're gonna have a bunch of breakups in your life, and if you treat every girl who dumps you..."

"What makes you think I was dumped? Is that what she told you?"

"...or who you dump, as the enemy, you're gonna waste a whole lot of your life being pissed off. Trust me, that's not a good lifestyle choice. I'm not saying you've gotta be best buddies with her, but you'll earn enough enemies in your life who deserve to be hated, so why add to the list?"

I can't help falling into lecture mode, and so I share Richard Nixon's words when he stepped down from the presidency: "Always remember, others may hate you, but those who hate you don't win unless you hate them, and then you destroy yourself."

"Okay, professor, I'll make a note of that. So, what makes you think I can help? I already told you, we broke up weeks ago and I haven't seen or heard from her since."

I'm starting to lose patience. The clock is ticking, and the stink of failure hovers over me. Kent's a hostile witness and I see no indication that's going to change. I need to change my approach.

"Listen, Kent, we've all been there. That doesn't mean you get to be an asshole. Why not be a stand-up dude? It might be a better life choice for you."

His scowl is his answer. Hey, he wants to be an asshole the rest of his life, that's fine with me.

"When I say Allie's missing, what'd be the first thing to cross your mind in terms of where she might be?"

"My honest answer would be, 'I don't give a fuck.'"

"She dumped you. You're pissed. I get it, kid. But this has nothing to do with your past relationship with Allie. It has to do with the safety of another human being. And the peace of mind of her parents."

He goes silent. Have I finally broken through? Is he at least thinking about helping?

He shakes his head. "I got nothing for you."

I feel like grabbing the little prick and squeezing him till the truth comes tumbling out of his weaselly little mouth. But for obvious reasons, I resist the impulse.

"Did she break up with you for someone else?"

"Fuck no. Absolutely not."

"Do you know if anyone's been stalking her? Has she mentioned anything out of the ordinary that happened to her lately?"

"You don't know Allie very well, do you? If anyone was stalking her, she'd either call the cops or kick the shit out of him herself. That's one of the things I always liked about her. She could fucking take care of herself."

"Can you think of anything that might help us find her?"

His shoulders droop. His body seems to collapse into itself, like the air slowly escaping from a punctured balloon. "Nope." He hesitates a moment. "And listen, man, I guess I should apologize. It's just that, you know, I really cared for her. What she did was so fucking cold. She just cut me loose. Left me fucking bleeding on the side of the road. Like I was roadkill. We didn't fight, or anything like that. She just announced we were done." He goes silent. And then he packs every possible emotion in one word: "Bitch."

I flash back to all those times I was rejected, and yes, I can actually feel his pain, because now it's mine too. Is this the price I pay for inserting myself into someone else's past?

"Did she give you a reason for the breakup?"

"She kept saying we were too different. Over and over again. I asked her what the fuck she meant, but she couldn't tell me. She said there were some changes going on in her life and she had to deal with them."

I perk up. "What kind of changes?"

"She didn't say. And to tell the truth, I didn't give a shit. Still don't."

The kid is no longer an object standing between me and finding Allie. He's been hurt bad. Maybe he deserved it, maybe not. Doesn't matter. I have to keep reminding myself I'm dealing with teenagers here, a stage when everything is more intense. Colors are brighter. Sounds are louder. Disappointments are deeper. Especially with guys who aren't fully formed yet. They can't control their emotions, much less understand them. They're up. They're down. They're all over the fucking place. They either lack experiences to teach them, to build on, or they can't process them successfully. It's easy for me to identify with someone like Kent, probably because I'm not so sure we ever outgrow that stage. Deep inside we're all that vulnerable teenager.

"Listen, Kent. I really appreciate your taking the time to talk with me. One last thing before I let you go. Does the name Alex mean anything to you? Like maybe a new friend of Allison's?"

"Guy, girl, it, or they?"

"Not sure. Name mean anything to you?"

"Not a clue, man."

"Anyone you think I should talk to, someone who might help?"

"Maybe her best friend? Lisa something."

"Milano?"

"That's her. Cute chick. After Allie dumped me, I thought about asking her out. You know, just to piss Allie off. But I figured it would kinda make me look bad. Like it was revenge or something."

You think?

"I've already spoken to her."

"Did she help?"

"Not really. Anyone else?"

"Allie was pretty popular, but the funny thing is, she didn't have all that many close friends. I know it sounds contradictory, but that's the way it was with her. She had trust issues. At least that's what she told me when we started dating."

He checks his watch.

"Gotta go, man. You're even one minute late, the professor locks the door and, like, he says even the Pope couldn't get in. Listen, I hope she turns up soon…she's not a bad person."

And just like that, I'm alone.

I walk slowly in the direction of my motel, my iPod plugged in, listening to the soundtrack of *The Last Waltz.* A feeble attempt to escape my thoughts. A couple blocks from my destination, I stop and wait for the light to change. Suddenly, an image flashes through my mind.

I'm floating in midair near the back of a half-empty train car. By shifting my weight, I can go in any direction. Lean to the left, I move left. Lean to the right, I move right. I feel the incredible euphoria of flight. I've never felt so free, so powerful. At first, the thrill of such complete freedom is intoxicating. It's like a shot of adrenaline. I'm defying all the rules of gravity. And I'm beginning to understand and learn the "rules" of my affliction. I can control where my body goes and the pace at which it moves. Ever so slowly, I move forward, until I reach the front of the car. I stop, turn, and look back. There, sitting alone, in an aisle seat three rows down, is a young woman. She's stooped over, staring at the screen of her laptop. Her fingers are poised above the keyboard. As I move closer, I recognize that it's Allie. I maneuver myself until I'm almost directly over her shoulder, hoping to see what's on her computer screen. But it's all a blur, and no matter how hard I try, I can't seem to get it in focus.

I look out the window. I see a thick border of trees. As the train moves forward, the vista opens up, and we're passing miles and miles of farmland. On the service road running perpendicular to us, I see a wagon pulled by a horse. At the reins, there's a man dressed in black, with a thick-brimmed black hat on his head. I'm in Amish country. Most likely Pennsylvania. And we're headed west, toward the setting sun.

When I try moving back to where Allie is sitting, the image suddenly disappears. It's like a balloon that's popped. Once all the air is gone, it's only a sad, deflated piece of rubber. There's only nothingness. A black screen.

Now, the inevitable questions. What's this all about? When is this happening? Am I seeing this in real time, or is it in the past? No matter when it is, it's obvious that Allie is alive and well and traveling, unaccompanied, on a train heading to an unknown destination.

The sound of car horns yanks me back to reality. Slightly dizzy, I lean up against a mailbox to steady myself. My breathing quickens. My heart is beating so loud and so fast it feels like it's going to burst from my chest.

Suddenly, all that changes. I feel strikingly calm. Like I've taken a Valium and the sweet effect of calm is kicking in. I can't remember ever feeling so at peace. Is this, I wonder, a sign that I've made a deep connection with Allie? That we're on the same wavelength?

If I have somehow dialed into Allie's psyche, then maybe I really will be able to find her. But even more exciting is that it appears I've made a personal breakthrough. For the first time, I realize I can have more control over this thing of mine than I've ever imagined.

Whether that's a good or a bad thing is to be determined. But at least I don't feel as much of a fraud as I have in the past.

Josh
Use It, or Lose It

I'm sitting in a window seat on Amtrak's Acela, heading home.

I'm exhausted. I can't ever remember feeling such fatigue. It's as if I've lived the past two days twice. All I want to do is shut my eyes and sleep. But if I do close my eyes, I'm afraid an image of Allie will take over my mind. The earlier scene of Allie on the train has disoriented me. It's as if I'm in two different places simultaneously. I've entered a new reality. A reality I've never even dreamed of. A reality I've only read about without any real understanding of what it means. It's called "quantum superposition." Somehow, in a way I can't possibly understand, researchers have caused a molecule made up of up to two thousand atoms to occupy two places at the same time. I don't understand it. I probably never will. But could this be what I'm experiencing?

I'm a different person from the one I was before meeting with Tony at Friedman's. For one thing, I no longer have doubts about my ability to *see* things from the past. Not my past, that's called memory. Other people's past. Now, more than ever, I'm—and right now I can't think of any better word for it—afraid. I probably should be thrilled that I might be able to help my best friend and his wife find their daughter. But I'm not.

It's a weird feeling. It's like I've been reborn. I'm someone else now. Someone who can see things most others can't. I cannot imagine ever again being the person I was.

Over the years, I've done my best to ignore this strange, inexplicable "power." No longer will this be possible. It's an integral part of me now, whether I want it or not. And so, as we pull into the tunnel that will take us from upper Manhattan into Grand Central, I yield to the dark forces. I make the conscious effort to embrace it.

Not for Rachel.

Not for Tony.

Not for Allie.

For me.

Josh
Slip of the Tongue

It's early Tuesday morning and I'm heading out to meet Tony and Rachel.

Tony calls it a debriefing. I think of it as a let's-clear-the-air-and-put-all-our-cards-on-the-table meeting.

Last night, a phone call was placed, and we agreed on time and place. I reminded Tony (and myself) about *our* secret and how it has to stay that way.

"I don't know what your problem is," he says, with no attempt to hide his irritation.

I've covered this multiple times, but obviously it hasn't sunk in yet.

"I don't want the world to know about this."

"Jesus, Josh, stop being such a fucking drama queen. You think the world gives a fuck that you can see into the fucking future?"

"That's exactly my point, man. I *can't* see into the future. But the minute you say anything about it, that's what everyone's going to think. I'll be labeled a weirdo, charlatan, liar, cheat, or worse, for the rest of my life. No one will ever treat me the same."

"Is that really what you want? To be treated the same?"

I'm tempted to hang up on him. I'll block his calls and his emails. I'll find a new best friend. I'll move away and change my name. Maybe that won't be so bad. A clean slate. A new life. I ask myself, where might I want to live…?

Okay, maybe I'm getting a little carried away. But if Tony can't figure out what the ramifications of this are for me, that's on him. Maybe this does teeter on the edge of Drama Queen territory. But instead of taking this discussion any further, I take a deep breath and try to explain myself. Again. For the last time, I hope.

"Listen, Tony, you're gonna have to take my word for it. I've played this out in my head a million times. The minute this gets out I'll be defined by it. People won't see me. They'll see a nut who thinks he can see into the future and commune with dead people or…"

"I know that's not what this is all about."

"You know. But no one else will. Do you think I've got the time or inclination to explain over and over again what I can and can't do? Do you think I want people looking at me and wondering if I can see right through them, to their deepest, darkest secrets? Do you think I want to be perceived as a freak? You might think this is a good thing, Tony, like it's some kind of divine gift. The ultimate parlor trick. But take my word for it, it's not. Case in point: what you're asking me to do. Suddenly, I'm not Josh the Friend. I'm Josh the Savior. The man who's going to bring his best friend's daughter back from wherever the hell she is."

"And your problem with that is?"

"Look, I'm happy to help. If I can. But the price of this help, keeping this strictly between you and me, is steep. If it gets out, my life is changed forever. Not for the good. People either believe me or not. If they do, think how I'll be treated. If they don't, I'll be vilified as a phony. Someone who takes advantage of those poor suckers who believe in this shit."

There's a moment of silence. I can practically hear a clanking sound coming from his head, while he tries to figure out the best way to get what he wants without causing too much collateral damage. He's between a rock and a hard place. As am I.

Finally, he speaks.

"I hear what you're saying, Josh. And trust me, man, your secret's safe with me. I promise. Now what's this meetup all about?"

"I want to catch you guys up on what's been going on."

"Good news?" he asks, in a strangled voice. Suddenly, something I've never considered pops into my head: *How am I going to tell him if there's ever bad news?*

"It's news. Not bad. Not good. Just news. And remember, Tony, you can't take anything I say as fact. It's all about possibilities. And whatever I say in front of Rachel, just play along, okay?"

"Got it. And Josh, I'm not very good at communicating appreciation, but I want you to know how much I appreciate what you're doing. I really do. You can trust me to keep your secret, my friend."

This should calm my nerves, but it doesn't. I know how disciplined Tony is, so I know there's no way he's going to spill the beans about me on purpose. When dormant, it's easy to keep this secret. But once activated, the chances of it staying between the two of us are pretty much impossible. I know this going in, but that doesn't make it any easier.

"Be careful about questions you ask me in front of Rachel. I'm going to try to cover myself, so I might be stretching the truth a little. I know how your mind works, Tony. You never let anything go. I also know how tough it is for you to give up control. I get it. But this time I need you to let things ride. Okay?"

"Yeah. Sure. Okay. See you soon."

Tony invites me to their place in Westchester, but getting on another train holds zero appeal. I want a quiet place, at a time of day when most people are at or on their way to work. Central Park fits the bill.

I arrange to meet them at a little outdoor café near the carousel facing the Heckscher Ballfields, where Tony and I used to play on a Sunday-morning softball team when he lived in the city. The fields are generally empty weekday mornings, and the café doesn't open till eleven.

It's that time of year in New York, mid-spring, when the weather is unpredictable. One day the temperature can be in the seventies or eighties, the next day there'll be a snowstorm. Which is why you're never quite sure how to dress. Today, it's somewhere in between, and I'm wearing jeans and a faded denim trucker's jacket over a black T-shirt I rescued from the laundry bin.

When I arrive, Tony and Rachel are already seated at a table in the back corner, directly under a tree, which serves as a natural umbrella from the sun. As I approach, I'm transported back in time by the sound of carousel music in the background.

I drag over a chair from an adjacent table and sit, facing the ballfields.

"I'd treat you to coffee," says Josh, "but as you can see, they're not open for business yet."

"Exactly why I chose it," I say.

"Of course," says Rachel. Her face is drawn, her expression serious. She isn't wearing makeup, and with apologies to the great Smokey Robinson, I can see what must be the tracks of her tears. Her dirty-blonde hair is tied back in a ponytail. She's wearing jeans, a light blue turtleneck sweater, and a black leather bomber jacket. She's always been striking in appearance, and even now, under these horrible circumstances, she radiates a quiet beauty. Her arms are folded tightly across her chest, as if that's all that's holding her together. Her body is rigid, which mirrors the distress she must be feeling.

"Any trouble parking?" I ask in a pathetic attempt at small talk, something none of us is interested in or good at.

"We took the train," says Rachel. "The last thing we wanted was to be stuck in traffic." She hesitates. "And keep you waiting."

I reach out for Rachel's hand and squeeze it gently. An electric jolt travels through my hand, up my arm, then down my spine. I know it's crazy, like something out the movies, but the first thing that occurs to me is that all her emotions are magically being transferred to me. I'm trying to make sense of this, but Allie's anxious parents aren't real interested watching me deal with my shit. I can't help but wonder if in embracing this ability I've unleashed other mysterious sensitivities I never even knew I had. I'm not at all religious, but still, just in case, I take the French philosopher, scientist, and mathematician Pascal's advice: If we don't know whether God exists, then we should play it safe rather than risk being sorry.

The thing unsaid, that elephant in the room, is that they're thinking the worst: that Allie is dead. If I can only accomplish one thing, let it be that they're able to "bury" this horrible thought. Whether or not I can help isn't the point. The point is, I *might* be able to help. And I realize that at this moment, this is just as important finding her.

"Can we skip the small talk, Josh?" says Tony. "What happened after I left you up there in Boston?"

This is one time I'm grateful for Tony's no-bullshit personality.

"A couple things. First off, I'm pretty sure Allison's safe…"

As soon as the words are out of my mouth, I realize I've said the wrong thing. Rachel, who up to now has been relatively quiet, is all over me, "Unless you've found her, Josh, how could you possibly know she's safe?" she scolds.

I shoot a look at Tony, hoping he'll jump in and help. But that isn't going to happen. His eyes are glazed over, and he seems to be anywhere but here.

Finally, after what seems like an eternity of awkward silence, Tony, who by now must sense my discomfort, says in a remarkably gentle voice, "Relax, Josh. We're not the enemy. It's just that… well, unless you're a parent, you can't possibly get what we're going through."

Ah, the "unless you're a parent" card. Not fair, but I understand why it's being played. From now on, I will weigh my words more carefully,

"Everything indicates she left on her own. I'm sure Tony told you about talking with her roommate, who saw her packing a bag to go away for the weekend. So, the chances of foul play are really slim. Wherever she is now, she's there of her own volition. I've spoken with a couple of her friends, and none of them sent up any red flags." I take a breath. Here comes the Big Lie. It's not a good one, but it's the only one I can come up with, because I want to give them something tangible to tie Rachel's hopes to. I'm hoping she won't question the logic or the reality.

"On a hunch, I went to South Station. Eventually, I found a ticket seller who was on duty Friday. I showed him a photo of Allie, and amazingly, he recognized her."

Oh, man, what am I thinking? No way Rachel is going to buy this. I don't even believe it. I mean, who doesn't purchase their tickets online nowadays? I should have come up with something more believable, but instead, I've folded under pressure.

Out of the corner of my eye, I see Tony roll his eyes, a gesture I'm sure he picked up from living with a teenager. He knows I'm lying. He knows Allie would most likely have purchased her ticket electronically. But we're both hoping Rachel, desperate for encouraging news, won't question it. Turns out, we dodge a bullet. She doesn't. Most likely because she isn't totally tuned in.

"I guess that's something," says Rachel, leaning back, her body relaxing slightly. "Did he say where she was going? And was she with anyone?"

"He didn't remember details."

"But where did she go and why?" says Rachel.

I shrug.

There's an awkward silence I'm compelled to fill, hoping we can move on to something else. "After you left, Josh, I went back to Allie's room. I thought we might have missed something."

"Did we?"

"I think so."

"Like what?" says Rachel.

"Has Allie ever mentioned hooking up with one of those genealogical services? The ones where you spit in a tube and they tell you everything you never wanted to know about all your ancestors?"

"Not that I know of," says Tony.

I turn to Rachel. "Did Allie ever mention those services to you?"

She looks away. Her right leg begins to jackhammer. I think I've maybe hit a nerve.

"Rachel?" says Tony.

"Um, not that I'm aware of."

"That's something she would have mentioned, isn't it?" says Tony.

"I guess," says Rachel. "But if she did, I don't remember it."

Tony glares at her. He's picking up on something, something only he would notice. But the last thing we need right now is to get derailed by a familial spat. "Kids have all kinds of things they keep from us, right? I mean, they live this life we know nothing about. I don't know about you guys, but I never told my parents anything. And to be honest, I think they preferred it that way."

Before she passed away, I asked my mother if I was an emotional kid. If I showed anger or sadness. Her response was, "No. You were like this." She passed her hand flatly through the air. "I never knew what you were thinking." I showed great restraint by asking, "Why didn't you just ask me?"

Tony smiles. "Definitely a need-to-know basis. And when it came to me, they didn't need to know anything."

I glance over toward the ballfields. Half a dozen young men are taking fielding practice on the diamond closest to us. I'm reminded of how much I miss softball. It was a much-needed way to deal with frustration and take my mind off failure. Every play in the field, every at-bat, was another opportunity to succeed, if not shine. At this moment, there's nowhere I'd rather be than out there with those guys. It was an uncomplicated time in my life, a time where I could shut out everything else going on. It was all so simple, so black and white. You either made the play or you didn't. You either got the hit or you didn't. And you knew, no matter what happened, you were going to get another crack at it.

A question from Rachel jerks me back to the here and now.

"Why are you bringing this up, Josh? What does it have to do with her disappearance?"

"Probably nothing, but I saw an ad for one of those services stuck in one of her books and thought it might be important."

Rachel becomes agitated. She squirms in her chair. Something's wrong. She's keeping something from us. I debate with myself as to whether I should follow up, but before I can say anything, Tony swoops in and saves the day when he asks, "Anything else?"

"I think that's it. Why don't we give it another day or two, and then you guys should contact the cops."

"What's the point? They're not going to do a damn thing," says Rachel.

"You need to get it on the record."

"Once we do that," says Rachel, her voice infused with sadness, "it's like we're admitting something's seriously wrong. That she's in...trouble." She's choking on her words. Her breathing gets heavier, more labored.

Tony places his hand on Rachel's. I'm touched by his concern and envious of their close and loving relationship, something I've never been able to emulate.

"So, you're saying there's absolutely nothing we can do?" says Rachel.

"We're not doing nothing, Rachel. Josh and I are on the case."

"You're not cops, you know," she says, with a sharp edge in her voice.

"But we're trained journalists. We use the same tools cops do," says Tony.

I'm neither a crisis manager nor a marriage counselor, but at this moment I feel the need to be a bit of both. And so, fearlessly (or foolishly) I jump in.

"How about this, Rachel. Give us a couple more days, and if we don't make any progress, we'll not only go to the cops, but we'll hire a professional."

"Like a private detective?"

I look at Tony, whose expression reads, *I don't know where you're going with this, pal, but be my guest.*

"Sure. A private detective."

"Do you have someone in mind?" she says.

I don't, but one more lie can't hurt. I mean, how hard can it be to find a PI in this city?

"Sure. A friend of a friend."

This appears to calm Rachel. She closes her eyes and drops her head into her hands, as if in prayer. The only sound I hear is the crack of a bat as a guy dressed in sweatpants and a Yankees shirt with Derek Jeter's number on the back peppers the ball to the infielders.

"All right. But I need you guys to keep me posted. I'm her mother, and I have every right to know exactly what's going on. You keep nothing from me, okay? Promise me that."

We both nod in unison. But I can't help thinking it's Rachel who's keeping something from us. I tell myself it's just a feeling, and I could be wrong. But it seems so real to me.

"Is there a bathroom around here?" Rachel asks.

"Yeah," says Tony. "It's on the other side of the ball diamonds." He points south. "Just follow the path. It's right behind that little playground. We'll wait here for you."

"Okay. Be right back."

I watch as Rachel heads toward the bathroom. Her head is down, her pace slow. Halfway there, she sits down on a bench and takes out her phone. Is she checking her email? Is she calling or texting someone? Does it have something to do with Allie's disappearance?

I look over at Tony, wondering if he's also watching her. But no. He's a million miles away, thinking about God knows what. I decide not to call attention to Rachel's behavior. It can only cause a problem and potentially load more stress on their marriage.

"So, what's with that bullshit about finding the ticket seller?" he says. "I mean, Rachel's no idiot. If she wasn't so preoccupied and not thinking straight, she'd see right through that." He shakes his head. "You're gonna have to up your game, Josh. Now, what's really going on?"

"I'm sorry, man. I should've come up with something way better. But let's face it, I'm just not a very good liar. Especially under pressure."

"So?"

"I had one of those *things*."

"What things?"

"Shit. You're gonna make me say it, aren't you? Visions."

Damn it. I sound like I'm a cut-rate Hildegard of Bingen, who saw images since she was five. "That word makes me sound like I'm some kind of religious nut."

"What did you see?"

"She was a passenger on a train, sitting by herself, in front of her open laptop."

"Where was she going?"

"Don't know."

"So what good is that information, if it's even true?"

He's challenging me. And I don't like it.

"The thing is, Tony, she was alone and she's alive and safe. Wherever she's going, it's by choice. But I couldn't come out and say that in front of Rachel, could I? So, I had to come up with something, and that's the best I could do on short notice."

"Let's hope you do better next time, brother. What's next?"

"I'm not sure why, but I think this genealogy thing is important. Did you see Rachel's face when I mentioned it?"

"I'm sitting next to her, dude. How'm I supposed to see her face?"

"Her expression changed when I mentioned Allie did one of those spit-in-a-tube things."

"So?"

"I think it meant something to Rachel. Maybe you should talk to her about it? Unless you want me to do it?"

"No. I'm the one who should do it."

"Obviously, I can't access the genealogic report, but I think you should sign up for the same service. That way, you guys should be able to access Allie's information."

"You do remember I'm not her birth father, right?"

"Have Rachel do it. It's probably nothing, but right now it's the only lead we have. If I'm right about Allie, and there's nothing criminal going on, you really can't get the cops involved. Which means it's pretty much up to us to find her. It's either that, or we just sit back and wait till we hear from her."

"That's not an option. How reliable do you think this image you had of Allie is?"

There's the answer I should give, and then there's the truth. My gut tells me it's 100 percent true. But the thing of it is, if I'm wrong, then this whole vision thing is bullshit, which makes me nothing more than a twenty-first century P.T. Barnum, selling snake oil and broken dreams to friends. But if true, then maybe I really can help find Allie.

"We'll find out, won't we?" I say.

"I sure as hell hope so," says Tony.

At this moment, both of us are filled with hope. But the truth is, I'm not sure either of us believes in happy endings.

Allie

The Truth, the Whole Truth, and Nothing but the Truth. Maybe.

I haven't slept in two days. That's not hyperbole. That's the truth.

I hate being lied to. I mean, no one likes it, right? But I really, really hate it. And when it comes to a lie as big as this one, well, let's face it, it changes everything. I mean, how could you trust anyone after something like this?

I remember the first time I caught my mother in a lie. I'm sure it wasn't the first lie she told me, only the first I found out about. It was a small lie. Insignificant in the large scheme of things. But still, it was a lie. One night, she made fried filet of sole for dinner. I am not a fish person. Maybe it's the smell. Or the texture. Or the yucky idea that I'm eating something that's been swimming around in water that's likely polluted. But when she dressed it up with a heavy coating of bread crumbs, and then used lemon to camouflage the smell and the taste, it wasn't so bad. When I ate it, I could see the smile on Mom and Dad's faces. Like they'd won the lottery. Like somehow my life was forever going to be changed because I was eating a creature from the sea. And so, every so often she'd rotate filet of sole into our meal cycle, and when I balked, she'd proclaim, "It's filet of sole, honey. You like filet of sole, don't you?" That was an exaggeration. More like I tolerated it. But then one day I opened the refrigerator and I spotted the package of fish. Instead of "filet of sole," it was "flounder." Huh? What's going on here? Only later did I learn filet of sole was expensive, while flounder was much cheaper. She figured that under that heavy blanket of bread crumbs and lemon, I wouldn't know the difference. Maybe she was right, but the feeling of betrayal was heavy. I never said anything about it, and I ate the fish dish as she prepared it. I know this is kinda silly, but I'm not exaggerating when I say it was a life-altering experience. I mean, that she could lie so easily to me, well, it kinda shook my world. I'd lost a little confidence in my mother. I mean, if she could lie about fish, she could lie about anything, right? So, what's the moral? Don't ever lie to your kids, but if you do, make damn sure you cover it up really, really well.

I was kind of hoping the gentle swaying back-and-forth and the soothing chug-a-lug sound of the train riding the rails would act like a cradle rocking a baby to sleep. No such luck. Sleep is out of the question. Closing my eyes and feeling at one with the movement of the train doesn't help in the least. I can't seem to clear my mind enough to let sleep take over.

It reminds me of the time I was in the hospital overnight with a broken leg I got playing soccer. I swear, every fifteen minutes someone was in the room checking my vitals. Giving me medication. Asking me to choose a number on the pain scale. How anyone ever gets better in a hospital is beyond me. I mean, your body's supposed to heal itself during the sleep cycle, right? But how's any healing going to take place when your room is like Grand Central Terminal?

I didn't count on the train stopping every other minute to pick up or drop off passengers, or to let another train pass. And so, even when it seems like I might be dropping off to dreamland, I'm jolted awake. But mostly, it's the voices in my head. Like the imaginary conversations I'm having with my mom.

As we're crossing into Pennsylvania, I take out my phone and Google train quotes and this one by Paul Simon seems appropriate: "There's something about the sound of a train that's very romantic and nostalgic and hopeful."

Too bad I can't reach out to old Paul and tell him he's full of it and that he's putting fake news out there about the virtues of train travel.

But why blame all this on Amtrak? The real blame lies with my mother, who somehow thinks it okay to lie to her daughter about something so darn important. I mean, after this, how can I possibly trust anything she says? Ever? The answer's easy: I can't.

And so, all kinds of things are keeping me awake. Anger. Confusion. Resentment. Confusion. Resentment. Fear. And maybe most of all, lack of forward motion.

Thanks a lot, Mom.

But then, when I recite Simon's quote again and again to myself, I start to look at it from a different angle. Especially that part that says "hopeful." Because, when you get right down to it, isn't the journey I'm on now—and I love that word *journey,* because it connotes that there's a specific destination to be reached—isn't this all about hope? But the hope is at the end of the journey, not the journey itself. In this case, it's the hope that by finding my birth father, I can also find out something very important, maybe even essential, about myself.

One day, I'll cut through the imaginary conversations I have with my mom in my head and confront her about her lies. Maybe she'll be able to explain what she was thinking and why she lied to me. I'm not sure how it'll go, because she's pretty slick when it comes to things like that. After all, she's spent most of her adult life spinning lies for politicians and large corporations. And getting paid pretty darn well for it, I might add. I wonder when what started out as a practical tool to attain a better life became a lifestyle.

But right now, I've got other, more important things to do.

Allie
That Somber City with Big Shoulders

I've been to Europe twice. South America twice. Wait. Costa Rica is Central America, right? So, it's South America once, Central America once. Los Angeles twice. Montreal once, when we visited McGill, which was high on my college list. I almost chose that school, until I got the acceptance letter from Yale. I mean, how could I turn that down? But it was close. I think if I'd chosen McGill my mother would have killed me, while Tony would be laughing hysterically. Not that he's into homicide, of course. Although he's reported his share of it.

The point being I've never been to Chicago, or any other part of the Midwest. It's like there's this gigantic hole in the middle of the country that's a total mystery to me. Pretty much all I know about the city of Chicago, for instance, is that it's nicknamed the Windy City and the City of Big Shoulders. The first one, I get. I thought it was pretty obvious. They get a lot of wind. But when I looked it up, I found it wasn't the actual wind they were talking about, but the wind coming from blowhard politicians. (Some things never change, right?) The other one turns out to come from a poem by Carl Sandburg. The big shoulder reference is to the hardworking tradesmen and physical laborers instrumental in making Chicago the industrial center of the Midwest. I once asked my high school English teacher, Mr. Schwerner, about Sandburg. Schwerner, who was a poet himself, sneered, shook his head, and said with a dismissive wave of his hand, "No one reads him anymore." So, of course, being who I am—my mom calls me stubborn and ornery and probably a lot worse behind my back, but I think she knows where I get it from—I bought a book of Sandburg's poems and read it cover to cover. Okay, so he's no T.S. Eliot, Sylvia Plath, or Emily Dickinson, three of my personal favorites, but he's not anywhere near as bad as Mr. Schwerner made him out to be. When I raised my hand and told him what I thought, he praised me for being enterprising enough to look it up and then admitted that these kinds of conclusions are subjective rather than objective. (I loved the way he turned these things into what he liked to call "teachable moments.") And then he added, "But if you wind up reading as much poetry as I have, and written as much as I have, you'll see I'm right."

Kinda cocky, wasn't he?

The real reason I know anything at all about the city is because my stepdad, Tony, is originally from there. He's a huge fan of *The Adventures of Augie March* by Saul Bellow. I mean huge. He admires it so much he's even memorized parts of the book, including the first paragraph, which he's likely to recite at the drop of a hat. In the beginning, it was kinda cute. But after the zillionth time, well, it really wore kinda thin. Still, it's catchy enough so it eventually got to the point where after hearing it so often, I can quote that beginning word for word.

"I am an American, Chicago born—Chicago, that somber city—and go at things as I have taught myself, freestyle, and will make the record in my own way: first to knock, first admitted; sometimes an innocent knock, sometimes a not so innocent. But a man's character is his fate, says Heraclitus, and in the end there isn't any way to disguise

the nature of the knocks by acoustical work on the door or gloving the knuckles."

I've always loved Tony. He's the only father I've ever known, and he's really good to my mother. And me. Actually, they fit really well. She once told me he saved her life. I was too young and self-absorbed to ask how—maybe she meant it metaphorically—and someday, when I'm talking to her again, I probably should. Tony's always treated me the same as his own flesh and blood, my half brother Dougie. In fact, sometimes I think he actually bends over backward to be nicer to me and harder on Dougie. That's probably why, when I was maybe fourteen, I read the Bellow book, mostly to bond with Tony. Turns out I actually liked it. And it led me to pick up a couple other Bellow novels. But after a while, they got kinda boring, so I moved on.

But I'm not going to Chicago as a tourist, or an *Augie March* lover who wants to walk in the footsteps of that headstrong, ambitious young Jewish boy. I'm going there to see if I can track down my biological father, a father I've always been told was killed in a "tragic" (no one ever refers to it without adding the word "tragic") automobile accident.

Although I have absolutely no memory of him—I wasn't even born when he supposedly died. But that doesn't mean I haven't thought about him from time to time. Well, he really wasn't a *him.* More of an "it." FATHER. In big, bold caps. The only way I knew him was through a handful of photos I found buried in a shoebox in the back of my mom's closet. I've never told her I know of their existence because I always knew that bringing up my father would only make her sad. Or worse, upset. Of course, that didn't mean that in my teens, when my mom and I couldn't even be in the same room without one of us starting a fight, I didn't use it to my advantage. You know, like, "Well, if my *real* father hadn't died, I wouldn't…" Fill in the blank. Of course, this wasn't fair to Tony, and it was really hurtful, I'm sure, but back then I wasn't thinking about anyone's feelings but my own. After a while, when I saw this tactic resulted in diminishing returns, I found something else to use to get under my mom's skin. Believe me, I've never had much of a problem coming up with something that irritates the heck out of her. My thinking has always been simple. *Why should I be the only one who's miserable? After all, I'm the child of a broken marriage, and not by choice.*

Over the years, I've asked my mom about him, but she'd get this faraway look in her eyes and say something like, "Nothing to tell, Allie. The truth is, we didn't know each other all that well." I'd bring it up with my grandparents, but they insisted they hardly knew him. Nevertheless, even though I knew virtually nothing about him, over the years I've had plenty of imaginary conversations with my dead mystery dad. But now, sitting here on the train, staring out the window at the changing scenery, the imaginary conversations filling my head are more of a rehearsal as to what we might talk about when (or if) I ever track him down. I mean, for all I know by this time he might really be dead.

I keep thinking maybe I ought to write questions down, but I never do. Probably because there's a part of me that's in denial. I mean, what if the man isn't my father? And if he is, why has my mother lied to me all these years? And why did he never try to get in touch with me? And what's Tony's place in all this? Did my mom lie to him too? And what if it's a mistake? What if I'm barking up the wrong tree? What if there's been a DNA mix-up? I mean, that could happen, right? But then, when I think about it, that's ridiculous. This is science. And science doesn't make mistakes. Man does, but not science. The proof is right there on paper, a paper that's folded up and tucked into a safe place in my backpack.

DNA does not lie.

People lie.

I never would have found out about this if it hadn't been for my best friend, Lisa, who has all sorts of weird, fun, exotic stories about people who go on these genealogical sites. She kept daring me to do it. "Maybe you'll find out you're related to some famous person," she said. "Or maybe you'll find you've got a long-lost brother or sister. Wouldn't that be cool?"

"One sibling is more than enough, thank you very much."

"But he's only a half," she said, and we had a good laugh.

I'm not laughing anymore, because here's the thing: My place in the family, in the world, is shaky enough without digging up a brand-new family. Mostly to shut her up, I spit in a tube and send it off into the DNA world, pretty much forgetting about it as soon as I drop the package in the mailbox.

When the results arrive, I don't pay much attention. The unopened envelope sits on my desk for almost a week before I work myself up to the point where I open it. Only because as soon as Lisa learns the unopened letter is just sitting there on my desk, she keeps asking if I've checked out the results yet.

"What are you waiting for?"

"Been a little busy, Lisa," I lie, offering the lamest of excuses.

"Aren't you even the least bit curious?" she presses.

"Not really. I probably should be, right?"

"It's like opening a surprise package and finding a treasure."

"Or something like anthrax."

"You're sooo negative, Allie."

"Oh, please, Lisa. I mean how could whatever's in there possibly change my life? I already know everything I need to know about my relatives."

"What about your biological dad? Do you know anything about him or his family?"

"Nope. And to be honest, I really don't care."

"How could you not care, Allie? What if you're heir to a huge fortune? Or what if you're related to someone like Taylor Swift? Or Steve Jobs? You know the story about Mona Simpson, right?"

I do. Mona Simpson, the writer, turned out to be the younger sister of Jobs, who was put up for adoption.

"But what if I'm in a long line of serial killers?"

"You mean like maybe Ted Bundy was your uncle?"

"Or my dad…"

"Ha! Very funny."

I want to join her and laugh too, only when I think about it, I realize it isn't very funny. It's like I'd voluntarily entered into a genetic lottery where the prize might be life-altering, but not in a good way. I'm sorry I did it in the first place. And to be honest, I feel a little guilty for going behind my mom's back. Not that she would have or could have stopped me.

Lisa finally convinces me I'm making way too much about this.

When I do read the letter and digest the results, I notice something strange. There are several people related to me with the same last name as my dead father: Piedmont. That's not surprising, I guess, but it kinda hits me like a ton of bricks, because for the first time, ever, it sinks in that I'm part of another family, a family I know absolutely nothing about. And so, I start Googling some of the names. Just for fun, really. But the deeper dive I make the more I want to put together a complete family tree that includes the Piedmonts.

I wind up spending half the night on this Internet fact-finding mission. I'm someone who's never, ever had to pull an all-nighter—I mean, why give up sleep just to get a higher grade? But I get hooked on the search. I can't rest until I put together an extensive family tree, as if it will help me understand who I am and where I fit in. I focus on one name, Google that name to see if there's any info on them out there in cyberspace. Kinda like putting together a giant human jigsaw puzzle.

That's what I'm doing when I notice something strange. In messages on the genealogy site between my new "family" members, I see the name Daniel keeps coming up. You know, like, "Daniel will get a big kick out of that…" Innocuous stuff like that. What stops me in my tracks is that my birth father's name was "Danny," or the more formal Daniel Piedmont. Sounds like one of those snotty, upper-class bank president guys in a cheesy sitcom. At first, I think, wait a minute, families often pass down names. Maybe this person, whoever he is, was named after my birth father, because he died so young. But the way they keep referring to this Danny person, in the present tense, makes me pretty certain he's still alive. And guess what, turns out he's about the same age my father would be if he were alive. Coincidence? Maybe. Maybe not.

All kinds of weird thoughts begin shooting through my brain. I mean, what if my birth father really is alive? But if he is, why has my mom been keeping it a secret all these years? Why has she made up some ridiculous story about him being killed in a horrible traffic accident? And if he is alive, what's he doing now? Where's he living? Does he even know he has a daughter? And if he does, how could he have stayed away from me for so long?

The more I try to *not* think about it, the more I can't think of anything else.

I have to find out. So, I dive headfirst into solving this mystery. I start by Googling my birth dad. I don't have much to work with. I mean, it's not like he was famous or anything. And I know practically nothing about him because it's not like my mom ever talked about him. On the few occasions I asked, she never gave me a direct answer.

I find out he grew up in a rough neighborhood in Chicago. And this leads to finding his name turn up in some newspaper articles. A half dozen of them come from the *Tribune* and the *Sun Times*, and they have to do with some kind of fraudulent scheme that bilked a lot of people out of a lot of money. It wasn't a Ponzi scheme—I know all about those from the Bernie Madoff thing—but some kind of complicated fraud I don't quite understand. And even though there were several mentions of Danny Piedmont, I can't quite figure out how he fit into this scheme. Eventually, the story begins to fade from the papers to the point where his name completely disappears. No matter how deep I dig, I can't find anything else about him. It's like he never existed.

But the damage is done. Because I let Lisa talk me into spitting into a tube, my whole world has been turned upside down.

Every new bit of information results in a bunch of new questions to be answered. For the next few days, I hardly sleep or eat. Instead, practically every waking hour is spent on the Internet searching for more information.

Finally, it gets to be too much. I'm starting to feel like my brother when he was addicted to those electronic games.

The first order of business is to make sure it's true. Second, I need to find out why my mom has lied to me all these years. But there's no way I'm going to confront my mother now. I know her too well; she'll deny, deny, deny. Or, because this is what she does for a living, give it a completely different spin. It'll only result in a battle, and that's not something I want or need right now. Especially since lately my relationship with my mom has improved so much. I know the only way I'm going to clear this up is to track down this Daniel Piedmont guy.

And the best way to do that is to find and visit some of his (now my) long-lost relatives in Chicago to see what I can find out.

Allie
The Last Mile

Nerves. I've got them. And they're driving me crazy.

As soon as I get off the train, the seriousness of what I'm doing hits me. My stomach is flip-flopping. I'm feeling dizzy. Dizzy enough to grab a spot on a bench in the station, where I try and steady myself. I'm beginning to wonder if I've thought this all the way through. I mean, what if this is a big fat mistake? What if I've misread the genealogical findings and messages? But it gets worse. What if it isn't a mistake? Do I really want to lift this rock and see what crawls out from under it? Maybe my mom has a really good reason for lying to me. Like maybe she's trying to protect me from something? But all these questions don't help. Bottom line: I don't like the idea of being treated like a baby. Like I can't like handle the truth.

To be honest, I'm really, really, really tempted to get back on the train and take it all the way back to New Haven, where I can go back to my old life, where my mother's alive, my birth father is dead, and my stepfather is Tony.

But I don't.

As soon as I arrive at Chicago Union Station, I check the address I've jotted down on the back of one of the pages of my genealogy report. The woman I'm looking for is Jeannette Piedmont Kopecky, who, if I'm reading this right, looks to be a cousin or maybe an aunt. She lives in the Lincoln Park neighborhood.

I'm on a tight budget, so before I leave, I find a place on Craigslist within walking distance from where this Jeannette woman lives. It's advertised as a room in a large apartment in a prewar building.

I pay for everything by cash, because I know Tony can track me down by following the money, something he took great delight in explaining to me one night when we watched *All the President's Men.* It's one of Tony's favorite movies. He claims it inspired him to become a journalist.

Tony is probably beating the bushes looking for me. He's always boasting that given enough time he can find anything or anyone "dead or alive." He loves making all kinds of ridiculous claims about what he can and can't do. But over the years I've found he's not just bragging. He really is that good. I Googled him once and found that he's won all kinds of awards and honorable mentions. And get this. He's never, ever mentioned any of them. I brought this up with my mom once and she explained, "He's embarrassed. I think part of him doesn't believe he deserves them. And there's the part of him that's afraid if he does start to believe all this stuff about how good he is, he won't try as hard and his career will be over."

I guess I should let them know I'm okay. I mean, I know how worried they must be. And believe me, I'm not unaware of the ramifications of my actions. I mean, like that wasn't pounded into my head enough growing up? If I'm being honest with myself, I'd have to admit I'm kinda enjoying the fact that they must going crazy with worry. I guess it *is* mean. But to be honest, it's the only way I can think of right now to punish my mom for lying to me all these years. I'm sure she has her reasons, but whatever those reasons are I still think it's pretty crummy lying to me about something so important. Fish is one thing. This is another. Maybe I'll give them a call after all this is settled. Or drop them an email or text. But if I do, when I do, I won't tell them where I am or why I'm not back at school. They deserve it.

When I arrive at Jeannette's building, I give my name to the dude at the front desk, who opens up a book, finds my name there, then hands me an envelope with my name and the apartment number typed neatly on the front. Inside, I find the key, a crudely drawn map of the apartment layout, and two paragraphs of instructions.

"Could you point me toward the elevator, please," I say.

"Sure thing, honey," he says, with a big smile on his face. "Honey" sets my teeth on edge. Even though I'm tempted to say something, I don't. Which, believe me, is definite progress when it comes to self-control. If I weren't on the road, trying to duck under the radar, it's the kind of thing where I'd immediately tell my mom and we'd laugh ourselves sick.

"You know there's no one up there, right?"

"No one said anything about that."

"Gone for a long weekend. She said everything you'd need to know is in there." He points to the envelope in my hand. "Don't know why she bothers. Not like she needs the money."

I might be there forever, but I'm saved when the phone rings. When he picks it up, I hike my backpack over my shoulder and head toward the elevator while I silently mouth the words "Thanks so much." He nods, but I don't think he really hears what I'm saying.

I unlock the door and step into the foyer. It smells a little funky. Like an old person's apartment. I drop my backpack down on a small table beside the front door and read the letter, which includes an almost perfectly drawn map of the sprawling three-bedroom apartment. An X and my initials mark the room I'm to use. I've never been in an apartment this spacious. And neat! Nothing seems out of place. If it were my mom's or even worse, mine, this place would look like a cyclone hit it.

The last page has the word *WARNING!* written on the top in big, black letters. "*Allison, I don't want to freak you out but there are a few cameras placed strategically in certain places of the apartment. They're all in plain sight, and there aren't any cameras in your bedroom, or any of the bathrooms. It's purely for security reasons, so I hope you don't take it personally. Which is why I wanted to make a point of warning you. Please don't hesitate to use any of the common rooms, living room, kitchen, dining room. And if you have any problems, either speak to someone at the front desk or here's a number where you may reach me, if there's an emergency—or you have a question only I can answer. Sorry I won't be able to meet you. I had to go out of town for a family event, but perhaps you'll visit another time...*"

I'm happy to be on my own. But there's something kinda creepy about being alone in someone else's apartment, surrounded by someone else's stuff. The upside is I won't have to tiptoe around and have polite, meaningless conversations with someone I don't know.

I grab my backpack and follow the blue line on the map to what is to be my room, which is at the very back of the apartment, right by the service entrance.

The room is tiny. I'm a shade under five-six, and if I sit on the edge of the bed and the bed was in the middle of the room, I'm pretty sure I could spread my arms out to the side, like I'm an airplane, and, no exaggeration, touch one wall with my left hand and my right hand on the other. Either people were a lot shorter, like hobbit-size, back when the building was built, or they just didn't care about where the "help" lived. Maybe both.

There's a dark blue futon up against one wall. On it are neatly folded top and bottom sheets, a pillow and a pillowcase, and two white towels, one face-size, the other bath-size. There's also a small dresser and a night table. I pull out the drawer to find it's empty.

I'm not the kind of girl who needs creature comfort. During that month last summer I spent in Costa Rica working for Habitat for Humanity, we often wound up sleeping on the floor. I never complained. In fact, I kinda liked it. I felt like it gave me better insight into how people outside the US live. Americans are so spoiled, and I think every teenager should have to spend at least a month in what our ridiculous ex-president called one of those "shit-hole countries."

I dump the contents of my backpack onto my bed and arrange them neatly—if my mom saw this, she'd probably keel over from shock—use the bathroom, and then head out to visit Jeannette.

Chicago isn't hard to navigate. I don't get lost even once. This may not seem cause for celebration, but for me it is. I have the world's worst sense of direction. If it wasn't for GPS, I'd probably be lost most of the time. My mom likes to remind me there was a time, not so long ago, when there was no such thing as smartphones or the Internet. Once she makes that clear for the zillionth time, she inevitably launches into this big speech—I've heard it so many times I can practically recite it word for word—about how lucky I am and how we have to be responsible because all these new-agey (yes, that's the actual phrase she uses) inventions that supposedly make life easier are really making it not just difficult but impossible to live in "peace and harmony." I don't think she means to lecture, but that's the way it comes out.

"There's no such thing as privacy anymore, Allison. Just assume that wherever you are, there's a camera aimed at you. So, be careful what you do. And what you say. Big Brother is always watching."

I don't argue with her. At least not about that. What's the point?

I didn't figure out how to handle my mom till I was a junior in high school. But once I did, and I learned to let my mom run down like that non-Energizer Bunny, it gave me a real sense of power. That's when it seemed the balance of power between us started to shift. I realized that if I used the right strategy, I could manipulate my mom, and you know what, it probably works on other people too. All I have to do is figure out what people want, and then use that against them. I know it sounds kind of cynical, but that doesn't mean it isn't true.

Rather than surprise Jeannette, I contacted her a few days ago using the messaging service on the ancestry site. I told her I was going to be visiting a friend in Chicago for a couple days and, if she had the time, I'd love to meet her. She wrote back right away saying it would be her "pleasure" and that she was "really looking forward to meeting" me. I didn't tell her the real reason I want to meet her. I was afraid that would freak her out.

I'm not far from where she lives, and the weather is pretty good, so I decide to walk. I'm nervous, of course. Butterflies are crashing into each other in my stomach. Half a dozen times I'm tempted to turn around and go home. I keep asking myself, *Allie, do you really want to open this Pandora's box? Maybe you should just leave it alone.* After all, let's say he's alive and I can locate him, what will I have accomplished? How will anyone's life be any better? Maybe I should sit down with my mom and have it out with her first? Maybe she has a very good explanation—or excuse—for lying to me all these years?

In the end, I decide I've come too far to give up now. And so, I keep walking, feeling very much like that guy on death row heading toward his own execution.

Allie
Who's Your Daddy?

Jeannette answers the door wearing a ratty flowered housecoat. Her hair, dyed to some unrecognizable color halfway between brown and red, is up in curlers. Kinda scary, actually. At first, I think maybe I've knocked at the wrong door. I mean, who dresses like that when they're expecting company? In fact, who dresses that way ever?

Although I've alerted her to my visit, Jeannette seems shocked to see me. And so, we stand facing each other for several seconds, speechless. It feels so awkward. Neither of us seems prepared to meet the other.

Jeannette is probably somewhere in her late fifties, but the deep wrinkles that crisscross her face make her look way older. Some makeup would probably help. Of course, I'm not the best judge of age. At a certain point, maybe it's when you reach forty, especially if you're going grey, everyone starts to look like a senior citizen to me. My mom jokes about that. "To you, Allie, anyone with even a strand of grey hair should be making burial plans."

She's exaggerating, of course. But not by much, I guess.

I expect her to be a little standoffish, but I'm not expecting how she just stares super hard at me, like she's trying to look deep into my soul or something. Super creepy. Maybe she's studying my face to see if she can recognize a family resemblance. Whatever it is, it kinda creeps me out.

I'm still having second thoughts. What do I hope to accomplish with this visit? Is it really so important that I track down information about my birth father? Why should it matter? Why not just leave things alone, instead of upending everyone's life? Suddenly, standing there facing a woman who might be my aunt, I come to understand the meaning of that old saying, "Let sleeping dogs lie."

What must she be thinking about me? How can she possibly know I'm just a harmless girl on a quest to find her family? What if, in her mind, I'm some kind of con artist?

I stand there, hands folded demurely in front of me, hoping she'll ask me in while at the same time hoping she doesn't. Because once I step inside that apartment, there's no turning back.

It's like we're in a staring contest. Eventually, one of us has to blink. And it isn't going to be me. I hate to lose. I'm a poor loser. That's why no one wants me on their team in PE. My mom calls me stubborn, and she's right. And so, even though she doesn't know it, this poor woman doesn't stand a chance.

It reminds me of when we got our first kitten. I'd been bugging my mom and Tony for months, and finally they caved. My mom's a charter member of any group that wants to, like, save the whales. Or save anything. That meant it had to be a "rescue" animal. Okay. I get it. No problem. Tony took me to the local shelter and I picked out a beautiful calico and, although she was a female, I named her George—cause she looked like a George. I chose her because she showed absolutely no interest in me or any of her fellow felines. In her, I saw a reflection of me: independent, self-reliant, and at times aloof. Only then did negotiations begin. I had to promise this. I had to promise that. My mom made it very clear: It was my cat. She was going to stay in my room, and I would be totally responsible for her. I think this was probably her way of making a life lesson out of it.

That first night was hell. Starting around 3 a.m., George started meowing. I wasn't sure why. I mean, what did I know about cats? I figured she must be hungry. But I'd laid out some dry food for her, so if she was hungry, why not eat that?

When she kept at it, I thought maybe I was being tested. So, I decided I'd just let her meow all she wanted and eventually, when she saw it wasn't working, she'd give up, and I could go back to sleep, knowing I'd shown that stupid cat who was boss.

No way. She kept it up for five minutes, ten minutes, fifteen minutes. If anything, she got louder and came closer to the edge of my bed. I put a pillow over my head to shut out the noise. Didn't help. So, here I am, in the middle of the night, it's pitch dark, and I'm in a battle of wits with a cat!

Finally, after maybe a half hour, I realize this cat's gonna meow all night till she gets what she wants. So, I drag myself out of bed, go to the kitchen, get a can of fresh cat food, empty the bowl of dry food, and replace it with the wet food. I come back to my room, put the bowl down, and hop back into bed. Sure enough, it works! She stops meowing. After more than an hour engaged in a battle of will with a cat, trying to bend her to my will, just the opposite happens. And so, every night, around three, I'd wake up, stumble into the kitchen, and fill her bowl with fresh food. Lesson learned. Training complete.

After maybe ten, twenty seconds, Jeannette shifts her gaze to over my shoulders. Like she's checking to see if I've come alone or with a posse.

Finally, she speaks. "So, you're Allison."

"That's right. But you can call me Allie."

We stand there a few more awkward seconds, before she finally says, "Would you like to come in, Allison?"

Okay, so she doesn't want to call me Allie. That's fine. Maybe it's her way of maintaining a discreet distance between us. Like maybe she doesn't trust me. Like I could be some kind of slick con artist who preys on ladies in flowered housecoats and curlers, getting them to sign over all their property. I have to laugh—to myself, of course—at the thought of me conning anyone out of anything. My mom keeps pounding it into my head: "Know your worth, Allie! Because if you don't, no one else will." I guess I'm still working on that.

I follow Jeannette through a long, poorly lit hallway, which opens up into the living room. Suddenly, it's like I'm yanked into another time, another place. You know, like those cheesy, old-timey movies where the screen gets all wavy and the music gets really scary, and you get sucked into, like, the inside of a cyclone, and it spins you around and you go through like a time warp thing. It's the kind of living room your grandparents, if they came over from the "old country," lived in. One wall is covered with a floral-print wallpaper that reminds me of Rousseau's jungle paintings, which in turn kinda reminds me of Jeannette's housecoat. Wouldn't that be something if this woman has color- and theme-coordinated everything in her life! It kinda feels like any minute some jungle animal is going to jump out from the wall. There's a deep green couch with a plastic cover over it, end tables on either side, a coffee table, a large easy chair, a couple other chairs, and on the wall there are these tacky still-life paintings that look like they've been purchased at a garage sale.

She points me toward the leather couch while she plops down in an easy chair with a flowery pattern that matches the wall. I feel like if I listen carefully, maybe I'll hear jungle sounds.

"Would you like something to drink, dear?" Her tone softens, maybe because she no longer considers me a threat.

"Thank you very much, but I'm fine."

"Well, if you change your mind…"

"Of course."

She folds her hands in her lap and leans forward. "To be honest, Allison, I'm not quite sure why you're here."

"Okay. Well, you know, I'll get right to the point. It's like, I signed onto this genealogy site, you know, the ones that use DNA to tell you all about your ancestry. So, I thought maybe it might be fun to connect with some of my long-lost relatives. You know, like to maybe learn something about my heritage."

She laughs. "I'm not sure I think of myself as lost, dear. And as for heritage, well, I'm afraid if you're looking to see if you're related to someone important or famous, you're going to be very disappointed."

"Oh, no…I didn't mean it that way."

She smiles and reaches her hand across the table, grabbing my wrist and squeezing it affectionately. "I know, dear. I'm just pulling your leg. But I'm still not sure for the reason for your visit."

"To be honest, Jeannie—is it okay if I call you Jeannie?"

She blushes. "That's what they used to call me when I was a kid."

It's starting to sink in that I'm part of a family I never knew I had. A family with history I'm not part of. I'm not sure how I feel about this.

I swallow and plow ahead. "I'm here about my father."

Her body stiffens and the muscles in her face tighten. Now that she knows why I'm here, I'm afraid she's going to throw me out. But instead, she asks calmly, "And who might that be?"

Is she playing with me, or does she really not know what I'm talking about?

"Umm, I'm pretty sure Daniel—I think maybe he's your nephew—is my birth father."

I look for a reaction. Any reaction. But her expression stays the same. "I think you may be confused, dear, because as far as I know, Daniel doesn't have any children."

"Actually, I'm pretty sure he does—and I'm pretty sure that child would be me. But I don't blame you for not knowing. I've always been told he passed away in a car accident not long after I was born."

She shakes her head.

"We can't possibly be talking about the same person, dear, because Danny is still very much alive and kicking. And as far as I know, he's never been in a fatal car accident." She smiles.

"I guess it's possible I'm mistaken. Would you mind looking at a photograph I have of him?" I reach into my backpack and pull out an envelope, open it, take out a faded Polaroid and hand it to her. "I think this was taken on a trip they made to the mountains. Is this your nephew Danny?"

She takes the photo from me and holds it a few inches from her eyes. "Excuse me," she says. "I can't see a damn thing anymore without my glasses." She gets up and disappears into another room. A few seconds pass, and then she returns carrying a pair of horn-rimmed eyeglasses. She sits back down and puts them on. "I'm afraid I'm at the age when everything seems to be falling apart. It's like suddenly the warranty has run out, and of course that's when everything starts falling apart."

She looks at the photo. Looks back to me. Then looks at the photo again.

"Well, this really is strange, dear, because this is a photo of Daniel. But I have no idea who the woman in the photo is."

"That would be my mom."

"And you say they were married?"

"Actually, it's very possible they were never married."

She shakes her head back and forth, then hands the photo back to me.

"I don't know how to tell you this, dear, but Daniel, the man in this photograph, the man you say is your father, is very much alive. At least he was a year or so ago, which is the last time I heard from him, or anything about him. But I certainly can't imagine he could have kept something like this from his family."

My stomach churns. Suddenly, this is all very real. This *is* my father and he *is* alive. He might be across the street. Or across the country. My face flushes. My heart beats quicker. I'm afraid it's going to burst out of my chest. I feel like I'm going to die. I try to center myself. I take a deep breath and exhale.

"I'm sorry," I say. "But this is *so* confusing."

"I imagine it is," she says.

For a moment, I forget where I am and why I'm here. Jeannette says nothing. It's up to me to keep things moving.

"It means my mom hasn't been telling me the truth. Why would she do something like that?"

"Like that?"

"Like lying to me about my father?"

"I'm afraid this is something between you and your mother, dear. If it's true. After all, if she's lied to you about whether he's alive or dead, she could be lying about him being your father, couldn't she?"

It's one thing for me to call my mom a liar, but it's totally something else for a stranger to call her a liar. Suddenly, I feel protective toward my mom, and I'm about to defend her, when I realize maybe it's best to keep my mouth shut, because I don't want to offend Jeannette before I get the information I'm here for.

Jeannette removes her eyeglasses and lays them gently on the coffee table. "I can't tell you how many pairs of these I've scratched up so bad I can't use them anymore." She picks them up again and uses the hem of her housecoat to wipe them clean. She holds them up to the light and, satisfied she's cleaned them sufficiently, she puts them back on.

"If it's true, Allison, and I'm not saying it is, I might have an explanation for it. But to be honest, I'm not sure I should be the one telling you about this. I mean, it's really none of my business."

"I need someone to be honest with me, Jeannie. I mean, you can't imagine how awful this is. It changes everything I've ever known. My world is turned upside down."

To my surprise, I'm on the verge of crying. I try to check myself, but obviously it's not working because Jeannette reaches over and takes my hand to comfort me.

I'm lost and I don't know how to find myself. I look over at Jeannette, and I'm moved by her gentle touch and the sympathetic look in her eyes. I'm feeling guilty. I've disturbed this sweet woman's life and she's done nothing to deserve it. I should thank her, get up, and leave. I'll never forget this happened, but maybe she can.

I want to stop, but I can't. I've come this far and I know I have to follow through.

In high school, thinking maybe I should be an actress—it was appealing because I thought that meant I could live in a fantasy world and get paid for it—I took a drama workshop class and found I was actually pretty good at faking tears. Well, not really faking it, because the tears are real. I realized I was good at faking emotion, which would bring on the tears. It was like having a superpower: the power to turn on a gusher of tears at will. All I had to do was think of something really, really sad. Like when Georgie died. It was the first time I experienced death on such a close, personal level. I knew what it was, of course. But it was never real to me until Georgie passed away. Even now, when I feel the need to cry, I think about Georgie and the tears arrive.

Years ago, I read an article Tony wrote about the actress Meg Ryan. She said that when she was starting out in soaps, she was able to cry on cue. Once the producers and writers found she could do this, every Friday they'd have Ryan cry, just so viewers would come back Monday to see if she was okay.

"Please, please, please. I need to know..." I beg Jeannette, hoping she'll take pity on me. This approach is nothing new. It worked pretty well for me until I was twelve or thirteen, which is when my mom figured out what was going on. After that, every time she saw me reaching for my secret power, she'd beat me to the punch by making a crying face and moving her index finger from her eye down her cheek, like it was a falling tear.

Today, I decide to stop short of the waterworks. It seems so tacky and dishonest to use this to get what I want. I mean, it was one thing when I was a kid, but I'm an adult now, and manipulation doesn't feel all that good. Instead, I call on my "lost puppy look," hoping Jeannette's maternal instincts will kick in. I can't believe I'm turning into such a manipulative bitch.

Surprise! It works.

"All right, dear. But promise me if this gets too much for you, you'll tell me and I'll stop. Are you sure you wouldn't like something to drink?"

"Thanks. I'm sure," I say, wiping away an imaginary tear.

She leans back and folds her hands, then settles them on her lap. "Where to begin? Where. To. Begin. Daniel was, oh, how can I put it? Well, he was always the black sheep of the family. From the time he was a teenager he was in trouble. Always in trouble. Nothing big, you understand. But if there was trouble to be found, Daniel would find it. That boy sure had a knack for trouble."

"What kind of trouble?"

"Oh, you know. Same old story. Hanging around with the wrong element. Little things. Shoplifting, underage drinking, cutting school. Only weeks before he was due to graduate—he was smart as a whip, by the way—he was thrown out of high school for selling drugs. It was only marijuana, but still.... That boy just loved money, and he didn't seem to care how he got it."

I can't believe it! My father was a juvenile delinquent. A drug dealer before he was eighteen!

"But he never went to jail or anything like that, did he?"

"Umm," she hesitates, which signals what she's about to say isn't good. "Not real jail. You know, one of those juvenile-detention places. But he didn't have a violent nature. Which was surprising because Danny wasn't the type to ever walk away from a fight. The thing about Danny is that everyone liked him. He could charm the pants off you." She laughs. "And I'm sure he did. He stood up for himself, when he had to. So, he did get into more than his fair share of fights. Lots of people tried to help him along the way. A gym teacher thought he'd harness some of that anger and aggression and tried to convince him to take up boxing. But that wasn't his thing."

"Did he have a 'thing'?"

"Just stupid teenage stuff. We always said if Danny would just put his mind to serious matters, he could have been a huge success. I mean, he really did have it all. Brains. Good looks. Charisma." She shakes her head. "He just couldn't stay out of trouble. As soon as he turned eighteen, he moved out."

"Do you know where he went?"

She shakes her head no.

"Has he been back to Chicago?"

"Honestly, I have no idea. I haven't seen him since he disowned the family…or we disowned him. I can't remember which. Probably a little of both. Occasionally, someone in the family will report back on our prodigal son. Years ago, his sister, Blanche, claimed he was 'riding the rails.' You know, like the hobos used to do. I don't know if that was actually true, or just a story Blanche concocted. Every so often, he'd call home, so his mother didn't worry. But that stopped after she passed away. With Daniel, you never knew what was true and what was made up. He had a knack for telling you just what he wanted you to know, and I'm afraid it wasn't always the truth. I stopped wondering what was true and what wasn't, when it came to Daniel. I mean, what was the point?"

"So, he was an unreliable narrator."

"Excuse me?"

"I'm sorry. Just a term I learned in a lit class."

"You're still in school, dear?"

"Yes. I'm at Yale."

She reaches across the table again, grabs my wrist, and squeezes tight. "Aren't you the smart one?" she says. "You might be the first one in the family to make it through all four years of college."

I'm not sure why, but I'm feeling a little icky. Like I've done something wrong by going to college. Like I was betraying the family. Like I was the family weirdo.

"Daniel never attended college?"

"One of my friends once ran into him in New York City, down by Washington Square Park, and said Danny was taking classes at NYU. Who knows if it was true? Daniel's always been impatient. As a child, he was always moving. He never walked. He ran. His mom spent so much time chasing him. I once asked my sister, his mother, the difference between Daniel and his sister and she said, 'If I wanted them to stop doing something, I'd say, "You better stop, or else." That was enough for his sister, who would stop. But not Daniel. He'd ask, 'Or else what?' Always weighing the consequences. At one point, she actually got one of those retractable dog leashes and attached it to him, so he couldn't wander off too far." She laughs. "But that didn't last long. One day, it just disappeared. You can draw your own conclusions as to how that happened."

I smile at the thought of this man who is very likely my birth father being walked like a dog as he pulls at the leash.

"When did his mother die?"

"Sylvia, God rest her soul, passed away right around 9/11." She makes the sign of the cross. "His father left the family about the same time Danny did. We still have no idea where he is or even if he's still alive. If you ask me, he probably drank himself to death. Neither of them was easy to get along with. Sylvia was the oldest, ten years older than me. She was so bossy. It's no wonder Daniel turned out the way he did. Oh, my, I can't believe I'm telling all this to a total stranger."

"Well, we're family, aren't we?" I say with a big fat fake smile plastered across my face.

"Yes, I suppose we are."

Last week, these people were nothing to me. Now, they're my family. Suddenly, I have this weird sense of loss, even though up until a few minutes ago, I didn't even know these people existed.

"Oh, my. I know it's a little late, but maybe I should be asking you for some kind of identification, proof of who you are. I mean, you hear all about these horrible scammers…"

"Of course," I say as I reach for my wallet and show her my Yale ID and my driver's license.

She puts on her glasses and examines them like she's one of those TSA security people. "I'd love to meet Daniel's sister, my aunt. Would that be possible?"

"Blanche?"

I love the sound of it. Blanche. So old-timey. "Yes. That's a pretty old-fashioned name, isn't it?"

"It's from some play. You're the one in that fancy Ivy League college, so you must know who I'm talking about."

"*A Streetcar Named Desire*. Blanche DuBois was one of the characters," I say. "Maybe you saw the movie? You know, the one with Marlon Brando. *Stella! Stella!*" I do my best impression. I watched that movie with my family and for days after I'd walk around the house screaming, "Stella! Stella!" It cracked up Tony and my mom, until they got pretty sick of it.

"That's it. She hated that name. Thought it was an old lady's name. When she was a teenager, she made everyone call her Marcy. The family still calls her Blanche, at least behind her back. If you call her that to her face, she'll bust a gut. That girl has a temper! We'd steer clear of her when we thought she was in one of her moods."

It's so weird hearing intimate, inside stories about people I'm related to but have never met.

I'm pretty much done. Not because I don't have any more questions, but because I have too many. My mind is racing in so many different directions, I realize I have to stop and let this new information sink in.

I think maybe I'm on the verge of a panic attack. I need to get the heck out of here before my head explodes. I check my watch and say, "Oh, my, I didn't realize it was getting so late. I'm supposed to meet up with that friend I came to Chicago to see. But before I go, could you give me Blanche's contact information? I'd love to connect with her and maybe find out some more about my..." I can't quite get the word "father" out of my mouth. "Daniel."

"Blanche isn't easy to find, dear. She moves around a lot. She's been married four times. That I know of. I can give you the latest phone number and email I have for her, if that'll help."

"That would be great."

She gets up and disappears again. When she gets back, she's holding a small piece of paper, folded over once, the way we used to do it in elementary school when we were voting for something using a secret ballot. "Here we go, dear," she says, handing it to me.

I unfold it and see she's written down her name, "Blanche/ Marcy," a phone number, and an email address.

"I have to warn you, she might just up and refuse to talk to you. I'm not even sure you should mention where you got this. We had a pretty serious falling out a few years ago, which is why I can't be sure where she is or how cooperative she'll be." She leans forward and in a half whisper adds, "Our family is like a version of the Hatfields and McCoys."

I'm not quite sure who they are, but I'll look them up later.

I refold the paper and stuff it into my jeans pocket.

My heart begins to beat faster. I feel like I'm going to jump out of my skin. I feel lightheaded and I begin to gasp for air.

All I can think about is getting the heck out of here.

Josh
Ever Seen a Dream Walking?

It began with a nightmare so vivid, so real, I couldn't be sure it hadn't actually happened.

Wait. That's not quite right. The nightmare part, I mean. Strictly speaking, it wasn't what we usually think of a nightmare because I was wide awake.

I was a kid. Seven, eight years old. I can still see it, as clear as if it's happening right in front of me. But what stands out is how I felt. Frightened. Creeped out. Confused. Anxious.

I'd had nightmares before. Those monster-in-the-closet or monster-under-the-bed kinds. Quickly forgotten once awake. This was different. For one thing, I wasn't asleep, or anywhere near a bed, when it arrived, seemingly out of nowhere.

It was a cold, windy, rainy day. I was on the bus heading to school, staring out the window, mesmerized by the tiny raindrops striking the window then, gripped by gravity—something we'd learned about earlier that year—slowly sliding down the pane until they disappeared from sight. That's when, out of the blue, this vivid, powerful image pops into my head.

I see my father and mother, looking much younger than I'd ever seen them, standing in front of Doctors Hospital (I can read the words on the awning) on the Upper East Side, steps from Gracie Mansion, where the mayor of New York City lives. My mom is very pregnant. She's wearing a camel-hair coat and feathered hat. She's smiling, and yet I can see great concern etched on her face, while my father, stoic, sphinxlike, impenetrable as always, is walking several steps in front of her. He's carrying a small suitcase. He pushes open the hospital door, motions to my mother to move faster, then leads the way inside. I watch as they approach the front desk. My father seems agitated. He says something to the nurse at the front desk, but I can't hear the words. He waves his hand and points back to my mother, standing quietly behind him. And then, as sudden as it arrived, the image disappears, and I'm back watching the raindrops make their downward journey on the bus window.

At the time, I have nothing to compare this to. But now, some forty-odd years later, I can best describe it as being like one of those virtual reality gizmos. That's how real it felt. That's how much I felt a part of it, even though I wasn't born yet.

In the days after it happened, the discomforting sense that something was out of whack stayed with me. It wasn't the nightmare itself that made it stand out. It was my relationship to it that was so disturbing. It was like stepping into another dimension. It felt like I'd crossed over into what seemed like a higher consciousness.

I was already an anxious kid, and this would make me even more anxious. At that age, you're looking for commonalities between you and the other kids, not differences. You want to be part of a group. Not on the outside looking in. If I took this "vision" thing any further, I'd be more of a freak than I thought I already was.

For days after, I was afraid to close my eyes, lest I saw something I didn't want to see. I was fearful it might return and, in an attempt to ward off any unwanted visions, I made as much noise as I could, hoping I could scare it away. If I felt something coming on, I'd go to the bathroom and open the sink and bathtub water taps full blast. As if that wasn't enough, I'd drop the toilet seat several times, in the hope the noise would protect me. I'd turn on the radio and turn up the volume. All this did the job. I knew the visions were probably still there, but I'd found an effective way of keeping the lid on them.

Years later, long after my father passed away (his weakened heart from a childhood bout of rheumatic fever gave out and he died while they were attending a Sunday-evening wedding), I questioned my mother about that day. I asked if she remembered what she was wearing. She laughed and said she hardly remembers what she wore last week, let alone decades ago. She said she had other things on her mind. I asked if she ever owned a camel-hair overcoat and feathered hat. She stared at me wide-eyed. Like I'd performed a particularly astounding magic trick. "Yes. That's right. How could you possibly know that?" I lied, telling her I'd seen them in photos from the period.

"Seeing" Allie on the train results in the floodgates opening and the visions are coming fast and furious. It's like they've been bottled up for years, decades even, and now they've been freed.

Until now, by sheer act of will, I've been able to stem the tide of images by willfully shutting them down as soon as they begin to appear. The strategy is simple: Maybe it's a case of use it or lose it.

Now, because of Tony's plea for help, my life has undergone a sea change. No longer am I a journalist. I've morphed into a psychic detective.

Yesterday, standing in line at the supermarket, I had a vision of Allie. She's walking down a city street. At first, I don't recognize it, but I know it's not New York. As I follow her, hovering above her like a tiny drone, I recognize it as Chicago, my ex-wife's hometown. I continue to follow her, as I note the various street signs and landmarks she passes until she finally stops in front of an apartment building. She enters. I make a note of the address, but as soon as I try to follow her inside, the vision fades.

When I mention this to Tony, he lights up.

"You think she's in Chicago, man?"

"I can't swear to it, but it appears that's the case. But remember, I don't know how accurate these 'visions' are, and I don't even know how current they are. I mean, I might be seeing something from the distant past…or something that never even happened."

"No. It's gotta be now because Allie's never been to Chicago before."

"Any idea why she'd be there now?"

"Not a clue. But she's heard me talk about the city for years since I grew up there. Maybe she just wanted to check it out."

"That doesn't sound right to me. Why now?"

"I guess we'll get the answer once you track her down. Tell me exactly what you saw."

I describe the scene in as much detail as I can—enough so that Tony is over the moon.

"You're going to Chicago," he announces.

"You want me to go to Chicago simply because of what I saw?"

"It's crazy that I have more faith in you than you do. We'll pay for everything. Even your time there. I'm really pumped, Josh. I mean this is pretty amazing."

"Tony, please, let's not overdo it. I don't want you guys to be disappointed. Besides, you're putting a lot of pressure on me."

"Look, Josh. I don't understand this *thing*"—he uses air quotes—"of yours any more than you do. And I don't know if we mere mortals ever can. Either we accept it or we don't. Faith, man. It's all about faith. You know me, J. I'm pretty levelheaded and down to earth, right? I've spent my life trying to keep my feet planted firmly on the ground, only accepting facts I can verify. But this is different."

"Different how?"

"Different because you've obviously got some kind of 'gift.' And because of that gift, you're in the unique position of being able to help us. Without you, Josh, what else can we do? You're all we have right now. Can you leave tomorrow?"

I want to say no, a thousand times no. I want to help, but at what cost to me? I have to tap into a part of me that is frightening. I am different, that's for sure. But if I pursue helping Tony find Allie, I'll have to learn more about myself and my place in the world. That scares the hell out of me.

Eventually, friendship trumps fear, so I agree to go to Chicago.

And so, it is with a mixture of fear, anticipation, and excitement that I now sit in an aisle seat on a flight heading to Chicago's O'Hare.

During the flight, I try coming up with a plan of action. But it doesn't take long to realize making such a plan is impossible without knowing certain facts. Like, why Allie is in Chicago. What drove her to disappear, to leave New Haven without telling anyone, especially her parents, where she was going and why? Is the address of the building she entered even real?

Without answers to these questions, making a plan is pointless. The best I can do is find a starting point, follow the crumbs, and hope they eventually lead to Allie.

I'm too wound up to read, so I'm forced to spend time in the air inside my head. If I'm going to be any help at all, I have to try to harness this thing, figure out how I can summon it at will.

Finally, my mind still racing, I try to slow it down. I shut my eyes and try to get into the rhythm of the constant thrum of the plane, hoping it'll put me into some kind of trance-like state. The more I try, the more I fail. Until I finally give up.

Josh
Josh Green, Psychic Detective

After I check into my no-frills hotel, splash water on my face, and check my phone for messages, I hit the streets.

Step one: Find the building Allie was visiting in my vision. Step two: Find out who she's visiting and why.

Using Google Earth, I'm able to zero in on the neighborhood, then the right building. It's only a mile or so from where I'm staying, so I decide to walk, hoping the exercise will help me focus.

I'm experiencing a curious mix of excitement and anxiety.

If I'm able to find her, it'll be a win for Tony, Rachel, and Allie. And when it's over, they'll slip back into their familiar everyday life. For me, this will be impossible. I'll have finally embraced a world I've spent a lifetime pretending isn't there. And the rub? If it is there, I'm not sure I want to be part of it.

As I amble down the Chicago streets, following directions downloaded from Google Maps, I'm in a heated conversation with myself. *Why not get out now, while you can?* asks an imaginary me. It would be so easy to report back to Tony, "Sorry, buddy, but nothing seems to be coming through." I'll be off the hook and can return to life B.A.D., Before Allie Disappeared.

It reminds me of the first book deal I scored. The contract was signed. The first payment check arrived. Only then did it become real, and when it did the task ahead of me seemed frighteningly formidable and ultimately undoable. What was I thinking? I'd never written a book before. What made me think I could do it now? Did I even know enough words to fill a book? I'd never written anything longer than a true crime piece about the illicit diamond trade for *Vanity Fair.* How could I possibly now churn out three hundred or so pages that made sense?

I hadn't set one word to paper yet, but I was already desperately searching for a way out. I could return the advance money and move on to something else, something I could handle.

But that I did not do. For one thing, I needed the money. Besides, I'm no quitter. At least that's what I told myself. All my life, I've tried to meet challenges—the tougher the challenge the harder I'd try. I knew I'd never be the most talented journalist, but I could be the hardest working. I just had to keep my head squarely on my shoulders and move forward. So, after losing a couple nights of sleep, the *Eureka!* moment struck: What if I tackled each chapter as if it were an individual magazine article? By the time I had a dozen or so magazine articles strung together, I'd have myself a book.

Easy peasy.

It worked. With the completion of each chapter, the anxiety slowly melted away until it finally disappeared. After six months, I had a book. Maybe it will work the same way when it comes to dealing with this troublesome, extraordinary extra sense of mine.

It doesn't take long to find the right block, then the building. I know it's right because although the actual address is 206, the 2 on the awning has faded, so it looks like the address is 06, the same way it appeared in my vision.

I approach the doorman, who instead of manning his post out front, guarding the wretched souls who live in the building, is sitting on a folding chair in the vestibule, immersed in the sports pages of the *Chicago Tribune*.

I step directly in front of him, but he doesn't look up.

"Excuse me, sir, but I wonder if you can help me?"

He puts the newspaper down, and with a look of disdain for daring to interrupt him, eyes me up and down. "Do what?"

"Excuse me?"

"You asked if I can help you. Help you do what?"

I reach into my pocket and pull out my phone. I hold it at his eye level and swipe through, showing him the various shots of Allie, who from the expression on her face doesn't fancy being photographed.

"Recognize her? I think she was here the other day."

He takes the phone from me and with two fingers flicks the screen, enlarging a photo of Allie taken in front of her dorm. Forever frozen in time, she is dressed in a pink tank top with "Yale" across the front and tight blue bicycle shorts. She's smiling, holding two thumbs-up. In the background is Tony, his back to the camera, his arms full of clothing, as he heads into the building.

"She looks kinda familiar."

"She visited someone in this building in the last few days."

He hesitates. Is he waiting for me to make it worth his while? If so, what's the going rate for dispensing relatively useless information to anyone else?

Before I come up with an answer—twenty bucks seems fair—he says, "What's today? Thursday, right?"

He isn't negotiating. He's trying to remember when he saw her.

"Right."

"Yeah. She was here. Couple days ago. Like maybe Monday. Truth is, one day's no different from the next. Ask me what today is, I'm not sure I can tell you. But yeah, had to be Monday 'cause I was off yesterday. And that was Tuesday, right?"

I refuse to lower myself into an Abbott and Costello routine. Instead, I offer my hand and say, "I'm Josh."

"Ralphie."

"Like Kramden."

"Who?"

"Never mind. Can you tell me who she visited?"

He stands up, places the newspaper on his stool, and retreats behind his official podium. Now at eye level, he leans forward and asks, "You a cop?"

First time I've ever been accused of that, and for some reason it makes me feel more important than I am. The road-not-taken thing. "Nope. But I'm flattered you think so."

"If you are, you'd have to tell me. That's the law, ain't it?"

Another citizen schooled in law enforcement rules and regulations from watching *Law and Order* or *Judge Judy*. I don't have the heart to tell him that so-called rule was more appropriate for women of the night asking the question of an undercover cop.

"If I were a cop, I'd know that. But since I'm not, I really don't know the ground rules."

"Why you got to know who she visited? What she done wrong?"

"Nothing. She's my best friend's daughter. She's missing, and I'm helping find her."

"Little old to be running away from home, ain't she?"

"You're never too old to run away from home, Ralphie. I'm guessing plenty of times you've wanted to pack a bag and get the hell out of Dodge, right?"

He nods. His lips curl into a smile. Ralphie and me. Two peas in a pod.

"Jeannette Davis. That's the lady she came to see. Up there an hour, maybe hour and a half."

"Is Jeannette home now?"

He shrugs. "Been on since eight this morning, and ain't seen her go out, so she's probably up there."

"I'd sure like to talk to her, Ralphie. She might be able to help us find the girl."

"Sorry. No can do without her permission."

"Keeping the riffraff out of the building."

He smiles. "Yeah, that's pretty much the job description."

Power has been thrust upon Ralphie. I need something, and he alone can give it to me. I've given a gift to a man who for most of his life has been controlled by others. Well played, Ralphie. But there are, I'm told, several ways to skin a cat, though I have no idea why anyone would want to do that. As a journalist, I have plenty of tricks in my bag for getting people to cooperate. Bonding is one of them.

"I get you're just doing your job, man. But how 'bout this?" I point to the housephone. "You give her a buzz and tell her someone would like to talk to her. That way, you're doing your job and you're helping me out at the same time. The ball would be in her court. What do you say?"

He removes his cap, scratches the top of his totally shaved head, then puts it back on. "Guess there's no harm in that."

"I really appreciate it, man," I say, patting his shoulder. "And you know what, when I speak to the girl's parents, I'm gonna be sure to mention how helpful you've been."

"What do I tell her? She ain't gonna let some stranger come up. Don't blame her. You'd be surprised how many weirdos there are out there. You ain't from around here, are you?"

"How'd you know?"

He taps his eye, then his ear.

"I got a second sense for that. Pennsylvania, right?"

"You've got a gift, Ralphie."

He smiles. "Don't know what it's like where you come from, but crime in this town is off the friggin' charts, and I got a ringside seat here..."

"Tell you what, how about you buzz her, hand me the phone, and I'll do the explaining."

He ponders a moment, then reaches for the housephone, fixes it between his cheek and shoulder, and punches in a number on the base. Couple seconds pass, he looks up and flashes me two thumbs-up.

"Miss Davis, there's a gentleman down here wants to see you."

I grab Ralphie's arm and reposition him so we're facing each other. I curl up four fingers of my free hand and wiggled them in the universal "come to papa" gesture.

He shrugs and hands me the phone.

"Miss Davis," I say, "first off, I want to apologize for interrupting your day. My name's Josh Green, and I'd like a few minutes of your time. I'm not selling anything. I believe the young woman who visited you the other day is the missing daughter of a friend of mine, and I think you might be able to help us find her."

She mumbles something about letting strangers into her apartment.

"Yes, ma'am, I totally get that. And you're absolutely right, you really can't be too careful. So, what I'm gonna do is show your doorman here…"

"Ralphie," he says as he leans into the phone. "It's me, Miss Davis. Ralphie…" He puffs up his chest, like a Russian weightlifter preparing to hoist hundreds of pounds over his head.

"…some identification." I take my wallet from my back pocket and wave it in front of Ralphie. "I'm gonna let Ralphie hold on to my wallet and I'm gonna let him take a picture of me with his phone. That way, you'll know everything you need to know about me in case things go…well, in case your safety is compromised. What do you say?" I hold the phone out toward Ralphie, to make sure he can hear her answer.

A moment of silence passes and then, "Can you hear me, Ralphie?"

Ralphie moves his head closer to the phone and shouts out much louder than he needs to, "Sure thing Miss Davis." I hand him the phone.

"Yes, Miss Davis. Don't you worry. I got everything under control."

He whispers, "The wallet."

I dangle it in front of him. He takes it, opens it, checks my driver's license. He reaches behind the podium, picks up his cell phone, and snaps a picture of me.

"Everything's A-OK, Miss Davis. I got his wallet here," he says, waving it in front of the phone like she can see it. "Got a picture too. You don't got nothing to worry 'bout."

He winks at me, his coconspirator.

Ralphie hangs up, slips my wallet into his jacket pocket, then points behind me, where there's a cluster of chairs and a round table with a vase of flowers on it. Beyond that there's a bank of elevators. "Fourteen B. And remember, no funny business."

I don't press him for his definition of "funny business."

"You got it, Ralphie. Absolutely no funny business. Scout's honor." I raise my hand as if I'm being sworn in. "Besides," I say, pointing to the pocket where he's stashed his cell phone. "You got the goods on me, pal." I throw up my hands in the universal gesture of *I give up.*

He smiles and starts to wave me through but stops midway.

"Hold on a sec," he says. He reaches into his jacket pocket, pulls out my wallet, opens it, removes the cash, and counts it. It's not much. Seventy, eighty bucks, tops.

"I don't want no future accusations after the fact. Way things are today, you can't be too careful. It'd be your word against mine as to how much cash was here. I don't need trouble like that. You got two choices. Either I give you the cash and hold onto the wallet, or we write down how much is in here, and both sign."

It seems ridiculously complicated for no reason, but if it's going to lead to me getting a chance to speak to this woman, it's worth it.

"I know we've only just met, Ralphie, but there's something about this face of yours that screams, *Honest man!* So, why don't you just hold onto the wallet and the cash."

"Okay, but just so's you know, you ain't back down here in thirty minutes, I'm callin' the cops."

I give him a thumbs-up and turn toward the elevator bank.

"Hold on. Miss Davis wants you to give her a few minutes before going up."

"Time for her to stash the drug paraphernalia?"

"Huh?"

"Just kidding. I'll sit over there and catch up on emails."

"Sure thing, chief. I'll flash you the high sign when you can go up."

I have no idea what Ralphie considers a "high sign," but I say, "Sure."

I plop down into a well-worn leather chair, pull out my phone, and scroll through a bunch of new emails, most of which are spam urging me to buy something or sign up for something I have absolutely no need for. There are a couple from Tony, touching base, he says. I check the day's headlines. Same old, same old, proof the world is, indeed, heading for a fiery end. I check my watch. Five minutes have passed. I figure that's plenty. I look to Ralphie for the high sign, but his head is back buried in his newspaper.

The elevator deposits me on the fourteenth floor. Jeannette's apartment is at the end of the hall, which has a heavy odor of chicken soup and cleaning solution. I press the buzzer. No response. I know she's in there, so I knock a couple times. I hear footsteps followed by the sound of multiple locks unlatching. The door opens as far as the security chain will allow, leaving the chain in place.

I can only see a sliver of her face.

"What is your name, please?"

"Josh Green."

She removes the chain and the door swings open.

Jeannette looks to be in her late fifties, early sixties. She's dressed in a pink and blue tracksuit. She's applied enough makeup that she reminds me of a circus clown. And she reeks of cheap perfume with a slight hint of Pledge.

"Can I see some identification?" she asks.

"Well, that's a little tricky. Ralphie took my wallet hostage."

"Oh, yes." She takes a long, hard look at me. "Well, I guess you seem okay."

"I am." I raise my hand. "Can I come in?"

"Okay," she says. She steps aside, clearing a path into the apartment, then steps in front of me, leading our way through a long, dimly lit hallway.

Before we reach our destination, she stops short, turns around, looks up at me—I have her by at least half a foot—and asks, "Why is it you want to see me?"

"I think you can help me find my friend's daughter."

She stares me down for a moment, then turns and leads me into the living room.

It's a sunny day, but the blinds are down, so the only light in the room comes from two lamps placed on either side of the couch.

"Please, have a seat," she says. "Would you like something to drink?"

"No thanks." I pull a half-empty plastic water bottle from my jacket pocket and wave it in front of her. "Brought my own. Like to keep hydrated."

I sit down on what reminds me of every grandmother's couch. It's so soft it practically swallows me up, like a Venus fly trap.

Jeannette sits opposite me in what my maternal grandparents, who were in the furniture business, referred to as a wing chair. As a kid, I was fascinated by the name, imagining that if I sat in it the right way, it would take off, like Aladdin's magic carpet, and fly me through their apartment.

"I really appreciate you're taking the time to see me, Ms. Davis."

"Jeannette."

"Jeannette. Like I said, the reason I'm here is I'm looking for the young woman who visited you the other day." I pull out my cell phone and call up the photo of Allie. "This is her, right?"

Jeannette takes the phone from me. She studies the photo, but seems lost as to how to enlarge it so she can have a better look. I take the phone back from her and use my fingers to enlarge the image and then scroll down to another photo of Allie. I hand the phone back to her. She puts it down on the table, holds up her index finger, and says, "Please excuse me. I'll be back in a minute."

She disappears for a moment or two and when she reappears, she's clutching a pair of glasses. "I can never find these darn things. My son suggested I get a pair for every room; they're pretty inexpensive, you know, and that way I'd never be without them. That only made things worse because somehow, by the end of the day, all five pairs wound up being in the same room. Same thing with lists. I make them, but can never find them. When you get to my age, every time you forget a name, or where you put something, you're sure it's an early sign of dementia."

I know exactly what she means. I'm only in my mid-forties, yet I'm always looking for a sign I might be losing mental acuity. Probably because my mother suffered from early-onset Alzheimer's. By the time she was in her early seventies, she was pretty much gone. She hung around till she was seventy-seven, but when asked at what age did she pass, I say seventy-two, which was the age at which we pretty much lost her to this insidious illness that so mercilessly robs us of our personhood. For those five or six years, she was one of the walking dead.

Jeannette puts on her readers and picks up the phone.

"Keep swiping right, Jeannette, and you'll find more photos."

She smiles, nods, takes one look at the screen and without looking at any other photos, hands the phone back to me. "Yes, this is the young woman who visited me the other day. But then she's not really missing, is she? Because she was here."

"True. But her parents haven't heard from her in over a week and they have no idea where she is..."

"Kids are like that," she says. "Here today, gone tomorrow..."

"I understand. But this is unusual for Allison. She and her mother are very close."

"Well, I guess you can all rest easy now, since you know where she is."

"I know where she *was*, not where she is now. To her parents, she's still very much missing."

"She's an adult. If she doesn't want her parents to know where she is, maybe she has a good reason."

I'm not expecting pushback, and I wonder why Jeannette is trying to minimize the situation. Is there something she doesn't want me to know?

"Why are you looking for her and not her parents?"

"They're doing everything they possibly can, and because of certain skills I have, they've asked me to help out."

"What kind of skills?"

"I'm a journalist."

"Why do *you* think she's missing?"

The interview is getting away from me. Suddenly, I'm the one answering questions, which isn't getting me a damn bit closer to finding Allie.

"We don't know. One minute she's at school, the next minute she's gone. Maybe if I find out why she took off without telling anyone I'll be able to track her down. What was she like when you saw her?"

"Like?"

"Disoriented? Confused? Angry? Sad?"

"She seemed perfectly fine."

I'm getting frustrated. Jeannette has obviously chosen not to cooperate. Why?

"She might appear to be okay, but unless we find out why she's disappeared, we won't know. The family is quite worried. She's very close to her mother—they talk all the time—so it's unlike her to take off without an explanation."

She nods, but I can see from the expression on her face she still isn't sold on cooperating. I need to change this, which means finding the right approach. Early on in my journalism career I learned the best interviews come when you make it a conversation, not an interrogation. It's best to create an air of cooperation, where both parties are vested in helping the other.

Trouble is, I can't seem to find common ground between me and Jeannette.

"How is it you got to me?"

This is a question I was hoping would never get asked because the answer of "I get these visions, see, and in one of them I saw her going into your building" is utterly ridiculous. So, I ignore it.

"Why was she visiting you, Jeannette?"

Silence.

"How about this, Jeannette? We continue chatting, and if there's a question you'd rather not answer, well, that's fine. We'll just move on."

This suggestion, which gives her a sense of empowerment, seems to work. The muscles in her face begin to relax. Her hands, crossed, rest demurely on her lap. If I don't rush it, I think I've got a fifty-fifty chance of getting her to tell me everything she knows.

"I think the key to this, Jeannette, is to find out why she visited you. Why she abruptly left school, without telling anyone where she was going and why."

"Children don't always have logical reasons for doing things, Mr. Green."

"She's not a child. She's a very smart, sophisticated, responsible young woman. She didn't show up on your doorstep for no reason."

I can't read minds, but I'm having no trouble reading Jeannette's. She's torn between a mysterious loyalty to Allie and a responsibility as a parent to help Allie's parents. Question is, why does she feel a duty to protect a girl she's met for the first time only a few days ago?

"I'm sure she had a good reason…" she says.

"Good reason or not, her parents are very worried. Do you have kids?"

She holds up two fingers.

"Then I'm sure you can appreciate how worried her parents are. If you could tell me about her visit, it would go a long way to putting her parents at ease. There are no dire consequences for Allison, so by cooperating with me, you're not betraying her. They don't want to punish her. They just want to make sure she's okay."

"I understand," she says, her voice trailing off. I have her on the ropes. She's close to giving me what I want. I need to take a step back and gently reel her in.

"If you're worried about confidentiality, Jeannette, I promise whatever you tell me I'll only share with her mother and father."

"What if it's something she doesn't want them to know about?"

"If it's such a touchy subject, and it's in Allie's best interest not to divulge this information, that's fine. I don't need the 'why' as much as I need to know 'where she is'...and that she's okay."

"I'm not sure it's my place to tell you..."

She removes her readers, folds them, and gently places them on the coffee table.

"I'm not sure, Josh—I hope it's all right to call you that."

"Of course."

"I don't feel comfortable talking about this. I can tell you this much: It's a very, very private issue. But so far as I know, there's no danger involved."

"Did she specifically ask you not to tell anyone?"

"Well, not exactly. Not in those words."

"Then you're not breaking a confidence, Jeannette. Look at it this way. What if one of your kids was missing and I had information as to where he or she might be? Wouldn't you want me to share it?"

She sighs.

"I see your point. But I do hope you don't spread this around. I mean, people are allowed privacy, right?"

"Absolutely. As a journalist I know all about protecting sources. Especially when it comes to sensitive family issues."

I can see she's struggling, which probably means she has important information. Even if she doesn't know exactly where Allie is now, I suspect she can point me in the right direction. But instead of pressing her, I say nothing, hoping she'll fill the void. Nature abhors a vacuum. So does conversation.

It only takes a few seconds before she starts to open up. At first, she speaks in a voice so soft I have to lean in to make sure I catch it all. She begins by telling me about an introductory phone call from Allie.

"Did she explain why she wanted to see you?"

She hesitates a moment. "She said we were related."

"Related? How?"

"She didn't say when she first called."

"How about when she visited?"

"Yes..." She hesitates again. I'm growing impatient. But I know pressing her will be counterproductive. To help her along and reassure her, I reach over and touch her hand, in a gesture I hope will connect us.

"She told me she's looking for her...her...birth father," she says.

"Excuse me?"

"Her birth father."

"Allie's birth father is dead. He died in a car accident shortly after she was born."

She shakes her head no.

"Let's back up a little, Jeannette. Exactly what did she tell you?"

"She said she was always told that her birth father died, but she recently learned that isn't true..."

That genetic report. That must be what started all this.

"...she told me that my nephew, Daniel, is her father."

I'm stunned.

"Did you know Daniel had a child, Jeannette?"

She shakes her head no.

"Do you believe it's true?"

"Uhm. I suppose it's possible."

"I don't mean to press you, Jeannette, but it's either true or it's not. Which one is it?"

"I guess it's true."

Suddenly, my mind is awash with questions. If true, this means Rachel has been lying to the kid—and maybe everyone else—for years. Does Tony know? It seems unlikely, because if he does, as soon as I told him about the letter from the genealogy company, he'd have known exactly why she left. And why lie in the first place?

These are questions Rachel can answer.

I push Jeannette to give me every detail she can remember. After close to half an hour—and no, Ralphie doesn't come bursting in the door, with the cops close behind him—I pretty much have all I need in terms of explanation as to why Allie disappeared: She's searching for her birth father. Which means if I find him, I'll find her. I try to get as much information as I can from Jeannette that might help me track him down.

"Tell me about Daniel. What's his full name?"

Jeannette falls silent. I ask again. Still nothing.

"Why aren't you answering this question, Jeannette? You know eventually I'll find out."

"He's family, and in my family, we don't talk ill of blood."

"It's not about talking ill, Jeannette. It's about reuniting a girl with her parents. I don't know if she's in danger, because I don't know who Daniel is and why Rachel saw fit not to tell Allison of his existence."

"His birth name was Daniel Piedmont."

"Why do you say *was*?"

"Because he changed it. Maybe even more than once."

"Why?"

She shakes her head.

"That doesn't have anything to do with this."

"Of course it does. I can't find him if I don't know his name. Why did he change it, and what is it now?"

"I honestly don't know."

"You must know why the change."

"He got himself into a little trouble."

"What kind of trouble?"

"I really can't say."

She means *won't* say, and I'm not about to browbeat her, especially since I'm not sure any answer she gives me will be true.

"Do you know where he is?"

"No idea."

"Why not?"

"He got into some trouble a while back…and then he kind of disappeared."

She starts to say something more but changes her mind. From the pained expression on her face, I can tell she's anguished. She probably thinks she's already said way too much. There's something, maybe a lot about Daniel, she doesn't want me to know.

"I have no doubt you know more than you're telling me, Jeannette. But you know what, I'll eventually find out, so why not save me a lot of time and trouble?"

She shrugs. "Do what you have to do."

I can see from the tight expression on her face that we're done. But I give it one last shot. I'm not going to get anything more about Daniel, so I put the focus back on Allison.

"Do you know where Allie is now? And Jeannette, I have to tell you that after a career in journalism I'm pretty good at telling what's true and what's bullshit."

Silence.

"How did your meeting end? What direction did you point her in?"

I think she wants to help, but doesn't know how much.

"She asked who might know where Daniel is, and I told her that if anyone might know, it would be Blanche, Daniel's sister. I told her I didn't think Blanche could help, but I'm not sure she was listening. My kids are like that too. You tell them something and you're sure they're hearing it, but then they go and do the complete opposite."

"Does Blanche live here in Chicago?"

"She moved to Minneapolis about a year or so ago. But we haven't been in touch for a while, so she might not be there anymore. Blanche has trouble staying in one place. She has what they call wanderlust. In the past few years, she's moved at least half a dozen times."

"And you think that's where Allie's headed?"

She shrugs. "Maybe."

"Do you have an address for Blanche? A phone number? An email address?"

"I think so. But it might not be up to date."

"That's fine. Just give me what you've got, exactly what you gave Allie, and I'll take it from there."

Josh
Tapping the Source

Thanks to Jeannette, I know why Allison disappeared without telling Tony and Rachel. But I still have to find her, and that won't be easy.

First, I have to decide whether or not I tell Tony and Rachel why Allison hit the bricks. I struggle with the decision, but eventually decide it's better to hold off for a while telling them everything I know. My priority is to find Allison and if and when I do, it becomes a family matter, and I can bow out.

Finding Blanche is the next step.

The closest I'd ever been to Minneapolis was an hour-and-a-half layover at the MSP airport, on my way to a "guys'" weekend in Vegas. Far from the *Hangover* or *Weekend at Bernie's* variety, it was more like three literary nerds looking for something to write about. Journalism legend Clay Felker, founder of the first city magazine with *New York*, once proclaimed, "The best stories are between New York and Los Angeles." Turns out, it's true. Not New York. Not Los Angeles. But in the heartland. Places like Minneapolis, which in my geography-challenged mind, feels like it's smack-dab in the middle of the country, though that isn't technically true. Wanna impress someone? Casually drop the information that the precise geographic halfway point between the East Coast and West Coast is a couple miles northwest of Lebanon, Kansas. Which reminds me of the time I profiled actress Amanda Plummer when she was costarring in a production of Tennessee Williams's *The Glass Menagerie.* We met in a downtown dive bar midafternoon, early enough so that we were the only people in the joint. Sitting across from each other in a booth that smelled of stale beer, we had a pleasant conversation. At one point, I asked her where she'd like to visit that she'd never been before. "Kansas," she said. When I asked why, she explained, "Because there's dirt there." Seems like an odd answer, except that after sitting with her for more than an hour, I knew exactly what she meant. It was a "real" place with "real" dirt, not like the hyper version of reality in places like New York and LA, or even the bar we were sitting in.

Questioning Jeannette wasn't easy. She felt compelled to closely guard family business. I understood and, as a result, I tried to be as gentle and patient as possible. Eventually, my patience was rewarded when I was able to pry a little information out of Jeannette about Blanche, including her present last name.

"I can't keep up with all the marriages she's had," says Jeannette, "so who knows which name she's using now. But when I last spoke to her, even though she dumped the asshole, she was still using his name. Hellman."

Jeannette provides a phone number for Blanche, albeit with a caveat.

"We had a kind of falling out a year or so ago," she explains. "And I haven't spoken to her since. She's living in Minneapolis. Lord knows why. It's not like we have any family there."

"Maybe she's a fan of ice fishing."

She provides me with the last email address she had. "Changes that all the time. I don't know what's wrong with that girl. Between her and her brother..." She shakes her head, never finishing her sentence.

Back in my room, armed with this information, I put my research skills to the test. I hop on the Internet, type in "Blanche Hellman, Minneapolis." Fortunately, the name is distinctive enough in the land of Scandinavians that I'm able to come up with an address.

I send Tony a noncommittal text. *"I've got a good lead that's taking me to Minneapolis. Will call you once I'm there and explain everything."* Almost immediately Tony texts back, "Thanks."

Inspired by reading Kerouac's *On the Road* when I was a teenager, I've always loved the idea of long road trips. There's the starting point and the destination. But in between there's the intoxicating possibility of adventure.

It's a six-and-a-half-hour drive from Chicago, and since I do some of my best thinking behind the wheel, I decide to embrace the romance of the road. I rent a car rather than fly, which adds at least three hours to any journey.

Minneapolis is well known as home to the Mall of America, the largest mall in the country (nowhere close, by the way, to the largest in the world, which is the Iran Mall). Large enough to house a working roller coaster under its roof.

Why do I know so much about malls? Because I love them. I know most people feel just the opposite, but those people grew up with malls as the social center of their lives. Not me. I'm a New Yorker, born and bred. We don't have malls, which makes them all the more exotic. Everything you can possibly need or want is under one humungous roof. It's akin to being in the womb, where everything you need to survive is supplied by your host.

In malls, weather and time stand still. At the Mall of America, it's always a cool seventy degrees, thanks to a passive solar-energy system provided by 1.2 miles of skylights and heat generated from lighting, store fixtures, and body heat. No snow, no rain, no wind. And yet, seasons are reflected in the mall, especially the Christmas and New Year's holidays, when you'll find plenty of elves and Santa Clauses, not to mention Christmas music piped into every square inch of the mall.

Malls remind me of giant snow globes.

Even though I'm hoping this will be a quick in-and-out proposition, I promise to reward myself with time to visit the mall. I don't have a bucket list, but if I did, the Mall of America would top the list.

By the time I arrive in Minneapolis, it's midafternoon. The temperature is in the low seventies, and there's not a cloud in the sky. Instead of checking into the motel I've chosen, due to its proximity to the Mall of America, I head straight to the address I have for Blanche.

It's a residential area and the neighborhood is eerily quiet. I park across from a small two-family cookie-cutter house that looks to have been built in the 1950s. While I screw up the courage to knock on the door, I find the NPR station and sit there, keeping one eye on the house as I browse the Internet on my phone. Half an hour passes, and a car pulls into the driveway. A middle-aged woman, wearing jeans and a blue windbreaker, gets out, opens the trunk, removes a couple large brown paper bags, and heads into the house.

Although I don't have a description of Blanche, this must be her. I wait a few minutes for her to get settled, then head across the street. I climb the steps that lead to the porch and knock on the door.

A dog barks.

I hear a loud "Shhh. Shut up!"

The dog stops barking.

I knock again.

A woman's voice asks, "Who's there?"

"I'm looking for Blanche."

A moment of silence.

"No Blanche here. You got the wrong house."

Before I answer, I'm struck with a weird, unsettling feeling. It's impossible to describe, but it's rapidly followed by an image of Allison, standing in the very spot I'm standing. Is my mind playing tricks on me? Or am I actually feeling and seeing her presence?

"I just need a few minutes of your time, Blanche. No one's in trouble. I promise. I just came from meeting with your aunt Jeannette. Check with her, and you'll see I mean no harm. I just need a few minutes of your time."

"If you don't leave, I'm calling the cops."

"If you get the cops involved, it'll only make things worse for your family, Blanche. Right now, this is private. Between you and me. Call the cops, and it's not."

Silence.

"Just a few minutes, Blanche. I promise."

The door opens slowly. I take a couple steps back. A little dog, a Shih Tzu or a Havanese—I can never tell these tiny dogs apart—rushes out onto the porch. It looks up at me with bulging Marty Feldman eyes, sniffs my leg, then gives a couple short barks. "Okay to pet him?" I ask.

The woman eyes me suspiciously.

"Her. She only bites salesmen, mail carriers, cops, and people who don't mind their own damn business."

"Then I'm safe."

I kneel down and pet her.

"Cute dog. What's her name?"

"Chloe."

I rub Chloe's chin and in return she nuzzles my leg. Seems like I've made a friend.

Blanche, who's changed into a maroon Vikings sweatshirt, has her arms folded across her chest. She's a handsome woman, but her face reflects plenty of hard times.

I stand up. "Mind if I come in?"

"I don't like strangers in my house." She points to a couple beach chairs at the far end of the porch. "We can sit over there. But I don't got much time."

"This shouldn't take long."

I take a seat and, after angling the other chair so it faces me, she sits opposite me.

"What's this all about?"

"It's about your brother, Daniel."

The expression on her face tells me everything I need to know about their relationship. This is not going to be an easy interview.

"What about him?"

"I'll make this short and sweet. I have a very close friend whose college-age daughter, Allison, disappeared last week, without telling anyone where she was going or why. I'm helping track her down, and I think her disappearance has something to do with finding her birth father."

"What's that got to do with me? Or Daniel?"

"Apparently, your brother, Daniel, is her birth father."

"Daniel don't have kids." She crosses herself. "Thank the Lord. If he did, it would probably be the child of Satan."

"Well, like it or not, looks like you're an aunt. She signed up for one of those genealogical sites, and that's where it popped up."

"What popped up?"

"That Daniel is her birth father. It surprised her, I'm sure, because she'd always been told he passed away shortly before or right after she was born."

"If only. But even if it's true, I don't see what it's got to do with me."

"Your aunt pointed Allison in your direction, so I'm pretty sure she's either met you or spoken to you."

"What's it your business?"

"Allison's my goddaughter," I lie, hoping it'll add to my bona fides, "and her parents asked me to help find her. All they want to know is that Allie's safe."

"She's fine. Case closed. I got things to do." She begins to get up, but I stand and block her way.

"Look, Blanche, no one's in trouble here. All I need to know is how to get in touch with Daniel, so I can verify that Allie's okay. It would help if you'd tell me what you told Allie."

She sits back down. Chloe jumps into her lap and begins licking her hand.

"If I tell you what you want, you'll get the hell off my property and leave me and my family alone?"

"Absolutely."

She gently puts Chloe down, whereupon the dog scoots over to the other side of the porch and starts drinking from a bowl of water.

"First off, there ain't no Daniel Piedmont anymore."

"You mean he's passed away?"

She snorts. "No such luck. Far as I know, he's still alive and kicking...probably someone or something."

"So, what did you mean he's not Daniel anymore?"

"You do one of those Internet searches on him?"

"I did."

"And what did you come up with?"

"Not much, other than it seems he was in a little trouble a ways back."

She laughs. "Seems like? A little trouble? That's a good one. No such thing as little when it comes to Daniel. He's an asshole, and he's been nothing but trouble since the day he was fucking born."

As much as I'd like to know more about that, it's not going to help me find Allison, so I try nudging her back on track.

"Were you able to help her find him?"

"Let me tell you something about Daniel."

"I'm all ears."

"He was always trouble, but it was little shit. Shoplifting. Kiting bad checks. Breaking and entering. Real low-level shit. But a while back he graduated. He got himself involved in something way more serious. Only a matter of time, you ask me."

"Serious how?"

"Water seeks its own level. Got hisself involved with a bunch of low-life, assholes..."—she presses her nose to one side with her forefinger, indicating someone in the mob—"...who thought they were a big fucking deal. He got into plenty of trouble before he hooked up with them, but mostly kid stuff. This shit was way over Daniel's paygrade. But Daniel's a survivor. It's like what they say about roaches, when it's all over he'll be the last guy left standing. All his life he's managed to adapt hisself and come up smelling like he swallowed a fucking bottle of Chanel number five. He's got a very strong sense of self-preservation. The thing about Daniel is, he never knows when enough's enough. It's always push, push, push. But when it all comes tumblin' down, and it always does, he's disappears. Poof! Always leaving someone else holding the bag."

"What was in that bag?"

"Huh?"

"What was he involved in?"

"No fucking idea. Some kind of high-level scam. And because these guys were such fuckups, I mean none of them were members of that genius thing..." She reaches for the word.

"Mensa."

"Yeah. That's it. Anyway, the cops found out about it and they had all the goods to pin it on Daniel. But like I say, he's a slippery motherfucker, always working the angles. He saw an opportunity to save himself by cooperating with the feds and they dropped him from the case."

"So, what happened to him?"

"Thing about Daniel is, he never thinks about consequences. Never. These were not the kinds of people to fuck with, so they put a target on his back. But the feds got wind of it—some wiretap thing, I think. They let Daniel know and offered to put him into the Witness Protection Program."

"And he took it?"

"Like I said, Daniel's always been a survivor. Between you and me, I think he loved the idea of getting a new identity and starting over. But Daniel is Daniel, so that didn't mean he was going to make good on having been given a new life. You know, like taking the opportunity to do the right thing. No fucking way. Daniel took it as a Get Out of Jail Free card, and from what I hear, after a while he just picked up where he left off."

"Which meant?"

"Taking shit that don't belong to him."

"When did all this happen?"

"I'm not good with years, every time you turn around, we're changing the date on our checks. But it's gotta be at least ten, twelve years ago."

Allison was only six or seven at the time, which meant the decision to keep the information from her that her father was alive was made well before he got in trouble and entered the Program.

"Has he spent any time in prison?"

She shrugs. "A little here, a little there. Nothing that amounted to more than a few nights, maybe a week. Daniel's like that Houdini guy when it comes to escaping consequences. But one of these days, it'll catch up to him, and he'll get what he deserves."

"Was he ever violent?"

She shrugs. "Depends on what you mean by violent. Is he capable of it? Sure. But if you're asking if I ever seen him throw down, the answer's no. But that don't mean under the right circumstances he wouldn't be violent. Depends on the stakes."

This is not good to hear.

"Do you know where he wound up once he entered the Program?"

"No fucking idea. That's the point, right?"

"From what you're telling me about Daniel, he wouldn't think twice about breaking the rules. I'm guessing you've been in touch with him over the years and, in an emergency, you'd know how to reach him, even if he's in the Program."

"He's not."

"Why not?"

"Got tossed out. Knowing Daniel, I doubt he was able to follow the rules."

"Did you tell any of this to Allison?"

"Who says I told her anything?"

"Come on…"

"Maybe I told her I'd try to get a message to him that she was looking for him."

"Did you?"

"Did I what?"

"Tell Daniel his daughter is looking for him."

"What's that thing they say when someone doesn't want to incriminate himself?"

"The Fifth."

"Right. We done?"

"What if I ask you to get a message to Daniel?"

"Can't stop you from asking."

"Consider it asked. Tell him I'd like to talk to him." I open my wallet and take out my business card and hand it to her.

Without bothering to look at it, she stuffs it in the back pocket of her jeans.

"Maybe there's some kind of reward involved?"

"I'm sure her parents would come up with something to show their appreciation. But the information would have to lead to her being found."

"How much we talking?"

"Not sure." I pull a number out of thin air. What the hell? It's not like I'm under oath. "Maybe five grand?"

"That all the kid's worth?"

I get up. "I'm not going to sit here and negotiate with you, Blanche. Either you help or you don't."

"So, we're finished here?" she says.

"I think we've gone about as far as we can. You've got my card, so I'd appreciate it if you'd give me a call, or shoot me an email if you have information for me. And Blanche, this kid means a lot to me, and her father's very well-connected."

"What's that supposed to mean?"

"It means he's owed a bunch of favors from some important people. The kind of people who can make it tough on someone who refuses to cooperate."

"You threatening me?"

"Absolutely not. Just telling it like it is. I'm leaving town in the morning, so it would be nice to hear from you before that."

She takes the card out of her back pocket and looks at it. "This your cell?"

"It is."

I take a step toward the stairs, but turn around before I reach them.

"Oh, and what's the new name he's going by?"

"Even if I knew, you think I'd tell you?"

I smile. "I had you pegged as a good citizen, Blanche."

She laughs. "Wrong peg."

As I step down onto her front lawn, I look back and see she's examining my business card.

"I ain't making no promises," she says.

I don't tell her that even if she did, I wouldn't believe her.

Daniel
The Prodigal Father

"How'd you get this number?"

"I don't want to get anyone in trouble," she says in a soft, whispery little girl voice.

"Fucking Blanche, right?"

"I…I…"

"Don't worry. You're not in trouble. She is. She knows better than to give my fucking contact info to anyone."

"Uhm, I think maybe she thought this was, like, a special circumstance."

"Fuck it. What's done is done. I'll deal with her later. So, who the hell are you and why are you calling me?"

She doesn't answer right away. Although I'm sorely tempted, I don't hang up on her. At least not till I find out what her story is and what I have to do with it.

Lucky for her she's caught me when I'm sitting poolside, catching up on a little paperwork, replenishing vitamin C.

I think I've intimidated her, because all I hear is the soft, rhythmic sound of her breathing.

"Come on. I don't have all day."

"Uhm, I don't know if it means anything to you, but, uhm, my name is Allison. My mom's name is Rachel..."

She doesn't have to say anymore. I know exactly who she is. And I have a pretty good idea why she's calling. The question is, how do I play it? I can deny, deny, deny. I can play dumb. Like I don't know what the hell she's talking about. I can just hang the fuck up on her. But it's too late for any of that. She's obviously done her homework. She's nailed me, and it's not like I never thought this day might come.

"Okay, kid. Let's get right down to it. What do you want from me?"

"I...I'm not sure. But I'm pretty sure you're, like, my birth father."

And there you have it.

I quickly calculate she must be around nineteen. She's really nervous. Fearful even. I can waste time denying the truth, but what's the point? She's smart enough to get this far, so it's too late to deal with it any other way.

"Listen, I'm not going to insult your intelligence and waste my valuable time playing around. Where are you now?"

"Uhm, I'm in Minneapolis. Where are you?"

I smile. Does she really think I'm dumb enough to out myself?

"Not in Minneapolis. So, you've met Blanche."

"Yes. She's the one..."

"I know. Let's cut to the chase, kid. First off, I'm guessing your mother has no idea you're in touch with me."

"How do you know?"

"I don't have to be a fu..." I start to say the word, but catch myself. "...genius to figure that one out. So, what do you want?"

The simple answer is money. Which, like they say, is what makes the world go round. Like reparations for all those years I wasn't around. Only somehow, I don't think that's what this is about.

"You mean ultimately?"

Her voice is gaining strength. She's starting to relax. She's made contact and the house hasn't fallen down.

"Yeah. Ultimately."

"I'd like to meet you. I'd like to get to know you."

I choke back a laugh. I mean, the last thing in the world I want is for anyone to get to know me. I'm very happy, ecstatic even, cruising under the radar. Unfortunately, that ship has sailed.

"I'm surprised it took so long."

"To?"

"Find me."

"Uhm, that's because I didn't know you, like, even existed."

"How's that?"

"My mom said you were killed in a car accident right after I was born."

This time, I can't help but laugh.

"That sounds like Rachel, all right."

"Uhm, yeah, I guess."

"Was it a bloody, painful, slow death?"

"Excuse me?"

"My death. Did she describe the accident?"

"Well, actually, no."

"One point for her."

"Excuse me?"

"Never mind. Okay, so you found me. Now what?"

"Uhm, well, like I said. I'd really like to meet you. Like, in person."

"Why's that?"

She hesitates. She's obviously not prepared for this question.

"Well, like, you're my father. Isn't that reason enough?"

"Kid, after you've been around the block a time or two, you'll be able to answer that question real easy. But since you're only what, eighteen, nineteen years old, I'll answer it for you. No. It's not reason enough."

There's a moment of silence. Have I insulted the kid? Maybe. But if I did, so what? If she doesn't know by now that life is a series of insults and that it's how you deal with them that matters, maybe now's the time to find out.

"Aren't you curious to meet me?" she asks in that whiney, manipulative voice kids have.

She isn't going to like the answer, so I ignore the question.

"Uhm, may I ask where you are? Geographically, I mean."

I ignore that one too. And ask one of my own.

"What did Blanche tell you about me?"

"Like, in what way?"

"Like why she doesn't know where I am, only how to contact me. In an emergency. And by the way, in no way does this qualify as an emergency."

"Uhm, I didn't think to ask her why."

"Ever hear of the Witness Protection Program?"

"That's the thing the government does when they give you a new identity, when no one's supposed to know where you are."

TV and movies have pretty much made everyone think they're an expert on all things crime and punishment.

"Right. And you know the kind of people who are in the Program, right?"

"I guess."

"Let me hear you say it."

"Uhm, criminals?"

"Right. And let me put it as plain and simple as I can. I had information the government wanted, and the only way they were going to get it from me was make sure I'm safe. Which is a pretty good clue as to the kind of people I've been associated with. Pretty sketchy characters, and I've done some pretty sketchy things. But this is not the time to get into that, and besides, that's all in the past. Officially, the government has washed their hands of me. I'm in my own Program now. Which is why I don't advertise where I am and what I'm doing. Or, my new name."

"Do you think it would be possible for us to meet? I have so many questions to ask you."

I'm not sure what to answer. Part of me is curious about the kid. I mean, she does share half my DNA. But another part is very aware that getting involved with her, even to the extent of just meeting her, will complicate my life. And I like things as uncomplicated as possible.

"To what end?"

"You know, to kind of get to know you."

I don't bother telling her that's the last thing I want of anyone. I mean, there's no reason to be nasty. At least not yet.

"I don't know. I'll give it some thought and get back to you."

"Is this one of those things adults tell kids all the time? 'I'll think about it,' which somehow always turns out to be 'no'?"

"I'm new at this parenting thing, kid. I don't know all the tropes and trite sayings."

She mumbles, but I think I make out something like, "You're learning pretty quick."

"What was that?"

"I said you're a quick learner."

I like how she's standing up to me. She's way out of my weight class, but she's not afraid to stick in there. And maybe this is why I'm starting to think that maybe I'll cooperate. To a point.

"How's your mother?"

"Do you really care?"

I laugh. Kid's no dummy. "Not really. Just seems like the kind of question I ought to ask."

"Aren't you the least bit curious how I turned out?"

Truth is, no. I mean, it's not like I've ever given it any thought. This whole thing about blood connections never made sense to me. The only way my family gives a fuck about me is that they hope I don't embarrass them. And that ship sailed a long time ago. That answer seems gratuitously cruel. But I know if I say yes, there's no way I'm gonna be able to justify not meeting up with her. So, I punt.

"Does your mother know about this ridiculous quest of yours?"

"Not really. I'm kinda pissed at her for lying to me all these years."

"You do know she was probably trying to protect you, right?" I don't know why I say this. I mean, it's not like I need to cover for Rachel. She certainly wouldn't do it for me.

"From what? From you? Are you that dangerous?"

More than you can possibly imagine, baby.

"I'm a pussycat, Allison—that's your name, right?" I say, doing everything I can to keep from laughing, because that's not the kind of feline I'm usually associated with.

"Yes. Nice of you to remember."

Snark. I love it.

There's a pause in the conversation. She's obviously not finished with me yet, but she doesn't know how to keep the conversation going.

Finally, she comes up with, "You know, I'd really appreciate having some kind of relationship with you. And it's not like I *need* anything from you. Like money, for instance."

What I don't say, what is the honest-to-God truth, is that she's way better off hanging up and never having anything to do with me. If I said that, it'd probably be the closest I'd ever get to protecting her. But then, before I say some version of this, I have an epiphany, though certainly not the religious kind. Maybe I'm being too hasty. Maybe there is a place for this kid in my life. It couldn't hurt to find out, right? Even though that would mean getting to know her. And her me.

"You know, maybe you're right."

"About what?"

"That it wouldn't hurt if we met."

"You mean, like, we can meet?"

"Yeah. I think that is what I mean."

"That's so cool. And I promise, it's not like I want anything from you—other than getting to know you a little, I mean. Like, everyone should know where they came from, right? Thank you so much. Now, how do we make this happen?"

Daniel

Family Ties

"Is this number the best way to reach you?"

"Yes," she says.

"Okay. I need you to promise me something, kid."

"What is it?"

"You don't say anything to your mother about this—or anyone else. And that you lose my number. Understand what I'm saying?"

"Yes. Of course."

"And you promise you'll do it?"

"Uh-huh."

"Say it."

"Yes. I promise I won't tell anyone, especially my mother, and I'll lose your number. But what if I need to get in touch with you?"

"You don't."

"Uhm, okay, I guess. But I'm not going to hang up and then never hear from you again, am I?"

"No guarantees in life, kiddo. Remember, I'm the one driving this car. Not you. Not your mother. Not Blanche. Not anyone else. Do we understand each other?"

"I guess."

"No. Allison," I say, slipping into my best authoritative, tough-guy voice. "You either do or you don't."

"Uhm, okay. Yes, I understand."

"And I can trust you on this?"

"Yes. But you promise you won't just disappear? Because you know, if you do, I'll just find you again. I'm very stubborn, and I'm very resourceful."

Tough chick. Probably gets that from me, though her mother is no slouch in that department.

"Doesn't surprise me," I say. "You say you're still in Minneapolis?"

"Yes, but I guess I'm on my way back to New Haven."

"What's in New Haven?"

"It's where I go to school."

"That's where Yale is, right?"

"Yes."

"That where you go?"

"Uhm, yes," she says, like she's ashamed of it.

"Fucking A. Aren't you the smart one? Unless your family donated a shitload of dough to the school, like that Kushner asshole."

She laughs. "Unfortunately, we don't have that kind of money."

"What do you know, I got a kid in the fucking Ivy League."

"It's not as big a deal as you might think."

"A good life's lesson there, kid. Nothing is."

You would think this would end it, but it doesn't. She doesn't want to get off the phone. She says she's got "so many questions" to ask me. I tell her I'm too busy to answer them now.

"Okay," she says, and I can hear the disappointment in her voice. "But I'm really glad I found you…"

Before she finishes, I hang up.

One thing I now know for sure: It's not going to be so easy to get rid of her.

Time to deal with Blanche. We've never gotten along. As the older sister, she was supposed to look out for her kid brother. That didn't happen. She hated me from the day I was born, five years after her. Before me, she was Queen of the Hill. Suddenly, the *Queen* had to share the throne. No fucking way she wanted to do that. I was her subject. She used to dress me up, like I was her little doll, and force me to do these ridiculous "skits" with her. And when I got old enough and big enough and wouldn't do her bidding, she instituted a reign of terror. It worked until it didn't. Once I realized I could fight back, and win, it was over.

The old man flew the coop as soon as he learned my mother was pregnant with me. Never heard from him again. Like, he disappeared from the fucking planet. Not that it was any great loss. I didn't take it personally, but no way I ever wanted to find him, the way this kid does with me.

Blanche's way of getting back on top was to become the annoying goody-two-shoes kid. Ratting out her younger brother became a full-time job. The more she ratted me out, the more shitty crap I did.

Until the kid shows up, I haven't thought about Rachel in years. We met in a Fort Lauderdale dive bar. She was with a bunch of her college buddies, celebrating their last spring break before graduating. She was a real looker, and the fact that she tried brushing me off a few minutes after I started hitting on her made her irresistible. I love challenges. So, as soon as she left the bar, I cornered one of her friends, and for the price of a drink, I learned she was going to NYU, that she grew up in some ritzy town in Connecticut. That was more than enough.

I was a few years older than her and was down there to pick up a few extra bucks selling coke and weed to spoiled rich kids. Penny-ante stuff, really. I grew to hate that state with a passion, so once break was over, I followed her up to New York. I hung around Washington Square Park until one afternoon I spotted her and a few friends sunning themselves while watching a couple kids breakdancing. I knew she was way out of my league, but that only fueled my desire. When I approached her, she remembered me, and after chatting her up she finally agreed to go out with me. It took three dates before I got her into the sack.

The whole thing lasted a few months. It ended abruptly when she announced she was pregnant. I left thinking she was going to take care of the kid, but obviously she didn't. So, when the kid tracks me down it's not exactly a shock, but it is a surprise.

As soon as Blanche picks up, I let her have it.

"What the fuck, Blanche?"

"Excuse me?"

"What the fuck were you thinking? You tell a kid you don't know from fucking Adam how to get in touch with me? What if she's a fucking plant working for people who want to find me? You know they're out there, don't you? You think I disappeared just so you can point some girl who claims to be *my* kid in my direction? Fuck no! I know you're out to make trouble for me any chance you get, but to drag some poor kid into this…"

"You flatter yourself, Daniel. You think I give two fucks about you? The kid has every right to know who her father is and that he's a piece of shit. If anyone should be pissed at me it should be the kid for putting her in touch with you. That's why I didn't tell her where you are now."

"You don't know where the fuck I am, Blanche."

"Don't be so sure…"

"From now on, Blanche, just keep your damn mouth shut. And just in case you're wondering, you call this number again and you're gonna get one of those fucking 'no longer in service' messages. And remember this, Blanche, I'm perfectly capable of showing up on your doorstep one day and, sister or not, fucking you up. And you know I'll do it, don't you?"

"If anything, I owe the kid an apology. The best thing that ever happened to her is that you took off. The worst, that she found you."

"If you weren't so fucking pathetic, I'd take care of you once and for all. But I don't have that kind of time to waste."

I hang up before she can say anything else.

Allie
My Two Dads

One minute I'm flying high, the next I'm having trouble getting out of bed.

That's pretty much the definition of manic depression, right? Only I know that's not my problem. In a way, I wish it was because there are all kinds of pills for that. Too bad there's no pill for the roller coaster I'm on.

I think of the time before I found Daniel as the halcyon days, the days when the only thing I had to worry about was what I was doing for summer break or whether I should switch my major from literature to something more targeted to an actual career. Those were the days when I had one dad, not two. Those were the days when I trusted my mother to tell me the truth about everything. Those were my *Days of Innocence.*

But those days are gone, never to return. Welcome to the Adult World, Allison.

Everything changes the minute I make that phone call to Daniel. Not only do I suddenly have another father, I now have a brand-new middle-American dysfunctional family. As my mom always says, "Be careful what you wish for, Allison." Now I know what she means.

I was hoping to meet Daniel in person, but after speaking with him I know the chances of that are pretty slim. Still, this is just the opening act. If I don't crowd him, and if I can convince him I don't want anything from him...well, I guess that's not technically true. I'm not quite sure what I want, what kind of relationship I'd like to forge, but if I can keep him engaged, if I can keep him from disappearing on me, I think it'll work itself out.

I have so many questions, and although I need Daniel to answer them, it doesn't mean I can't do a little digging on my own. For instance, why is he so secretive about where he is and what he's doing? Fortunately, from the time I was a kid, I liked nothing better than solving mysteries.

I devoured the *Nancy Drew* books. Twice! After I ran through them, I moved on to the *Hardy Boys* (Joe and Frank were pretty cool, even though they were boys). From there, it was the classics by Raymond Chandler, Dashiell Hammett, Agatha Christie, Ross MacDonald, and Nero Wolfe. I loved those books because by the end, the detective always solves the crime and puts a messed-up world back together. And by guessing along with them, sometimes figuring out whodunnit, I felt like I was part of the solution.

I Google Daniel and get more questions than answers. One of the biggest stumbling blocks is his name. Or should I say various names. There's his birth name, which I know from Jeannette. But at a certain point, that name disappears and doesn't return, which means he either went completely off the grid, or changed his name.

It might have to do with something else I learn. About a dozen years ago, he was involved in some kind of mob conspiracy having to do with a massive art fraud. Fake works of artists like Salvador Dali, Joan Miró, Pablo Picasso, Jackson Pollack, and a bunch of other famous artists.

I have no idea what role Daniel played in this scam, which was a complicated mob operation that eventually resulted in arson and ultimately violence. I'm able to find several articles in the *Chicago Tribune* that name Daniel as an active participant in the scheme. But what's weird is that his name suddenly disappears from these stories. The articles give no explanation for this, but maybe it's because Daniel cooperated with the authorities and was given immunity for ratting out his colleagues. On YouTube, I'm able to find a few TV news clips of the trial, one of which shows a man in heavy shadows, his voice electronically altered, testifying against his former colleagues. I suspect this is Daniel. If it is, no wonder he's trying to fly under the radar. How about this: I have a birth father who's not only a criminal, but has a big, fat target pinned to his back for ratting out his coconspirators. I guess that explains his talking about Witness Protection.

I know I should be appalled, frightened even, but for some reason the emotion I have isn't fear but pride. I guess that explains my state of mind when Lisa insisted I sign up for that genealogical report. If I had the choice between having a father who's an anonymous citizen or a notorious criminal (short of murder, of course), I would certainly prefer the latter. And maybe that's what fuels my desire to meet Daniel and find out as much about him as I can.

So, now that I've found him, what's next?

There's only a week left till the end of the semester, and I've got a couple papers due, but I'm not worried. I'll contact my professors and talk my way into extensions. I'm much more worried about how I'm going to deal with Mom and Tony. They've left a ton of phone messages, each one more frantic than the last, as well as emails, texts, and DMs, each one reflecting their escalating range from mild concern to anger, then serious worry. I probably should answer them, but to be honest I'm not sure what to say. My mom would flip out if she finds out what I'm doing. But it isn't only that. I guess, if I'm honest with myself, I kinda want to see her suffer a little. Punish her for lying to me all these years. I'm afraid that confronting her about it now will only make things worse. It's probably better for all of us if I cool down before I interact with her.

Besides, if Daniel does get back in touch with me, and maybe even if he agrees to meet with me, I don't want my mom raining on my parade. Which she surely will.

Besides, I'm afraid they'll pressure me into coming home, and I'm not ready for that. I don't want to be convinced or threatened or cajoled. I'm an adult and I'll do what I want to do, when I want to do it.

In the meantime, I'm not quite sure what to do, so I take myself to a movie, have dinner at a cheapo restaurant near the apartment, and try not to think about plans until tomorrow.

The next morning, at 7:30 a.m., the sound of Taylor Swift singing "I Knew You Were Trouble" on my cell wakes me from a deep sleep. The call is from an unfamiliar number. It's probably one of those spam calls, but I take it anyway.

"Hello," I say, my voice raspy with sleep.

"Morning, sunshine. Hope I didn't wake you. I know how you kids stay up all night partying and love to sleep in."

At first, I have no idea who I'm talking to, and I'm too embarrassed to ask, so I play along.

"Actually, I did have trouble sleeping last night."

"I wonder why."

It's Daniel! And my heart starts to race. Oh, my god, what is going on with me. I feel like a teeny-bopper who's just received a call from her secret crush. I'm at a loss for words.

"Told you I'd get back to you, didn't I? Surprised?"

"Uhm, no. Well, yes, I guess..." I'm so excited, I jump out of bed and start pacing back and forth in the room.

He laughs. "I've given it a lot of thought, Allison. I admire the trouble you've gone to in order to find me. It tells me a lot about your character, and you know what..."

He stops. Have we been cut off?

"Are you still there?" I ask.

"I think we should meet."

"Really?"

"You bet."

"You're not kidding, are you?"

"Why would I do that?"

"I don't know..." I stop myself because I have no good answer. "That's so cool. When? Where?"

"Do you have to get back to school, home or something?"

"No. The semester's over." Nothing wrong with a little white lie, right? Officially, there are still a couple weeks.

"How about back home?"

"No. I'm fine."

"You're sure?"

"I'm sure."

"Okay. Here's the deal. I'm in Florida for a business deal. How about you fly down here, we spend a couple days together, and get to know each other?"

"For real?"

"You bet."

"Uhm, you want me to come down there?"

"I'll send you a plane ticket to Fort Lauderdale—ever been there before?"

"Uhm, my dad's mom, my grandmother, lives in Hollywood, Florida, and I've visited her a couple times."

"Great. Can you come down tomorrow?"

"Sure," I say, even though I'm not even sure what day tomorrow is.

"Give me your email address and I'll send you the ticket."

I'm so excited, but I don't want to come off like some giddy teenager.

"Sounds good," I say, in a tone meant to be solemn, though I'm afraid it just comes out like weird. It's like in junior high when some boy calls you up for a date and you're so embarrassed you can hardly speak.

"When you arrive, I'll meet you outside baggage claim. I'll text you if there's a problem."

"That's it?"

"Don't forget to bring a swimsuit."

"Uhm…"

"Just kidding. If you need one, we'll just buy you one when you get down here. One more thing, Allison. Does your mom still not know where you are and that you've been in touch with me?"

"Uhm…" How much should I lie? "I haven't, like, told her yet."

"Good. Let's keep it that way. At least for now. Otherwise, I'm afraid she'll put the kibosh on the whole thing. The last thing I need is her on my ass. Agreed?"

"Yes. Agreed. You know, Daniel, I'm really excited about meeting you and getting to know you."

"Me, too, kid."

"I've got so many questions…"

"I bet. What's your email?"

I give it to him.

"Okay. You'll hear back from me within the hour. See you tomorrow, kiddo."

I hang up, sit down on the bed, and I remain there for I don't know how long with a super huge smile on my face.

Josh

Hot On the Trail

If I were a cop or PI in a really bad movie, I might describe myself as being "hot on the trail."

But the truth is, I have absolutely no idea how close or how far I am from finding Allie. Sometimes, it feels like I'm just around the corner. That I can reach out and touch her. Other times, it feels like this whole search thing is a fiasco. Especially when I step back and admit that the only reason I'm even this close is because I have this ridiculous ability to *see* things other people can't. For some strange reason, it feels like cheating.

I never hear back from Blanche. Not that I expect to. Instead, I get another vision. In this one, Allie's on the move again. I *see* her sitting in an aisle seat on a plane. Her head is back, her eyes are closed, and there's an open magazine in her lap. I maneuver myself so I can see that it's a Delta inflight flyer. There's no way of telling where this flight is headed, but it does indicate she's left Minnesota. I'm hoping she's on her way back to New York City, and that we can put a period on this whole misadventure. I imagine getting a call from Tony thanking me for all I've done, ending with, "We are no longer in need of your services." Words that would be music to my ears.

I'm not sure whether I should head back home or sit tight and wait till I get some indication as to where Allie is headed and then follow her. I'm paralyzed by indecision. And so, I await divine intervention, which, by the way, I know is never coming.

As promised, I make my nightly check-in call to Tony.

Before he can ask me his usual question—"Have you found her yet?"—I ask, "Any chance you guys have heard from Allie?"

"Of course not. If we did, don't you think I would have led with that?"

"I'm sorry. Stupid question. Chalk it up to not enough sleep."

"Why do you even ask?"

"Just checking."

"Are you fucking kidding? What's going on, Josh?"

"Well, to be honest, I've kinda reached a dead end here. She was here all right, in Minneapolis, visiting a woman named Blanche."

"Who the hell is Blanche?"

"The sister of the man she's looking for."

"She's looking for a man?"

"Yup."

"Who is he, and why's she looking for him?"

Shit! Unintentionally, I've dropped information I'm not ready for Tony to know. But now I have no choice but to spill everything. Tony's much too smart and perceptive to let me shine him on.

"You've gotta promise this stays between us, Tony."

"You don't want me to tell Rachel?"

"Not yet."

There's a moment of silence before he says, "That's a tall order, compadre."

"I'm pretty sure you're up to it."

"You know me well enough to know that keeping my mouth shut isn't my forte. I've been keeping your secret for years; I'm not sure how I'll deal with a second. Besides, Rachel can read me like a book…but okay. Consider her in the dark. For now."

"Allie signed up with one of those genealogical websites. After she got the results, she mucked around and found evidence that seems to indicate that her birth father, who she believed to be dead, might still be alive. She's a smart kid, Tony, so she tracked the family down to Chicago and then Minneapolis, which is why I'm here."

"Wait a minute. You're telling me Allie believes her birth father is alive and she's looking to hook up with him?"

"Yup. And I'm guessing the reason she hasn't told you and Rachel any of this is because she's really pissed at her, and you too, if you knew about the lie."

"This is crazy. As far as I know, the dude is dead. Has been since she was born. I can't imagine Rachel lying about something like that."

"Unfortunately, she has. And it appears Allie's going to keep looking till she finds him."

Silence.

I don't know what to say, so I keep my mouth shut.

Finally.

"Why the hell didn't she just come to us?"

"First off, you've got to remember she's still a kid. Even at her age, I'm not sure their brains are fully formed. I think the only emotion she feels right now is anger. Angry because she feels she's been betrayed. You can see why I'd rather you didn't tell Rachel, right?"

"Yeah."

More silence.

Finally: "Has she made contact with him yet?"

"Don't know. But I can tell you this, if she hasn't yet, she won't stop till she does. And the thing of it is, I'm not sure he's a model citizen."

"What the fuck does that mean?"

I get it. He's pissed at me, at Allison, and probably everyone else in the world.

"I'm not Joseph from the Bible, Tony. I don't dream answers to these things."

"Yeah, yeah. Okay. No dreams. What do you know about him?"

"Not much. I checked him out, of course, and it appears he was in some kind of big trouble ten, twelve years ago."

"What kind of trouble?"

"Something to do with an art scam. I think the mob might have been involved."

"Jesus. The mob? Is he dangerous?"

"Don't know."

"What else?"

"That's the weird part. He's mentioned in newspaper articles but then, suddenly, his name disappears. That leaves two possibilities. Either he was cleared or..."

"He cooperated."

"Right."

"Send me everything you know about him. And I'll get on it. I've got a few sources that might help."

"That's the thing, Tony. If you use his real name, Piedmont, you won't come up with anything more than I just told you. Somewhere along the line, he changed his name."

"To what?"

"Don't know."

"Great."

"I'm not giving up, Tony. I'm getting closer to finding her. Just finished talking to his sister, who wasn't much help. There's no love lost between the two of them. But I do know Allison met with her. I just don't know how much information was exchanged."

"How much longer you need?"

"I feel like I'm close. But please keep all this from Rachel. She'd only complicate things, and get in the way. But I am damn curious as to why she lied to everyone all these years. I'm assuming you didn't know the truth?"

"Absolutely not."

"The most important thing is that she's safe."

"For now."

"Yes. For now. Just give me another day or two and I promise I'll get to the bottom of it."

"You've got forty-eight hours, and after that, all bets are off."

I'm tempted to argue the point, but he hangs up before I can argue for an extension.

Allie
Daddy Dearest

I haven't been this excited since waiting for Christmas morning to arrive when I was a kid. It was a morning that would be filled with promise, joy, or grave disappointment—sometimes all three—but it never seemed to arrive. Back then, time was elastic. A minute could seem like an hour. A day like a week. And nothing I could do or think made it come any quicker. Whenever I'd get too antsy, my mom would warn, "A watched pot never boils." I didn't get it then, but I sure get it now.

I know this sounds silly, but I'm dizzy with anticipation. The minute I step off the plane, I begin to worry about how I'll recognize Daniel. I should have asked him what he looks like. Or what he'll be wearing. Or the kind of car he has. But I didn't. If I had a cell number for him, I could text him that I've landed, what I'm wearing, what I look like. But I don't.

I can't help wondering if he'll recognize me in his face. Will we have some kind of immediate, magical blood connection, creating a mysterious magnetic-like force that will pull us together?

What if he doesn't show? What will I do? He's only provided me with a one-way ticket. At first, I think this is ominous, like I'm making a trip I'll never return from. But then reality sets in and I realize the reason it's a one-way ticket is that he has no idea where to fly me back to. Minneapolis? New York? New Haven? I'm starting to get, like, pretty sick of myself, so I decide from now on, I'll try giving him the benefit of the doubt.

For the first time since I left New Haven almost a week ago, I start missing my mom and Tony. I feel bad that I'm treating them this way. I'm still angry with my mom for lying to me, but I promise myself that no matter what happens today, I'll get in touch with them very soon. I'll apologize for what I'm putting them through, and assure them I'm fine.

When I get inside the terminal, I look for signs pointing me toward the baggage area. But before I can figure it out, I hear my name called. I look up to see a man who appears to be in his mid-forties, about five-ten, very trim. He's wearing faded blue jeans and a brightly colored Hawaiian shirt. He kinda looks like Magnum's older brother. He's wearing aviator sunglasses, and there are several silver bracelets dangling on his right wrist and an expensive-looking watch on the other. The pièces de résistance are the bright red Chucks on his feet. This has to be him, and if it is, it looks like I've got myself a pretty cool-looking second "dad."

I'm surprised at hearing my name called out, so I reflexively take a step back.

"Relax, kiddo. It's me. Daniel. Your…"—he flashes a big, fat smile—"…brand-new and improved father."

I'm, like, totally disoriented, so I'm sure I look like an idiot, standing there with what I'm guessing is a really goofy expression on my face. Part of it is that nobody's supposed to be at the gate unless they have a ticket. So, I can't help wondering *how* did he make it through security? But more than that, it's the shock of hearing him say those words. *Your father.* All I can think of is that Darth Vader line from *The Empire Strikes Back*.

But it's more than just being taken off guard. The man standing in front of me is more like a sperm donor than father. Tony's my dad, and he always will be. But then, if I feel this way, why am I bothering with this stranger in front of me?

When I can finally focus on him, I see he's very handsome, and when he removes his aviators, he's got the bluest eyes I've ever seen. Like Paul Newman blue. I have blue eyes too, but they're a pale, washed-out version compared to his.

I feel like a total dork. I'm not quite sure what I should do. Should I hug him? That seems like a pretty big leap. Should I shake his hand? Seems kind of formal. Should I do neither? I start to extend my hand but before I get far, he says, "I think we can do better than that, kiddo." He bypasses my outstretched hand and, arms out in front of him, he moves in for a hug.

I stiffen as soon as he touches me. He holds on a few seconds, then releases me and steps back. "Loosen up, kiddo. I promise I won't bite."

"I'm sorry," I say, though I'm not sure why. I mean, it's not like I'm doing anything wrong. It's an awkward situation. Why wouldn't I be a little stiff?

"Nothing to be sorry about, kiddo. I gotta say, you look like a younger, even prettier version of your mom." He shakes his head. "I can't believe the resemblance."

You would believe it if you hadn't disappeared from my life.

But maybe I'm not being fair. After all, I don't know the circumstances. Maybe he wasn't even aware of my presence on earth. Maybe he was out of our lives before my mom gave birth to me. Maybe he didn't *choose* to leave. Maybe he was pushed. The older I get, the more I understand life is not black and white, but shades of gray. What is truth, anyway? I mean especially when we all have our "own truth"? So, in that split second, I make the decision to bend over backwards and give him the benefit of the doubt. At least until something changes my mind.

Meanwhile, I'm super focused on everything about him. The expression on his face. How he cocks his head slightly to one side, which is what I do sometimes. The shape of his nose, which is very much like mine. Even the sound of his voice. It's annoying and unfair, treating him like some kind of specimen under glass. But I can't help myself. Maybe my personal experience will finally answer the question: Nurture or nature?

"Any checked bags?" he asks.

"Everything's here in my backpack," I say.

"A chip off the old block. Always travel light, and never, ever check bags. Come on, kiddo, let's get the car then bust out of this shithole. Here, give me that," he says. He grabs the strap of my backpack and strips it off me.

My first reaction is to resist, though I'm not sure why. Maybe because it's a little too personal? Maybe because it feels like he's violating me? Maybe it's because I think he's going to steal it? Maybe because it makes me feel like he's simply a driver picking me up at the airport? All ridiculous, but I can't seem to help myself.

I protest. "It's okay. I'm used to it."

"Danny Peacock's kid doesn't carry her own bag."

I'm confused. Who's this Danny Peacock person? I thought his last name was Piedmont. This must be the name Daniel is using now. Kind of a crazy name to choose, but it's also kinda, like, cute. And it kinda fits him too. I mean, he looks like he puts a lot of time and thought into how he presents himself. Not necessarily in a vain way, but in the way some people naturally have in presenting themselves once they've, like, created the image for themselves they want to project to the world. I'm not one of those people, but maybe if I hang around Daniel Peacock long enough, I'll pick up this trait. Maybe I'll even decide to change my last name. Allison Peacock? Allison Flamingo? Allison Hummingbird? Allison Warbler? Allison Bald Eagle? The possibilities are endless, but I have to stop because I'm beginning to sound like Rain Man.

"Come on, let's hit the road," he says. This is what my mom always says when we're getting ready to leave someplace. And without fail, if Tony's with us, he'll start singing "Hit the Road Jack."

I start trying to picture what the two of them, my mom and Daniel, would look like standing side by side. Walking down the street holding hands. Staring longingly into each other's eyes. And this morphs into a picture of Tony and mom doing the same thing. Whoa, Allie. You're obsessing, and you have to stop!

We head toward the exit. I let him set the pace, and he moves quickly and gracefully, weaving in and out, passing through people heading toward the baggage conveyor belt. I'm in pretty good shape, though I haven't worked out in more than a week. But I have to strain a little to keep up with Daniel, who obviously takes good care of himself.

"By the way, how'd you get them to let you come to the gate? Don't you need a ticket for that?"

"Not if you're me." He winks.

"What do you mean?"

"First fatherly lesson: *Where there's a will there's a way.*" He smiles, leans over, and whispers, "Let's just say, I've got the ways and means. Which brings us to fatherly lesson number two: *Rules are made to be broken.*"

"What's that supposed to mean?"

He smiles again. "Secrets of the trade, Allison. Let's just say I make it my business to make sure things work to my advantage. You've got a lot to learn, kiddo."

And you're going to be the one to teach me?

He puts his arm around my shoulder. I've only just met this man. I know absolutely nothing about him. And yet, his arm around my shoulder makes me feel…like, protected.

"You know, I was kinda surprised when you called me back the other day," I say, as we step onto one of those moving sidewalks. It's actually kinda fun. Like we're on some wacky Disney World ride;

I'm even tempted to do the Michael Jackson moonwalk backwards. But I don't.

"Why's that?"

"Oh, I don't know. It seemed like you were going to blow me off."

"What if I told you I considered that?"

"You did?"

He smiles. "Maybe for like a second and a half."

I don't mean to, but I can't help smiling. Daniel's a stranger, and yet it feels like I've known him all my life. Pretty crazy, right? He seems so comfortable with himself. Or maybe it's his sense of humor. He's making this a lot easier than I thought it would be.

"So, what's the plan?" I ask.

"You must be hungry, right?"

I'm too nervous to think about food. But now that he brings it up, I realize I haven't eaten since breakfast, and that was seven or eight hours ago.

"Uhm, yes, I guess I am."

"Then that's our first stop."

As we make our way to the parking lot, I can't think of anything to say, so I say nothing, which is just as well since Daniel is busy checking his phone. His car's a very expensive-looking snazzy red convertible BMW. I don't know much about cars, but I do know an expensive one when I see it. Probably a skill I picked up growing up in an "upscale" bedroom community outside New York City, where everything is measured not by inches or feet or yards, but by dollars. And where a car like this wouldn't stand out.

I confess I'm a little confused. If he's in some kind of trouble, why would he draw attention to himself by the car he chooses to drive and the clothes he chooses to wear? Maybe this is a sign everything's okay.

"Nice car," I say as I settle into the passenger seat and strap myself in.

He fiddles with the temperature button. "Here we go," says, flipping a switch. "It'll take a minute or two to cool down. The heat down here can really get to you. Can you imagine what it would be like without air-conditioning?"

I'm not sure if this is a question I'm supposed to answer, or just a statement of fact. But just so he doesn't think I'm ignoring him, I answer with, "I'm okay…uhm, is this, like, yours?"

He laughs. "You think maybe I carjacked it?"

"No. No. That's not what I…"

He reaches over and puts his hand on my shoulder. "Relax. Just kidding. Guess you're gonna have to get used to my sense of humor."

"I guess."

"It's a rental."

"Excuse me?"

"The car. It's a rental."

I'm trying hard as I can to pay attention, but my mind is racing in all directions. *Calm down, Allison,* I tell myself over and over. Maybe that should be my new mantra.

"Oh, yeah…of course." I know I'm beginning to sound like a big, ol' dork, but I can't help myself. Maybe I am better off just keeping my mouth shut. "By the way, I really like your…outfit."

He laughs. "Never thought of it as an outfit." He looks over at me and winks. "More like a statement."

"Of what?" I ask, immediately afraid I've crossed some kind of imaginary line.

"Let's just say, to be the part, you got to look the part."

I'm not quite sure what he means. But I don't think this is the time to ask for an explanation.

"Ever been to Florida before?" he asks.

"Once. I was a kid and we visited my grandmother down here. Oh, and we went to Disney World…in Orlando."

He smiles. "Yeah, I know where it is."

"Oh, sorry. Course you do."

"You apologize way too much, kiddo."

"I'm…" I stop myself and smile. "It's a bad habit, right?"

"Pretty much all habits are bad. Strive to be unpredictable, Allison. Once people have your number, it's all over, baby blue."

I feel like I should be taking notes. Like it's *Life Lessons from My Birth Father Who I'm Meeting for the First Time.*

"One thing I'll tell you, kiddo, you never get used to the damn heat. Especially now that we're coming up on summer. Humidity's off the charts. It's the closest thing to hell I've experienced."

I don't ask him, but I did wonder how often he's down here. And if he hates it so much, how come he's here now?

"How long will you be here?"

Tony calls this small talk. He hates it, but says it's sometimes necessary. "It's a way of connecting with people, Allie," he tells me. "Some people are good at it, some aren't. It's one of those social skills that's good to have. It's a way to fill the silence." I don't ask him why that's necessary.

"Not much longer. I've got business up north."

"Like up north where?"

"Maine."

I want to know more, but I don't want to make this sound like an interrogation, so I keep my mouth shut. Which for me, isn't easy.

"So, where do you feel like eating? And please don't tell me you're one of those vegans."

"Uhm. Not really. But I don't eat much red meat."

"Guess that scuttles the idea of a steakhouse."

"Oh, no, that's fine. I can always find something to…"

"Relax, kiddo. Just kidding."

I force a smile. "Oh. Right." I can't help wondering if I'll ever be able to tell the difference with him between kidding and serious.

"I know just the place. By the water. You're in Florida, might as well take advantage of what little Floridians have to offer. It's a shithole state. Third highest state for serial killings. And that fucking governor, we have..." He turns to me and smiles. "Aren't you glad you got me started."

I smile back. I think maybe I'm beginning to get his sense of humor. At least I'm trying.

"Do you live down here?"

"Are you kidding? I wouldn't live here if they paid me, which they're not, by the way."

"Then..."

"Business. Been here a few weeks and, God willing, I'll be out of here in a couple more. As soon as my business is over, it's sayonara, baby."

"Where *do* you live?"

He stops, turns to me, and says, "I know you have a shitload of questions, Allison—or do you prefer Allie?"

"Either's fine."

"Know what? I'll test out a few and then we can decide what suits you best. Anyway, about the questions. Let's just put a hold on them for now and then, once we've got something in our stomachs"—he pats his—"you can ask away."

"Sounds good. And I'm sorry about all the questions." I smile. "And I'm sorry about being sorry."

He laughs. "At least you're working on it. Ninety percent of apologies are total bullshit. People aren't really sorry. It's just something they've been taught to say because that's what people want to hear. They think it wipes the slate clean of something they've said or done. Like a Get Out of Jail Free card."

"Is that what you want to hear?"

"Looks like I've got a live one here. Here's something you should know about me. I've got a very high-functioning bullshit detector. I've been around enough liars and cheats in my time that I can always tell the difference between truth and bullshit."

"I'll try to remember that. Do you ever lie?"

He smiles. "If I say no, I might be lying. And if I say yes, I also might be lying. Right?"

"I guess that's true. But it's kind of cynical, isn't it?"

"Sure, it is. When you get to know me, if you get to know me, you'll find I don't have a very high opinion of my fellow man… or woman. And you know what? That outlook goes a long way in terms of self-preservation."

"How do you ever get to know anyone if you can't tell whether they're lying or telling the truth?"

"I suppose you can't."

I feel like I'm back in class with Daniel in the role of teacher and me, his student. But I am finding out stuff about him. I just don't know whether it's good stuff or bad stuff.

"I guess you're right. But I do have so many questions…"

"I'll try to answer as many as I can. But for now, how about we both relax."

He reaches out and turns on some music. It's the Rolling Stones. Not my favorite group, but I've heard it all of my childhood because they're one of Tony's favorite bands. He even took me to one of their concerts when I was a kid. I pretty much know all the lyrics to "Sympathy for the Devil," and a bunch of their other songs. And I've seen *Gimme Shelter* at least three times, thanks to Tony. He loves to school me with concert movies. His favorites are *The Last Waltz* and *Rolling Thunder.*

The rest of our ride is spent listening to the Stones and other old groups from the '60s and '70s while I stare out the window, trying to remind myself to be careful what I say. But there's a little voice in my head that says, *Pay attention, girl. This guy might have some really valuable stuff for you to learn.*

Daniel
Every Day Is Father's Day

One day you're childless, the next day you're sitting across from a grown-ass woman who's carrying half your DNA. That's the fucked-up world we live in.

When I decide to hook up with the kid, I don't know what to expect. I figured she'd be smart and, if she takes after her mother, she'd be okay in the looks department too. But to be honest, I'm surprised how well she seems to have turned out. I'll give the Devil her due. Rachel, and maybe the guy she hooked up with, did a pretty good job.

I get that the kid has all kinds of questions she wants answered. But in order to know how much truth to tell her, I need to know how much she already knows. Let's face it. She's way too smart not to eventually see through bullshit.

The kid doesn't disappoint. As soon as we fill our plates from the buffet table—hers mostly salad-y stuff, mine a collection of foods that'll eventually earn their revenge on me, shortening my life by who knows how long—and come back to the table, the kid wastes no time going on the offensive, her aim straight for the jugular.

"Before the other day, did you even know I existed?" she asks, a forkful of salad poised in front of her mouth.

"Jeez, I thought maybe we could ease into the tough questions, kid."

"How do you know the rest of my questions aren't even tougher?"

"Good point."

"And by the way, I'd kinda appreciate it if you didn't refer to me as 'kid' or 'kiddo,' because it's kind of demeaning and it sets up a false dynamic between us. We're not father and daughter. We're two adults having lunch."

"Good point…*Allison.* I can do better."

"I hope so."

"Got enough on your plate?" I tease, hoping to lighten the mood. I should have known better.

"Nice try."

"Excuse me?"

"I know when someone's changing the subject to avoid answering a question."

"I guess I shouldn't even try, right?"

"Right."

"You gonna believe what I tell you?"

"If it's the truth, I will."

"How will you know?"

"I'll assume you're lying till you're not."

"I can see I'm not gonna win many arguments with you."

She shrugs. "Maybe none. So, why try? How about the answer?"

"Can you repeat the question?"

"Before the other day when we spoke, did you even know I existed?"

"I knew Rachel was pregnant when I left. Didn't know if she kept it. You."

"Now you know."

"And now I know."

"You didn't care?"

"You're asking me to tell you my state of mind what, twenty years ago?"

"Yep."

"It was a tumultuous time, Allison. I had a lot going on."

"Like what?"

When I hesitate, she interprets this as weakness and, like Mike Tyson, she doesn't back off but instead goes in for the kill.

"Did you leave of your own choice or did my mom throw you out?"

"A little of both. Either way, let's just say it was for the best."

"You're going to have to be more specific."

"You'd make a good lawyer—not that we need more of them."

"You're doing it again."

"What's that?"

"Changing the subject."

"Yeah. Right. Force of habit. Okay, here's the truth. First off, it's not like Rachel and I were a match made in heaven. We had that heavy animal attraction thing going, but once we started to get to know each other, that began to wear off and we realized it would never work. We were too different. We wanted different things. And..."

"You were in trouble with the law."

The kid's no pushover. There's a lot of her mother in her. It's like it's Rachel, not Allison, sitting across from me giving me the third degree.

"Why would you say that?"

"You must know I did a little research on you, right?"

"I'm an open book," I say.

"Is that why you left? Because you were on the lam?"

I laugh.

"What's so funny?"

"You talk like you're in a Jimmy Cagney movie."

"Who's that?"

"An Ivy Leaguer doesn't know who James Cagney was?"

"There are lots of things I don't know. I try to focus on important stuff."

"For the record, he was a movie tough guy in the forties and fifties. You realize I don't owe you an answer, right?"

"That's debatable."

"I wasn't ready to settle down and have a family. By the time I found out she gave birth, it wasn't like there was an option to come back and do the right thing. I'd been excommunicated. Once your mother closes a door she double-locks it and there ain't no one getting in."

She slowly nods her head, so I know she recognizes it's true. I wonder if this is something she inherited from her mother.

"She decided she didn't want me in her life and she made that very clear."

"Once you found out there was a baby, did you send child support?"

"She didn't want anything from me. Basically, I was treated like a sperm donor."

"That doesn't mean you couldn't have sent money every once in a while."

"I had my own life, Allison. My own needs. If she wanted something from me in those early days, she knew how to find me. And she's not the type who's shy about asking for something she wants."

"Weren't you at all curious about me?"

"I could lie and say yes, but the truth is it was very easy to convince myself you didn't exist."

"Even though you knew…"

"Yes. Even though I knew."

She turns quiet as she uses her fork to move salad around her plate. I think maybe she's run out of questions, but it turns out that's not even close. She's just deciding what to ask next. Still, this is getting a little too close for comfort. I need to change the balance of power.

"Mind if I jump in here with a few questions of my own?"

"Uhm. Okay. Sure."

"Why did you decide to look for me? And what do you expect to get out of this?"

"That's two questions."

"It is. But I figure it might be the only questions I get before you jump back in. Besides, they're connected. So, let's call it a two-part question."

She smiles. "You think I'm monopolizing the conversation?"

"What do you think?"

"Okay. Maybe. A little. So, why did I decide to look for you? That's an easy one. You're my birth father. I'm curious. Like it or not, half my DNA is yours. I think it's pretty natural for me to want to get to know you. And as for part two, I'm not sure what I expect. Maybe because I wasn't sure I could track you down and if I did, I wasn't sure you'd agree to meet with me."

"Do I get points for that?"

"You mean, like extra credit?"

"Sure."

"Absolutely not. Don't you think you owe it to me?"

"That's not the way I operate, Allison. I don't owe anyone anything and no one owes me anything. If I want something, I take it. Because no one hands you anything in this life, at least not without strings attached. I've got a few rules to live by, and one of them is that it's not that 'You get out of life what you put into it.' You get out of life what everyone else is stupid enough to put into it."

"Wow! That's pretty cynical, isn't it?"

"It's the truth."

"You mean, it's *your* truth. Why are you smiling?"

"Because if we don't go too far with this line of questioning, it could almost be fun."

"I don't get what you're saying."

"This whole *your* truth thing. It's either the truth or it's not. Otherwise, you'll have as many truths as the eight-billion population of the planet. Kind of corrupts the idea of truth, doesn't it?"

"No. It doesn't. Truth is a matter of perspective. What I see as the truth isn't necessarily what you see as the truth."

"Okay. Let's just agree to disagree. I can see it's going to be a challenge getting to know you. But you know what, I think I'm up to it."

"I don't see it the least bit challenging."

"Well then, let's just call it *my* truth."

She smiles. She's got a sense of humor. She's intelligent and likeable and yeah, kind of charming. Very useful qualities.

"By the way, what exactly is it you do for a living?" she asks.

"That's complicated."

"Complicated how?"

"Let's just say I have my fingers in a lot of pies."

"I have no idea what that means. Sounds like to me it's just a way of saying you're unemployed."

"I'm a freelancer."

"Freelancing in what?"

"Whatever I decide to get involved with at any particular time."

She shakes her head, and I can tell by the expression on her face she's frustrated. Fine with me. Keeps her off balance, something I thrive on. I check my watch. It's close to three o'clock.

"You know what, I'm starting to wind down a little, and I've got an appointment at four. What say we drop the third degree and talk about what the next day or two is going to look like. And then I'll take you back to where I'm staying."

"Where's that?"

"Airbnb on Collins, across from the Diplomat Hotel. I've got two bedrooms. There's a pool, and if you prefer the ocean, it's across the street."

"You act like I'm here on vacation."

"I know why you're here. But why not take advantage of the situation? Kick back and enjoy what little Florida has to offer."

"Then what?"

"We take a day or two to do that father-daughter bonding thing, then I put you back on a plane to wherever you want to go."

She's silent—a welcome change.

"I guess that's okay. You know, I'm not here to, like, cramp your style or anything."

"I never said you were. Look, Allison, this whole thing is unscripted. I'm not sure what your ultimate goal is, and I'm not sure you know what it is either. But I'm gonna give you a little fatherly advice. Keep your expectations low. Very low. If you think this is a fairy tale with a happy ending, I'm gonna bust that bubble right here and now. It's not. I may be a lot of things, but parent material isn't one of them. There's a reason I don't have any other kids, or at least that I know of, and it's a conscious choice. Consider it my gift to humanity. This world is fucked up enough without me adding to it."

I see from the sad expression on her face that maybe I've gone a little too far. Better that than give her false hope.

"Are you saying that after tomorrow you're going to just disappear into the ether? And, like, I'll never see you again?"

"I'm just warning you to temper your expectations."

"So, you're pissed I found you?"

"I didn't say that. I'm not. At least not yet. If it's something you had to do, then I'm glad you did it. So far, I'm okay with whatever this is." I wave my hand back and forth between us. "But my life is pretty full now and this isn't some feel-good sitcom with one of those sappy, happy endings."

I know this isn't what she wants to hear, but I'm not sorry I've said it. The lower her expectations are, the better. For both of us.

Josh
Moon over Miami

When I was young and single, I got all kinds of advice about how to find true love—not that I was looking for it. I won't bore you with the unsolicited wisdom—most of it useless—but I did have a least favorite. "When you stop looking, that's when it'll happen. When you least expect it."

I didn't believe a word of it then…or now. But to be honest, I favored that piece of advice because it absolved me from doing anything proactive. In effect, I was, as my religious friends might say, putting myself in "God's hands," despite the fact I don't believe in a conventional God. Or at least the kind of God who's going to fix me up with the woman of my dreams. I had all kinds of possible scenarios, my favorite being I'd answer my door one day and there would stand my soulmate. She finds herself at the wrong apartment…but it turns out she's in the absolutely right place—my reward for doing absolutely nothing.

This comes to mind now because I'm having an impossible time trying to coax out a vision that will help me locate Allie. The harder I try, the more I shoot blanks. And so, after spending a lifetime running away from these visions, by pretending they aren't there, I'm doing everything I can to make one appear. I am not unaware of the irony.

I try to empty my mind (as if that's possible) and wait for a "picture" to appear, which is like waiting for a long-anticipated film that's never been made to arrive at a local theater. I get nothing. I try thinking of mundane things, hoping these thoughts will launch a scene with Allie in it. Still nothing. I try to jumpstart the process by staring at a photo of Allie on my phone. Nada.

And so, I reach for another tool in my toolbox and resort to the kind of legwork I use when I'm on a story. This is what leads me back to Blanche.

I'm afraid she won't speak to me, but when I get through to her, I'm pleasantly surprised. She seems almost happy to hear from me. I stretch the truth a little by telling her I've found that Allie is with Daniel, but I don't know where they are. Does she have even the slightest idea of where he is now? Or where he might be?

At first, she hems and haws, but if there's one thing I've learned early on as a journalist, it's perseverance. After asking the same question every possible way I can, I try directly tapping into her strained relationship with her brother.

"I suspect if anyone knows where Daniel might be, it would be you, Blanche. And I'm just as sure he'd much prefer you keeping it to yourself."

"I don't have anything to do with him anymore. And if you're smart, you'll do the same. He can be...dangerous."

"I don't mean to disrespect you, Blanche, but I'm pretty sure you know more than you're telling me."

"What makes you think that?"

"I've been doing this a long time, and if you're good at something, and I am, you acquire instinct. My instinct tells me you have a good idea where he is. I know your relationship is, er, strained, so I'm not quite sure why you're protecting him."

"He's an asshole," she says.

This is it. The crack in the doorway where I can insert my foot. Both love and hate are potent motivations. And I can practically feel her hate for him through the phone.

"Look, we both know Daniel has a pretty sordid history of getting in trouble with the law. I'm afraid he's going to lead Allie into something that'll get her in trouble. That's why I think it's so important to find her now, before he leads her astray."

Silence.

"All I need from you is your best guess as to where he is. And remember, this is your niece we're talking about. Your flesh and blood."

She hesitates, like she's weighing consequences. Then, "I think he's in Florida."

"What makes you think that's where he is?"

"Doesn't matter."

"Where in Florida?"

"Around Fort Lauderdale maybe. We had an aunt who lived down there. We visited her a couple times when we were kids. Daniel was attracted to the lifestyle. He especially liked going to the dog races and jai alai, because they were legalized gambling, which meant all kinds of opportunities to fix games. She lived in a town called Hollywood. We used to joke that she was the unlikeliest person to make it to Hollywood. When I spoke to him, I made a joke about him running into her. He said he sure hoped not, which makes me think he might be in that area."

I don't want Blanche to suddenly get a case of family loyalty, resulting in her giving him a heads-up, so I quickly thank her and hang up. I call up a map of southern Florida and find that Hollywood is just north of Miami Beach and south of Fort Lauderdale.

I book a flight to Fort Lauderdale, hoping this might jumpstart my uncooperative "power."

Daniel
Kids Today

We make a quick stop at a shopping mall to pick up a swimsuit for the kid. She's got her eye on a skimpy number that looks like it belongs on the cover of the *Sports Illustrated* swimsuit issue, and I surprise myself by doing the "dad" thing and nix it.

She laughs. "What's wrong with it?" she says, holding it up.

I check the price tag. "You gotta be kidding. They're certainly not charging for the cost of the material."

"Pretty awesome, right?"

"How about we find something a little less awesome."

Reluctantly, she puts it back. "Yes, *Dad*," she says, rolling her eyes. Is this what I've been missing by not having kids?

"When you start paying for things, you can choose whatever you want. Meanwhile, I have some say in the matter."

Are these words really coming out of *my* mouth? Have I suddenly turned into Jim Anderson of *Father Knows Best*? I need to get a grip. But for now, I'm sticking to my guns.

"Are you living in a church or something?" she says.

I smile. Kid's got a good sense of humor. Maybe she gets that from me, since I don't remember her mother being a bundle of laughs. Truth is, this genetic thing is beyond my paygrade.

We settle on a bright red two-piece that even though it has twice as much fabric is still suggestive of something other than swimming.

By the time we get to my place, it's creeping up on four o'clock. I settle her in the guest room. "Take a nap. Go for a swim. Watch TV. Do some homework…"

"What am I, twelve?"

I can't help smiling. Maybe it'll be fun having her around for a couple days.

"Where are you going, Pops?"

"Business."

"What kind of business?"

"The none of your damn business kind of business."

"Jeez, pretty touchy, aren't we?"

"We know each other what, less than twenty-four hours and you want to get all into my personal business?"

"Got something to hide, Dad?"

For a moment, I'm a little disoriented. I've been called many things over the years, but "Dad" isn't one of them. I wonder if I'll ever get used to that? And then I think, *Why the fuck am I looking at this as a long-term thing? Why should I have to get used to it?*

"Pretty much everything. I should be back in a couple hours, three at the most."

"Don't worry about me. I can amuse myself while you're gone."

"Try staying out of trouble, okay?"

"Sure thing. I'll leave that up to you."

I want to smile, but I don't want to encourage her. Truth is, she's beginning to grow on me. More important, there's an idea forming in the back of my mind on how I might be able to fit her into my life.

I'm halfway out the door when I realize there's a question I haven't asked.

"By the way, exactly what does your mother know about all this?"

"Depends what you mean by 'all this.'"

"You. Here. Me."

She smiles. "Nothing. She has no idea where I am or what I'm doing."

I take a step back toward her. "You're telling me your mother hasn't heard from you in over a week?"

"That's right."

"Don't you think she's worried?"

"Of course she's worried."

"And you don't care?"

"I care. Kinda. It's just a little payback..."

"For?"

"For lying to me all those years."

"I'm sure she had her reasons." Reasons I know all too well.

"Maybe when I was a kid. Not now."

"You do know she's probably looking for you, don't you?"

"Sure."

"There's even a chance she's called the cops."

"She wouldn't do that. First off, I'm an adult. I don't have to check in with anyone, even her. And I think you've got enough experience with the cops to know the last thing they're worried about is some upper-middle-class, Ivy League kid gone missing. And she knows I haven't been kidnapped or anything."

"How would she know that?"

"All she had to do was talk to my roommate, Kevin. He saw me packing and I told him I was going away for the weekend..."

"You're living with a guy? I don't know if I approve of that." I'm smiling when I say this, of course.

She laughs. "He's way not my type. And you know what, Pops, it's not like olden times. Girls and guys room together all the time. Even share bathrooms. You are aware we're not in the Dark Ages?"

"No one tells me anything."

"Besides, when I was a kid, I ran away from home a couple times. If the cops checked they'd find out about that and I'm pretty sure because of my history, they wouldn't touch this with a ten-foot pole."

"You've got all the answers, don't you?"

"Not all." She cracks a huge smile. "But enough of them."

"Okay. I'm outta here. And if you get in any trouble, just dial 911."

"Like what kind of trouble do you expect I'd get into? Like set the place on fire?"

"I have no idea, Allison, but I'm pretty sure you can come up with something. Oh, and if you do decide to contact your mother, like to tell her you're okay, I'd appreciate it if you kept me out of the conversation."

She makes a zipping motion with her finger, running it across her pursed lips, then mimes throwing away an imaginary key.

"If you get hungry there's a bunch of takeout menus in the drawer next to the refrigerator." I grab my wallet from my back pocket, pull out a credit card, and hand it to her. "This is just for dinner, okay? Not for online shopping sprees."

"You think I'm gonna steal your card, run up a huge bill, then disappear?"

"Oh, and don't open the door for strangers."

"Stranger danger. Got it." She mimics an imaginary pad and pencil and writes an imaginary list. "Any other obvious instructions, *Dad*?"

I want to smile, but I don't want to encourage her, so I just turn around and head out the door.

Daniel
Workin' Nine to Five

"You're late."

"Watch broke," he says. He shows me his wrist. It's bare, except for a faint tan line where a broken watch might or might not have been.

"Get a new fucking watch."

"Yeah, I'll get right on that," he says, not bothering to mask his sarcasm. I don't mind attitude so long as it's mine.

"Got a phone?" I say.

"Sure…" he says tentatively, not sure where I'm going with this.

"Take it out."

He sticks his hand in his jacket pocket, pulls out an older-model iPhone. The screen has a big crack down the middle. I should take this as a warning sign of carelessness and walk away. No harm, no foul. But time is short, and we're not talking a lifetime commitment here. When it's done, I wave goodbye and cut the cord.

"Activate it," I say.

He does.

"What's that in front?"

He holds up the phone for me to get a better look. "You mean this?" he says, pointing to the numerals.

"Yeah."

He looks at me like I'm from another planet. "It's the time."

"You're a fucking genius, Frankie. Next time you're late will be the last time you're late. And just so you know, in my world, ten minutes early is late. Anything after that you're wasting my time."

"Why are you bustin' my chops, man?"

"Because this isn't a game, Frankie. This is business. There are rules. My rules. And being on time is one of those rules. You don't like it, there's the fucking door."

"Okay, okay. I get it. So, what's this job?"

It's late afternoon and we're sitting across from each other in a sparsely inhabited Popeyes Louisiana Chicken. It's too late for the lunch crowd, too early for the Early Birders. I'm in the midst of putting together a crew. Frankie's been recommended by someone I've never met, which is the way I like it. Plausible deniability. That's one of the safeguards for any successful business venture. At least the kind of businesses I'm in.

Before I can say anything, Frankie pipes up. "Hey, you know what? I haven't eaten all day. Maybe I'll get myself one of those three-piece combo meals."

"We're not here to feed your face, Frankie. You wanna eat, do it on your own time."

"Okay," he says. He's getting a preview of what it's like to work for me. This is a good thing, because another feature of any successful venture is everyone knows their place. This tough-guy thing is pretty much an act, essential to establish the pecking order upfront.

I scooch back my chair and get up. "Come with me."

"We're leaving?"

I ignore his question.

He follows me to the back of the restaurant, to the parking area. I point to two large metal drums chained to the ground, a few feet from the back entrance to the building.

"Know what these are?" I ask.

"Oil drums?"

"Know what's in 'em?"

"No fucking idea."

"Get closer."

He moves closer.

"What's that smell?"

"Like grease, maybe."

"No. It's the smell of money."

He looks at me like I'm crazy.

"I don't get you."

"Come on." I grab him by the arm and lead us back into Popeyes, where we sit down at our table.

"I thought this meeting is about a job, not to see how good my fucking sense of smell is," he says. "I'm fucking confused, man."

"That's cooking grease in those barrels and they're chained up for a good reason. This shit is like bitcoin. It's valuable, if you know what to do with it."

"I don't get it."

"Years ago, used cooking grease, after it was cleaned up, was used by livestock farmers. They'd spray it on animal feed to fatten up hogs, chickens, and cows. So, it had value. Not a lot, but something. Not enough for restaurants to give a damn what happened to it. Trucking it away was doing them a favor. But once they found there was another use for it, and there was value in it, that changed. Now, it's cleaned, filtered, and chemically modified into biofuel, which makes the value skyrocket. One company is valued at two billion dollars."

He whistles.

"So, what do you need me for?"

"You'll be part of a crew I'm putting together to liberate the grease."

"Then what?"

"Deliver it where I say."

"So, let me get this straight. You just need me to grab a bunch of drums filled with fucking dirty cooking grease and deliver them somewheres?"

"All I care about is what's in those drums. You can get yourself a pair of bolt cutters to remove the locks on the container lids and steal the whole drum, or use vacuum hoses to suck the grease into empty drums. I don't give a fuck. I just want the grease. How you get it is up to you."

"That's it?"

"That's it."

"Sounds doable."

"It is, unless you screw up. And Frankie, we're in the twenty-first century. Everyone's on *Candid Camera* all the fucking time. So, if I were you, I'd make sure you either disable the cameras or make damn sure you don't get recognized. I figure you can collect up to three, four grand's worth in half an hour."

"What's the split?"

"Seventy-thirty."

"Seems a little out of whack, since I'm taking all the risk."

"The stuff's worthless unless you know what to do with it and who to sell it to. I'll take care of all the logistics, and I'll be the one who chooses where you hit. I'll also provide you with everything you need to know about the target. All you gotta do is get the goods and deliver them where I say."

"How many these places you want me to hit?"

"Sky's the limit. In or out?"

Allison
Father-Daughter Reunion

As soon as Daniel's out the door, I start snooping.

I don't know what I'm looking for and yes, I know it's a serious breach of privacy, but I don't, like, care. There's something about Daniel I don't trust. Why should I? He abandoned me…and my mom. Add to the mix that he's been in trouble with the law. I don't know how much trouble and how serious it was…or is. And I don't know if he's still involved in anything illegal, cause what's that old saying about tigers not being able to change their stripes? Or is it leopards and their spots? Obviously, I'm not an animal person.

On the other hand, I actually kinda like the guy. I have this really weird feeling when I'm with him. Like I feel protected. I'm not sure why. Maybe it's because he, like, kinda oozes self-confidence. And I'm not sure how to explain this, but I'm almost proud of him. Makes no sense, right? I mean, what have I got to be proud about? Maybe it's all about this undeniable charisma thing he's got going. He kinda reminds me a little of Ryan Gosling or Jake Gyllenhaal. Okay, it's a little gross thinking about your father as a hottie like Ryan or Jake, but that's the point. I don't see him as my dad. Maybe

I will someday. Maybe we'll grow into, like, a father-daughter relationship. Not like now, but maybe sometime in the future. Anyway, like them, he's got this "bad boy" vibe going for him. My mom has warned me over and over again about getting involved with "bad boys." More than once she's preached, "No matter what I say, Allison, you're going to be attracted to these kinds of boys and men. Almost every woman is at some point in our lives. So, I guarantee you'll go through that phase too, but if you're lucky you'll come out of it unscathed and hopefully wind up with one of the good ones."

"Who says I want a good one?" I'd answer, mostly just to get under her skin. She'd smile, but I don't think she found it funny. All she did was shake her head in that way that says, *What on earth am I going to do with this girl?*

Now that I've met Daniel and spent some time with him, I can see my mom speaks from experience. Maybe she's right. Maybe it's a phase you grow out of. After all, she did wind up with Tony and yes, he really is one of the good ones.

I go through his bedroom closet first. There are a couple jackets, shirts, and pants, hanging there. On the floor there's a suitcase. I'm really, really tempted to open it up and look through the contents, but after thinking about it, I chicken out. It's just a bridge too far to rifle through that suitcase. Besides, what if I find something I don't want to see?

Just as I'm about to give up, I notice a small brown paper bag stuffed in a corner of the closet. I pick it up. It's surprisingly heavy. I stand there for a moment or two, debating with myself whether or not to open it. Turns out, I don't have to, because when I move my hand across the bag I can feel the shape. It's a handgun! Whether or not it's loaded, I don't know, and I don't want to find out. Quick as I can, I put it back in the corner of the closet, making sure it's in the exact position where I found it.

I try to forget about it, but I can't. This is troubling. Very troubling. But maybe Daniel has a good reason. Like for protection. I mean, who knows what kinds of people he's involved with. Or maybe he's had a bad experience and needs to know he can protect himself if he has to.

After finding this, I don't have the stomach to keep looking and, speaking of stomach, I'm hungry. I go back into the kitchen and order a pizza from one of the takeout menus Daniel left. When they ask for payment, I pull out the credit card he left with me. When I read off the information, I'm surprised to find the name on it is Daniel Peacock. It's official. One of my two dads has an alias.

Turns out, I'm not as hungry as I thought, so there's plenty left for Daniel if he wants it. My body is tired, but my mind is not. I turn on the TV, hoping it'll help me relax and stop thinking about that pistol in the closet. I wonder, has it ever been fired? And if so, has it ever been fired at someone? And if so, what happened to that someone? Should I say something to Daniel? But if I do, he'll know I was snooping, and he'll probably waste no time putting me on a plane back up north. I'm definitely not ready for that to happen. So, I decide, at least for now, to keep my mouth shut.

Finally, the day catches up with me and I manage to fall asleep on the couch, with a half-empty box of mutilated pizza slices on the coffee table in front of me.

It's pitch-dark when I'm awakened by the sound of the front door opening. I'm disoriented, not sure where I am and, as a result, I'm so startled by the sound that I nearly fall off the couch.

A light comes on, and I see it's Daniel.

"Sorry, kiddo," he says. "Didn't mean to wake you…"—he checks his watch—"…at eight-thirty in the evening."

"I've been up since early this morning, so I figured I'd take a little nap. It just lasted a little longer than I thought it would."

"Sleep when you're tired, eat when you're hungry, and never miss an opportunity to use a bathroom."

"You really do offer a lot of wisdom, don't you?"

I can hear his keys jingling as he moves toward me. I sit up and try to straighten out my T-shirt, which got bunched up because of the funny position I was in.

I see him eying the pizza box. "There are a few slices left, if you're hungry. It was pretty good. Not as good as New York or Connecticut pizza, of course."

"Thanks, but I grabbed something on the way back. How long you been out?"

"Couple hours, I guess. I'll go to my room and get out of your way."

"Stay where you are. We can talk a little, if you like."

"Really?"

"If you spend enough time with me, Allison, you'll find I hardly ever say things I don't mean."

If that's true, he's the only one in the world who doesn't. But I don't say that.

"I'm gonna grab a beer. Want one?" he says.

I'm not much of a drinker. But I'm not going to give up an opportunity to bond with Daniel. I want to get to know him better before I blow him off.

"Sure."

He disappears into the kitchen. I hear the refrigerator open and close, and he reappears holding two bottles of Coors. Like I say, I'm not much of a drinker, but I do know a couple things about Coors. One is it was Paul Newman's favorite drink—this factoid was told to me by Tony while we were watching a documentary about the dreamy actor and his super talented wife—and the other is that the Coors owner is a right-winger. And although the temptation to attack Daniel for his choice of beer is strong, I hold my tongue.

He twists the caps off both, hands one to me, and sits down on the easy chair opposite the couch.

"So, I guess this is the time we start getting to know each other," he says as he takes a swig.

"I guess."

"A father-daughter chat," he says, but I know he's just kidding around. "I'm sure you've got plenty of questions."

I do, but for some reason I can't think of a single one. Maybe it's because my mind is still foggy from sleep. Or maybe it's because this scene, me drinking beer with a man who's my birth father, a man I hardly know, is really weird. But he's opened the door, so I might as well come in.

I should probably proceed slowly, but I am my mother's daughter and so, instead, I go straight for the jugular.

"What were the circumstances of you leaving my mom?"

"Whoa! You don't waste any time, do you?"

I'm not looking for approval from Daniel, but for some reason I feel empowered after he says this.

"So, what was the deal?"

He takes another swig of beer. "We weren't a good mix."

I smile. At least he doesn't use that ridiculous *we just grew apart* line.

"That's pretty vague. Besides, right mix or not, taking off as soon as you found out she was pregnant wasn't cool."

"First off, you assume I knew she was pregnant when I left. I didn't. I only found out after, and it wasn't your mom who told me. If it were up to her, she would have been very happy if I'd never known, if I just disappeared from her life. And that's pretty much what happened. But if I'd known, it's unlikely that would've changed anything. Believe me, Allison, the way things turned out are much better for you than if I'd stuck around. If we'd gotten hitched, we'd probably have been in divorce court in record time. Either that or one or both of us would have been dead. And I'm not so sure it wouldn't have been me."

"Okay, but what was the real reason you walked away?"

"I was a jerk. A wild child. I was way too young to be tied down with a wife and kid. I might have been a dumb asshole, but I was smart enough to see the likely future if I stuck around and tried to shoehorn myself into a 'normal' relationship." He uses air quotes. "I grew up in a bad part of town in Chicago, and it's a story as old as time. I hooked up with the wrong element and wound up getting in trouble."

"What kind of trouble?"

"The kind of trouble you don't want to get into."

"You're so good at avoiding answering questions."

He shrugs and takes another swig.

"Were you, like, in a gang or something?"

"We called it a social club."

I laugh. "Good one," I say. "And what kind of things were you guys into? Socially, I mean. Like dances and hanging out at the mall?"

He smiles. We're actually having a conversation!

"Pretty much everything you can imagine. It started small, but it didn't stay that way. I don't want to go into details, because, to tell the truth, it's embarrassing and not germane to this conversation. Eventually, it turned into some pretty serious shit. I was just a dumb kid, and eventually I got caught, and the only way I could get out of it was to cooperate."

"Like rat on your friends?"

I know I'm being a little obnoxious, but I want to see how he handles it.

"You don't pull your punches, do you?"

"I don't, like, see the value of beating around the bush."

"These were some dangerous dudes, so part of the deal for me testifying was they'd put me in the Witness Protection Program."

"That's how you got the name Peacock."

"How'd you know that?"

"Your credit card."

"Clever girl."

"How'd you come up with that one?"

"It seemed to fit my personality. In case you haven't picked up on it, I don't exactly shun the spotlight."

"Are you still in the Program?"

"Nope. Bombed out of that pretty quick."

"What do you mean?"

"I don't want to get into details. Let's just say I've never been very good at following rules."

He's outing himself as a bad guy. And yet, there's still something so appealing about him. Maybe this has something to do with my mom's "bad boy" warning? There's so much to unpack here, so much more I want to know. I'm impatient, so I jump ahead.

"So, what kind of business are you in now, and why are you down here?"

"Excellent questions. And you can keep asking them over and over again, in a whole bunch of different ways, but you're going to get the same response from me. For your own protection all I'm gonna say is that right now I'm in commodities."

"Huh?"

"You know what commodities are, right?"

"I'm at Yale, Daniel. And although economics is far from my favorite subject, I do pay attention enough to know that 'commodities are basic goods and materials widely used and not meaningfully differentiated from one another. They include agricultural products like wheat and cattle, energy products like oil and natural gas, and metals like gold, silver, and aluminum.'"

"You really are an egghead, aren't you?"

"I've got kind of a photographic memory. I read something, it sticks with me." I hesitate for a moment for dramatic effect. "Same goes for the spoken word. So, consider yourself warned. If you don't want me to remember something, best not say it in front of me."

"Thanks for the heads-up," he says in a tone I recognize as sarcastic.

My face is turning warm, a sure sign I'm blushing. I hope this isn't apparent to Daniel, because I'm trying to play it cool, like I'm so, so sophisticated that nothing shocks or surprises me. But I guess it's not working. I know Daniel is playing with me. I also know he's holding something back. Probably a lot. And who knows what's true and what isn't? This only makes him even more of a challenge.

He's a complicated guy. I get that. And he's got this patina of mystery that surrounds him. There's part of me that wants to get out of here as quick as I can. It's the part that keeps warning me to heed that flashing redlight *DANGER* sign. But there's this other part that makes it more likely I'll stick around.

For one thing, there's so much more I want to know. So many questions I want to ask. But I can see Daniel is starting to guard. Still, I keep at it. Because how many other chances do I think I'll get?

"Now that you know I have an understanding of what commodities are, how about being a little more explicit about what you do?"

"One thing you should know about me, Allison, is I'm excellent at keeping secrets, especially when they're mine."

"Are you saying that by not going into details about what you do, you're somehow protecting me?"

He smirks.

"Guess you're not going to give me an honest answer, are you?"

"I think we've reached a stalemate. And you know what, even though I'm kind of enjoying this conversation, it's been a long day for me, so I think I'm gonna turn in. We can pick this up in the morning."

That's what he says, but I'm pretty sure tomorrow isn't going to make much of a difference. He's only going to tell me what he wants me to know, and I'm not sure even that's going to be the truth.

He starts toward his bedroom, but stops suddenly. "By the way, when do you think you'll want to get back to *your* life?"

"Excuse me?"

"Let your mom know you're safe and head back home or to school or wherever you should be."

"You want to get rid of me?"

"It's time both of us get back to our lives. You found me. We've interacted. I'm not sure what else you're looking for."

Truth is, I'm not sure either. But for some reason, this, whatever this is, feels incomplete. There's more, I'm just not sure what that is.

"Okay. How about we spend the day together tomorrow, and then I'll get out of your hair."

"Let's sleep on it, and we'll figure it out in the morning."

Look at that. He's been a father for less than twenty-four hours and he's already mastered all the lingo. I won't tell him this, but I think maybe he's a natural parent.

Josh
Giving In to a Higher Power

Putting faith in visions is akin to putting faith in religion. You can't control it. You have no idea how it works. You have no idea *if* it works. You're either a believer or you're not. Either way, you're bound to be disappointed.

As of now, I'm forced into the believer column when it comes to these random visions. It's a very uncomfortable place to be. When it comes to organized religion, I'm a skeptic. I don't want to be one of those people who *hears* "voices," and *sees* things, like burning bushes that aren't burning and aren't even there. And yet, here I am. Having to rely on something I don't understand. All because I'm trying to help a friend. What keeps coming to mind is Clare Boothe Luce's wise warning: "No good deed goes unpunished."

In the past, I spent way too much time and energy in denial. Now, not only am I a reluctant believer, but I'm frustrated I can't call upon this strange ability at will.

It reminds me of a time in life when I suffered from severe nerve pain. Well-meaning friends would ask if the pain was dependent on outside forces. Is it affected by the weather? Is it more prevalent at certain times of day? The answer was always, no. It was totally random. This, I could see, was hard for people to understand or accept. They meant well. They were hoping if it could be understood what affected the pain, this would lead to controlling it. Sounds reasonable. But pain is uncooperative. One day, for no apparent reason, it's worse. Another day, again for no apparent reason, it's better. There is no rhyme or reason. The days it's better are the dangerous days. They dare you to believe you're on the way to eliminating the pain altogether. Alas, that is the biggest and most dangerous lie of all. As Emily Dickinson wrote, "Pain has an element of blank." It is a clean slate ready to be defaced.

Living with this ability means I have to learn how to let go. I must give in to the mystery of how it works, when it works, and why it works. The only way to coexist is to live my life as normally as I can, while allowing myself to be open to these images when they come, randomly and uninvited. In other words, I have to cede control to a power I don't understand.

I'm not sure if this new attitude has anything to do with it, but while waiting in the

airport security line, a sudden image pops into my head. In it, Allison is sitting at a kitchen table, an open box of pizza in front of her. Hoping to pick up some clue as to where she is, I allow myself to enter this scene. Suspended in midair, I slowly circle her.

As I hover over the table, I lower myself until I get close enough to see that on top of the pizza box there's a slip of paper with an address on it: 1328 Wiley Street, Apt. 1C.

This is where I will begin.

Allison

What Happens in Florida Stays in Florida

It's almost 9 a.m. when I finally stumble out of my room. I've had almost ten hours' sleep, but I'm still tired. The only reason I'm even up now is that I forgot to pull down the blinds, so the sunlight streaming into the room woke me.

Daniel is in the kitchen. The seductive aroma of coffee fills the air.

I'm wearing jeans and a faded green T-shirt, the only things I have fresh enough to wear. Which reminds me to ask Daniel if there's a communal laundry room in the complex. Having no idea how long I'd be on the road, I've brought only a bare minimum of clothing, which amounts to a couple pairs of jeans, a few tops, a sweater, a few pairs of underwear, and the same number of pairs of socks.

"Well, well, the princess arises," says Daniel as I enter the brightly lit, surprisingly clean, uncluttered kitchen.

I don't know why I feel the need to apologize, but I do it anyway. I know Daniel hates when I do this, but old habits are hard to break.

"I'm sorry. I never, ever sleep this late."

"You obviously needed the sleep. Coffee?"

"Yes. Please."

"Milk? Sugar? Or do you prefer the fake stuff?"

"Straight, please," I say, hoping an unadulterated cup will give me enough of a jolt so I can make it through the day. Or at least the morning.

I sit down at the kitchen table and pick up today's copy of the *Miami Herald* that's sitting in front of me. I take one look at the depressing headlines and push it away.

"Ugh," I say.

Daniel, carrying a steaming hot mug of coffee in each hand, places them on the table, one in front of me, the other by the seat opposite me. He starts to sit, but catches himself.

"How 'bout some breakfast? I think I've got eggs, English muffins, maybe even bacon."

"No thanks. I'm never hungry when I get up. But I do need this," I say as I lift the mug, "to wake me up."

Daniel smiles.

"I know. I know. My grandmother hates that I don't eat breakfast. 'It's the most important meal of the day,' she says, like over and over again. And I always go, 'The most important meal of the day is the one in front of me.' It became this running joke with us."

"Never met your grandmother."

"Too late now. She passed away a few years ago."

"So, I guess it's a little late for a condolence card."

I smile. I like that he's joking around with me. It relaxes me. And I need it. I've got this empty feeling in the pit of my stomach. When I was twelve, my mom sent me to a therapist—it was after I ran away from home the first time. I kicked and screamed, but it turned out I actually liked the woman. It felt good telling her things I couldn't tell anyone else. Not my mom or Tony or anyone. She said I suffered from free-floating anxiety, that it was very common, and that eventually, when I'm able to pinpoint what the anxiety is about, I'll be able to deal with it. But it's more than half a dozen years later, and even though I recognize it when it happens, I still can't do anything to control it. I know it's natural. Everybody suffers from it at one time or another. But this time, I totally know what's bringing it on. I mean, what could be more anxiety-provoking than meeting your birth father for the first time? Plus, I feel like I'm a little too old for running away from home, which is, when you think of it, exactly what I'm doing.

Daniel pulls out a chair and sits opposite me. His hands surround the mug, like he's trying to keep them warm. His fingernails shine, like he's just had a manicure. It seems so counter to the way he comes off. The kind of man who gets a manicure, I mean.

"So, what's the plan, Stan?" he says.

I look at him like I'm asking, *What the fuck is going on with the rhyming*? I know what he's alluding to. Tony's a big fan of Paul Simon. Before we convinced him to get earphones for the good of the family—like we all don't have the same taste in music—he used to play his music all the time.

"Plan? You mean like what to do, like, today?"

"Veni, vidi, vici. You've come, you've seen, you've conquered. What's next?"

"You're quoting Julius Caesar?"

"Don't look so surprised. I may not be as smart or as well-read as you or your mother, but I can read without moving my lips… too much."

Imagine that. My birth pops has a sense of humor. And he can quote Shakespeare.

"I'm guessing you got what you came for, to make sure I exist, right?" He reaches his arm across the table. "Give a touch."

I smile and touch his arm, just above his wrist. It feels warm and I get this crazy sensation. Like electricity. But not electricity.

Is it possible this has something to do with our sharing blood and DNA? Suddenly, I have this image of two different streams of blood connecting and making one large river of blood.

"Yup, you're real all right."

I don't know what else to say, so I say what's on my mind.

"I don't think I'll ever get to know who you really are, no matter how much time we spend together. Not that I wouldn't try."

"To what end?"

It's a question I'm not expecting and one I don't have a ready answer for.

"To be honest, I'm not sure."

"Look, there are two things that can happen if we spend time together. One, you find out I'm a major asshole. Obnoxious, offensive, whatever bad thing you can think about another person. And, you wisely choose to never to see me again."

"What if it turns out I like those traits?"

"That brings us to the other option. After spending time with me, you start thinking, 'This is the most interesting, fascinating, generous, intelligent girl I've ever met.' You start to bond with me. You find you like having me around. Until I do something that makes you realize it was a huge mistake. And then comes the emotional trauma. You feel so bad, you want to kill yourself. Or me. See where I'm going with this?"

"This from some college class you're taking? Because you're pretty young to be so perceptive about relationships. In the end, we're screwed no matter what, right? You really are frigging smart, aren't you?"

He has me on the road to another blush.

"Okay, let's cut to the chase. You want to spend time with me. Honestly, I don't see the point. I think it's a waste of time, yours and mine. But I've got an open mind. Like this much." He takes his thumb and his index finger and holds them about a quarter of an inch apart.

"With that attitude, you might be right. But I'll take the chance. Maybe just a day or two, and then I'll head back?"

"You want a bring-your-daughter-to-work day?"

"I know you're being sarcastic, but that'd be great. I promise I won't get in the way. And this way, I'll be able to learn more about you. And maybe you'll learn something about me?"

"Let's not assume either of those things is a good thing."

"I see it as a win-win situation. By the end of the day, I'll either like you or hate you."

"Nothing in between?"

"Nothing in between."

"Is that supposed to be a desired result for me?"

"Oh, come on. I promise I won't get in the way. It's another forty-eight hours of your life. That's not so much, is it?"

I'm ashamed of myself. I mean, resorting to being a whiny, obnoxious kid just to get what I want. It's something I haven't used since I was like eleven. And I doubt it worked then. But it's like a muscle memory. It's always there when you need it. Manipulation is deep in our DNA. Just shows how low I'm willing to go. And you know what? I'm shameless in that I don't feel the least bit guilty about resurrecting this tried-and-true tactic.

"That's not what I'm worried about."

"Oh, I see. I get it. You're afraid I'll see something you don't want me to see. So, how about this, we'll invoke the cone of silence. What happens in Florida stays in Florida."

He laughs.

"Oh, and don't worry, no matter what they do, they'll never get me to talk."

"They? Who's they?"

"Just a figure of speech. They. Like whoever's out there who might be interested."

Somehow, I don't think I'm helping my cause. He's got me on the defensive. And the thing of it is, he does it so effortlessly and skillfully. I have a feeling he's toying with me, but it's actually, like, fun.

"So, you think I'm involved in something that's against the law?" he says.

"Oh, no, no, no. It's just that..."

He puts up his hand, palm out, in a "stop" gesture.

"Even if you are, I'm your daughter. I can't be forced to testify against you."

"That's not a thing, Allison. There is no father-daughter confidentiality. Someone hasn't been watching enough *Law and Order*."

"So, what have you got planned for us today that you don't want me to see?"

"A classic 'When did you stop beating your wife' question."

I'm not sure what that means, but I make like I do.

"So, what about it? Please. Please. Please." I clap my hands together in a prayer position.

"Okay. One day with a mutual option for one more. And I'm going to respect you as a fellow adult, Allison. I won't be taking you to something like an amusement park...or the playground..."

"Good decision. I'm nineteen, not nine."

"Thanks for reminding me. But I've got a couple ground rules."

I'm excited. He's really going to let me hang with him.

"What are they?"

"For one thing, that cone of silence thing is definitely invoked. Not necessarily for my good, but for yours."

Alarm bells should go off, but I'm so excited, I don't ask him to tell me what he means by that.

"Okay. And?"

"No judging me. I am who I am, and I do what I do. I'm not going to be putting on a show for you. What you see is what you get. Anytime you want to opt out, just ask."

Another red flag to ignore?

"Okay."

"One more thing. At the end of the day, you'll contact your mother, tell her you're okay, without a word about finding me or spending time with me, or anything about me. Capiche?"

"Capiche! Let's get started! What's our first stop?"

Daniel
Gone Fishin'

"When someone says to you, 'I've got nothing to hide,' run for the hills."

"Why are you telling me this? Have you got something to hide?" she says as we sit in the front seat of my red Chevy Camaro rental.

"Everyone's got something to hide, Allison. Everyone."

"Hey, how about putting the top down?" she says as she straps herself in.

"You're okay with your hair blowing around?

"How vain do you think I am?"

"In my experience, it's a common complaint coming from your gender. But I'm fine with it, if you are."

"You do know you're not supposed to say things like that? Or think them."

"You mean the gender crack?"

"Yes."

"Not woke, right?"

"Right. But then I guess your generation has a lot to learn."

"My generation?"

"Yes. You're like what, a boomer?"

"How old do you think I am?"

"I don't know. Were you born between sixty-five and eighty?"

"I was."

"Then I apologize. You're Gen X, not a boomer."

"And what are you?"

"Gen Z."

"You do know all this alphabet soup stuff is ridiculous, don't you?"

"If you say so."

She whips out her phone and types something.

"According to Wikipedia, 'Generation X is known as the middle-child generation because of its small size in comparison with the baby boomer and millennial generations. Gen Xers are typically described as resourceful, independent, and good at maintaining work-life balance. They were the first generation to grow up with personal computers.' Sound familiar?"

"Slightly. What about Gen Z?"

She reads, "'Gen Z characteristics: They're growing up; they're prioritizing saving money; they love to travel; they're prone to anxiety; they shape culture through social media.'"

"True?"

"I don't like labels."

"Ten seconds ago, you labeled me a Gen Xer. Get your facts straight, kiddo."

"You're very exasperating."

"Yet another heretofore unknown characteristic of us Xers."

The kid is tough. I like that. Every time she says or does something, I can't help focusing on it, deconstructing it, wondering if it's something she's gotten from me. I don't know why. I mean, what difference does it make?

I push the button and the top begins to recede.

"What's our first stop?" she says excitedly.

I turn to face her.

"Look, I agreed to spend the day with you, but if you're going to question my every move, this isn't going to work. Why not just sit back and let the experience of spending a day with me waft over you?"

"So, no questions?"

"I'm not into rules. I'm just warning you that I am what I am and I do what I do. No matter what, you're going to judge me. I'd just appreciate it if, unless I ask, you keep it to yourself."

She folds her arms across her chest. I think maybe she's sulking.

I'm beginning to second-guess myself. Why am I letting this happen? The warning I gave her is true. No one's going to benefit from this. No one. And yet, I forge ahead.

Maybe I should just put her on a plane to wherever.

So, why don't I?

It's not about a familial obligation or even an attempt to create a relationship with her. It's something else. Deep in some dark recess of my mind, I'm thinking that having a kid, this kid in particular, might be to my advantage. She's good-looking, well spoken, and she makes a good first impression. And she's whip-smart. I can't help thinking about that movie, *Paper Moon*, where Ryan O'Neal's kid is not a daughter but a partner.

Should I consider bringing the kid into the family business? If so, is this an audition?

The bottom line is, I've been with her less than twenty-four hours, and yet I feel a mysterious connection to her.

We head over to Collins Avenue and make a right, and head south toward Miami Beach.

"Okay if I talk now?"

"Sure. What you got?"

"Well, I'm really curious about your past..." She hesitates and looks away from me.

"And by that you mean my rap sheet, right?"

"Uhm."

"It's okay. I'm not ashamed of my past."

I see the beginnings of a smile. "Maybe you should be."

It's a beautiful day. The humidity hasn't hit yet and there's not a cloud in the sky. As we drive down A1A, I can't help wondering what other drivers might be thinking of us. Middle-aged dude sitting next to a young, very pretty brunette. I doubt anyone pegs us as father and daughter, but that doesn't bother me. And I don't mean it in an incestuous way. It's all about appearances. And in this case the appearance is, *What a fucking lucky dude this guy is.*

She's opened the conversation, but now, suddenly she's grown mysteriously quiet. She's staring straight ahead, but I'm not sure she's actually seeing anything. Is she trying to form a question? Has she realized that maybe she doesn't want the answers? I'm not sure why I don't leave well enough alone, but I don't. Maybe it's the provocateur in me.

"Cat got your tongue?"

"Just thinking."

"About your next question?"

"Maybe."

"Tell you what, kiddo, because you're blood, I'm gonna help you out by giving you the *Reader's Digest* version of my adult life. Seems kinda pointless to complain about my shitty childhood, so I'll skip that. We've all got our own version of that, don't we?"

She immediately perks up. "Uhm, mine wasn't so bad. I'm not saying it was idyllic, but I don't really have anything to complain about.... Unless it has to do with the lies my mother's told me. Who knows how many there were? But I don't mind the CliffsNotes version of Daniel growing up."

"Maybe another time. Right now, since I'm the one giving the tour, I'll set the ground rules. Okay?"

I don't mean it to sound scolding, but somehow it comes out that way. Maybe it's the fatherhood DNA?

"Sure."

"You're not gonna be too shocked, are you?"

"I may look like a kid, but I promise you, I'm not," she says firmly, as if trying to convince me and herself.

"Like I said, I got in with what most people would call the wrong crowd. But at the time, I needed to belong somewhere. I didn't have a family at home, but I realized I could make one of my own. And it wasn't going to be anything like my fucked-up family. We started out small. Stealing anything that wasn't nailed down. Eventually, small stuff turned into bigger-ticket items, like cars, jewelry. Anything we could turn around for a quick buck. I even broke into a few homes. It gave me a tremendous rush, a rush I'd never felt before. It was like a drug, and it didn't take long till I got hooked. Besides belonging to something bigger than me, it gave me a place in the world. Made me feel important. Gave me purpose. I turned out to be very adept at taking things that didn't belong to me. Eventually, when the excitement wore off, I looked around and saw a lot of the people I was hanging out with starting to get pinched—arrested. It was the first time I considered consequences. The idea of spending time behind bars didn't much appeal to me. I told myself I was way too smart for that. Besides, I knew if I kept it up, it would eventually escalate into violence. When that happens, no one wins. You begin to stop thinking about consequences. You're forever looking over your shoulder, because you know, even if you're not a moron, that eventually that shit catches up to you. That's when I learned a valuable lesson…"

"Which was?"

"I realized it's pretty damn easy to get people to give you things rather than having to take it from them. If you're really smart, you can even get away with it. Let me tell you something, Allison: The biggest suckers are the ones with the most money. It's like pool… you play?"

"We have a pool table in our basement. Tony taught me how to play. I'm actually pretty good. We ought to play some time. For money, of course."

"Then you know it's all about angles and thinking ahead. The good players aren't playing the ball in front of them. They're playing two, three, four shots ahead."

"Is that what you do? Thinking four shots ahead?"

The kid's engaged. She's paying attention.

"Can't help myself."

"We're talking like metaphorically, right?"

"You learn the most about life by looking at the edges. If you want to know about someone, you don't ask them, you find the peripheral people in their lives and ask them. Like doormen or concierges. They know every tenant's intimate secrets. They know what makes people tick. There's an art to it, kiddo. Find out what people want or need, and give it to them. Or at least make them think you're going to give it to them. Not all of it. Just enough to keep them interested. Sometimes, all you have to do is let them think they're getting what they want. Now they see it, now they don't. So long as you accept the possibility that you might get caught, that there can be serious consequences, it makes you better."

"At what?"

"Doesn't matter."

"Interesting. Or, as my dad might say, 'Food for thought.'" Her mood seems to have brightened. "So, what's on our agenda today?"

This is the make-or-break moment, and I don't want to screw it up. How much do I tell her and when? I have to keep reminding myself: Right now she's not my daughter, she's just another fish in the sea.

"We're going to see a man about a horse."

"You mean you're gonna buy a horse?"

I laugh.

Her face turns bright red.

"So, by horse you mean something else?"

"I do."

"Like what?"

"Doesn't matter. It's all a commodity…and we've gone through that, remember?"

"But in this particular case, what kind of commodity?"

I glance over at her again. She looks so damn earnest. It's like her mouth is wide open and she's ready to chomp down on the bait. Question is, do I reel her in now or keep her dangling on the line? And if I do reel her in, do I keep her or throw her back in? All good questions, but I'm not ready to answer them yet.

"Enough details for now. But remember, kiddo, you asked for this. All you have to do is say the word and we'll turn around and I'll drop you at the airport."

"I don't think I'm ready to get back on a plane. How 'bout we talk a little about your run-ins with the law?" she says.

"Patience, little one. Patience. When the time is right, you'll know everything you need to know. Promise."

Under her breath she mutters, "Oh, I doubt that."

Which only goes to prove I'm right about her. She might turn out to be a very valuable commodity.

Daniel
Gobble, Gobble, Gobble

"Ain't she a little young for you, Danny-boy?"

"She's my kid, asshole."

Allison, her arms folded across her chest, is standing several feet behind me, to my right, far enough from us so she can't hear what we're saying. He leers at her like she's an underage girl dressed in one of those Catholic-school uniforms, not well-worn faded blue jeans and a Yale T-shirt.

"If you say so."

"I say so."

"So, what's she doing here? This here's between you and me, Danny-boy. I don't like an audience."

"Live with it."

He stares me down. Or tries to. I've been around too long, seen too much to be intimidated by this two-bit punk. The company I keep is definitely the downside of what I do. Under other circumstances, I might play along. But this is my kid, not some cutie-pie along for the ride. For a split second, I wonder if maybe I'm making a mistake bringing her along. But that's the point, isn't it? To give her an honest look at the kind of life I lead and why she should run not walk back to her Ivy League life.

Finally, when he sees he's getting nowhere, he gives it up.

"Okay, okay. Let's talk turkey."

"That's what I'm here for," I say.

"You don't mind talking about this shit in front of..." He jerks his thumb in the general direction of Allison. "...the kid."

I look back at Allison. I can't tell if she's in shock or enjoying herself.

"Nope."

"Okay. Your funeral, if something goes wrong." He looks over my shoulder. "What's that they say? Little pinchers have big ears."

"Talk to me, not her."

"Okay, man. But if something goes wrong, it's gonna be because you screwed up, not me. When do we get started?"

I rub the thumb of my right hand against my index finger. At that moment, it occurs to me that maybe I ought to check to see if he's wired. I doubt it, but better safe than sorry. In this world I live in, you trust nobody. Someone once said, "You trust your mother, but you should still cut the cards." Even if he's not wired now, he might be next in the future. This'll put him on notice of how thorough I am.

"Mind if I pat you down?" I say.

"What's a matter, you don't trust me?"

"It's not you, Teddy. I don't trust anyone. Two things can happen if I do, and neither one of them is good."

I see from the expression on his face that he has no idea what I'm talking about, but that's fine. The last thing I want is someone who questions everything I say or do. He takes a couple seconds to register his defiance, then raises his arms above his head and wiggles the fingers of his left hand in a gesture that says, *Bring it on.*

So, I pat him down. He's clean.

"Satisfied?" he says with a smirk on his face. "You know, I'm a little insulted that you'd think I'd drop a dime on you."

"I'll live with it. Maybe you should too."

He shrugs. I feel like punching him in his fucking face. Maybe I would have if the kid hadn't been there.

"So," he says, "I need half of what we agreed on upfront. Otherwise, my people won't work."

"Find other people."

"Maybe I should. But truth is, it's been pretty slow and I could use the scratch."

"A quarter."

"You drive a hard bargain."

"Take it or leave it." I turn as if I'm going to walk away. I wink at the kid, and she drops her head, hiding the beginnings of a smile. Kid's got good instincts. What's this strange feeling I'm getting? Could it possibly be pride?

Teddy takes a step forward and places his hand on my shoulder.

"Hold on, man. Don't be so damn sensitive. We're negotiating here."

I stare at his beefy hand on my shoulder. He's got a pinky ring. Who the hell wears a pinky ring? That alone should be a good enough reason to walk away.

"How do I know you won't stiff me?"

"Ever hear of honor among thieves?"

He looks at me like I'm from another fucking planet. Like he's never heard anything like this before.

"I'll give you a few hundred up front. Think of it as a down payment. Good faith money. This is a contract, Teddy...." I reach for my wallet in my back pocket, open it, count out six fifties, and hand them to him. "Once you take this, we're officially in business together. Got it?"

He reaches out, grabs the fifties, counts them, snaps them, holds each one up against the bright, blue sky, then stuffs them in his pocket.

"I guess we're partners now," he says, reaching out his hand. I know he wants to shake on it, but I ignore the gesture.

I look back at Allison. It looks like she's frustrated, probably because she can't hear what's going down. Maybe this isn't such a good idea. Do I really want to be responsible for putting this kid on the road to a life of crime?

"No way I can do this alone."

"That's your business, Teddy. Hire whoever you want, but anything you pay them comes out of your pocket."

"You gotta be kidding."

"For that I'd have to have a sense of humor, Teddy. Do I look like I'm a funny guy?"

"Shit. Okay, when do I start?"

"The sooner the better." I reach into my pocket and pull out a sheet of paper folded in half and hand it to him.

"What's this?"

"A list of the places I want you pick up from."

He unfolds it and reads.

He whistles. "Whew, you don't fucking fool around, do you? Must be a dozen places here. You want me to hit all of them?"

"The more you hit the more you get."

"What do I do with the stuff once I have it?"

"You call the number at the bottom."

It's a burner phone.

"Once you deliver a load, you'll get paid for that load. No more advances."

"How do I get the dough?"

"I'll give you a place when you make the call. The quicker you work, the more you earn. Congratulations, you're now part of the American Dream."

"If I run into a problem...?"

"There aren't going to be any problems, Teddy. All you have to do is fulfill our contract. If there's a problem, it's your problem not mine, which means you deal with it. I'm only interested in results. You want to back out, now's the time."

He thinks for a moment. "Nah. I'm good."

As soon as we're back in the car, Allison says, "That looks like it was pretty rad, Pops. I couldn't hear anything, so what was it all about?"

"Business."

"Yeah, but what kind of business?"

"My kind."

"This sucks…"

"If I discuss this with you, we're past the point of no return."

"What's that mean?"

"In legal terms, it means you can be held complicit."

"Complicit to what?"

"Look, kid, before this goes any further, say the word and we head to the airport and I put you on a plane back home. No harm, no foul."

"I'm not ready to go home yet, so…"

"This isn't a negotiation, Allison. This is the life I've chosen for myself, and sometimes it falls into a grey area. I don't go out of my way to hurt people. But sometimes people get hurt as a result of what I'm involved in."

"Doesn't that bother you?"

"No. If you're asking if I have a conscience, the answer is, I don't know. I am what I am and I do what I do. I provide a service. I have a knack for seeing where the money is and figuring out how to get a piece of it for myself. And before we go any further, I need you to know something."

"What's that?"

"I'm not a good guy. What I'm doing now, taking you around with me, is not something a good guy would do."

"At least you're honest."

"I'm not about to sugarcoat this. I'm a con man. I'm only honest when it benefits me. You've got a lot of potential, kid. You've got a good head on your shoulders. You're good-looking. You've probably got a rosy future ahead of you. Not so much if you take one step into my world."

"Okay, how about as a spectator?"

"It might start out that way, but mark my words, eventually the vortex will suck you in."

"Gee, Pops, that's almost poetic. You know, it might have the opposite effect on me."

I can see it already. This kid is trouble, with a capital T. She has the gift of gab. She kinda reminds me of myself when I was that age. Maybe there is something to this genetic thing.

If I was a different person, I'd hustle her back into the car and head straight for the airport.

But I'm not, so I don't.

Josh
Dream a Little Dream for Me

I wake up suddenly, my body springing to an upright position.

Where am I?

Nothing looks familiar.

Panic sets in.

Am I losing my mind?

Am I in the midst of a dream?

A nightmare?

Why am I not in my own bed, my own room, my own apartment?

Have I been kidnapped?

I gently rock back and forth, hoping this will help regain my equilibrium.

Seconds pass.

Maybe it's minutes.

The answer is far more mundane. I'm disoriented because I'm spending yet another night in yet another nondescript hotel room.

It's still dark outside. The only light comes from an unknown outside source, bleeding in from between a gap in the curtains, casting dancing shadows in the room.

I lie back and stare at the ceiling.

It's only then that I realize I was startled awake from a very vivid dream. A dream unlike usual, a disjointed, hyperreal dream, filled with symbolism waiting to be decoded.

In my dream, Allison is with a couple men I've never seen before. She stands several steps behind them, watching as the two men are deep in conversation. The atmosphere is charged. I sense danger. But I'm not sure what the danger is and who is at risk.

I close my eyes and try to concentrate on the image of Allison and the two men, hoping to recreate the scene so I can become a part of it.

Unlike in the past, when I'm happy to move on, I don't give up. Eventually, I'm rewarded when I find myself hovering above them. I look around and see they're in the parking lot of a large mall. I see a Publix supermarket, a Target, a T-Mobile store, a building identified as Memorial Healthcare Systems.

I turn to see the Hollywood Hills Plaza sign.

I move back in to Allison and the two men, still in conversation. One of the men is wearing a frayed orange T-shirt and his potbelly hangs over faded jeans. He's unshaven and his hair, matted and dirty, is in disarray. He looks to be in his mid-thirties. The other man, perhaps in his late forties or early fifties, in much better physical shape, is wearing a yellow and green Hawaiian shirt, dark blue Bermuda shorts, and sandals.

The man in the orange T-shirt offers his hand, but the man in the Hawaiian shirt ignores it. He turns, and with Allison, they leave. I try to float higher so I can see where they're going. Perhaps to a car, which will help me locate them. Unfortunately, they simply disappear from sight.

I'm so anxious I can hardly breathe. I know Allison is close. She doesn't seem to be in distress or imminent danger. The man in the Hawaiian shirt must be her birth father.

The dream and subsequent vision energize me, giving me hope in finding her by providing me with clues.

I grab the small motel pad and jot down all the details from the dream I can remember.

I brush my teeth, splash water on my face, get dressed, and make myself a cup of motel-room coffee.

I take out my phone and type in "Hollywood Hills Plaza," then follow the instructions to the mall, which will be Ground Zero for my search.

It's a big world, but it seems to be getting smaller.

Daniel
The Sinful Pippin

"How's about listen to some tunes," she says in a way that makes it sound like an order, not a request. Frankly, I'm fine with it because I'm in no mood to answer any more questions. Maybe music will soothe both our savage breasts. I smile to myself when I say this because I'm sure this Ivy League chick sitting next to me would be impressed that I say to myself breasts not beasts.

Meanwhile, I'm still busy questioning my judgment in bringing her along. What did I think I would accomplish? Was it an unconscious move to make her reject me? To wash her hands of me and walk away? Or was it something else? I'm not sure.

"Hey, Pops," she says, snapping her fingers by the side of my head. "Anybody home?"

This gets my attention.

"Passenger's choice, right?" she chirps as she reaches out and fiddles with the radio dial.

"Go for it," I say. Anything to keep her busy while I try to figure out what my next move will be.

"Are you a Swiftie?" she asks.

"Would it surprise you to know I know exactly who you're referring to?"

"More like shocked."

"I don't reside in a Russian gulag, you know."

"I'm pretty sure the Russians, even in the gulags, know who Taylor Swift is. By the way, what's a gulag?"

"Oh my god! I've stumped the Ivy Leaguer. It's a Russian political labor camp."

"Oh, yeah, right. That's where they sent Aleksandr Solzhenitsyn, right?"

"If you say so."

She fiddles with the dial and finds a station playing Taylor Swift. At least I assume it's Taylor Swift, because after she's found it she starts bouncing around in her portion of the front seat, snapping her fingers. I adjust the rearview mirror and see she's dramatically mouthing the words of the song.

"What's this one called?" I ask.

"'Cruel Summer.' It's an oldie but a goodie. I thought you said you're a fan."

"Didn't say I was a fan. Said I know who she is."

"So, who's your favorite? Frank Sinatra? Tony Bennett? Barbra Streisand?"

"Very funny."

"No, seriously, who are your favorite singers or bands?"

"The Beatles, the Stones…and I like country music. Patsy Cline, Johnny Cash, Loretta Lynn…"

"I have no idea who any of those people are."

"Oh, and I left out Snoop Dogg and Busta Rhymes."

"Hilarious."

"I'm serious."

"Yeah, well, maybe we'll do karaoke some time and we can rap together."

"Absolutely."

She shakes her head, indicating I'm obviously a lost cause.

The song changes and she sings along to this one too. It's as if she doesn't have a care in the world. Maybe she doesn't. Evidently, what she's just witnessed hasn't soured her on me. Good news? Bad news? I'm not sure.

"What's this one?" I ask.

"Do you really want to know, or are you just making conversation?"

"Just making conversation."

"Ha!" she says, and she punches me on the arm. Not hard, but hard enough to know I've been hit.

"It's called 'Guilty as Sin,' and it's from her latest album."

If I were paranoid, I'd think even Taylor Swift was against me. But I'm not, so I chalk it up to coincidence.

"What is it you like about her music?"

She stops gyrating, and the expression on her face turns serious.

"She writes about *real* things. She writes from the heart. She doesn't hold back. She writes about stuff my generation is experiencing or thinking. You must have some singers like that."

I decide to have a little fun with her. "Afraid not. If I can dance to it, I like it. And the less meaning there is in the song, the better."

She looks at me like I'm some kind of pathetic loser. And then she breaks into a smile.

"Nice work, Pops. You had me there for a minute."

She goes back to "dancing" in her seat.

When the song ends, she reaches out and turns down the volume.

"So, what was that all about?"

"What?"

"That so-called meeting with that ridiculous man. He looks like an extra from *Goodfellas*."

"What do you know about *Goodfellas*?"

"It's one of Tony's favorite movies. He shows it to me at least once a year."

"Who's Tony, by the way?"

"My father."

My initial reaction is to stop the car, look her in the eye, and remind her in no uncertain terms, "*I'm* your father." But I don't. Not because it isn't technically true, but because, let's face it, I'm not her father. I'm just some random sperm donor dude.

"So?"

"So?"

"Are you going to avoid talking about what I just saw?"

"Maybe."

"You wanted me to see it. And I think I know why."

"Why?"

"Because you want me to be so disgusted with you that I disappear from your life."

"Exactly how would what you just saw accomplish that?"

"When I was a kid and tried playing dumb with my parents, Tony would always say, 'We didn't just fall off the turnip truck.' I didn't know what that meant until I was older and realized it was a way of saying the person wasn't dumb, or oblivious, but that they knew the score."

We approach another one of Florida's ubiquitous malls.

"Hey, there's a Baskin-Robbins. How 'bout we stop and grab a midafternoon snack?" I say.

"Are you trying to bribe me with ice cream? I'm not seven, you know."

"For future reference, would it work?"

"Absolutely not! I'd take your ice cream and then do whatever I was going to do."

I can't help smiling. What she's saying is that she's as corruptible as anyone else.

I'm beginning to wonder just how far this apple has fallen from my tree.

Josh
In Search of a Needle

As a result of the signage, it isn't difficult to track down the mall I saw in my vision, and now I'm standing in front of the Publix supermarket. It's only then that the enormity of the task ahead of me makes me realize how supremely ridiculous and unlikely this is.

I've found the haystack, but what about that needle? Just because Allie and those two guys were here recently doesn't mean they'll be back. So, what comes next? Do I really think going into every shop in the mall and showing her photo is going to bear fruit?

Of course not.

So, what's the alternative?

Driving around the area in ever-widening concentric circles?

Yeah, that sounds like it'll be real fruitful.

And so, what first appears to be a step forward might really be taking two steps back.

I'm stumped and stymied.

I get back in the car, turn up the air-conditioning, lean my head back on the headrest, and close my eyes.

I'm not tired. I'm much too wired for that. But as a last resort, I'm hoping something more recent will pop into my head. Something that'll point me in the direction of where Allie is at this very moment.

Suddenly, a sense of guilt overwhelms me. But guilt for what? And then it strikes me: I'm feeling guilty because putting this "ability" of mine to good use seems like cheating. I know that sounds ridiculous, but I can't help it. It's like athletes who "juice" in order to give themselves an advantage over the other players. Unless everyone juices, it's an unfair advantage. And why should this bother me? Because, once again, I have concrete evidence that I'm different from most everyone else. Not better. Just different.

Before I can examine this epiphany any better, there's a tapping at the window. I look up to see a man in a security guard's uniform motioning me to roll down my window. I oblige.

"Hey, buddy, you okay?"

"Yes. I'm fine."

"Thought maybe you'd passed out or something. Keeping your windows closed like this can be pretty dangerous, you know. Dogs, kids, people sometimes leave them in a car with the windows up on a hot day—like today. Happened a couple years ago when I was working security over at the Hollywood mall. Father gets out of the car, forgets he's got a kid in the backseat, locks the car with all the windows up, comes back a half hour later, and the kid's dead. Real tragedy. Made all the papers and TV. Wasn't me that found her, but even so it ain't something you're likely to forget. Just making sure nothing like that happens on my watch."

"Well, I'm fine. Just needed a little alone time to think some things out. But I appreciate your concern. Thanks for checking on me."

"No problem. You sure you're okay, sir?"

"I'm sure. Air-conditioning's on, and from now on, you can be darn sure I'll remember to crack a window."

He smiles, tips his cap, then continues on his rounds.

Should I have tipped him for making sure I'm alive? For potentially saving my life? I consider chasing after him and giving him a few bucks. But by the time I've got my hand on the doorknob, I've lost him. And the last thing I need now is someone to add to my list of people to find.

I have no idea what to do next, until I realize I should check in with Tony. So, I give him a call. The minute he picks up, I realize this is a mistake. I have no idea what I'm going to say. I consider hanging up, but he knows it's me and he'll just call me back. I am hoisted on my own petard.

"Hey, Tony, we haven't spoken for a while so..."

"This is unbelievable," he says excitedly. "I was just getting ready to call you."

"Really? What's up?"

"Just got an email from Allie."

"You're kidding.... What does she say?"

"Not much. Just that she's all right."

"Did she say where she is?"

"Nope. But at least we know she's alive."

"And you're sure it's from her?"

"Absolutely. She uses the nickname she gave me when she was a kid."

I'm curious as to what the nickname is, but it doesn't seem like the right time to ask.

"Actually, that's what I was calling about. I'm pretty sure I know where she is and who she's with."

"What? Where? Who?"

"Is Rachel with you?"

"No. I'm on location. Just checked my phone and saw the email."

"Did she send it to Rachel too?"

"Jeez, I never thought to check. Wait a sec..."

A moment later, he's back. "Nope. She only wrote me. Not Rachel."

"I'm not surprised."

"Why not?"

"I think she's still pissed at her."

"Pissed? Why?"

"I'll explain everything soon," I say, but I'm not sure he hears me, because he keeps talking.

"I'll give Rachel a call and tell her about the email."

"Don't hang up yet, Tony. Let's hold off on that a bit."

"She's Allie's mother, Josh. She's crazy with worry. She has a right to know everything, and as soon as possible."

"I know. I know. But I think we should know more before you talk to Rachel."

"I'm not getting you. Exactly what is it we need to know but don't? And where the hell is she?"

"I'm pretty sure she's in Florida, which is where I am."

"Florida? What the hell's going on?"

I'm not sure this is the right time to go into this, but there's no way I can avoid it now that Allie's been in touch with Tony.

"Are you somewhere you can talk privately?"

"I'll just step away." In the background, I hear him say, "Be right back, guys. Okay. Shoot."

"I'll try to make this as clear and concise as I can, Tony. But please, just listen. No third degree."

"You're asking a lot, J."

"I know. Here goes. When Allie got the report from that ancestry service, she somehow figured out her birth father was alive, that he hadn't been killed in an accident. She decided to track him down, which turns out wasn't so easy. Evidently, he was in some kind of trouble with the law a while back and then just disappeared. My guess is he went into Witness Protection. Allie was able to trace the family back to Chicago, where she found the guy's aunt. From there, she found his sister in Minneapolis."

"You've spoken to these people?"

"Yes. But getting information from them wasn't easy. Talk about family dysfunction. Anyway, she's in Florida now because that's where he is."

"Shit. This is a fucking nightmare that just seems to get worse. Do you know exactly where she is?"

"Not yet. But I'm pretty close."

"I'm coming down to help."

"I don't think that's a good idea, Tony. Give me a couple days to see what I can come up with, and maybe then it'll be good for you to come down. In the meantime, you can really help by digging up as much as you can about this guy." I give Tony the name I have but warn him that he's probably had several aliases.

"Use your contacts in law enforcement to get the scoop on this guy."

"Okay, but I still think coming down to help you is the way to go."

"I think you'd only get in the way. I think she's more likely to run if she sees you."

There's a moment of silence.

"Okay. Maybe you're right."

"I really think I am. And I promise to get back to you as soon I find her. But before you hang up, did you know about Allie's birth father being alive?"

"Absolutely not."

"Rachel never told you the accidental death story was bullshit?"

"Absolutely not. I swear. If she had, I would have urged her to come clean. I can't believe she's kept that from me. I have to ask myself why."

"That's between you and Rachel."

"You think I should confront her about it?"

"There's no way I'm getting in the middle of your marriage, Tony."

I hear him inhale deeply. There's nothing I want more than to get off this call. But before I do, I give in to the urge to patch things up between Tony and Rachel.

"I'm sure she had good intentions, Tony. We often do the wrong things for the right reasons. I think maybe we need to cut her some slack."

"Maybe you're right. But I really think I ought to come down there and help."

"You'll be a lot more help digging up all the information you can on this guy. That might even give us a clue as to where they are."

In the end, I'm able to talk Tony off the ledge and buy myself a day or two, which I'm hoping will be enough. And if not, then it probably is best for me to hand it over to Tony.

Meanwhile, all the pressure is on me to find Allie as soon as I can.

Allison
Father Knows Best

I'm not sure what just went down with Daniel and this skeezy-looking guy, but I have to admit it was kind of exciting.

I'm dying to ask him about it. But I don't want it to come off like I'm minding his business. Besides, I'm pretty sure he won't tell me anything. And so, I keep my mouth shut on the ride home. And believe me, that's not easy. Tony once bet me I couldn't remain quiet for thirty minutes. It was right after I'd asked him for money to go to a Beyoncé concert.

"Never heard of her," he said, but I knew he was just saying that to get a rise out of me. Tony's one of the smartest people I know. In that huge brain of his he's able to collect all kinds of information, including keeping track of everything cultural. He reads four newspapers a day: *The New York Times*, *The Washington Post*, *The New York Post*, and *The Los Angeles Times*, not to mention all kinds of magazines like *The New Yorker*, *Vanity Fair*, *The New York Review of Books*, and *New York Magazine*.

Tony loves teasing me, and to be honest, I've grown to like it, because I know it's his way of telling me how much he cares about me.

"She's really great. And how many chances am I going to have to see her in person?"

"Gee, maybe I should check her out."

"I'll download some of her music for you. But there's nothing like seeing her in person."

"How much are tickets, Allie?"

"Well, they're completely sold out, so I guess whatever a scalper is selling them for—maybe a hundred dollars?"

He smiled.

"When I was a kid, I could see people like Paul Simon for free in Central Park."

"That was back in the Dark Ages. Right? Before music videos, right?"

"Tell you what," he said as he opened his wallet and counted out five twenties, which he called Jacksons, "if you can say nothing for half an hour, this is yours."

"You mean all I have to do is keep quiet for thirty minutes?"

"That's right."

"Sure. I'll just go to my room and…"

"No way, Jose. You've got to be with other people. Like dinner tonight. If you can sit there for thirty minutes without saying a word, the money's yours. And, as a bonus, I'll drive you to wherever the concert is and I'll pick you up when it's over."

I think I made it to the twenty-minute mark, but Tony swears I didn't even break double digits. By the way, he still gave me the money, and he did chauffeur me back and forth.

I can't hold back anymore. Big surprise, right? "So, what's next on the agenda?"

Daniel looks at me and smiles.

"Haven't given it much thought."

"You know, you don't have to entertain me. I just kinda like hanging out. So, if I wasn't here, what would you be doing."

"Plotting and scheming."

"Excuse me?"

"Just kidding. I don't plot and I don't scheme. I make it up as I go along."

"I wish I knew what you're talking about. Like what *it* is."

"Who was it who said 'I am what I am'?" he says, cracking a huge smile.

"I think that's from the Bible, actually."

"How do you know anything about what's in the Bible?"

"Sunday school. Not that I paid all that much attention. But sometimes, information soaked in. No one knows this, so you've got to promise not to tell anyone..." He crosses his heart. "I used to cut Sunday school all the time. Never got caught. Not even once."

"Jeez, it's like I'm sitting next to Public Enemy Number One. Very Impressive. How do you account for that?"

"I guess I'm just good at keeping secrets."

While we're talking, I'm checking Google on my phone.

"Here we go," I say. "'According to the Hebrew Bible, in the encounter of the burning bush (Exodus 3:14), Moses asks what he's to say to the Israelites when they ask what gods (Elohiym) have sent him to them, and YHWH replies, "I am who I am," adding, "Say this to the people of Israel, 'I am has sent me to you.'"'"

"I was thinking more along the lines of Popeye," says Daniel.

"Who's Popeye?" I say. I think I've heard of him before, but I'm not sure who he is.

"Are you kidding? What's the deal with your generation? It's like anything and everything before you were born is a total mystery. Where's your knowledge of cultural history?"

"I think maybe I was absent that day."

He laughs at my little joke. I think maybe I'm starting to grow on him.

"So?"

"I know this place near the beach where we can have a drink."

"You mean like margaritas and mojitos?"

"You old enough to drink?"

"Of course."

"I hope you have your ID with you."

"I have *an* ID with me."

"What's that supposed to mean?"

"To paraphrase the Bible, it means what it means."

He laughs. "You're a slick one, aren't you?"

I'm not sure how he means this, but I'm taking it as a compliment.

"For someone who skipped out on Sunday School, you seem to be very familiar with the Bible."

"It's probably that photographic memory for the spoken word thing."

We pull into a parking lot adjacent to the beach. We park, and Daniel leads the way onto a pier with a restaurant midway across it.

When the waitress comes to take our order, Daniel orders a frozen margarita, no salt.

"I'll have a pina colada."

"Sorry, hon, but I'll have to see some identification."

"Sure thing," I say, taking out my wallet and showing her my fake ID. Well, it's not really fake. It's just not mine.

She takes a quick look—actually, I don't even think she pays attention—smiles, then hands it back to me.

"Anything else?" she asks.

"I think we're good for now," says Daniel.

As soon as she walks away, he says, "Where'd you get that thing?"

"Thing?"

"That ID. That's not your picture on it."

"Well, that's kind of a funny story."

"I love funny stories."

"Okay. Well, a friend of mine was in the police station one day and she saw this ID. sitting on someone's desk and she, like, grabbed it and put it in her pocket. She used it for a couple years, and then she turned twenty-one and didn't need it anymore. She was going to return it to the police, but we kinda talked her out of that. So, she gave it to me. You know, like a hand-me-down."

"Lemme see it."

I hand it to him.

"The picture looks nothing like you, kiddo."

"It doesn't, right?"

"The girl is Asian."

"That's the thing. When these places ask for it, they really don't look at it too close. All they're interested in is the date of birth."

He smiles and shakes his head. For some reason, it kinda feels like I'm scoring points with him.

Because we're on a pier, surrounded on both sides by the water, it feels like we're on a ship in the middle of the ocean.

When the waitress, who doesn't look much older than me, comes back, Daniel asks her to bring us chips and salsa.

"So, what do you think?" he asks.

"About what?"

"About me. About the situation."

"Oh, well, it's like, I've got to get used to it. I mean, a week ago I didn't even know you existed. And now, well, here you are."

"And here you are." He raises his glass. I raise mine. "Here's to our new life," he says. We clink glasses.

"So, have you thought about what you want to do with the rest of your life?" he asks.

"When I was a kid, I wanted to be all kinds of things. A veterinarian. A marine biologist. A lawyer. An actress..."

"And now?"

I shrug. "The way I figure, I don't have to commit to anything now, right? I'm taking all kinds of courses and I'm hoping eventually it'll kinda reveal itself."

"Good plan. I'm sure you'll be a big success, no matter what you choose," he says. I can't be sure if he's serious or not.

He raises his glass. I raise mine. We clink them together again.

"Of course, the way the world's going, any choice I make might be superfluous."

"I hear ya," he says. "So, what do you think of me?"

"You're putting me on the spot."

"I am."

"I don't know. You seem okay. But I don't want to make any snap decisions."

"So, as of now it could go either way?"

I laugh. "That's right. So, you better be on your best behavior."

"Not my strong suit," he says.

He's silent for a few moments. He looks like he's in deep thought. Finally, he says, "I've got a proposition for you."

"What's that?"

"Well, it's the end of your semester, right?"

"Pretty much."

"Have you made any plans for the summer?"

"I've been looking for a job, but the only thing I can find so far is as a waitress at one of the local country clubs."

"How do you feel about that?"

I make a face.

"That's what I figured. How about this? I hire you as, like, an intern."

"You're kidding, right?"

"Dead serious."

"Like, what would I be doing?"

"All kinds of things. You're a smart kid, you present very well, and I think, from what I've seen, you can handle yourself on your feet."

"What kind of situations would you be putting me in?"

"See? That's just what I mean. You don't just jump into things before you know what you're getting into. You're not impulsive."

"I don't want to do anything...like...illegal."

"You think what I do is illegal?"

"I don't know what you do, but I would hope it's not."

"Here's what I think, Allison. I know we're related by blood, but not knowing you exist till now might be a good thing in terms of the relationship we forge in the future. What I mean is, I don't see you as a daughter..."

"Good, 'cause I've already got a mother and father."

"Of course. And that's never going to change. I'm seeing you as a person. A person who has an incredible amount of talent and potential. I think working with me—not for me—you'll learn things about the world, about people, about yourself, that'll hold you in good stead. Even if it's only for a few months."

"I'd have to move down here?"

"I move around, kiddo. You'd come with me wherever I happen to be."

"How would I afford that?"

"I'd take care of all your expenses and you'd get a salary, of course."

"How much?"

He smiles.

"See? You ask all the right questions. How's, like, two-fifty a week? To start."

"I think three would be better."

He laughs.

"Okay. You win. Three hundred a week, it is."

"Cash?"

"Of course. Cash is king."

I reach my hand across the table and we shake on it.

"These are delicious. I could go for another," I say.

"Not while you're working for me," he says.

Daniel

You're Hired!

It isn't something I planned.

It was all instinct. And who knows if it was blood talking or simply a way to keep the kid in my life. But I'd like to think it was because I see something in her that could work to my advantage. After all, I'm not exactly known for selfless acts. I'm more of a me, myself, and I kind of guy.

And if I believed in God, which I don't, I'd probably think this kid showing up on my doorstep was a divine gift.

In the end, the reason doesn't matter. I see a road in front of me and I take it. If it turns out to be the wrong road, well, I just turn around and take a different road.

Oh, and it doesn't hurt that the kid seems so enthusiastic.

Of course, there are details to work out. One of the first is figuring out how to deal with the elephant in the room by the name of Rachel. That's what I need to address first.

"So, where do we stand with your mother?" I ask.

"What do you mean?"

"I'm assuming you still haven't gotten in touch with her."

"You assume wrong. I sent an email to Tony, telling him I'm okay."

"Did you tell him where you were and who you're with?"

"Nope."

Can she hear that sigh of relief?

"What about your mother?"

"I'm sure he'll tell her."

"Why didn't you write or call her?"

"Because I'm still not sure how I feel about what she's done. Lying to me all these years. I have to work that out before I want to have any contact with her. But..." She hesitates. "I still love her, and I don't want her to worry about me."

"Do you really think they're going to stop looking for you just because you told them you're okay?"

"Course not. But I don't know how they'd find me. I mean, it's not like I'm leaving a trail of breadcrumbs. Besides, you don't want me to tell her I'm with you, do you?"

"If you do, she'll have the fucking FBI, Interpol, the CIA, and the KGB out looking for you. And she'd probably hire a team of hitmen to take me out of the picture."

She smiles. "I think you're exaggerating...maybe only a little bit? Besides, I'm over eighteen, and she can't control my life anymore. So, what kinds of things would I be doing? I mean, if you intend on sending me on coffee runs and taking care of your dry cleaning, you've got the wrong girl."

"Don't worry. I've got much more important things for you to do."

"Like?"

"Anxious, aren't you?"

"I kinda want to see what I've got myself into."

"Smart girl. Okay, how about we put you on the payroll right now."

"I like the sound of that. Oh, by the way, what do you want me to call you? Boss? Sir? Pops? Daddy-O? Daniel?"

"What say I give that some thought and for the time being, let's just go with Daniel or Danny."

She salutes. "Aye, aye, sir. I mean Danny. Hey, Sir Danny. That has a certain ring to it, right?"

Much to my surprise, I'm actually enjoying this.

"Okay, here's what I want you to do. I've got a deal pending, and I need you to put together as much information as you can on the American eel."

"The American eel? Are you serious?"

"As a heart attack."

"I didn't even know there was such a thing."

"See, you're already learning something new—and you didn't have to sit in a stuffy classroom to learn it."

"Why do you need to know about that?"

"This is a good time to set ground rules. Number one, you don't question what I ask you to do. You don't have to do it if you think it's illegal or immoral, or you have another good reason. That's fine. But I need you to know that this isn't a partnership. I make all the decisions. That doesn't mean you can't ask questions. It just means I don't necessarily have to answer them."

"Just one rule?"

"Nope. There are plenty. But let's just go with one at a time. We'll deal with them if and when the situation arises. You in or out?"

"Before I give you an answer, let me make sure I've got this right. You won't make me do anything I think is illegal or immoral, or if it makes me feel icky, right?"

"Right. Although I'm a little vague about the 'icky' thing. But yes. I will not make you do anything you're morally or ethically opposed to."

"Like clubbing baby seals?"

"I didn't know there was such a thing, but if there is, yes. No clubbing baby seals."

"And I can ask questions, but you don't have to answer them, right?"

"Right."

She thinks for a moment and then extends her hand. I shake it.

"Welcome to the firm, Allison. Now about that American eel thing. I need you to find out everything you can about them. And I'd like you to get it done as quickly as possible."

"Okay. One more thing. Where do I stay?"

"As long as we're down here, you can stay with me—that second bedroom is yours. When I move on, I'll make sure you have a place of your own. And I'll be paying for that."

"Sounds good, Pops." She smiles. "Whoops. I mean Daniel. Oh, and one more thing."

"Yes?"

"When do I get my first paycheck?"

Josh
Needle in the Haystack

I feel it.

Allison is close.

Question is, how do I find her?

After not too much thought, I come up with a plan: The only way to find her is not to look for her, the needle in this haystack, but instead look for the man who is her biological father.

I find him, I find her.

For this, I can fall back on the lessons I learned as a journalist. But the key might be to harness and learn how best to use this thing I have.

I'm in uncharted territory. If I'm going to make this work, I have to "learn" how to use what I have. In effect, I have to attend ESP school, and to do this I have to find a teacher. Someone who shares this strange "power." Someone willing to teach me, in a short amount of time, how to use this "gift" more efficiently. Instead of garbage in, garbage out, it will be pertinent information in, pertinent information out.

A decade or so ago, I was asked to write a profile of a woman who worked with the cops to solve crimes. A clairvoyant. At first, I was reluctant to take the assignment. For one thing, it was much too close to what I'd been experiencing, and since I was doing everything I could to deny this "ability," it would be counterproductive to get involved in this kind of story. But as a freelance writer, one of the first lessons you learn is to never say no.

And so, I didn't.

Her name was Evelyn. She was a New Jersey housewife, mother of three, who came to her "power" rather late in life. In her late thirties, she was awakened by extremely violent, startlingly vivid dreams. They were so intense they remained with her for days, sometimes weeks. One day, after a series of these disturbing dreams, she came across a newspaper story about a woman who'd been violently assaulted and killed. Many of the details seemed eerily familiar to Evelyn, and eventually she realized this was because she recognized some of the details from dreams she was having. At first, she thought it was coincidental, but when the dreams kept coming, gaining in intensity and detail, she realized it was more than that. She was perplexed, of course, but filed it away as being one of those weird intersections between the real world and the dream world.

Several weeks later, Evelyn read a newspaper story about a missing woman. That night, she had a dream about the woman, a dream in which she not only "witnessed" the woman's brutal murder, but "saw" where the body of the missing woman was.

She decided to go to the police, knowing full well they'd probably dismiss her as either crazy or an attention seeker. But when she described the area where she "saw" the body, they checked it out and, sure enough, there it was: the body of the murdered woman.

Over time, the police began to trust Evelyn and came to her with especially vexing cases. One involved a young woman police believed had run away. Evelyn thought otherwise. She was certain the woman had been murdered and her body buried deep in the desert. A year later, the young man who killed her confessed and led police to her grave in…the desert.

Eventually, these visions came to Evelyn while awake. When I interviewed her, she made the audacious claim that she was able to *control* the visions.

My profile of Evelyn never ran. I was told it was a space issue, but I think the magazine got cold feet, afraid the story would hurt their "high" journalistic reputation. I tried selling it elsewhere, but had no luck, and so it sits in my computer's memory.

I haven't been in touch with Evelyn for almost ten years, but now it occurs to me she might be able to help. I email her and ask if she'll FaceTime with me. I hear back immediately. "Of course. Is now good?"

Within minutes, we're staring at each other through our respective phones.

"Thanks so much for doing this, Evelyn. You know, I'm still pissed they killed that story. But that's not why I called."

"I think I know why you called, Joshua."

"You haven't added mindreading to your resume, have you, Evelyn?"

She laughs. "No time for that, I'm afraid. But I do know why you're calling."

"You do?"

"Yes. You want to share something about you. Something that's very troubling for you."

"How could you possibly…?"

"I knew you had the *gift* within the first ten minutes we met."

"You did?"

"I did."

"Why didn't you say something?"

"I knew you were struggling with it, and I wasn't going to interfere with that process. Because that's what it is. A process. I'm guessing that finally, after all these years, you're ready to come to grips with it."

"I am."

"The only thing that surprises me is that it's taken this long. I could tell when we met that you were aware of what you could do but were frightened by it. You're not alone. To outsiders it seems this ability we have, which, by the way, is just an extension of the other five senses, is a cool gift. We know better. It doesn't make life any simpler. In fact, it makes it more difficult. And complicated. But I'm not telling you anything you don't already know. Now, how can I help you?"

"I remember you telling me you learned how to control this…" I struggle for the right word.

"Let's just refer to it as a 'gift.'"

"I was hoping you could give me some information and maybe a few tips."

"For another story you're working on?"

"No. This is personal. I need a little guidance."

"There's no better use of my time than to help someone in need, Joshua. So, before I answer your questions, I need to know a few things about your visions. How do you get them? When do you get them? How detailed are they? Do they include sound? Smells? Are they stills, like a Kodak moment, or are they animated, like a video?"

After answering her questions, I feel like a tremendous weight has been lifted. It's the first time I've ever been able to speak with someone who knows what I'm dealing with from her personal experience. It's like we're part of a very exclusive club. Her responses are simple and to the point.

"You're a very raw talent, Joshua. You have an amazing ability, but you're in kindergarten in terms of knowing what to do with it and how to use it."

"Exactly. I need to graduate to first grade."

She proceeds to give me a master class. Before talking to her, I'd always thought what I got was what I got. But Evelyn insists there's so much more available to me, if I dive deeper.

"I'm not sure what you mean."

"For instance," Evelyn explains, "you tell me you see a green car. I'd say, 'Well, that's real helpful, honey, but what can anyone do with that information?' You have to focus on the details, what's going on around you. For instance, there are thousands of green cars. So, I'd ask what kind of car is it? Is there anything about it that would make it stand out? Bumper stickers? Dents? See what I mean?"

"I do."

"Our ability is interactive," she says, meaning I can literally "enter" a scene, as if I'm actually there—which I have experimented with a little in the past. Furthermore, I can "control it," though I can't turn these visions on or off at will. I'm not an "open" channel. "You're not *on* all the time, Joshua. Sometimes it comes out of the blue. Other times, you can coax it along. Other times, you'll draw a blank no matter what you do. It's more of an art than a science."

She tells me things I already know, like when I shake a person's hand, I'm not going to pick up anything. "It doesn't work that way. We're not trained seals, Joshua. What you must remember is that like fingerprints or snowflakes, we're all slightly different. What works for me might not work for you, and vice versa. In the end, you have to find your own way. And if you're diligent and serious about it, you will. It'll be frustrating at times. It's not infallible. You'll be wrong sometimes. And I'm sure you'll be tempted to give up. I hope you don't, but if you do, please, feel no guilt. Having this ability can be a privilege, but it can also be a curse. It's not right for everyone, and if that's the case with you, if you think you'll be happier tamping it down, then please, I urge you to do that."

"If I choose that path, will it just disappear?"

"What you're really asking is, 'Will I ever be normal again?'"

I laugh. "Yes."

"I'd like to say yes, honey, but the truth is, I don't know because I decided rather than fight it to embrace it. But if you take that path, let me know how it goes."

"I will."

"Oh, and one more thing before we hang up. And you don't have to answer this, but is there a special reason for this call?"

I want to be truthful, but I don't want to invade Tony and Rachel's privacy. So, I make my answer as generic as possible.

"The daughter of a good friend is missing and I'm trying to help find her."

"I see. I wish you luck, and if there's any way I can help…"

"You've helped plenty already, Evelyn. I truly appreciate taking the time…"

"Please. I'm happy to do it."

We end the conversation forty-five minutes after it begins. While we speak, I'm taking copious notes, four pages' worth, which I'll go through later. Armed with this information, and a newfound confidence about what is possible, I leave the woo-woo world and do a deep dive into the real world of Daniel.

Just as I'm into my research, Tony calls. He's put together a pretty impressive dossier on Daniel, who now seems to have taken Peacock as his latest last name.

"He's had several names or aliases over the years, but this seems to be his latest. The dude's a bit of a shadow who shuns the spotlight, but I was able to get enough information to maybe help you find him."

Tony gives me a pretty good profile, despite a three-year gap where he seems to have been swallowed up by the earth. "He was in the Witness Protection Program," says Tony. "Usually, that information is off-limits, but I have a contact over there—we did a story on them a few years ago—so I reached out to her. I had to swear secrecy, of course, and you will too."

"What happened?"

"I don't have the details, but evidently, he didn't exactly leave of his own volition. My source says he was involved in something illegal and when they found out, they turned him loose. That was four or five years ago. Evidently, it's not unusual. These folks are the proverbial fish out of water, and they feel trapped. So, they either opt out voluntarily or they wind up doing something illegal. For many of these people the only thing they know is breaking the rules."

"Do you know where they stashed him?"

"Somewhere in the Southwest. She wouldn't be specific, but if I had to guess I'd say the Scottsdale-Phoenix area."

Tony feeds me a little more information about Peacock, but nothing that'll help me find him now. And not much that allows me to learn more about what he's like as a human being.

"There are a couple ways to track someone. By their credit history—assuming they use credit cards rather than cash—and through their cell phone usage. It's amazing how much information is packed into those smartphones. You can pretty much construct a person's entire life. Both methods are pretty much beyond the capabilities of civilians like us. But I was able to call in a couple favors—unofficially, of course. Through his credit card use, he was tracked down to Florida. He rented an Airbnb in Hollywood. I'll text you the address."

"Perfect."

"A few days ago, he purchased a ticket from Minneapolis to Fort Lauderdale, which is the closest airport to Hollywood. I'm thinking it was for Allie. I've got a call into someone I know at Delta…"

"I'm pretty sure she's down here with him."

"You think you can track him down now?"

"Sure," I say, surprising myself at my bravado.

He hesitates a moment. I can practically hear him thinking.

"Listen, J, I'm coming down there. I can't stand being up here and not being able to do anything. And believe me, it's no picnic being around Rachel. Especially since I'm keeping shit from her."

"I can't stop you from coming down, Tony, but I strongly advise against it. I understand how you feel. I'm sure I'd feel the same way. But…"

"Okay. Okay. You're probably right. I've got a couple things to finish up work-wise, but I've already booked a flight for the day after tomorrow. Email me where you're staying, and I'll see if I can book a room there."

I'm a little pissed, but I certainly understand how he feels and, if I were in the same position, I'm sure I'd be on the next plane down.

"I've got a comfortable couch where I'm staying, and I can pick you up at the airport as soon as you send me all the info."

And so, the conversation ends, leaving me two days to locate Peacock and Allie on my own. Tony's a bit of a hothead, and I'm afraid he'll get in the way, so the more I can get done before he arrives, the better.

Daniel
All A's

I give the kid an assignment and by breakfast she presents me with a detailed report, which she hands to me handwritten, on three pages of yellow legal-pad paper.

"Hope you can read my handwriting. I would've printed it out, but you don't have a printer here."

I give it a quick look and can see how much work she's put into it.

"How late were you up working on this?"

"I don't know. Maybe till around two. But that's nothing. I've pulled actual all-nighters. So, I'm kinda used to it."

I take another look.

"Where'd you get such good penmanship?"

Her face reddens.

"I've kept journals for years. I've worked on my handwriting so I could actually read what I write. I hope it's what you're looking for. I know you wanted it quick, so I'm sorry it might be a little, like, all over the place."

I sit down on the couch and begin to read her report.

"The American eel, also known as Anguilla rostrata, is a facultative catadromous fish found on the eastern coast of North America. It lives in fresh water and estuaries and only leaves these habitats to enter the North Atlantic Ocean to make its spawning migration to the Sargasso Sea which is their natural home. (fyi, there's a wonderful novel by Jean Rhys called Wild Sargasso Sea. You should read it sometime).

The American eel is found along the Atlantic coast, including the tributaries of the Chesapeake Bay, the Delaware River and the Hudson River, and as far north as the Saint Lawrence River.

The eels begin life the length of an index finger and the circumference of a bean sprout. They're translucent, like jelly-fish. Its nickname is glass eels, but they're also known as elvers.

Elvers mature into adults that can be as much as two to three-feet in length, and they have the girth and coloring of a slimy bicycle tire.

As the water warms up, hundreds of millions of the glass eels arrive each spring on the coast near Maine.

In an effort to preserve the species, elver fishing without a license is a federal crime. There are approximately four hundred and twenty-five licensed elvermen who are allowed to harvest slightly more than 7,500 pounds of them during a strictly regulated fishing season, which runs from late March to early June.

Maine is the only state that has a major number of elvers. They can also be found off the coast of South Carolina, which has a much smaller number of elvers.

Once caught, the baby eels are shipped live, mostly to Hong Kong, in clear plastic bags of water and pure oxygen, very much the same way goldfish are "packaged" for kids' fish bowls.

The American eel is a delicacy and they're sometimes worth more than $2,000 a pound, because of their high value to Asian aquaculture companies. They're of extreme importance to the worldwide supply chain for Japanese food.

Eels are also in demand because they can help reduce wrinkles, improve skin, hair and nail condition due to its high collagen content.

Japan, which consumes more than seventy percent of the global eel catch, consumes at least 100,000 tons of freshwater eel, or unagi, which is enjoyed kabayaki style—butterflied, marinated and grilled."

I look up from the report.

"This is incredible, kiddo. You really nailed it. You've already earned your first week's salary."

She turns a light shade of pink. "It's not like it was a difficult assignment. Heck, you could have like fed it into ChatGPT and pretty much gotten the same thing, only, like, a zillion times quicker."

I stand up and give her a hug.

"So, like, why do you need this?"

"I'm considering investing in a little deal."

"Selling eels? Hope you don't actually have to touch any."

"I'm kind of a middleman."

"Exactly how does that work?"

I smile and say nothing. If the kid's going to stick around, I have to set boundaries. Put limits on what she knows. Not only to protect me, but also to protect her.

When she sees she's not going to get an answer, she smiles and says, "Need-to-know basis?"

"Exactly."

"Okay, so what's next?"

I put my hand in my pocket, take out the car keys, and flip them to her. She catches them, like a pro.

"What's this for?"

"I've got a few calls to make. Why don't you hop in the car and take a spin. Maybe to the beach. Get some use out of that new bathing suit. Or the mall. Wherever."

"Really?"

"Really."

"But what if I get into an accident?"

"Got your license?"

"Yes."

"How long you been driving?"

"Since I was sixteen."

"Been in any accidents?"

"Not really."

"Then I'd say the odds are with me."

"But what if something you know, like, happens? I mean, I'm not on the paperwork. They might think I've stolen it."

"Don't think so negative. You're putting bad juju into the air. We'll deal with it if it happens, which it won't. Listen, kiddo, you've got to stop making up excuses as to why you should or shouldn't do things. You're young. Now's the time to take chances. You know the saying 'Live fast, die young, leave a good-looking corpse'?"

"Nope."

"Know what it means?"

"I can guess."

I smile. She's just exhibited two very important qualities: She's not afraid to ask questions, and she's smart enough to figure things out without me having to waste time explaining every little thing.

I rip off a piece of the yellow-lined paper and scribble down the number of one of my burners. I hand it to her. "Here. Now you've got my number. Give a call if you get in any trouble. Just don't get into any trouble, okay?"

She smiles.

"By the way, who said that good-looking corpse thing?" she asks.

"No idea. But someone who knew the score."

Allison
How to Win Friends and Influence People

Daniel has given me plenty of food for thought.

I actually enjoy doing this research project for him. It's similar to stuff I've done so many times before, and yet it's different because this has a point to it. I'm not sure what that point is, but I know there is one, otherwise Daniel wouldn't have asked me to do it. And I'm guessing if I stick around long enough, I'll find out what it is. Doing schoolwork is more about preparing for the future, with very little connection to the here and now. Supposedly, it gives us skills to use in the real world. But what if you've already got those skills? Isn't it time to use them? Isn't it time to get into the *real world*?

Something tells me I can learn more from Daniel in a week than I can learn in a semester or maybe more of college. So, if this works out, why should I even go back to school? I mean, if I choose to drop out, it's not like I can't go back later, if I think I've made a mistake. Look at athletes. They used to have to go through four years of college. Now that's changed. Some of them don't even make it to college before they turn pro. And most of them don't spend four years in school before joining a professional team, right?

But all this is worthless if Daniel decides I can't cut it. So, if I want to stick around, l have to make sure I perform so well he can't do without me. That would make me indispensable. And when that time comes, I can make the decision whether I stick or boot it.

The longer I stick around, the more time there is for me to get to know him better. And maybe, since I've got half his DNA, I'll learn stuff about myself I wouldn't otherwise been able to know. And I'm not just talking about, like, health stuff. More like that nurture-versus-nature stuff we learned about in school.

Of course, Mom and Dad will kill me if I drop out. And honestly, that'd make me real sad. Disappointing them, I mean. And maybe they'd be right. But maybe not. The bottom line is, if I make a mistake, I make a mistake. Like Tony always says, "That's why they put erasers on the ends of pencils."

Daniel obviously loves what I've given him. As soon as he finishes reading it, he pulls out his wallet and counts off two one-hundred-dollar bills and a fifty—he calls them Grants and Benjamins—and hands them to me. I can't ever remember having that much cash in my hands. Actually, I can't ever remember seeing a Benjamin before. My first thought is, *What am I going to do with this?* I mean, it's not like I can walk into a store and buy a candy bar with a hundred-dollar bill, right?

Daniel must sense my concern because he asks, "Kiddo, you have a checking account, right?"

"Uhm, I've got a savings account at Chase that my mom set up, but I don't think I have a checking account. I mean, who uses checks anymore, right? I pretty much use my credit or debit card."

"If you've got a savings account, chances are you've got a checking account too. What I'd do if I were you, and this is just a suggestion because it's your dough and you can do anything you want with it, I'd put the money in the bank, maybe half in checking and half in savings."

"You know, like, I can put it in one and transfer it electronically, if I have to?"

"Right."

He's probably giving me good advice, but I think I'm just going to hang onto the cash. It makes me feel pretty good to have that much cash in my wallet.

"What's next?" I ask.

"Good question."

"And the answer is…?"

"I gotta think this out, kiddo. Right now, I'm leaning toward sending you back home, finishing the week or so left in the semester, and then we'll figure out the rest from there. Meanwhile, you'll still be on the…" He smiles. "Payroll."

"Cool." Though I can't say I like the going-back-to-school part.

"While we're at it, Allison, my timetable's been pushed up. My work down here is pretty much done and I'll be heading up to Maine."

"Anything to do with this elver stuff?"

He smiles. "Maybe."

"So, won't you need to have me around. I mean, like, with you?"

"Haven't thought about it."

"I can be a lot more help to you if I'm with you. Besides, I know what you do is pretty secret, and if I'm not with you…"

I don't have to finish the sentence because before I can he says, "I get it. Look, I've got some stuff to take care of around here, so why don't you take the car and go shopping, do a little sightseeing, or go to the beach again. You won't have very many other opportunities, unless you're considering resettling down here amongst the old Jews, snowbirds, and retirees."

"Are you trying to get rid of me?"

He laughs. "If I were, I wouldn't be subtle about it. I'd just tell you to get lost."

"Good to know," I say.

Josh
Stakeout

The clock is ticking.

Make that two clocks.

One counts down the hours till Tony, who's booked a flight to Fort Lauderdale tomorrow, arrives. The other clock ticks off how long Allison remains in place.

The address Tony texts is a two-story garden apartment complex on Wiley Street, adjacent to a golf course.

Is this where the search for Allison will end? Will I finally be able to get back to my own life? Which leads to a far more troubling question: What will that life be now that the gates to my subconscious have flung wide open?

I choose not to get ahead of myself. Instead, I try focusing on what's directly in front of me. And so, with little time to waste, I hop in my rental, double-check my phone for directions, and head off to Wiley Street.

I'm not quite sure what I'll do once I get there. It doesn't seem productive knocking on every door. What would I ask? *Any chance,* pointing to a photo of Allison, *you've seen this young woman, along with a much older man going in and out of one of these apartments?*

Instead, I decide to park across the street from the building entrance and wait for Allie to go in or out of the building.

With no idea how long I'll have to sit there in my car, I try to anticipate all my needs. I find the nearest Publix and pick up a couple sandwiches and a half a dozen bottles of Gatorade. One of the bottles will be repurposed as a receptacle to pee in. Next, I hit the local CVS, where I purchase a thermos, packages of plastic utensils, napkins, and small paper plates, as if I'm going on a picnic. Then, I find an ice machine and fill the thermos with ice.

I make sure my iPad is fully juiced, then find the closest electronic store, where I purchase one of those extra power devices. Nothing worse than running out of power on a stakeout, only to find there is something worse: crippling boredom.

I grab a spot across the street from the complex with a good view of the front entrance, park, find the local NPR radio station, and make myself as comfortable as possible.

I check my watch. It's a little after 10 a.m. I'll hang out till I can't take it anymore, or 5 p.m. Whichever comes first.

And so, both clocks begin to tick.

Daniel
Peacock and Daughter

"Loose lips sink ships."

That's what posters warned the Allies during World War II.

Which explains why I work alone. Trust no one, because trust is the beginning of the end. Or the end of the beginning. Better to outsource. But even this only when absolutely necessary.

This longstanding rule might have to change, because with Allison's arrival on the scene, certain possibilities become apparent. And so, despite all the reasons to send her back to where she came from, there are a few good ones to hold onto her. At least for a while:

1. She's smart as a whip.
2. Her age and the image she projects—pretty, innocent, earnest, honest—can work to my advantage.
3. She's blood, and for that reason she might be more inclined to have my back (not that I ever turn it).

So far, she's done nothing to make me think she can't be an asset, and yet having a partner will take some getting used to.

She doesn't seem inclined to confide in her mother, but at some point, that'll change. And so, I have to be careful about what she knows or can learn about me and what I do. This means living with the possibility that everything she sees or hears might be shared with Rachel. So, moving forward, I'll be performing a very delicate balancing act. I have to appear to be respectful of their relationship, while at the same time do my best to subtly create a wedge between them.

While the kid's out doing whatever she's doing, I begin to clear up the dangling threads here in Florida. Once this operation is in full swing, it should take only a week or so before all the barrels of cooking grease reach their destination. At that point, I'll cash in, cut ties with the operation, and I'll head up to Maine to make the necessary contacts for the American Eel Caper. I'll bring the kid up there with me and make sure I find tasks that'll keep her busy and challenge her.

There's no way Rachel doesn't have people out looking for her, which means they're on my tail too. The faster I move, the better. I even consider taking separate fights up to Portland. But just as I'm about to book our flights, I change my mind. Instead of flying, I'll rent a car and we'll drive up together. That way, there won't be any paper trail pointing to where we're going.

Allison
Miami Vice

I don't do drugs. Unless you include the occasional hit on a blunt, just to be social.

It's not that I have anything against them. To each her or his own. It's just that I guess I'm a bit of a control freak, and the idea of getting high and losing control is kinda scary.

When it comes to drugs and alcohol, my mom and dad have set a pretty good example. I mean, if they are into it, they've done a super job of keeping it from me. But they've never given me one of those "Just Say No" speeches. They're big into letting me decide for myself. In fact, before I left for Yale, my mom actually took me to a liquor store and bought me all kinds of stuff like those flavored hard seltzers. It was pretty hilarious the way they actually set up a bar in our living room and had me sample a bunch of alcoholic drinks. They wanted me experience it and, in case I did want to drink, know what my favorites were and how they affected me. I guess that's what qualifies as "good parenting" today.

The reason I bring this up is to describe how I was feeling as I left the condo that day. It's a combination of excitement, empowerment, the sense that everything is good with the world. I'm looking as this—I don't even know what to call it, because it's certainly not a partnership—new connection with Daniel as opening up all kinds of opportunities. Daniel is treating me as a peer, not as some ditzy kid, and certainly not someone who isn't capable of dealing with responsibility. He's not "hiring" me because we share DNA. He's hiring me because he thinks I can do the job. And do it well.

That's how I'm feeling when I hop into the car. The only thing is, I have no idea where to go. It's overcast and there's a hint of rain in the air, so it's not exactly a beach day. And I don't feel like hanging out at a mall. So, I decide I'll head down to Miami Beach and check out the scene. When I was surfing the web looking for stuff about South Florida, I kept reading about the renaissance of the downtown area. It looked really cool. With lots of people my age. Time to check it out.

I turn up the radio, still tuned to yesterday's pop station, and head south.

Josh
Cherchez la Femme

I don't have to wait long.

A little after 11 a.m., a bright red convertible, top up, pulls out of the parking area behind the complex. There, sitting behind the wheel, is Allie. And she's alone.

This is not the way I pictured finding her, so I have to scotch my original plan, which was without warning, to step out of the darkness and confront her. I haven't quite worked out what I'm going to say, but I'm confident I'll come up with something unthreatening and supportive when the time comes.

I duck down as she passes right by me. And then, as soon as she has about a block head start, I begin to trail her, careful to maintain a discreet distance between us.

I wonder where Daniel is. I wonder why he's not with her. And I wonder where she's going.

I feel like I'm in the midst of some high-stakes thriller and to be honest, I'm starting to enjoy myself. But fifteen minutes later, as I find myself tooling down Collins Avenue, I'm starting to lose that sense of adventure, and in its place is the feeling that this is ridiculous. Why am I following her? What will I do once she reaches her destination? Should I confront her? Or should I wait till she gets back to the complex and confront both of them?

Without answers, all I can do is continue following Allie, delaying any meaningful decision until I see where she lands.

Allison
Journey to Nowhere

I'm cruising down the road in a bright red convertible, my hair blowing in the warm Miami breeze. I have to pinch myself to make sure I'm not dreaming. A couple weeks ago, I was rushing to make a class I couldn't care less about.

I've only known Daniel a couple days, known he existed for only a couple weeks, and yet he's changing my life. Well, I guess it's not him who's changing it. It's me.

For the first time in my life, I see a clear path ahead of me. A future. I'm not sure what that future will be, but that's okay. In fact, that's progress. Just like with this ride, I'm not sure what my destination will be. I'm heading in a direction I didn't even know existed. But for some reason, that's okay.

For the first time in a long time, I'm feeling forward motion. And it's a good feeling. Kinda like this is the first day of the rest of my life. Corny, I know. But true.

I've always been a little afraid of the unknown. I've always felt like there's a path I'm supposed to be on. I just didn't know what it was. Now, for the first time in my life, I realize I don't need to have a specific plan. So long as I'm moving forward, a plan will eventually reveal itself. I have Daniel to thank for this. Because he represents opportunity. He also represents the fact that I can accept or reject that opportunity. That makes me powerful.

Like today, I don't have a specific plan. But that's okay. I'll keep driving, till I get to the Miami Beach area. Maybe I'll grab some lunch if I can find a spot with a view of the ocean. Who knows what'll come after that. Maybe I'll head back to see what the next thing is that Daniel has in store for me.

And right now, that's the only future I have to worry about.

Josh
Miami Blues

There's a smile on my face, and for the first time since my breakfast meeting with Tony, I'm actually having fun.

Well, maybe fun isn't the right word. I mean, it's not like I'm on vacation. I'm here to find Allison, which it appears I have. So, now what?

I'm filled with a sense of adventure. A sense that not only do I have a future, but that I'm in control of that future. Maybe looking for then finding Allie is a gift. Instead of continually running away from life, I'm learning to embrace it. That's a gift, right?

Following Allie down A1A brings back memories from my junior year in college. Winter break, I headed down to Florida to visit my grandmother who, with my grandfather, moved down after they retired. They were married when he was twenty-seven and she was fifteen. And they both worked every day of their lives. He eagerly looked forward to retirement but, alas, he was only able to enjoy a couple years before he succumbed to a heart attack. Now, in her mid-sixties, my grandmother was forced to go it alone. She adjusted remarkably well. What helped, I'm sure, is that her daughter, my mother, who was only fifteen years younger than her mother, visited often, sometimes for a month or two at a time. They were more like sisters than mother and daughter.

After my grandfather's death, my grandmother felt isolated living in the garden apartment complex. In part, this was because she never learned to drive. So, always a problem solver, she moved into a two-bedroom apartment in a high-rise across from the Diplomat Hotel, where everything she'd need would be within walking distance.

As her first grandchild, I held a special place in her heart. Especially rewarding for her was my chosen career as a writer. Despite only having a junior-high-school education, she loved reading and revered writers. She was a remarkable storyteller. When we traveled, I would sit in the backseat of the car listening to every word, as she used those words to recount a recent movie she'd seen. She was so adept at storytelling that it was even better than seeing the movie myself. Experiencing up close the power of words is what might have led to my chosen career. Telling stories, and telling them well, is a special kind of superpower. Maybe this thing of mine is simply a logical extension of that power.

During the day, I'd sit by the pool, reading paperback novels. Every meal I spent with my grandmother, who, a working woman her entire life, never learned how to cook. But once she moved down here, she insisted on preparing meals for my grandfather. Mostly, they were disasters, a result of a hybrid of advice from other women in the building who'd spent their lives cooking meals for their families. Here was my grandmother, eager to cook meals, while those teaching her were more likely to line up for Early Bird Special dinners than spend any time in the kitchen.

My only break from this routine was evenings when, after clearing the table and washing the dishes, I'd hook up with a couple college buddies who were staying in whatever cheap motel they could manage down in Miami Beach. Without a car, my only means of transportation was to hitchhike down to meet them in the same area Allie appears to be heading.

This is what I'm thinking about as, seemingly without a care in the world, I follow Allison down the highway.

Even though it's midday, the traffic is relatively heavy, so it's not difficult to keep up with her while maintaining a discreet distance.

Once she hits the beach area, she finds public parking. I hang back, waiting until she gets out of the car and heads toward the beach. Only then do I pull in and find a row far enough from her so she won't be able to see me when she returns to her car.

It's warmed up a bit, and the morning's overcast has burned off to the point where there's not a cloud in the sky. This, I'm told, is typical Miami weather. It can be raining on one side of the street and bright sunshine across that street.

Standing by the edge of the parking area, I watch as Allison removes her sneakers and, barefoot, meanders down the beach. At one point she stops and spends several minutes staring at the water. Perhaps she's thinking of what's on the other side of that vast, aqua-colored ocean. Perhaps it's the feeling explorers had centuries ago as they looked in the opposite direction, toward an unexplored world, wondering what treasures might await them.

It doesn't take long to realize that Allie doesn't have a particular destination. Instead, she seems to be simply enjoying the here and now. Perhaps the feel of sand between her toes is a sign of freedom. If so, I envy her. I feel like doing the same: removing my shoes and walking barefoot down the beach.

But unlike Allie, I'm not free. I have to keep reminding myself I have a purpose. That purpose, now that I've found Allie, is to somehow convince her to go back where she belongs.

I can't help wondering if she's killing time before she meets someone, but that doesn't appear to be the case. Perhaps she's thinking about how much her life is changing. Or maybe that's just me projecting. Because no matter what happens, one thing is for sure: Once this is over, my life will be changed forever. I won't be able to go back in time to when I didn't acknowledge this so-called "gift." Now, it's a matter of how I'll integrate this gift into my life. Will it consume me? Will it define me? Will it ultimately destroy me?

I have to make a decision. Do I stick with Allie or drive back to the complex and wait for her to return? If I do, that might be the perfect time to confront Daniel. Not something I'm looking forward to, but something that might be necessary.

I wonder if he's capable of violence. I wonder what this new-found relationship with Allison is like. And finally, I wonder if I have any right to interfere. She's an adult. She's broken no law. I can't force her to come home. I can't compel her to return to her previous life, and I can't make her reconnect with Rachel and Tony. At best, all I can do is reason with her. Tell her how much pain she's caused her parents. So far, it doesn't appear as if she's in any danger. Maybe I should just keep an eye on her and wait for Tony to arrive and let him handle it.

I watch as she turns and begins to walk back in my direction. I'm confident I'm still far enough away that she can't see me. But, just in case, I duck down and, hunching over, I make a hasty retreat to the safety of my car.

Before Allison reaches the parking area, she suddenly turns left and heads in the direction of an outdoor café. I lose sight of her when she enters. I wait a few minutes, then realize she's there for lunch. Curious as to whether she's alone or is meeting someone, I head toward the restaurant. I walk in and, keeping my head down, make my way over to the dining area. There, sitting alone at a table in the outdoor area, is Allison, checking a menu. I wait until I see a waitress take her order, and only then do I conclude she's eating alone.

This stakeout thing is wearing me down. I can't imagine what good it'll do for me to stick around for the rest of the afternoon. So, I make the decision to return to Wiley Street and wait there for Allison's return.

Allison
Easy Rider

For the first time in my life, I feel free.

Before now, I had no idea how unfree I was. Probably because I never took the time to give it thought until we had to read Socrates and a particular line jumped out at me: "An unexamined life is not worth living."

Maybe that's what's wrong with people today. They never stop to look at the life they're living and wonder, is this really who I want to be, what I want to do, where I want to go? I guess most people are too busy living life to take out time to reflect on it.

When I look back, I realize I'm living my life for everyone but me. I was in a constant state of worry about what my mom and dad would think, and as a result I was living the life they wanted me to live without ever giving a thought to how I want to live my life. Do well in school. Get into a good college. Prepare for a career. Don't drink too much. Don't sleep too much. Don't have too much fun. It feels like everyone is telling me what to do, creating standards they want me to live up to, then judging me on their terms.

I guess it's not their fault. They're all part of the system. Don't get me wrong. I not only love my mom and Tony, I admire them. They've made it in a world that, in order to control you, breaks you down. It's a system that makes you conform to silly standards you often don't even understand. Meeting Daniel has forced me to look at the world and my place in it differently.

Driving down the highway with the top down, the warm Florida sun beating down on me, the wind whipping through my hair, listening to my favorite tunes on the radio, everything seems to be coming together. It's a feeling I've never had before and one I want to keep alive for as long as I can.

Suddenly, it's like all this heavy baggage I've been carrying around has disappeared. I don't have to worry about classes. I don't have to worry about grades. I don't have to worry about what I'm going to do with my life. And I don't have to worry about dealing with my mom. I know eventually I'll have to confront her, but right now it's like I'm living in Wonderland. Meeting Daniel has not only opened up my life, giving me all kinds of possibilities for the future, but he's offered me the promise of a *new* life. A life I can have some control over. A life where there's no one to tell me where to be and when to be there. For the first time in my life, I'm the one making the rules, and I'm the one who gets to choose whether to obey them or not. I think this is the way Daniel lives his life, and it very much appeals to me.

After lunch in a lovely outdoor café, I'm not sure what to do with myself. So, I find a bench and begin Googling all kinds of Miami Beach things I can experience. I stumble across photos of Key West, and I'm in love. If I were truly free, I'd hop in the car and head down there, my destination Hemingway's house. But, of course, not all my strings are unattached. The truth is, I can't really do *whatever* I want, *whenever* I want. But for the first time in my life, I can at least identify what my dreams might be. I mean, what's to stop me from backpacking across Europe and Asia? Well, there's the lack of money, sure, but maybe after I work for Daniel a while I'll be able to save up and follow my bliss. Whatever I decide that bliss is.

I'm not far into my search when the phone rings. It's Daniel.

"What's up?"

"Where are you?" he asks.

"Miami Beach. It's wild down here. I…"

"Listen, I need you back here ASAP."

"Why?"

"Things are happening. There's a change of plans."

"What do you mean?"

"No time to talk about it now, Allison. Just hop in the car and get yourself back here. I'll explain everything when you get here."

I have no time to respond, because he hangs up.

His call results in a strange feeling in the pit of my stomach.

Maybe I'm not as free as I think I am.

Josh
Chicken Flees Coop

Before resuming my stakeout at the Wiley Street address, I'll make a quick pit stop to shower, grab a short, twenty-minute nap, then head back to Wiley, where I'll wait for Allie to return.

Freshly showered, I'm about to lie down when a picture flashes through my mind. It's Allison, and she's in a bedroom stuffing her belongings into her backpack. A man enters the room. I can only see him from the back, but I assume it's Daniel. It's the perfect time to experiment a little by maneuvering myself into a position where I can see his face. But before I can, the image begins to fade.

The message is clear; they're on the move.

Cursing myself for making this pit stop, I dress quickly, hustle out the door, get into my car, and head over to Wiley Street. Fortunately, it's only a couple miles away, so there's a chance I can get there before they're gone.

On the way, I call Tony.

"Hey, man, what's up?"

"They're on the move. I'm on my way over there to see if I can intercept them."

"How do you know they're leaving for good?"

"Allison's all packed."

"Any idea where they're going?"

"Not a clue. The airport, maybe? If so, we'll pretty much have to start all over."

"Shit!"

"I know…but maybe I can get there in time to follow them."

"Don't hang up, J. I need to know what's going on."

I lay the phone on the seat beside me, but instead of continuing the conversation, I concentrate on making it to Wiley as quick as possible.

Luck is with us. As soon as I get within site of the complex, I see the red convertible pulling out of the parking area. Allison's in the passenger's seat, and I presume the man at the wheel is Daniel.

"I see them. I was right. They're on the move."

"You'll follow them, right?"

"Of course."

"Damn it! I should be down there with you."

"Don't worry. I'll stick with them. Question is, if I get an opportunity to intercept them, what do I do?"

"I think you'll have to confront them, Josh. Do you have a problem with that?"

I do, but that's not what Tony wants to hear.

"I'll do what I have to."

A moment or two passes.

"What's happening?" Tony asks.

"They just pulled onto US 1. They're heading north."

"One goes all the way up to Maine, doesn't it?"

"I think so…"

"That means they could be headed anywhere in between."

"Right. I don't know what to do about this rental if they leave the state."

"Don't worry. I'll take care of everything. Text me the make and model of the car and where you rented it. I'll make sure you can return it wherever and whenever you land. Listen, I gotta get off the phone. Obviously, I'll cancel my flight down till I hear back from you. But you keep me posted, understand?"

"Absolutely."

"And Josh…"

"Yeah?"

"I really appreciate this, man."

Before I can say anything else, he's gone and I'm alone again.

I keep my eye on the red convertible, now two or three cars ahead of me. We settle in on a steady pace between sixty-five and seventy miles an hour.

My head is spinning, filled with all kinds of possibilities. What will I do when they stop? If I do confront them, what do I say? I'm driving myself a little crazy, so I find a podcast called *Crimetown*, which chronicles the history of crime in Providence under former mayor Buddy Cianci. I'm thankful for anything that can take my mind off what's in front of me.

We're on the road for almost an hour, and I have to pee. Bad. I've still got my stakeout shit sitting there on the backseat, but I can't just pull over to heed nature's call. I'm at the mercy of the red convertible. I slow down when it slows down. I speed up when it speeds up. I'll stop when it stops. And so, I keep the pedal to the metal until it does. All I can hope for is that Daniel or Allison have a capacity similar to mine.

Meanwhile, there's nothing I can do but suck it up and hold it in.

Daniel
Father Knows Best

When the kid returns from her little adventure, I explain plans have changed and we have to leave Florida ASAP. I can see questions all over her face but, surprisingly, she doesn't ask any of them. Good thing, because I don't like lying to her. Not because I'm an honest guy, but because she's too smart to buy any line of bullshit I might be shoveling. She catches me in one lie, she'll catch me in another. This is not a good basis for a possible partnership. So, it's better not to answer at all.

Besides, telling her the truth would result in all kinds of problems. Does she have to know Teddy fucked up? Does she have to know that because of his fuckup, not only are boys in blue after me, but because he opened his big, fat mouth my competitors also found out I'm horning in on their "thing"?

Truth is, I don't know if Teddy is just plain stupid or just the opposite. Did he decide to play two ends against the middle, which would be me? Did he not only tip off the feds, but also the mob? Is he smart enough to figure out he could make a shitload more by selling me out to both?

In the end, does it fucking matter?

The only thing that matters is to get out of Dodge as soon as possible. Which is exactly what we're doing.

I expect to be bombarded with questions, but the kid is uncharacteristically quiet. But once we're on the road, she can't hold back anymore.

"So, are we going to Maine?"

"What makes you say that?"

"You know, the elver thing."

"You got good instincts, kid."

"Do you call me 'kid' because you can't remember my name?"

I laugh. She's not afraid to stand face-to-face and trade verbal punches. This is a good quality. Up to a point. I have no use for a yes-man, but at the same time I don't need someone questioning my every move.

"So?" she says.

"Yeah. It's the elver thing."

"How come we had to get out so quick? Is there trouble? Is someone after you?"

"Know who Satchel Paige was?"

"Nope. Should I be taking notes?"

"He was an old Black pitcher, played in the Negro leagues and then the major leagues. He used to say, 'Don't look back, something may be gaining on you.'"

"Meaning?"

"Meaning don't waste time looking back. Keep your eyes on what's ahead." And I should probably add, mind your own damn business. But I don't.

"So, that works for you? I mean, you can do both at the same time, you know. That's why they have rearview mirrors in cars, right?"

"Touché"

"I guess this means you're not going to discuss it with me."

"Let's say it's on a need-to-know basis."

"Well, you'll let me know when I need to know, won't you?"

"Possibly."

We ride in silence for the next ten minutes or so, but I know it's only a temporary lull. Finally, she can't hold back anymore.

"You'd tell me if there's danger involved, right? I mean, that's something I should know, right?"

"If I think you're in any physical danger, I'll let you know."

"So, does that mean that hanging around with you might put me in physical danger?"

"You were brought up in New York City, right?"

"Until I was ten. Then we moved to the 'burbs."

"Why was that?"

"I don't know. Better schools, maybe?"

"Safer neighborhoods too?"

"I didn't get a vote. If it were up to me, I would've stayed right where we were. I liked growing up on the Upper West Side. It was fun. So, what's your point?"

"My point is, at one time or another we're all in physical danger. The trick is to know it when you see it, or don't, and either avoid it or deal with it. Your family dealt with it by moving."

"Is that why we're on the road now?"

"Listen, k—Allison, this is my life and I make no apologies for it. And I guess this is as good a time as any to tell you what I do, how I live my life, is not always on, shall we say, the up and up."

"You're an outlaw?"

I laugh.

"That makes me sound a lot more interesting than I am. But if you mean I sometimes skirt the line between what's legal and what's not, guilty as charged."

"Does that put you in physical danger?"

"Sometimes. But I promise, if I think that's a possibility, the first thing I'll do is ship you back home. Even though you weren't aware I existed until a couple weeks ago, you're blood, and that means something."

"Like what?"

"Like it or not, I'm responsible for your safety."

"Okay. I get your point."

She turns quiet—I'd say she's out of questions but I know that's only wishful thinking.

I settle in cruising around seventy, seventy-five miles per hour. I love driving. It relaxes me. It's a time to think, to unwind, to plan, to scheme, even reflect. Someone once said there are three times in a man's life that offer quality alone time: reading, masturbating, and driving. Too bad you can't do all three at the same time.

Meanwhile, I can't help thinking about the kid sitting next to me.

Most of what I know, I've learned from experience. But no matter how much experience I've had, I'd be nowhere without instinct. Early on, I realized I have a facility for reading people. I know what they're going to do before they do it. I know what they're going to say before they say it. I know what they're thinking before they think it. It's why we're on the road now, putting as many miles between us and Miami as quick as possible.

There's nothing mysterious about it. It's a well-earned talent that takes years of paying attention. And I don't take it for granted. It's something I work on all the time. I guess you might say it's my superpower. And having a superpower doesn't mean shit unless you use it.

After spending only a few hours with Allison, I think she's got it too. Maybe it's in the genes. She is, after all, my kid. She's got her mother's delicate facial features. She's built like her mother too. And I'm pretty sure she gets her smarts from the same gene pool. But from me, I think maybe she's inherited things you can't see. The things that make us who and what we are.

I was gonna dump the kid as quick as I could. But now, after getting to know her a little, I'm not so sure. And it has nothing to do with my natural parental urges. I know this because I don't have any.

It's for other reasons, very practical reasons.

Josh
Face-Off

We've just crossed the border into Georgia. Florida is now a not-so-fond memory. The future is somewhere to the north.

Just as my bladder's about to burst, the red convertible slides over to the right lane and slows down. I give silent thanks and follow suit.

A voice in my head warns, *Careful what you wish for, Josh.*

Because, let's face it, this presents me with what I'll call the "dog catches bus" dilemma. Otherwise known as, *What now?*

I follow them off the highway and slow to a crawl as the red convertible stops in front of a McDonald's. Allison hops out and heads toward the entrance of the fast-food joint as the car crosses the road and pulls into a gas station.

If I act quick enough, this is my chance to get Allison alone.

I park as close to the entrance as possible and jump out so fast I don't even bother to lock the doors. I glance over across the road and watch Daniel—who I'm getting a good look at for the first time—as he exits the car and moves to the gas pump. I figure I've got five, six minutes tops until he either heads into the restaurant or pulls back in front and waits for Allison to emerge. I'm hoping for the latter, because it'll give me more time to do whatever it is I'm going to do. In that split second, I wish my "gift" included seeing into the future.

When I get inside and don't see Allison, I assume she's in the restroom. I figure it'll take her longer than me, so I duck into the men's room, do my business quick as I can. When I emerge, I scan the restaurant and don't see her, which means she must still be in the ladies' room.

I station myself strategically between the bathrooms and the main dining area. A moment later, Allison, a huge smile on her face, emerges. I step in front of her, but don't say anything. As soon as she sees someone in her way, she looks up. The surprised expression on her face is priceless.

I smile, but say nothing.

It takes a split second for her to realize it's me. Her smile quickly morphs into one of those looks you have when you see someone totally out of context. You recognize you know them, but you don't know from where.

"Uncle Josh. What are you doing here?"

I'm not fond of being called uncle. I know it's an honorary familial title, but it seems fake, unearned. I'm always tempted to say, *I'm not your uncle*, but that seems like a hostile, insulting overreaction, and so I grit my teeth and smile, telling myself, *Don't be an asshole.* One of these days I'm sure I'll slip. But today's not that day.

"Looking for you," I say, trying to keep my tone light.

She checks out the room, probably looking to see if Josh and Rachel will be joining us.

"I'm alone," I say. "Your dad asked me to help find you. He has no idea where you are right now, in case you're wondering."

It looks like she wants to say something, but there's only silence. If this is going anywhere, I know I have to hit hard and fast.

"Allie, why don't you let me take you home. Your parents are crazy with worry. Whatever the problem is, I'm sure you guys can work it out."

"What makes you think there's a problem?"

"You disappear without warning, without letting them know you're okay, where you are and why. I'd call that a problem. But look, that's none of my business. This is between you and your parents. I just want to bring you home, so you guys can talk this out."

"You know, you can't make me go anywhere," she says defiantly, and I can't help picturing her as the stubborn, willful, rebellious kid we all knew and loved. When she was young it was cute and endearing, this three- or four-year-old standing her ground against any and all adults. Today, not so much. Probably because the stakes are so much higher.

"I know. And even if I could, I wouldn't. All I'm asking is that you consider your mom and dad's feelings."

"Like they've considered mine?"

"I'm not getting into that debate with you. I know all about this guy you're with…"

"His name's Daniel and he's not just some guy. He's my birth father."

"I know. And I don't want to say anything bad about him, but the truth is he's got a very problematic history, Allie."

"I don't even know what that means. But whatever it means, it doesn't concern me now. I know he's no Boy Scout, but he treats me well, like I'm an adult…"

"Fine. I'm not telling you not to have a relationship with him. I'm telling you that the way you're going about it sucks. Is he coming in?"

"I'm supposed to order food and meet him back in the car."

A quick thought has me wishing I could grab her, lead her out a back door, shove her into the car, and take off, like one of those cult deprogrammers. But, of course, that's not going to happen.

We face each other silently for what seems like forever before trying to stare each other down until one of us gives in. Finally, she repeats, "I'm supposed to grab food for us."

"Won't you even consider coming back with me?"

"That's not in the cards," she says, and I can't help smiling. The kid's got attitude, and it's hard not to admire that. But it also means there's no frigging way I'm going to change her mind.

"Look, why don't we get in line for whatever you're eating these days and at least I can chat with you a little, so I have something to tell Tony and Rachel."

"You can tell them I'm fine. It's not like I'm kidnapped or anything. And it's not like he's"—she waves the fingers of one hand in my face—"hypnotized me. Or filled me full of drugs. Or messed with my mind."

"Someone's been watching a little too much bad TV."

For the first time since she recognized me, she cracks a smile. "A little dramatic, huh?"

"More than a little."

"Okay."

"Okay what?"

"Okay you can stand with me while I order."

"You know what, I'm hungry too, and don't let this get around, but I'm kinda jonesing for a Big Mac and fries. But if you tell anyone, I'll deny it."

"Your secret's safe with me," she says as we head toward the counter, where there are a couple people ahead of us. I feel like I should take her hand, as if she's a lost child I'm bringing back home.

"Like, how did you find me?" she asks, her tone softening slightly.

"Trade secret."

"This is really, really weird," she says, shaking her head back and forth.

"I know. Like, surreal, right?"

"Exactly."

I look over my shoulder and through the window I see Daniel is still at the gas station, across the street. He's using one of those squeegee things to clean the windows, which is buying me more time.

"Where are you guys headed?"

"North."

"Yeah, I get that. But where specifically?"

She shrugs. "Not sure."

"Did I ever tell you about this bullshit detector I had implanted up here?" I say, tapping my temple.

"Really? How cool is that? Is it on now?"

"Can't turn it off. That's the downside. You don't know what a burden it is always knowing when someone's not telling the truth."

"Sounds pretty cool to me. Maybe you should monetize it."

"Good idea. But right now, the alarm is going off, like one of those smoke detectors. It's telling me you know exactly where you're headed."

She shrugs again as we inch forward in the line.

"Okay. Let's drop that for the moment. How about the bigger picture. What's going on? Why are you still with him?"

"I'm working for him."

"Really? As what?"

"His assistant."

"His assistant to what?"

"Whatever he needs." She smiles. "It's an entry-level position, but it pays pretty good."

"If he's still hiring, maybe I ought to apply. Work has been pretty scarce lately. Maybe I could use a change of profession."

"I think we're good for now, Uncle Josh. But we'll keep you in mind. So, let me ask you a question."

"Sure."

"What's next?"

"Next?"

"Now that you found me and I'm not going back with you, what are you gonna do?"

I look over my shoulder again and see Daniel leaning against the car, talking on his cell phone. As long as I was given this other "thing" of mine, why couldn't I have super-hearing and super-vision, as an add-on?

"To be honest, I'm not sure."

We're one spot away from being served.

"Do you, like, want to meet him?" she says.

This catches me by surprise, and I answer without putting much thought into it.

"Sure. Why not?"

It's our turn to order. When the order is rung up, I pull out my credit card and tap the machine.

"Hey, I was going to pay for that!"

"Next time. This one's on me. Do you want to ask him to come in and join us, or should we go outside and wait till he pulls around?"

"Actually, I don't remember his number. So, why don't you grab a table and I'll go out and bring him in."

I sense trouble. If I let her go out alone, I'm afraid she'll hop in the car and they'll take off in a trail of dust, like they've just robbed a bank. And if they get enough of a head start, they'll be able to ditch me and I'll lose her forever. But I'm not exactly in a good bargaining position. My best strategy might be to face this head-on.

"You're not going to just hop in the car and take off, are you?"

"Do you really think I'd do something like that to you, Uncle Josh?"

"This is not my first time around the block, Allie. I'm a journalist, remember? I've spent most of my life being ditched or avoided. Besides, you're not the one behind the wheel."

"But you're like family."

"So are your mother and father…"

"Are you going to hold that against me the rest of my life? They lied to me. You haven't. At least I don't think you have."

"I knew nothing about him, if that's what you mean," I say, jerking my thumb in his direction. When I do, I see Daniel's back behind the wheel, waiting for traffic to ease up so he can cross over to us.

The kid behind the counter hands the bag of food, along with three empty cups, to Allie, who then hands it to me.

"Grab a table and I'll go out and bring Daniel in."

She can probably see the dubious expression on my face.

"Don't worry. I'll bring him in. It's not like we're on the lam or anything. Besides, I think he'd actually like meeting you."

"Not so sure about that," I say, but I have to admit I'm feeling a little bit better about the possibility of being abandoned.

She hands me the two bags of food. "You can think of this as collateral. I mean, if we were going to boot, I'd take it with me, wouldn't I?"

Before I can say anything, she leans over and gives me a brief kiss on the cheek, then heads out the door.

Allison
Guess Who's Coming to Dinner?

Holy shit!

I can't believe it's him. I mean, how in the world did he find me? And how much trouble have I caused for Mom and Dad? Oh, and it keeps getting worse. I mean, on second thought, maybe it's a really, really bad idea to introduce Daniel to Uncle Josh. I'm guessing the last thing in the world Daniel wants is someone all up in his business. Worlds that collide wind up destroying each other. I don't have to be an Ivy League kid to know that. It's kinda like introducing fire to oxygen. There's the scary possibility of everything and everybody going up in flames.

But what can I do?

I'm stuck.

It's not like I can run out, hop in the car, tell him to go, go, go, and act like nothing's happened. Daniel's not stupid. The minute he sees me without the food, he'll know something's up. And to be honest, I'm still a little freaked out after finding that gun. I mean, I don't know where it is now, but it's probably either packed in our trunk, in the glove box, or strapped to Daniel. But no matter where it is, it's like having an invisible guest at a dinner party. You know he's there, though you don't know where, and you don't know what he's going to do or say or when he's going to do or say something that's going to end up in flames. What if Daniel pulls out his gun and starts firing? I can see the headlines: "Bloody Shootout in Local McDonald's Ends in Tragedy."

In the end, I have no choice. I'll tell Daniel the truth and see where that takes us. He can always say no, right? And besides, how likely is the shootout scenario?

I walk around to the driver's side and motion for Daniel to roll down the window.

"What's wrong?" he asks.

"How do you know something's wrong?"

"Where's the beef, baby?"

"Huh?"

"The food you're supposed to get. Where is it?"

"Uhm. About that. I think you should park and then we go inside and eat at a proper table. You know, like civilized people."

"What's going on, Allison?"

"Uncle Josh, my dad's best friend, is in there and he wants to meet you. He's already paid for lunch so"—I dig into my back pocket and pull out the fifty-dollar bill Daniel had given me to pay for the food—"here's your money."

Josh
Worlds Collide

Allie, with this guy trailing a step or two behind, enters the restaurant. She's walking quick, like she can't wait for this to be over. I can see from the look on her face and the way she holds herself she's very anxious. Me? I'm not sure what I am. Nervous. Anxious. Confused. All of it.

I have no idea what I'm going to say or how I'll say it.

I'm not sure what I expected, but the Daniel now approaching is not it. He's a shade under six feet, maybe 160, 170 pounds. He's clean shaven with a full head of curly salt-and-pepper hair. He's wearing faded jeans, a deep-blue Hawaiian shirt, and a lightweight Army fatigue jacket.

I feel like I should stand up, so I do.

"Uncle Josh, I'd like you to meet my, uhm, Daniel Peacock."

He offers his hand. I shake it. "Nice to meet you, Mr. Peacock," I say.

"Likewise," he says. "But let's make that Daniel. 'Mr. Peacock' sounds like a friggin' porn star."

"Have a seat," I say, like I'm hosting an intimate dinner party. I feel like a jerk. Like I want to start over.

Daniel sits opposite me. Allie is on my left, in the middle, like she's the referee.

I empty the two bags of food and put everything on the table. I'm too nervous to eat, but I unwrap my Quarter Pounder with cheese anyway.

Allie eyes the food for a moment, then grabs what she's ordered, a fish filet sandwich, and carefully unwraps it. Daniel doesn't make a move for his food. Instead, he folds his arms across his chest and stares at me. Is that a smirk on his face?

I feel like we're in a staring contest, where the first one to blink loses. Poor Allie, literally and figuratively in the middle, is obviously uncomfortable.

Finally, one of us breaks the awkward silence. And it's not me.

"So, what's your deal?" says Peacock.

"Deal?"

"You know what I mean. Why are you here? Why are you following us?"

"I'm not following you. I've been looking for Allison. And you damn well know why. She's been gone for over a week and her parents had no idea where she was or why she disappeared without telling them."

"I haven't kidnapped her."

"I didn't think so."

"In case you haven't noticed, she's an adult. She doesn't have to report to anyone. Even her parents."

"How long have you been a parent, Daniel? Fifteen minutes? Which means you know nothing about how a parent feels."

"How many kids you got, Uncle Josh?"

"Touché."

He smiles. "Look, I don't want to fight. Maybe we got off on the wrong foot here. I didn't ask Allison to look me up. I didn't ask her to find me. I didn't ask her, once she did, to hunt me down and hang out with me. Why don't we ask Allison what she wants and then maybe cut her some slack."

"Fair enough." I turn to Allison. She's staring down at her fish filet sandwich but hasn't touched it yet. I feel for her. She's caught in the middle. But don't ask me who's the rock and who's the hard place.

"What would you like to do, Allie?" I say, although I'm pretty sure what her answer is going to be.

"I want to be treated like an adult."

"And what, as far as you're concerned, does that entail?"

"Making my own decisions."

"I'm good with that," I say. "All I ask is that you come back with me, sit down with your mom and dad, talk to them, explain what you want and why you want it. They're not going to chain you to the bedpost and lock you in the house. They just want to be part of your life. If you want to be treated like an adult, you have to act like an adult."

Oh, Jeez, did I really say that? I sound like some old fogie guidance counselor. Too late to start over. But not too late to shut the fuck up.

Daniel

Wrestling with the Devil

This is not good.

The last thing I need is this dude on my back about the kid. The easiest and smartest thing to do would be to kick her loose. I mean, what the fuck? Do I need this complication in my life?

That's what I should do, but my competitive side kicks in and suddenly I find myself doing battle over a nineteen-year-old kid. But it's not about her. It's about winning. And it's about not letting anyone tell me what I can and can't do. So, you want a fight, Uncle Josh? A fight is what you'll get.

"So, Allison, what is it you want to do?"

I can see from her face her mind is set. I recognize the look well. It's the same look I have when I'm backed in a corner. Can expressions be inherited? Is this a DNA thing?

She puts down her sandwich and turns to Josh.

"I really appreciate all the trouble you've gone to, Uncle Josh. I wish my mom and dad hadn't overreacted..."

"I'm not sure they overreacted," he says.

"Okay, maybe that's the wrong word. And maybe I, like, shouldn't have disappeared. But I did. And now that I've found Daniel, I think I'd like to explore our relationship a little more."

I shift my gaze to the dude. It's like watching a tennis match. Hope I don't get whiplash.

"Two things can happen at the same time, Allie. No one's telling you not to explore a relationship with—" He looks over at me and he can't hide his disdain. He's walking a thin line here. He doesn't want to insult me. Or bring me down. He knows that'd be counterproductive. At the same time, he wants to "save" her from the big, bad wolf. And in order to do that, he must wrestle with the devil.

"...you can pick up where you left off. Go back to school. Finish up the semester. And maybe then you and Daniel can get to know each other. I'm pretty sure at this point your mom and dad aren't going to stop you."

"They can't stop me."

"True. But..."

"Like I said, Uncle Josh, I appreciate all the trouble you've gone to. And I can see I kinda fucked up. But what's done is done, and what I want to do now is follow through on this."

"On what?"

She looks at me and smiles.

"Daniel has offered me a job. And I've accepted. It's not like it's for life. And with summer vacation coming up, it's not like I can't give it a try and then, if it doesn't work out, I'll just go back to school in the fall. The timing is perfect, don't you think?"

Josh
Mano a Mano

How much does Allison know about Daniel's checkered past? Does she know he's been in and out of trouble (mostly in) for most of his adult life? Does she know he takes things that don't belong to him? Does she know he's been in then kicked out of the Witness Protection Program? Does she know he might be capable of violence?

Tony and I have only scratched the surface when it comes to this guy's criminal history, and I can pretty much guarantee that no matter what job he's given Allison, it's at best shady, at worst against the law.

But I can't tell any of this to Allison. Especially not with Daniel sitting only a couple feet across from me.

"Guess you were surprised when this one showed up," I say, giving Allison a playful push to her shoulder.

"You could say that," says Daniel. He's got this scary, menacing expression on his face that carries a definite don't-fuck-with-me vibe. I can't tell if it's a tactic to intimidate, or if he's in a constant state of being pissed off. Whichever it is, it's very effective in providing a chill to the proceedings.

Daniel's staring at me. Allison is staring at her fish filet sandwich. And me? I'm looking at anything that'll help take my mind off this very awkward conclave in the middle of the day in the middle of a McDonald's in the middle of nowhere.

Finally, I've had enough. I mean, do I really want to spend all afternoon engaged in a standoff, accomplishing absolutely nothing? So, I take the plunge, which makes me feel like one of those Polar Bear idiots whose idea of fun is taking a dip in the Atlantic Ocean in the dead of winter. No matter what they say, no matter how they rationalize it, it's fucking cold and there's no earthly reason to be doing it.

"Let's cut to the chase, Daniel. All cards on the table. I'm here to persuade Allison to come back with me. Her *parents* are worried sick, and she's only got a couple weeks left of the semester. So, why not just finish up, and then she can do whatever it is she wants to do."

Daniel takes a deep breath and I see the beginning of what looks like a smile. You know what? He's fucking enjoying this. "The way I see it, she's free to do anything she wants. And if her choice is to leave a couple weeks on the table, so be it."

"Hey, guys, I'm right here. It's really weird that you two are negotiating *my* future. The only one who has a say in it, you know, is like, me."

"She's got a point," says Daniel, now in full-smile mode.

"I'm not telling you what to do, Allie. I'm just telling you what I think you *should* do. The final decision is up to you. No one's disputing that."

"And if I don't go back with you, what will you do? What will you tell Mom and Dad? Will you keep following us?"

"To be honest, I haven't thought that far ahead. But if you want to stick with Daniel, I'll tell your mom and dad I found you, that you're with Daniel, that you appear to be safe and unharmed, and be on my way."

"She is safe and unharmed," Daniel says firmly, the smile gone from his lips. He knows he's close to victory, yet he's not very magnanimous about it. Not that I expect anything different from a guy with his history.

"So, what do you say, Allie? Are you going to do the right thing or…" I stop myself short of saying something that will alienate her even more than she already is. No, I will not make this a case of right or wrong, good versus evil. Ultimately, like all of us, Allie has to make her own mistakes. And if she's as smart as I think she is, she'll learn from them.

She puts her sandwich down and looks at Daniel, who's popping fries, one by one, into his mouth. "Can't beat these fries," he says.

"I really appreciate everything you've done, Uncle Josh. I really do. I know I've made some mistakes along the way. I probably should have discussed this with Mom before I went off on my own. I guess I should have been more attuned to their feelings. I fucked up. But I'm not sorry about what I've done. I'm not sorry about finding Daniel. It was something I had to do. And now he's given me an opportunity I can't turn down. If I'm making a mistake, well, as Tony always says, that's why they put erasers on the opposite end of pencils. And as for Mom and Dad, well, I'll do the right thing. I'll call them. And after I get settled, I'll visit them, and we can hash all this out in person."

"So, you're sticking with Daniel?"

She nods her head yes.

"And there's nothing I can say to change your mind?"

She nods her head no.

"Before you leave us, *Uncle Josh*," he says, his voice dripping sarcasm, "I want to congratulate you on tracking us down. Those are some super-detective skills you have. What's your secret?"

"Hard work and clean living."

He smiles. "Guess it's too late for me to acquire either of those traits."

"I don't know what's in this for you, Daniel, but if you have a decent bone in your body, you'll send Allison home, let her mend fences, and then, when things settle down, she can come work for you with a clean slate. That's what a decent person would do."

"Yeah, well, I am who I am. But for the record, Allison is making her own decision. I hope you make that clear to Rachel."

I look him straight in the eye.

"I hope to God this isn't about you and Rachel, Daniel."

"What do you mean?"

"I don't know what went down between you two years ago, and frankly, I don't care. But if this is some kind of sick revenge against her for some real or perceived slight, it really sucks." I turn to Allie. "And if it is, I hope Allison here takes that into consideration. In the end, character is everything."

I see in his eyes that he's seething. He wants to reach out, grab me by the throat, and strangle the life out of me. But he won't. Not because he doesn't want to. But because he knows if he does, he's lost. And this is a man who does not like to lose. I could try to bait him even more, in the hopes that he shows his true colors, but to tell the truth, I don't have the stomach for it. Not here. Not now.

I'll leave. I'll report back to Tony and Rachel and let them take it from here. My job is done. I did what I was asked. I found Allison, and I learned why she left the way she did.

Now, it's time to get back to what's left of my life.

"I guess we're done here," says Daniel. He packs up what's left of his burger and fries, stands, and puts his hand on Allie's shoulder.

"Let's finish this in the car, kiddo," he says. "Time's a wastin'."

"What's the rush?" I say.

"No rush," he says.

"Well, you seem a little anxious. Like maybe someone's after you."

He stares daggers at me. "What makes you think anyone's after me, Uncle Josh?"

"Nothing. Just seems like you're in a hurry to leave."

"I don't like driving at night."

"So, where you headed?"

"Like, how's that any business of yours?"

I throw up my hands. "Sorry. Right. No business of mine, at all. Just curious. I just thought it might be nice to be able to tell Allison's parents where she's going."

"Allison can do that herself. Can't you, Allison?"

She nods. "Of course."

"Okay," he says. "Time to hit the road."

"Okay," she says as she starts stuffing what's left of her meal in one of the empty bags. "I'm sorry about this, Uncle Josh. I hate that you had to, like, disrupt your whole life just to find me."

If she only knew.

"I'd say it was a pleasure, Uncle Josh, but we both know that would be a lie, don't we?"

As Daniel turns away, I notice a bulge just above the midsection of his back. There's no mistaking it: He's carrying a gun.

Allison
Family Ties

Oh, man, am I glad that's over. My stomach's still doing flip-flops as I follow Daniel out the door.

And it isn't till we get outside that I notice the bulge on his back, just above his beltline. I know exactly what that is. But why is he carrying it around like that? Would he actually use it? What if I decided to go back with Uncle Josh? Would he have used it?

Now, wait a minute, girl! Let's not let this thing get away from us. It could be something really innocent. Like, no way he'd want to leave that in the car while we're inside McDonald's. I mean, that would really be risky, wouldn't it? Or what if he just forgot that he was carrying it? And what if he's got a perfectly good reason for carrying a gun? I mean, look at that guy he was doing business with the other day. I'm sure it's all about self-defense, right?

I'm a little shaken up, but when I get back into the car, Daniel is all smiles.

"You okay, kiddo?"

"Yes. I'm fine."

"Pretty freaky, right?"

"Yeah. I was totally shocked."

"He seems okay, your uncle Josh."

"Well, he's not really my uncle."

"Like I'm not really your father."

I can't help laughing, which puts me at ease.

"Look, it's okay. It's nice to know you have people who care about you."

"He does."

"You want to put on the radio?"

"Sure."

"Choose your poison, kiddo."

I find the station I've been listening to and crank up the music. At this point, it's a lot better than having to talk to Daniel, because I'm afraid if I do, I'll say something about that gun. And you know what, I'm not sure I want to hear the answer.

Suddenly, I'm awfully tired. It's like I can't keep my eyes open. So, I fiddle with the seat so I'm a little more comfortable, lean my head back, close my eyes, and let the music waft over me.

The next time I open my eyes, it's dark out and Daniel is pulling into one of those cookie-cutter motels where, I'm guessing, we'll spend the night.

And maybe, after a real meal and a good night's sleep, I'll have a better idea of what the future holds for me.

I understand I'm taking a big chance, hitching my wagon, as Tony might say, to a man like Daniel. But I feel a kinship to him and with good reason. We're blood, and I feel like he's part of my destiny. I don't believe I'll ever be able to understand myself until I understand Daniel. And the only way I'm going to be able to do that is to choose him, right now, over my mom and Tony. I know it's a risk, but I'm young, and isn't that the time to take risks? Besides, how will I know until I try it out? And that means sticking with Daniel, at least for now.

But there is one thing I know for sure: Nothing will ever be the same.

Acknowledgments

I'd like to thank a few people for keeping me writing when my natural instinct is to do anything but. First, the Monday Night Zoom Boys and fellow crime writers: Reed Farrel Coleman (notice the one l in Farrel), Tom Straw, Matt Goldman, and Michael Wiley. Years after the pandemic, which got us started, we're still Zooming, still hanging out, still sharing our successes and disappointments, still watching each other's back. I'm also inspired by my colleagues in crime, S.J. Rozan, Peter Blauner, Peter Spiegelman, Gabriel Cohen, Dennis Tafoya, and Bob Reiss. And thanks to Christina Chiu, for always being there whenever I need her (and even when I don't). Sally Koslow, Angela Himsel, Dawn Raffel, Helen Zelon, Christina Chiu, and Elise Zealand, an unofficial writing group that saw the early beginnings of *The Beginning of Everything*, when it didn't even have a title, and encouraged me to keep going. SallyAnne McCartin, who did everything she could to make sure this novel didn't sink silently into the abyss for lack of readers. And to Pam Coronado who, without her knowledge, inspired me to create Josh, and patiently explained how she does what she does.

And a special thanks to Gretchen Young, Caitlin Burdette, and all the other folks at Regalo Press who helped give life to this novel.

About the Author

Charles Salzberg is a former journalist. His work has appeared in articles in *Esquire, The New York Times, Redbook, GQ*, and *Travel + Leisure*. He is also the author of *From Set Shot to Slam Dunk: The Glory Days of Basketball in the Words of Those Who Played It, Soupy Sez: My Zany Life and Times*, and a number of other non-fiction books. His first novel, *Swann's Last Song*, was nominated for a Shamus Award as was *Second Story Man*, winner of the Beverly Hills Book Award, and *Canary in the Coal Mine*. His novel *Devil in the Hole* was named one of the best crime novels of 2013 by *Suspense Magazine*. He's been a visiting professor of magazine and the S.I. Newhouse School of Public Communications at Syracuse University and taught writing at Sarah Lawrence, Hunter College, the Writer's Voice, and the New York Writers Workshop, where he is a founding member. He has also served on the board of the New York chapter of Mystery Writers of America.